GO FIND *Less*

RECOVERING GOOD GIRLS BOOK 1

THEA CLAIRE

Copyright © 2024 by Thea Claire

All rights reserved.

No portion of this book may be reproduced in any form without written permission from the publisher or author, except as permitted by U.S. copyright law.

This book is a work of fiction. Names, characters, organizations, places, events, and incidents are either products of the author's imagination or used fictitiously.

For more information on the Recovering Good Girls series, visit www.theaclaireauthor.com

Cover Design: Booked Forever

To people who feel like they have to make themselves small to be accepted: You're not too much. They can go find less.

And to JT – my favorite.

CONTENT WARNINGS

This book contains the following material that may be triggering to some readers: spouse/partner dying, death on scene (medical, no blood), terminal illness, hospital/medical setting (brief), cheating (not perpetrated by MCs), emotional and mental abuse, paternity questions/challenges, panic attacks, brief mention of sexual assault, homophobia, toxic family members, body dysmorphia.

Playlist

HEARTBEAT | DAVINA MICHELLE — 3:19

BAD BLOOD | TAYLOR SWIFT — 3:32

PURITY | LILYISTHATYOU — 1:53

KISS ME | SIXPENSE NONE THE RICHER — 3:29

STELLA | CEREUS BRIGHT — 2:53

MANDY | JONAS BROTHERS — 2:48

CONFIDENT - ROCK VERSION | DEMI LOVATO — 3:26

IF I DIE YOUNG | THE BAND PERRY — 3:43

WHERE DOES THE GOOD GO | TEGAN AND SARA — 3:37

FAVORITE T-SHIRT | JAKE SCOTT — 3:04

NUMB LITTLE BUG | EM BEIHOLD — 2:49

FIGHT SONG | RACHEL PLATTEN — 3:24

GRACE | HENRIK — 3:20

GO FIND LESS | RILEY ROTH — 2:41

CHAPTER 1

Piper

There are lots of things I'll do for my friends without protest: holding hair back in a club bathroom while they puke, serving as a designated driver, and boob-taping plunging necklines come to mind. Helping with the high school reunion I don't even plan to attend is not one of those things.

"Come *on*," Carla whines, leaning against my door frame in a huff. "You know they're going to ask about design and no one that's RSVPed is creative *at all*."

"I guess it's better to know you're being used from the get-go," I say dryly, looking at her in the reflection of my vanity mirror. She's dressed to impress, as much as she can for a windy Texas morning, in a stylish jacket with a pair of dark jeans and white pointed snakeskin boots she doesn't get to wear often. They're her favorite, I know, but they don't really pair well with scrubs.

"They won't use you." She crosses her arms, blowing a piece of freshly highlighted, straight auburn hair from her pale eyes. "Just your talents." She smirks and meets my eyes in the mirror, running her fingers along the neckline of the top she's wearing under the jacket. It's studded with short, black spikes, matching the dark silk of the bodice. One of my designs. "Come on, just this one meeting. You can show up, look hot, let the rest of them see what they were missing ten years ago, and call it a day. Just hear Jackie out."

I narrow my eyes at her.

Jackie. She has to bring Jackie into this.

Jackie is one of the sweetest people on the planet. Ten years after graduation, I still get an annual "Merry Christmas!" text from her with a little Bitmoji. Even her gangbusters career in neuroscience hasn't stopped her from continuing the same "love everyone" attitude she'd had all those years ago. She was nice to me, when lots of people weren't.

"*Please*, Piper," she whines again. I close my eyes and take a ragged breath, trying to weigh my options.

I haven't seen most of these people in a decade. I moved away from our suburban hellhole to avoid running into anyone from high school a long time ago. Especially now, years later, when I'd gone off the deep end and somehow doggy-paddled my way back to the shallows, the last thing I need is to go grocery shopping and run into someone who tormented me.

But *Jackie*. Jackie is kind, and when Carla told me weeks ago she was heading up the reunion, as class president and valedictorian, I wasn't surprised. I just didn't think I'd be asked to tag along. Truthfully, my plan had been to say I was going, and then bow out at the last minute, claiming some lingerie-schilling emergency at work.

Still in the darkness of my closed eyes, I try to imagine the girl I was back then. Too tall, still wearing heels nearly every day. Too curvy, foregoing yoga pants and Ed Hardy tee shirts for blazers and blouses I'd altered myself. Loud. Nerdy. Too much, I was told.

When I open my eyes, I stare at my reflection. The same blue irises stare back at me. Those haven't changed. But everything else has. The dyed, fire engine red hair was replaced with shiny, well-conditioned, dark curls that have grown more in the last few years than in the last decade. Sobriety and a regular diet will do that. While my face was still full, it had yo-yoed so much with depression induced weight-loss, and then weight-gain, that my body had finally settled on a happy medium of looking healthy. I traded my thick glasses for contacts, my drugstore makeup for high-end (ish), and had even stopped biting my nails after years of therapy and bitter nail polish.

My gaze flits down to the framed photo on the vanity in front of me. A different woman than either one on my mind smiles back. Gaunt. Tired. The floral dress hanging off her frame matches the bouquet in her hand; arms flung over the man in front of her, seated firmly in a wheelchair, a Kansas City Royals blanket thrown over his lap to cover his too-thin legs. He smiles too, but it's just as worn as hers. Tie askew. Face roughly shaven. But yet, they're happy.

You're not that woman anymore.

I feel like a car that had all of the exterior panels replaced. The repair job hid a once-broken, still somehow functioning engine that had been refurbished piece-by-piece.

I look at Carla again in the reflection. She can sense my hesitation, and brings her hands in front of her, pleading.

"I'll take you for fro-yo after the show tonight."

"You've resorted to bribery, I see." She smiles at my snipe, knowing she's extorted my weakness for sugar. "Must really not want to face Kyle alone." Her smile falters a bit, and I realize I may have gone too far, teasing about her decade-long crush on my neighbor growing up. "Fine." I sigh, shaking my head. "I'll go."

"Really?" My roommate claps and gives a little jump, before faltering in her boots and catching herself in the doorframe just in time for Bex, my tiny, black Brussels Griffon to saunter her way into the room, pink, sparkly collar jingling. "We can kill time before the show at the Shops or something." I roll my eyes, turning back to my reflection in the mirror. Always an opportunity to participate in a little retail therapy when Carla's involved.

As she walks back towards her room doing a little happy dance, I get to work on my makeup, wondering what I've just gotten myself into. "Give me twenty minutes and we can head that way," I call after her.

When we walk into the cafe an hour later, Carla makes a bee-line towards the back, and I see where she's headed - a long, low table, with a booth on one side and low chairs on the other. There are open spots on the booth and in the uncomfortable, narrowly braced metal chairs that go with the farmhouse aesthetic of the cafe, Rooster Ranch. This place wasn't here when we went to Southwest High School, but the tables are now littered with what looks like students from the very place we graduated. Carla clearly suggested it for the meeting. The vibe matches her farmhouse chic bedroom, and she looks fresh from a night out now, but that woman lives in scrubs under a frilly duvet.

My roommate squeals as she gets closer to the table, and everyone stands so I'm able to get a good look at who's here.

From the seats stand three women and a man. The man I immediately recognize as Kyle, who pulls me into a quick side hug - I ran into him last Thanksgiving as we both left our parents' houses, his arms laden with to-go containers as he made his way to what looked like a food service job, based on his outfit. According to my mother, the neighborhood gossip, Kyle only moved out because his parents made him, and he still lived just a few miles away working his latest job in a series of short stints. Long gone were his days of being the bad boy loner that Carla had lusted after, but she still manages not to make googly eyes at him over the girl she's hugging.

When they separate, I realize that it's Fallon, one of Carla's best friends from high school. They were in theater together, and while Carla was always the shining star, Fallon, with her long, blonde hair and girl-next-door smile, was a close second. She came over to the apartment when she was in town from Oklahoma City, where she manages a children's theater with her husband. She pulls me into a hug behind Carla, holding me at arms length and looking over the a-line dress I'd thrown on, a personal favorite, with pearls studding the collar and sleeves.

"You look fabulous, as always." I give Fallon a wide grin at her sincere tone.

Kyle gives Carla the same awkward side hug. The other woman I can't place at first, but when Carla says "Hey, Jess!" recognition hits me. Jessica Alverado. Being off social media for years has its pros and cons.

Pros:
Free time to read
Nonexistent FOMO
Lack of access for harassment by my shitbag former in-laws and their small town groupies

Cons:
Not up-to-date on current lingo
Hard to track fashion trends
Unaware of what literally anyone looks like in person anymore

So, when realization hits Jessica too, there's a second of pause before she squeals, like Carla, and barrels into me, pulling me into a tight hug. Her squeeze surprises me, and my tense body relaxes as I hug back, laughing.

The joy Jessica radiates in seeing me catches me off guard. I had expected to be rebuffed. Indifference, maybe. But not happiness. We never really cleared things up before graduation, and then, like the majority of people I walked the stage with, I didn't speak to her again.

"I've been keeping up with you on Penny's social," she says, grasping my hands in hers and giving me a sad smile. Oh. Well, that explains it. Penny, my older sister, was on the girl's basketball team with Jessica until she graduated the year before us. I hadn't really considered that the two might still be on speaking terms. "It looks like you're doing so well for yourself."

I blush. "Thank you," I mutter, watching Jackie stand from her seat on the booth and hug Carla. "What have you been up to?" Jessica's sad smile turns broad, and she lifts her left hand to show me the glittering diamond on her ring finger.

"My wife's pregnant with our first." Jessica is beaming, and I try my best to hide my astonishment. At the end of senior year, Jessica was dating Michael Valdez, the co-captain of the lacrosse team, a complete 180 from Andy, her ex - *our* ex. Clearly, things have changed.

"That's amazing." I grin, genuinely happy for her. She falls into the seat she was occupying, along with Kyle and Fallon, as Jackie comes up to hug me, that same sad smile as Jessica on her face. At this point, I'm used to it.

CHAPTER 1

"How are you doing, Piper?" she asks, gripping my arm when she lets go of our hug.

I swallow, my well-rehearsed line already on my lips.

"Really well," I say, meaning it, but also not wanting to tack on "considering the circumstances." Widowed. Recovering alcoholic. Stuck designing for a manager who wouldn't know silk from satin.

"Good." Jackie gives my arm another squeeze before taking her seat again, patting the space next to her. Gingerly, I step in front of her, pulling my skirt under me as I take the seat. Carla plops down next to me. "And how is Alex?" Jackie asks. I smile to myself.

"Counting the days until she can see her toes again." I set my tote on the seat next to me. Very, very pregnant with her first child, Alex, my best friend since kindergarten, is probably sitting by her phone, waiting for me to spill all the details of seeing anyone from high school. She knew how nervous I was to come after I filled her in on the way to this side of DFW. A waitress steps in from another table and leans over, notepad in hand.

"Can I get you ladies anything to drink?" She tucks a piece of hair behind her ear and poises her pen to write.

"Caramel macchiato, oat milk," Carla says, and I turn to the waitress.

"Make that two," I add.

She nods and looks around the table to make sure everyone else's drinks are topped off.

"We're waiting for one more." Jackie cranes her neck to look over the crowd, and her eyes narrow, then go wide. "Just kidding, he's here!" She stands, waving a hand excitedly at whoever she's looking at. I lean towards Carla and gaze between Kyle and Jessica. Then I spot him.

Sauntering towards us, gazing between his phone and a frantic Jackie, is Fitz Westfall, student body Vice President and first-hand-witness to the swift and complete takedown of my good girl reputation, and everything that followed.

CHAPTER 2

Piper

Ten Years Ago

I stared at the screen laying on the desk in front of me, open mouthed.

What. The. Fuck.

I was scrolling mindlessly through my feed as we waited for the last few minutes of AP History to tick by, the Friday afternoon before Labor Day weekend. Then, I saw it. It's like a bucket of ice water over my entire body. I sucked in a breath and leaned over, trying to get a closer look.

It was a photo. That's it, just a photo. But it's a photo of Andy, his arm slung over Jessica, both of them smiling at the camera in front of a fireplace, clearly about to head out on a date. The photo accompanied a status.

Andy Martin is *In a Relationship* with **Jessica Alverado**

Andy and Jessica.

Andy, who was seated two rows away from me.

Andy, who lived down the street from me.

Andy, who, not not 48 hours before, I'd hooked up with while his parents watched TV downstairs, none the wiser.

Slowly, I turned to look at him. His buzz cut was covered by a backwards baseball cap. He leaned forward, talking excitedly with Fitz, his best friend, who was twisted around in his chair to listen, same stoic expression as always plastered on his face. Andy's baseball gear sat next to his desk, piled high before practice the next period.

CHAPTER 2

Before I reacted in front of everyone, I turned to the front and raised my hand. Mrs. Calhoun looked up from her computer and eyed me.

"Can I please use the restroom?" I asked quietly. She narrowed her eyes. I'd only been in her class a few weeks, but my volume was never this low. It was probably suspicious. After a second, she nodded towards the door, signaling me to go. I could feel eyes on my back - probably Alex's - as I walked out as quickly as possible, my heels clicking against the tile as I hurried down the hall.

I found a corner in the back stairwell and slid down the cold wall, gripping my shaking hands together around my knees and putting my head down.

I knew getting involved with Andy was a bad idea from the beginning. My gut, and Alex, told me that it would end poorly. Andy had a reputation as a fuckboy long before I considered even thinking about him, but the slightest interest he showed made some insecure part of me satiated.

Until junior year, I was the token good girl. While Alex, Maria, and our other girlfriends snuck alcohol from their parents' liquor cabinets and downed shots, refilling the bottles with water before they noticed, I kept watch. I was the constant alibi, the nerdy best friend, Never Been Kissed in real life. Jonas Brothers level purity ring wearing, save myself for marriage like my Catholic upbringing told me to, blushed at the whisper of a penis, good girl.

Subtract braces, add hair extensions, learn how to work a sewing machine and suddenly I had more confidence than I'd ever experienced. It was subtle at first, but I found my footing, and even got my first kiss. Then, I went zero to 100 real fast, in true, Piper Delmonico fashion.

I was noticed. Not necessarily at school - no, these people have known me since I was 5. I hadn't ugly-ducklinged that hard. But while they were out using fake IDs to get into sweaty, strip-mall clubs, I found a place with my older sister's friends, going to drag races and stealing the jackets - and attention - of guys I'd had crushes on for years. In a matter of months I had my first boyfriend, one of Penny's friends, and very quickly rounded all the bases. Sex became my one vice, and I fell into it hard.

Andy, recently single from his long-term girlfriend, Jessica, overheard Alex, Maria, Vic, and me discussing my latest adventures - something I was still getting used to, as typically, it was the other way around. He was shocked to find that gone was the good girl. Secretly, anyways.

And then began a conversation that has repeated time and time again in my life. Casual discussion turned into a game of 20 Questions (men think they're so fucking clever), which turned dirty real fast, which turned into his asking when we could try some of the things we'd talked about in real life.

The summer passed by in a flurry of clandestine meetings and sneaking into his house late at night. We both knew it wasn't going anywhere serious - I still maintained my good girl image, if not for my own personal security, than the security of the privileges that reputation had earned me, with teachers, with my parents, with some students. And Andy, for all his attention in the times we met up, wasn't about to be seen with me in public.

Andy Martin, showing affection to a girl that notoriously wouldn't put out? Never.

But there I was, getting the thrill of having someone, anyone, who'd known me this long, looking at me the way he did when we were in bed together, like I was too sexy to stop looking at, made that little insecure piece of me so, so happy.

It's your own fault.

I stared down at my shoes - a pair of nude block heels, the sides of which I'd painted with red and green flowers. Very Lilly Pulitzer.

I hadn't expected him to stay single. I *had* expected him to tell me when he was seeing someone else, so I wasn't the side piece.

My head flew up as I heard a pair of heavy shoes rounding the corner into the stairwell, and to my utter horror, Jessica came into view, her dark brows knit together in worry. She saw me, and her eyes widened.

"Oh, shit," I stuttered, wiping at my eyes to catch the tears that were about to fall. Jessica raced over to where I sat and kneeled in front of me, her hand reaching out to touch my arm.

"Are you ok? I saw you come this way, you looked upset."

"I, uh." I continued to struggle for words as I looked up into her big brown eyes.

She looked happy. Why wouldn't she be? She was back with her boyfriend, back to being the it-couple they've been, off and on, since the 8th grade.

But looking into those eyes, seeing that happiness, something snapped. Not at her. But at Andy. I knew what I was getting myself into, but Jessica, she was innocent in all this. And she deserved to know.

"I've been seeing Andy." It was out of my mouth before I could stop it, and instinctively, I bit my lips together before I could blurt anything else out. Her head shot back, and she seemed momentarily startled. Her eyes searched my face, probably waiting for me to yell "gotcha!" But when it didn't come, she sat back on her heels.

"For how long?"

I swallowed. That was not the reaction I was expecting. Then, it dawned on me. She knew Andy's reputation. Hell, she'd been dealing with it for the last four years. So maybe she wasn't as unprepared for this as I thought.

"Since the end of last year," I answered shakily, digging my nails into my knees.

CHAPTER 2

"Until?" Her eyes met mine, and her look willed me to tell the truth.

"I was at his house Wednesday night." She closed her eyes, steeling herself with a deep breath. There was a moment of silence, and I could tell her mind was whirring. Mine was too. Then, she looked at me, and a smile plastered itself across her face. It's forced, but I could tell it's just as much for herself as it is for me.

"Thank you for telling me." She reached out and squeezed my hand, before standing and helping me up with her. I nervously brushed my backside off, still watching her as her hands ball at her sides. "I'm not mad at you, you had no idea, we weren't really telling anyone until we figured out what we were doing." She sighed, looking at the ground. "Clearly, we were on different pages." I fought the nervous giggle at the edge of my lips, and nodded instead. Her phone buzzed, and she pulled it out. "Listen, I've got to get back to the office to get my stuff before the bell. Can you get to class ok?" She gave my shoulder a squeeze. She was being much, much nicer than she should have been, given the circumstances. And I was incredibly grateful for it.

I nodded, and she gave me a final smile before turning on her heels and walking back towards the Freshman Vice Principal's office, where she was an aid this period. I made my way back to Mrs. Calhoun's room, taking my sweet time to kill the minutes I had to spend in the same room as Andy.

When I finally slid back into my seat, Alex turned and gave me a concerned look. I shook my head, nodding slightly towards Andy a few rows over, and her eyes narrowed. I moved my finger across my throat and without hesitation, she nodded. Friends this long, she could tell, I'm raging.

I heard a phone buzz on a desk a few rows over, and watched from the corner of my eye as Andy paused, mid sentence, and read whatever message just came through. Then, his head turned slowly towards me.

Fuck.

"Are you fucking kidding me?" My head snapped towards him, and it took me a second to register he's actually addressing me in public.

"Andy!" Mrs. Calhoun cried, standing at her desk and narrowing her gaze at him. He gave her a cursory glance before standing up too. I knew from how he was seething that Jessica must have said something to him.

"Are you seriously this much of a goody-two-shoes that you went and tattled on me?" he sneered, clearing the empty desk between us in two steps. He stood over me, and I shrank. Alex jumped from her seat, trying to step between us.

"Back off!" she warned. Behind him, Fitz and his baseball teammate, Ryan, stood too.

"I wouldn't have to tattle if you didn't give me something to tattle about." The second I said it, I regretted it, because if he was seething before, he was absolutely livid then.

"What did you just say to me, you cunt?" I drew back, realizing that the entire room had turned to watch us.

"Andy!" Mrs. Calhoun called again, walking around her desk and crossing her arms. "One more outburst like that and I'm sending you to Coach Tanger." He didn't even acknowledge that she spoke, instead, turning to Alex and looking her up and down.

"Did your killjoy nun-of-a-friend here tell you we've been fucking all summer? Or that she just opened her whore mouth and fucked me over with Jessica?" Alex glanced over at me before squaring up to Andy.

"I'm sure whatever she told Jessica was something you did to fuck up," she said cooly. "And yeah, she shared a lot about her experiences with you, including some of your, uh, inadequacies." She held up her pinky and wiggled it in front of her face, pouting as if it was the saddest thing in the world. If I wasn't being stared down by a six-two prime example of toxic masculinity, I could have kissed her. There was a snicker or two from across the room.

"That's enough!" Mrs. Calhoun said, her eyes wide. "Andy, go-"

Before she could finish what she was saying, Andy lunged towards both of us. Arms wrapped around both of his, pulling him back. He was spitting curse words, trying to break loose of their grip as the bell rang overhead, but nobody moves.

"Get out!" Fitz screamed, his hands wrapped tightly around Andy's forearm. His copper curls flooded around his face as he strained to hold his friend back. Alex grabbed my hand and dragged me out of the room, while behind us, Mrs. Calhoun pressed buttons on her phone. We didn't stop until we were far, far away, but the damage was done, and distance won't change that.

"Piper?" Jackie's voice breaks me out of my thoughts, and I turn to her. She's staring, eyebrows raised, and looks between me and Fitz, who's seated himself in the uncomfortable chair across from me. There was a perfectly good spot on the other side of Carla, but I notice he's moved the chair a few inches away from the rest. "I was just wondering if you remember Fitz?" she asks, as if his face hadn't been plastered across the school in his bid for office.

I turn to look at him. His once-longer red hair is short on the sides, leaving thick curls on top that are cut short. His face, while aged, and looking a little

CHAPTER 2

more worn than I'd expected, is nearly the same as it was when we graduated. Dark green eyes, framed by long red lashes, smatterings of freckles across his tan skin. He's wearing a gray Kitan suit that's worth at least three grand, with black Gucci loafers. Combined with his watch, his entire outfit is worth more than my car.

I always knew Fitz's family was comfortable, but I didn't realize they were *this* well-off.

I meet his eyes, and he gives me a curt nod before turning to Jackie.

"I don't have all day, we have six weddings, a bat mitzvah, a corporate conference, and a charity gala happening tonight." He rattles off the list coldly, like we're inconveniencing him by asking him to be here. The waitress returns to the table, and he turns to her. "Whatever your lightest roast is, black."

I purse my lips, settling back in my seat.

New decade, same Fitz.

For as long as I can remember, Fitz had been the quiet, stoic type. Even as a kid, he was never really a talker, but he knew how to get shit done, which is why he swept student body VP by a landslide. He wasn't warm and fuzzy, like Jackie, but he could deliver a speech with enough determination behind it to make anyone believe he was the man for the job. Any job, really. His cool, easy confidence had been his trademark, so why I'd expected anything less today is beyond me.

"Right," Jackie replies, eyebrows quirking. She looks down at her list in her lap. "Well, I was going to do introductions, but it looks like everyone knows each other so…I guess we can talk about what everyone's roles are?" She looks back up, and we all give reassuring nods. All, except Fitz, whose lips are set in a thin line. "Carla, I have you on guest list and big logistics with me, Fallon helping with that and entertainment. Jessica will handle marketing and updates to our social groups." She points to Kyle with her pen. "We'll have you help Piper with design, and-"

"Whoa, whoa, whoa." I put my hand up to stop her. "I'm just here for moral support. Maybe a graphic or two."

The waitress returns with Fitz's drink, and he takes it without so much as a thank you.

"Oh come on," Jackie says, practically pouting while she puts a hand on my knee. "We could really use your help. You're so talented." I feel heat rising to my face as she looks around the group. "Piper designed our homecoming shirts all four years," she says, and her tone of pride ingratiates me towards her that much more. "Now she's a big-time fashion designer."

"A lingerie designer," Fallon emphasizes, wiggling her eyebrows. I watch as Fitz, mid-sip, chokes on his coffee, and fight the urge to smile while he splutters.

Carla beams while the rest of the group just stares at me. Guess my mom never mentioned my career choice to Kyle's parents.

"And Fitz," Jackie continues as Jessica hits him on the back, trying to help as best she can, "will help us get the venue, food and bar situated, since WHG owns The Pine now." I quirk my head, looking at Fitz, who seems to have regained his composure.

So Fitz works for WHG. That would explain the continued seemingly lavish lifestyle.

In the Dallas-Fort Worth metropolitan area, there was one company that owned the places you wanted to marry, meet, or just generally party, and that was WHG. While I don't know much about the company, I know that the last three weddings I went to were all at WHG properties, and they'd recently acquired The Pine, a small, barn-style venue near where we all went to school.

"My staff is happy to help coordinate, I'm just here to make sure the initial information gets to them." He nods, as if adding finality to the distance he was putting between himself and his involvement in this group.

Not so fast, buddy. If I have to be here, so does your grumpy ass.

"Oh, I'm sure once we get into it, you'll have all sorts of ideas," Carla says. She reaches forward and gives him a reassuring pat on the knee. He stiffens, and then recoils like he's been shocked. So, not a fan of physical contact, are we?

As we discuss the beginnings of planning a reunion, one thing is clear—no one in this group has any business coordinating an event in the first place. Except, I'm sure, Fitz, who spends most of the time with his lips pressed together like he's biting back commentary. By the time we wrap up, we've set a tentative date, made a short list of entertainment ideas, and discussed a few possible themes, keeping with the rustic vibe of the venue.

"Ugh, this is going to be so much fun!" Fallon says as we all stand.

I sling my purse over my shoulder, and look at Jackie. "Thank you for putting this together." I give her arm a light squeeze. She takes my hand in both of hers.

"Thank you for coming! You'll jump in our Facebook group, right?" Immediately, she catches herself, and course-corrects. "Or - uh - why don't we start a group text?" She says the last part a little louder, looking around the group. There's a general grumble, and she turns back to me, grinning. "It's settled. And Piper?" She gives me a serious look. "I'm so sorry for your loss."

It really shouldn't surprise me when people say it anymore, but it does. So much so, that I'm temporarily at a loss for words as everyone gathers their jackets, getting ready to head out. After five years of widowhood, the pang still hits as fresh as it did the day the first person told me "I'm sorry for your loss."

Even five years later, all I can manage back is "Thank you."

I follow Carla back to her car, collapsing into the passenger seat and fighting

CHAPTER 2

the urge to run my hands through my hair. I'd taught myself a long time ago not to fuck up my well-tamed curls just because I was stressed.

"Did Fitz unclench his jaw at all during that meeting?" Carla breathes, her hands tight on the steering wheel in front of her. I try to take a deep, calming breath, knowing my entire body is triggered from the memories that flooded my head after seeing both Jessica and Fitz. Carla and I weren't close back then, but she must be able to tell I'm rattled, because she looks at me, then pulls out her phone and starts typing. "I don't know about you, but I need a meeting. Do you need a meeting?"

CHAPTER 3

Fitz

"You don't need to watch over me like this," José says, waving a spatula defiantly. "I know what I'm doing." I raise my eyebrows at him, and he gives me his signature, jolly grin, pointing his cooking utensil at me. "Something's got you in a mood."

Internally, I chastise myself for letting it show so plainly on my face. All I wanted to do was get food before hiding myself away in the office for the evening, but he was going to make me converse while he prepared my plate.

José has worked for WHG practically from the beginning. At one point, he was our head chef at the highest-grossing property we own in Texas—the Monarch Hotel, smack dab in the middle of downtown Dallas. But in recent years, he'd relocated to the venue closest to his grandkids.

Tonight, I find myself working from Cosette, a French Chateau style venue, far east from my home in North Dallas.

"I just don't want to be stuck here with you," I deadpan, looking down at my phone on the counter as it buzzes. He eyes me from between the shelves stacked high in front of him, already covered with tonight's entree of choice - French onion chicken with gruyere mashed potatoes. My phone continues to vibrate, over and over, as a series of texts roll in.

"That's a lie, and we both know it. You love working with me."

It's true, I do, not that anyone else would know that. José has known me since I was a boy, running around my father's ankles as they tried to confirm menus and pricing each year. And, he makes some of the best food I've ever had. That's coming from someone who regularly dines at MICHELIN-starred restaurants.

He points down to my phone, still buzzing. "Someone's popular."

(10) Messages reads across the front, alongside my other notifications, left unchecked since I came in here ten minutes ago, trying to snag a plate before service started.

CHAPTER 3

SportsWatch
Cowboys regroup after a disappointing season.

FitnessFix
You still have time to achieve your daily step goal!

Amazon
Your order has been delivered!

Oh, good. My book order arrived. I set a mental note to check the parcel box when I get back, which will likely be well after 1 a.m. Nothing says a wild Saturday night like glorified chaperoning and a stack of books on the fall of the Roman empire waiting for you at home.

"Not intentionally," I grumble, putting my phone in my pocket and taking the plate he holds out to me. French onion chicken, extra veggies, no cheese. I reach down to the counter, snagging a fork and knife out of the sorting bins, along with a handful of napkins, and make a beeline out of the kitchen before I get caught in the bustle.

"You're welcome!" José calls, and I roll my eyes at him over my shoulder.

When I settle at the desk in the admin office, far away from the reception starting in the main hall, I unfold a napkin in my lap and finally take a moment to scroll through all of my texts.

BETTY TIPTON
Thank you, again, for covering for me tonight.

Of course, I respond as I chomp away at my dinner. What was I going to do? Tell one of our longest-standing employees that, no, she couldn't go see her son home from his third deployment overseas? I mean, I know I've been more bitter than usual lately, but that doesn't mean I can't respect the needs of a valuable asset.

Divorce has made me, if possible, more cynical and detached than before. Years of commitment with the person I thought knew me best in the world, down the drain, for all the world to see. The epic crash-and-burn of my relationship with Olivia was a spectacle that met soap-opera proportions, having cheated on me with one of our oldest friends and then, as soon as the divorce was finalized, less than two years ago, promptly announcing her pregnancy.

We talked about having kids for years, but she told me it was never the right time. Part of me, I think, secretly hoped that having a child of my own would somehow give me the opportunity to right the wrongs I felt I'd experienced in my own childhood. The moments that made me cold and standoffish.

And it's not like I have anything better to do tonight, besides sit on my couch and scroll mindlessly through end of year P&L statements and annual employee reviews with Roscoe. I'd imagine even he finds that prospect pretty boring, and the most exciting thing in his life recently is new tennis balls.

I sigh, flipping to the chain where the rest of the unread messages lie. This many notifications makes me anxious. I'm relieved to see that I have the majority of the numbers already saved in my phone, at least. Some of the last names I know need to be updated, but I can tell them apart.

JACKIE GILLESPIE
Hi everyone, this is our reunion group chat! If everyone can please let the group know who you are, so we can save each other's numbers. - Jackie Anderson

FALLON NEWSBERRY
Love this! - Fallon Peters

JESSICA BAKER
Samesies! So excited. – Jessica Baker

CARLA MONTOGMERY
Great seeing everyone. – Carla Montgomery

KYLE HOFFMAN
Awesome catching up. – Kyle Hoffman

UNKNOWN SENDER
See you all soon. – Piper Davis

I feel my eyebrows knit together reading the last message. I could swear I have Piper's number saved from working on a group project senior year.

Piper. I hadn't thought about her in a hot minute, until today. Truthfully, I hadn't even recognized her when I sat down at Rooster's, and it wasn't until Jackie said her name that memories came streaming back.

CHAPTER 3

Ten Years Ago

The hallway was jam packed with people in the long passing period between lunch and the next class, when people stop by the school store to stock up on snacks for the afternoon. Most seniors made their way to their last class of the day before early release.

I leaned against a column outside the cafeteria, watching as Ryan tried to chat up some bleach blonde sophomore. I rolled my eyes when he said "Yeah, I mean, I got a bunch of scholarship offers, but I really just wanted to stay close to home." Lie. He got zero scholarship offers, and was going to our local community college until he could transfer to A&M.

"Incoming," Andy growled next to me, and I looked to see what he was staring at.

Down the hall, I saw Piper's bright red hair, bobbing along next to Vic. The two of them were heading towards the marketing classroom next to the school store, which was down the ramp in front of us. She carried a bundle of something in her hands, clutched to her chest in front of her binder.

Vic scanned the hallway, and he spotted us standing against the wall. I heard him mutter something to Piper, and while she didn't look up, she visibly stiffened, and walked faster towards the ramp.

"Where are you heading in such a hurry?" Andy drawled next to me, and he spit into his dip bottle before pushing off the wall. I followed, leaving Olivia, my girlfriend, chatting with her friends. Vic put a hand on Piper's back.

I could already feel my heart beating faster - whatever Andy was about to say or do, Piper didn't deserve it. She didn't do anything to earn his wrath other than tell the truth and save Jessica more heartache.

Truth be told, I was just as shocked as everyone the day we found out about Piper and Andy, if not more. Andy had been one of my best friends since kindergarten. While I didn't always agree with his tactics, or his sense of style, for that matter, he and his family, like Ryan's, were good to me when I was grasping at anything resembling a stable home life growing up. In exchange, I put up with a gregarious amount of camo, and, as we got older, Jager bombs.

But Piper, well, Piper deserved better than him. Hell, everyone deserved better than him, because one taste of attention from a girl years ago and his ego had inflated to the size of the sun. Jessica had tried - and failed - to keep his attention, and I wasn't really in the mood to continue supporting someone leaving a trail of fuckboy antics in his wake. I may not be an expert on love and relationships, but even I knew that the consequences of his actions would eventually catch up with him.

Sure, I didn't know Piper well. We'd steadily moved through school at the same pace, sharing the occasional class, lunch period, but she was mostly friends with the artsy crowd. She always dressed so well, especially compared to some of the choices people around school made. She had a reputation for being this prim and proper princess, trailing behind Alex in the same way, arguably, that I trailed behind Andy. But her personality was big - loud - and full of spirit. At least, until after that blowup. I only had one class with her, but it felt like someone had knocked the wind out of her.

Well, not someone. Andy.

The whispers around school had spread fast, and soon, even I couldn't tell what was true and what wasn't. A metaphorical scarlet letter was painted on her chest, no longer the prim princess.

"I said," Andy started, crossing the wide ramp in a few steps and coming to walk behind her. "Where are you heading in such a hurry?" He emphasized the last word with a swift kick to the back of her shoe, a pair of blue heels, and I watched as she nearly fell, grasping at the ramp's rail for support.

"Seriously?" Vic seethed, grabbing onto her forearm and urging her forward. Vic was small - probably just over five feet, and has always held a lean, muscular dancer's frame from years on the school dance team. Andy towered over him easily.

"Andy," I warned, my own arm reaching out to touch him. He shook it off, giving me a sideways glance before continuing.

"You got me three days of suicides from Coach Vaughn," he spit at her, aiming another kick. "You're lucky I didn't key your fucking car."

"It's your own damn fault," Vic threw over his shoulder.

"Shut up, you stupid faggot."

I recoiled, stopping in my tracks. Andy did a lot of fucked up things, but I'd never heard him use a word like that before. It made my stomach roil. I watched as he reached out his hand and shoved Vic, hard. Unprepared, Vic sprawled forward, landing on his hands as everything in his hands went flying. Snickering, Andy turned and landed a final kick towards Piper. She flailed, losing her grip on the railing. Her arm flew back and smacked Andy in the chest before she, too, fell forward into a heap next to Vic.

"Fuck," I breathed, pushing Andy away and jogging up to the two of them, offering Piper my hand. She lifted herself up on her elbows, her blouse gathered

CHAPTER 3

above her stomach, revealing a pierced belly button - *wasn't expecting that* - and a wad of fabric lay next to her. Piper stared at my outstretched hand, and then up to me, her eyes narrowing.

She didn't trust me. Understandable, I guess, given what I'd just let happen.

"What's this?" Andy said in a mocking tone, bending down to pick up the other heap of fabric sitting next to Vic. I felt a hand on my shoulder, and turned to see Olivia standing next to me, her books clutched tight to her chest. On the front of her binder, the strip of photos she made me take in a dark booth one summer night last year was clearly visible. It made me uncomfortable, that display of emotion, that last picture just barely covered by her arm with her nose pressed against mine.

Sometimes, it felt like she only had those on display for everyone else, like a trophy. Proof that somewhere, below the mask I wore, there's a real person inside. But I wasn't even sure if the guy caught in those intimate moments was a real person anymore.

She glanced between Piper and me, eyes questioning, and I pulled my hand back. There was a small crowd gathered around us, watching.

"Give it back," Vic demanded, gathering his belongings and pushing himself up. He grasped at the item in Andy's hand, which Andy promptly held over Vic's head like a fucking asshole, shaking it out.

"Is that a skirt?" Olivia asked, and I looked closer at it. It sure was. A red plaid miniskirt hung from Andy's hand, and he looked at it, disgust plastered on his face. Vic jumped, trying to grab the item, and Andy threw it at him like it was made of acid.

"Maybe Delmonico can lend you a pair of heels to go with that." Andy nodded at Piper, who was leaning against the wall, visibly shaken but fuming. A few people around us laughed, which fueled Andy to push on. "And if you're lucky, she'll let you rail her ass, so you can pretend she's a dude."

Vic lunged forward, but Piper gripped his arm, and he retreated just as the crowd around us parted.

"What's going on here?" Coach Vaughn, one of the vice principals, made his way through, crossing his arms and looking between all of us.

"Just a misunderstanding." Andy threw me a look that clearly begged me to help him out.

I stayed silent. For this, he deserved more ass whooping out on the field.

"A misunderstanding?" Piper cried. "Andy pushed us both down the ramp. He kicked me!" Coach's eyebrows raised, and he stared at his star player.

"Piper hit him too," Olivia said cooly, and I turned to stare at her. What the *fuck*? That wasn't a hit. That was flailing, arms trying to grasp onto something before she fell, and she fell anyway.

"Is that true?" Coach was asking Andy, not Piper, and he nodded, a glint of satisfaction in his eyes. I watched as Coach pinched the bridge of his nose before gesturing to Vic, Piper and Andy. "You three, in my office, now." Piper was spitting curse words in a language I didn't recognize as she trailed behind Vic. Both of them kept their distance from Andy as they followed Coach Vaughn back up the ramp and down the hall. I turned to Olivia.

"That wasn't cool," I said, so low only she could hear. She raised her eyebrows at me. "She was trying to keep herself from falling."

"Why do you care?"

It was a valid question. Why did I care? I mean, I'm human - it was unfair for Piper to get punished for defending herself. But if was honest with myself, it was more than that.

Over the years, we haven't interacted much, but I think everyone in our grade noticed when she came to school one day without her signature, lime green braces and had about a foot of hair added to her head. Alex, her best friend, had always been the more popular one - the flirty blonde artist was every emo kid's wet dream. But there was something about the new confidence she gained that made people, myself included, take notice.

Even Olivia, who isn't particularly observant of anyone she deems too lowly to be worthy of her attention, had said something off-handed about an outfit Piper wore one day at lunch. "Acceptable," she called it, which from her, was high praise.

It was more than that she doesn't deserve the shit Andy was doing to her. It was that I cared that she didn't deserve it. And that scared me. Caring meant having any moniker of feeling towards someone, and that isn't something I took lightly. It'd taken years for Olivia to weasel her way into earning the title of "girlfriend." Honestly, sometimes it was easier to fall into that role with her, someone who seemed to care more about the status it brought her than a true relationship, than it would be to try and find it with somebody else.

Besides, I was heading to Austin at the end of the year for college, Olivia by my side. Caring about anyone, besides the small group of people I'd already let see any fragile piece of me, wasn't something I was about to do.

"I don't." Lie. Absolute lie.

Olivia narrowed her eyes at me, considering my words, and then shook her head. She plastered that head-bitch-in-charge smile onto her face and took my hand forcefully in hers. I winced at the public display of affection, but didn't fight it. Anything to calm the storm she threatened to brew.

An hour later, I watched as Andy stomped across the parking lot, nearly clipping the side of his truck with his equipment bag.

"Coach told me to take the afternoon off to cool down," he sneered, throwing

CHAPTER 3

the bag into his truck bed. I raised my eyebrows at him.

"That's all he said?"

"He fucking told me if I get out of line again, I'll be benched in the spring." Andy's voice was gruff, like he'd been yelling. I tilted my head at him. Consequences for his actions, finally. "That stupid bitch nearly got me kicked off the team - oh don't look at me like that."

"Like what?"

"You're being a smug bastard, and it's weird when you're not 'Marble Man Fitz.'" I felt the corner of my mouth turn up slightly at the nickname. Years of being told that emotions make you weak will do that.

"Did she get in trouble too?" I asked, regaining my composure. Andy grunted, opening his car and reaching in to grab his can of dip. He pulled a pinch and slid it into his mouth before answering.

"Coach tried, her mom came into the office screaming when I left. Something about threatening to sue the district and taking Piper to Disneyland," he explained. I quirked my eyebrow. "No idea, dude, bitch is as crazy as her daughter." Internally, I winced. "I'm just praying at this point she doesn't tell my mom, she'll ground me until graduation."

"Why would she tell your mom?"

"Because, we - uh - we live down the street from each other. Her mom recognized me today." Realization hit me. That's how this happened so quietly. We all lived so close to each other, if the two of them had been spotted driving around together, someone would have put two and two together.

"So you, what, snuck over to each other's houses?"

"Sometimes," Andy answered truthfully, leaning against his truck and crossing his arms. I sat against the window of my dark BMW, unsure of how much of this I wanted to hear. "Sometimes I'd pick her up, she'd hide so no one could see her, and we'd go somewhere and fuck around in the car." A dark smile spread across his face. "One time, we did it in the field behind the rec center." I bit my lips together to keep the shocked sound at the back of my throat from escaping. The mental picture of Andy and Piper fucking in the field where we used to catch frogs as kids made me want to puke.

"Maybe you should lay off her, man," I suggested casually. He looked at me, confused, and I was quick to cover my tracks. "The last thing you need is to get benched for your senior season. Shelley would murder you in your sleep, and your sister would help her hide the body." He laughed - a short, loud noise - before relenting.

"I'll try, dude, but something about her gets under my skin. It's annoying, ya know?"

I did. I really, really did.

Piper looked so different today; healthy - glowing, even - compared to the last time I'd seen her, at graduation. Back then, she was smiling, taking pictures with Alex and Vic, tossing their caps in the air. But looking back at that time, I felt a twinge of guilt in the back of my head. She seemed...dulled. Like her sparkle had gone. I knew that Andy was a huge part of that. Today, it felt like it had come back to her. Like she had resumed whatever regimen of glitter, motivational quotes, and caffeine had fueled her the first decade I'd known her.

Hold on a second. Why did I even remember that? Or notice it, for that matter?

Sighing, I reread Piper's message a couple of times, shifting in my seat. It doesn't look right. Piper Davis. Wait. Her name wasn't Davis, was it?

I pull up my contacts and search her name, and sure enough, there it is. Piper Delmonico. The number is different, too.

Hmm, she got married. And she changed her number? Curious, I open Facebook on my phone and search both names. Neither come up for anyone living in the state of Texas. I browse for a moment, thinking, maybe, she moved back and hadn't updated her profile. I even try both phone numbers. Nope. Instagram. Nope. LinkedIn. Nope. I check everything I can think of before realizing that she must have her stuff locked down so tight I can't find her, even with the mutual connections we're bound to have, or she doesn't have social media at all.

In my browser, I type Piper Delmonico Davis and click search. A flood of results swarm the front page, and at the top, there's a carousel of images. The first one is clearly the Piper I'm looking for. Without clicking on the picture, I can tell that she's behind a man with her arms draped over him. This must be Mr. Davis. She holds a bouquet in her hand, and they both beam at the camera.

My eyes scan over the search results, none of which are social media profiles, and my heart lurches. I click on the first link.

Mickey Davis Obituary - Paulsville, KS | Avery-Collins Mortuary and Crematory

Mickey Angelo Davis, age 28, formerly of Paulsville, passed away on Saturday, May 16 at Humble Spirit Hospital in Fort

CHAPTER 3

Worth, Texas, following a brave battle with pancreatic cancer.

Mickey is the son of Oscar and Melissa Davis. He graduated from Paulsville High School, and pursued a bachelors in business management from Kansas State University, where he graduated with honors and played on the baseball team. Mickey began a flourishing career in automotive insurance after moving to Fort Worth, Texas.

Mickey married Piper Delmonico Davis on January 1 of this year, and she survives. Additional survivors include: his parents, Oscar and Melissa Davis, Paulsville, KS; an older sister, Elizabeth Brown and husband, Tyler, as well as nephews Michael and Mickey, Paulsville, KS; a younger brother, Zander Davis, Paulsville, KS; and his in-laws, Luca and Bianca Delmonico, Fort Worth, TX. He was an avid KSU and Kansas City Royals fan, and enjoyed spending time outdoors with the dog he shared with Piper, Bex.

Funeral services will be at 9 a.m. Saturday, May 23 at Avery-Collins Chapel. Burial will take place at Paulsville Community Cemetery. Visitation will be Friday, May 22 from 5-7 p.m. at Avery-Collins.

Pallbearers include Zander Davis, Tyler Brown, Brett Robinson, Nolan Calloway, Kenneth Perez, and Vic Montero. Memorial contributions may be given to "Erickson Foundation" in care of the mortuary. Arrangements are under the direction of Avery-Collins Mortuary & Crematory.

I roll my chair away from my desk, bracing my hands on the edges for support, taking a deep breath. Holy fuck.

Piper's husband died. *Died.* And based on the dates, they hadn't been married long before he was gone. I don't even know where to start. Part of my brain is telling me to text her separately and -

Wait, what am I saying? *Text her my sympathies?* Me?

Immediately, I steel my spine, shaking my head and trying to knock some sense into myself. Fitz Westfall doesn't do touchy-feely.

I'm about to close out of the screen in front of me, when I notice, at the bottom, a comment section. **(48) Comments**, it reads, and I instinctively scroll down.

> **Anonymous**
> We're going to miss you so much, Mickey.

> **Anonymous**
> Miss you already, bud!

> **Anonymous**
> Can't believe his wife left his daughter out of this.

> **Anonymous**
> R.I.P.

Wait. *What?* I scroll back up one comment, and read it a few times, making sure I'm seeing it right. Daughter? The comment was right in one regard - it didn't have any mention of a daughter, or kids at all, for that matter.

I see, right below, there are other comments just like it.

> **Anonymous**
> No mention of Kayla? Classy.

> **Anonymous**
> This feels like it's missing someone.

> **Anonymous**
> Piper keeps saying he doesn't have a daughter, but the proof is in the paperwork.

Attached to the last comment is a photo, and tentatively, I open it, praying I'm not about to download a trojan horse porn virus onto this WHG computer.

It's a birth certificate. I give it a quick once-over, and spy the name on the line for father. Mickey Angelo Davis. Under *child's name*, it reads Kayla Marie Lofgren.

Before I can process what's in front of me, there's a knock at the door, and someone walks in without waiting for my response. I'm poised to lose it, but see it's José, his white apron covered in what looks like chocolate.

"How was it?" He gestures to the plate in front of me and narrows his eyes, and I realize I've barely touched my food. "Everything ok? Not like you to go hungry."

"I'm fine," I reply quickly. Too quickly. He gives me a suspicious look as I glance between him and the computer screen between us. "Really, just looking over some numbers. How are things going down there?"

"About to start the dances," he murmurs, his face slipping into a dreamy smile. *Bleh.*

If I had it my way, Olivia and I wouldn't have even done any dances. No one would have. We probably would have eloped and taken a much-needed vacation in some wintery location, far, far away from both of our families. But no, she wanted the attention, and God forbid, a Westfall kid doesn't get married in a WHG venue.

"Holler if you need anything." At my words, he gives me one last piercing gaze, before retreating back behind the door. I let out a deep breath, my hands clasping behind my head. I wobble in my chair, my brain whirring.

It takes a special kind of vindictive person to keep a child away from their parent, let alone their dying parent. I know that longing to connect with a parent all too well, except mine died long before I had the opportunity to even remember them. I wonder if Kayla was treated the same way?

On the other hand, Piper doesn't really seem like the vindictive type. But, who am I kidding? I've probably spoken fifty words to the woman in the last twenty years. And for my own sake, I'm going to keep it that way.

CHAPTER 4

Piper

"So sorry we're late," Carla purrs, and slides into the seat next to Alex. At the high top table where she's perched, my best friend is half standing, hands resting on her protruding belly. Across from her sits Penny, my sister, who seems to be just settling in herself. I sit next to her.

"What else is new?" Alex throws over her shoulder, leaning back to put a hand over the one that Carla uses to squeeze her shoulder. "Meeting go well?"

"Yeah." I lace my purse strap through the hook underneath the table, thankful that this seedy bar has at least one bonus feature. "They were talking all about resentments."

"Which was ironic as fuck," Carla adds with an eye roll, "considering I don't think I've seen Piper so wound up since that time she saw *she who must not be named* on TV at that Royals game."

"I fucking love that name," Penny laughs, waving a waitress over. "Don't get me wrong, it fits, it just makes me think of the bitch with her nose cut off." I shrug in agreement. That was half the fun of using the nickname for my former mother in law, Melissa. I could picture myself sending a well-placed curse hurtling towards her with a flick of a wand for all the things she's said about me - to me.

The waitress saddles up to the table, and Penny says "Rum and Coke, double, and…" She looks at all of us. "Three club sodas."

"With lime," Alex adds, patting her stomach. The waitress looks at the two of us without a clear excuse for not ordering a drink, and I see her eyes twitch momentarily towards the ceiling before she walks away.

It took me a while to get comfortable going out to bars again after I stopped drinking. Long before I even took my first drink, I was dragged into places like this and forced to sip on a soda while Alex and our friends used their fake IDs or feminine wiles to drink the night away. I was on standby, as a designated driver and a wingwoman of sorts. But I was never really a public drinker. In the short period in which I drowned my sorrows with a bottle, it was always at home, which is why one of the keys to my sobriety has been working in the office nearly every day.

Living with Carla has been one of the best decisions I've ever made, leaving the house I shared with Mickey behind for our modest apartment. Carla's edging towards five years of sobriety, with myself just passing the three year mark. After countless hours and dollars spent towards processing my trauma and following substance abuse, the way my body - and my mind - felt wasn't something I was going to give up because of my temptations.

"Who all was there?" Alex asks as the waitress brings over our drinks.

"Us, Fallon, Jackie, Jessica - she's married now, did you know -

"Yeah, to a fucking gorgeous specimen of a woman," Penny says, taking a giant gulp of her drink, her thick, dark hair falling around her face. I eye her. "What? Mama's got one night out this week, I'm going to enjoy it before I go back to diaper duty. And if you saw Jessica's wife, you'd agree."

"Don't forget Kyle," Carla adds. "Oh, and Fitz."

Alex's eyes snap to mine, and I shoot Carla a glare.

"No wonder you needed a meeting," Alex mutters, taking a sip of her drink. "I thought you were just nervous about going in general."

"I'm fine," I say, and Carla gives my shin a kick under the table. "Fuck! Ow." I know what it's in response to - fine is sort of a curse word in A.A. It's the dismissal of emotions, which can and often will lead to resentments and development of further character defects, the foundation of the program. "I'm...I don't know." I take a deep breath.

"I mean, the man is still hot as fuck," Carla says nonchalantly, and I see Penny and Alex give her looks. Penny downs the rest of her drink, and motions to the waitress for another. "But he's a dick. A total dick."

"I don't think he's a dick," I argue, and all three of them look at me. "I mean, fuck." I stumble on my words.

Why was this so difficult to articulate? Arguably, Fitz is a dick. Or at least, he was a decade ago. He had stood by while his best friend made it his personal mission to tear me down, and it had left me...hollow. Small. In a time where I had every opportunity to thrive, I let Andy make me small. A phenomenon that happened again and again, especially with Mickey, until I stumbled, hungover, into a meeting three years ago, reconnecting with Carla and finding my sobriety.

Fitz wasn't to blame for my trauma, but he certainly didn't help when he'd had the opportunity. And the small sliver of the man I saw today wasn't enough to tell me one way or the other whether he was still the guy that stood by the sidelines while bad things happened in front of him. I could barely read his face, much less tell if the emotions behind it were any different.

On the stage in front of us, the lights start to brighten, and the band steps in from one side, taking their places behind their instruments. Forgotten is my struggle of explaining my current headspace. The waitress is just in time with Penny's drink - she takes it, holding it in one hand over her head while she wolf-whistles loudly. From the stage, Brett, her husband, looks up from his bass, squinting through the spotlight on him under the brim of his fedora. He grins when he spots her, and signs "I love you" enthusiastically before going back to what he was doing.

"Bleh," Carla wretches, squeezing her lime in her club soda. "You two are disgusting."

"You're just jealous." Alex gives Carla a sideways grin over her shoulder, adjusting in her seat, and then turning to Penny. "I think it's adorable that the two of you are still like this after ten years."

"Like you two aren't adorable too," Penny says, taking a smaller sip of her drink this time and clapping as the mics screech on. Alex gives a hazy smile and holds her belly tighter.

The two of them have grown close, something I never could have seen coming growing up. Penny and I fought like lions as kids, and Alex not-so-secretly loved helping me torment her and her friends whenever possible. But when you're married to best friends, like they were to Nolan and Brett, it changes your relationship. I should know. I was married to the other piece of that trio, even for the shortest of time.

When Brett's band starts playing, I let my mind tune out a little bit. Meeting up to support Brett and his music has been something we've tried to do regularly - to stay together and close after experiencing so much together. Carla was an added bonus, as the other single woman and my friend in sobriety. She hadn't been there with us as the shitshow that was the final months of Mickey's life unfolded, but she went through her own trauma that put her in my path, and we had all bonded over that.

In the years since becoming a widow, I had experienced my fair share of ups and downs, but the one thing that always pulled me through was the friends and family who stood by Mickey and me when his own family couldn't. Wouldn't, really.

That ease, that healthy understanding provided by my support system is what got me through - and continues to get me through - the best and the worst days, is why today was triggering, but not in the way I'd thought.

It was almost...positive? Like I was buzzing all over still, remembering the gushing words Jackie and Fallon had said about my career. I'd put a lot of work into getting where I was, especially after years of setbacks while taking care of

CHAPTER 4

Mickey. And the reaction on the faces of the people I didn't talk to - of Fitz, especially - made me feel powerful. I knew it wasn't what they had expected, which made it all the better. They probably thought I'd go into kid's clothing or something, with the way sunshine and rainbows practically shot out of my ass for years.

Fitz, though. Man, I hadn't thought about him in a long time. Is he still with Olivia? I hadn't noticed a wedding ring on his finger, but I also wasn't paying particular attention. I'm not about to ask Carla if she noticed, she'd never let me hear the end of it.

But there's a small part of me, I think, that has always wondered - what if? What if, instead of Andy having overheard my conversations with my friends about my escapades, if it had been Fitz? What if he had been the one I had found myself entangled with? Not that I would ever have been involved with someone knowing they had a significant other. History has shown that.

I shake my head, trying to refocus back on the room around me. Who was I kidding? Stoic, quiet Fitz? Our personalities would have clashed, even back then. With time and recovery, I'd become less restrained in my passion and excitement for life, even compared to the years before I started whittling myself away for men. That isn't something I'm willing to do again.

※

When I slide into my desk chair on a Monday morning a few weeks and several attempts to get out of reunion planning later, Vic pops his head over the cubicle wall and gives me a sly smile, his pristine eyebrows raised.

"So, how did it go?"

"Dismal," I say, kicking my heels off and throwing my purse on the hook on the cubicle wall. In the nearly four years I've been at AllHearts, my space has truly become just that - a reflection of my time at the company and the work I've done. The walls of the cubicle are plastered with some of my favorite designs, along with photos of myself with models, other designers, at events and conferences. Vic's, in comparison, looks like it's been sterilized for anything seemingly personal, with the exception of the small cactus I gave him for his birthday last year.

As design team leads, our heads were constantly in the sand together, so why they put a wall between us...well, it was probably because we talk too much, and often forget our volume.

Truthfully, I never thought I would work for a company like AllHearts. I was in marketing when Mickey got sick, and the flexibility that world offered me became all too important as his disease progressed. But my mind always came back to designing. Even before becoming sober, I was sick of promoting other people's designs instead of making my own. So when Vic told me about this work from home job on his team, I jumped at the chance. It wasn't until I was in office, actively seeking sobriety, that I flourished. I needed to be around people, to suck in their creative energy and use it to fuel my fire.

"That bad?" Vic asks, sitting back down and rolling his chair around the wall to face me.

"It just went like it always does," I respond heavily, fishing in my bag and pulling out a can of Dr. Pepper, popping it open and taking a long sip before continuing. "Things were going great, and then he wanted to know where I worked. He knew I was a designer." I sigh, shaking my head, spinning one of my rings around on my finger. "It's not like I could lie, so I just ripped the bandaid off, and it was like I'd flipped a switch. He couldn't focus on anything I said, literally just stared at my boobs like he had x-ray vision."

"Gross." He makes a face, drinking his coffee, his big brown eyes surveying me over the cup. "So I take it there was no sexy time?" I grimace, shaking my head in disgust.

"Absolutely not." It's not like the man wasn't hot. He was a firefighter, for fuck's sake. I was with a firefighter - or two - during the craziest time of my life, and, oh, the stamina. But I'd worn out my widow-ho phase a long time ago, and the way his eyes stayed steady on my chest while I spoke made me want to puke. Then when he'd tried to kiss me goodnight, I could practically feel the hard-on through his jeans.

"Have you put any more thought into the designs for the reunion?" Half-ignoring Vic, I turn back to my desk and sign into my computer.

"Not really." I look back at him over my shoulder. "Kyle and I are trying to find time in the next couple of weeks to get a plan together, but really, I need to go see the space, take some measurements. You know me. I'm visual." He nods.

"I do." Vic pauses, and I watch my messages load up.

Marketing
Q4 Social Roundup
Hi Team! Wanted to share EOY numbers with everyone, as...

Excalibur Park
Meatless Monday
Did you hear about our exciting Meatless Monday optio...

CHAPTER 4

Jerry Lake
EOY Departmental Revenue Reports
Good morning, please see the attached by-department rep...

"Have you thought about asking Fitz to go look at the venue?" I whirl around in my seat, facing Vic completely.

"I have zero intention of putting myself in a room with him again until the reunion, if I can help it. He's supposed to send the group his assistant's information." Vic shrugged, taking another long sip of coffee, eyeing me.

Vic nearly had just as much reason to be apprehensive about Fitz as I did. He was a victim of Andy's wrath in high school, sometimes more than I was, just for being gay, and I wouldn't have been surprised if he'd been understandably protective of me, like I would be for him. But when I'd told him about my encounter with everyone at the first reunion planning meeting, he'd swiftly reminded me of the work I'd done to face all of my resentments, even the ones I'd had towards him - because there had been some that I'd had to work through with my sponsor.

"Just a thought. Might get done faster if you're not waiting on him to get his shit together." I ponder the idea, scrolling through more emails until I feel a presence behind my back.

"Happy Monday," Brianna's voice comes out as a slow drawl, and I turn around to face her, plastering a smile on my face.

"Happy Monday!" we trill together. There is nothing happy about Mondays. Mondays can go die a slow, painful death at the bottom of the Trinity River. But Brianna, in her pant-suited, black-loafered glory, is not somebody I can say that to.

"Did you two look at the end of year revenue reports?" she asks, leaning casually against the other wall of my cubicle as if we're best friends. It's not that I dislike Brianna. Ok, I do. But that was mostly because nearly every conversation I had with her ended with being told to tame down my designs. To think more inside the box. To look at spreadsheets and numbers and build on current, popular designs instead of doing what I really want - make something spectacular.

"Yes," Vic pipes in before I can, and I'm glad he saves me from telling the truth - that I'd just rolled in after a night of drowning my post-date sorrows in a pint of Halo Top, half a season of True Blood, and a stint of leather-tooling that left my hands sore.

"Good." Brianna holds her china coffee cup up to her face, seemingly thinking before taking a sip. "I'm sure you saw that we're below our EOY goals by 12%."

"I did see that." His tone is measured. "But, I mean, after Roger-"

"I thought we discussed that we weren't going to talk about that again," she says, her voice now also devoid of emotion, like she's trying not to let anyone, including us, know that she's upset.

Roger might as well be the other they-who-shall-not-be-named in my life. Talking about the former member of our team, who left after about six months of struggling to fit in here. Flamboyant, extroverted, and opinionated, we got along swimmingly, but Texas is a difficult place to live when you're out and loud. I'm only loud, and I have a hard enough time finding good people to tolerate my lack of volume control.

Since moving to L.A. with his partner last fall, his position has been vacant, leaving our team scrambling to pick up the pieces after what we'd hoped would be a productive end to the last year.

Brianna seemed to regain her composure, straightening her suit jacket a little.

"We need something fresh for the winter line," she says finally. "Something...whimsical." I turn back to my computer, opening up a document to take notes. "I'm thinking, icy fairy, maybe...Ooh!" She stands up straighter, pointing at us. "Elsa!"

I turn my head towards Vic, who's doing a much better job of hiding his horror than I am. I type away, squelching the nausea that rolls. Yuck.

"Sure thing," I say, and wheel around to face her.

"I want rough sketches by the tenth of next month." She taps her finger on her chin, her green eyes searching. "Let's say...15 per person. We can whittle down from there." I stare at her. Our team was tiny but mighty - with just a few more outside of Vic and myself, plus an intern - but not that mighty. Between active revisions for our fall pieces, finalizing our summer launch, and that, I won't even have time to sleep.

Not to mention the reunion.

"We can do it," Vic says, though after knowing him for two decades, I can tell his tone is less than authentic. I feel him put a reassuring hand on my shoulder as I try to ensure my face doesn't give my emotions away. Without another word, Brianna turns on her loafers and walks away, leaving me to put my elbows on my desk, rubbing my temples.

"I need to get this reunion shit out of the way so I can focus on work. I literally don't have time for this." I look down at my phone, and then sideways at Vic. He's giving me a knowing smile. "Fuck off."

"Feisty," he says saucily, returning to his desk, and I look down at my own, where my phone sits.

Fuck it. I can't wait around forever.

CHAPTER 4

PIPER DELMONICO
Hi there. Any chance I can come take a look at the venue for the reunion? Kyle and I need to get started on a few items, but I want to get a good visual, take some measurements, etc. If not, it's totally fine-

I catch myself. No. It's not totally fine. He volunteered the venue. That's great. But I needed access to get my part done. I shouldn't dismiss that just to make him feel better. I delete the last sentence and press send. It's a few minutes before he responds.

FITZ WESTFALL
I can arrange for the venue manager to meet you there one morning this week.

I bite my lips. Mornings during the week. I don't want to bother them while they're getting ready for an event, which I'm sure they will be on a weekend, but I couldn't leave the office for this.

PIPER DELMONICO
I work 9-5 M-Th, but I have a half day Friday. Would 2 on Friday work?

It takes him a little longer to respond.

FITZ WESTFALL
That's fine. I'll get it arranged.

PIPER DELMONICO
Thank you!

FITZ WESTFALL
Of course. Let me know if you need anything else.

I reread the message. A few times, actually.
Let me know if you need anything else.
I don't think I've ever heard - or read - Fitz say something so...casual? But my worry is satiated, knowing that I can cross a few things off my list after this weekend.

CHAPTER 5

Fitz

"Roscoe!" From across the park, he comes running, his pointy ears flying back on top of his head, long legs bounding on the wood chips. My dog comes to a screeching halt in front of me, offering the tennis ball in his mouth, and I take it, tossing it back in the same direction. He goes off after it, and I fight the urge to roll my eyes as he nearly trips over a tiny pug. Settling down into the bench behind me, I sip at the beer in my hands, trying to let the last few weeks roll off my back.

Spring is one of the busiest times for us - everyone wants a spring wedding. But even more than that, corporate clients have renewed budgets they can spend, people are traveling for spring break, and the nice weather means more people coming to enjoy our in-house restaurants with city line patio views.

Which means we're swamped. I'm not boots on the ground as much anymore, but the day to day of fielding calls from our locations, sifting through insurance documents and repair requests, has been mind-numbing. When I was appointed Chief Operations Officer just a few years ago, I thought I would still get to do what I enjoyed - watching the work we put into events pay off, like a well oiled machine. But then I realized that the job was more paperwork than personal ROI, and after Olivia...I was exhausted.

Taking time like this away from the office, away from the home I shared with her, just me, Roscoe, a beer and the dog park, is essential to my wellbeing. Without it, I'd probably explode on Georgia, my assistant.

"Vic, I'm gonna kill you!" My head whips around at the familiar voice, and I scan over the picnic tables on the deck behind me, flanked on either side by rows of food trucks. Sure enough, there she is. Piper.

She sits at a table near the ledge overlooking the park, her hair pulled back from her face, revealing dark-framed glasses. She's overdressed - not that I'm surprised - in a pair of plaid capri pants and a blue, short sleeved sweater-shirt, looking like she just stepped off the set of Mad Men.

Around the table sit three men - one I instantly recognize as Vic, from high school. He's filled out since the last time I saw him, probably graduation, but his face is so similar. The other two I don't recognize, but one, with a fedora covering his head, has his arms wrapped around her shoulders, trying to hold her back as Vic dangles what looks like a piece of squid in front of her face.

I feel my face flame. Was that her boyfriend?

Where did *that* question come from? I bristle, turning away and taking another sip of my beer.

I tried to stop myself from looking into things further after my search the other night went haywire. I really did. But after laying awake half the night thinking about it, I'd finally pulled my phone out and continued.

The comments were bad. Like, really bad. Every platform I could find, every place his obituary was listed, there was commentary about Piper, Mickey and his daughter, Kayla.

The thing that really stuck with me was the baseball tournament they still held in his honor. I stumbled across the Facebook event after finding an old news article about it, and sure enough, at the top of the page, there was a picture of a little girl, flanked by a photoshopped image of who I'd come to learn was Mickey, complete with little angel wings, like he was looking over her.

A little part of me wanted to fucking vomit looking at it. I mean, sentimentality has never really been my thing, but that was just...a lot.

The tournament raised money for local cancer patients each year, and it looked like their donations were more sizable as time went on. Well, at least they were turning the experience into something positive.

I couldn't believe that the person who had recoiled at the idea of impropriety all those years ago was capable of cutting off a child from her dying father, but nothing I saw told me otherwise - and believe me, I looked. And seeing her here, my insides feel a little molten. With anger? I'm not sure.

"You ok, man?" I look up to see Todd walking slowly, his nearly overflowing beer in his hands as he balances it with a giant soft pretzel. I nod wordlessly as Roscoe runs up again, nuzzling my knee with his tennis ball filled mouth.

"Just saw someone I know, not a big deal." He sits down, and appraises me. Todd, my neighbor, and I had really only started hanging out in the last few years - since shit hit the fan in my life, and he found me taking a sledgehammer to the custom oak dining table I'd had made for Olivia for our 5th anniversary in our backyard. He, too, was recently divorced, and had stepped in to fill the role that Ryan vacated when he fucked my wife.

"Are you sure you're good? You look like you saw a ghost." Todd presses, staring between me and the vague area where Piper and her group are seated.

CHAPTER 5

Not a ghost. Or, maybe, just a ghost of a person I used to know, and not even that well.

But it all goes back to the question Olivia asked me all those years ago - why do I care? Why do I, Fitz Westfall, give a flying fuck what this woman did or did not do to an innocent child?

Maybe because a part of me relates to that child, for not getting to know a parent fully. And another part wants to believe that none of it is true in the first place.

"Oh, fuck, Fitz!" Savannah calls out in a hoarse whisper, her hips slamming against the edge of the desk as I grind into her, my hand holding her hair securely at the nape of her neck. Her fingers claw at the paperwork in front of her, nearly knocking over a contract I've been working on all morning.

"Careful," I seethe, pulling her hair harder. She lets out a whimper before finding balance on an empty part of the desk, pushing back against my cock. "I'm close." She makes a guttural noise, one hand reaching between her legs, I'm sure to further herself along, and when I feel my orgasm hit me, she's not far behind, muffling her cries by biting her lips. I stare silently at the ceiling of the office, mouth open, slightly dazed.

For years, Olivia was the only woman I'd ever slept with. But post-separation, I was bitter - well, still am bitter - out for revenge and the only way I knew how to get it was by fucking my way through the hardest time of my life.

There were other women - a good career, good car, good life from the outside, will do that - but Savannah was the safe option. She came on strong after the divorce, seemingly always around thanks to her former job at The Monarch and her friendship with my sister, Frannie. I knew from the beginning that Fran was well aware of both the fact that it was happening, and that it was probably better for me to vent my sexual frustration with her eager friend than a stranger.

Savannah knew, I *made sure* she knew, what this was from the start.

My phone in front of us starts to ring, and I flip it over to see Georgia, my assistant, calling. Savannah turns back to look at me, and I answer, my finger at my lips.

"Yes, Georgia?" I pull out of her slowly, and watch as her head falls back in a silent moan.

"Tif just let me know your two o'clock is there. She didn't want to disturb you. What are you doing locked up in-"

"Thank you, Georgia." I cut her off, hanging up the call and getting dressed hastily, adjusting my tie and throwing my jacket back on. I watch as Savannah pulls up her underwear, smoothing her dress out before leaning up to give me a kiss. I turn my head at the last moment, letting her lips fall on my cheek, and she pulls back, frowning.

"What-"

Before she can get out whatever she was going to say, the door handle jiggles, and I cross the distance, unlocking and opening it. Tif, the office coordinator at The Pine, at least has the audacity to look startled.

"I'm so sorry, Georgia said..." She trails off, and I make a mental note to say something to Georgia later - nothing too harsh, as she's one of the only reasons I've been able to stay afloat the last few years in this position.

"Don't worry about it, Tif," I say, turning back to Savannah. "We can talk later about the rest of that proposal." She catches on quickly, nodding.

"Sounds good, I'll be in touch, Mr. Westfall." She scuttles out of the room, and it isn't until I look back at Tif that I notice Piper behind her.

I realize, for the first time, how tall she is. While she's wearing heels, she would still have several inches on Tif without them. Her dark, curly hair is pinned off to one side, exposing her collarbone in a wide-necked purple blouse.

She looks surprised.

"Uh, hi," she says, blinking twice. "I thought I was meeting with Claudia."

"Claudia has another meeting, I told her I'd fill in." I see Tif give me a look out of the corner of my eye, and I will her not to say anything to correct me. In reality, I'd told Claudia to go supervise the tool company executives setting up their annual awards dinner in the event space. "We have quite a bit going on today, so I want her full attention with our paying clients."

She lurches back at my words, and I realize how harsh they sound. Paying clients. Like she wasn't doing us all a favor by taking on the design aspect of this event, something she clearly didn't want to do in the first place.

"Why don't we head down to the space and take a look before things get too hectic?" I gesture behind her to the door, and the look of surprise returns to her face. Tif scurries out of the frame, back to her desk outside the office.

"Oh, sure," Piper mumbles, and then pulls open her tote, reaching in to grab a large tablet. Her brows furrowing, she digs in the bag, before looking up and then to the desk behind me. "Do you mind?" She lifts her bag up, indicating she needs to set it down. I step aside, and let her move forward, setting the tablet down before digging in the giant, intricately-carved leather bag.

"That's a nice purse," I muse quietly, and she freezes, her eyes darting towards me before seemingly shaking herself out of whatever thought crossed her mind

CHAPTER 5

"Thanks." Her voice is clipped as she takes a handful of items out of her bag and lays them on the desk, cluttering it quickly. "I made it." I can feel my head tilt to the side, surprised. She made it?

I study it closer - the dark, rich leather is bordered on the top and bottom of the bag with deep set floral patterns, marking out lilies, tulips, and roses woven with vines. The straps are covered in the same design, the edges stitched with thick, dark string.

It must be a sturdy bag for all the shit she's pulling out of it.

"I can't find my..." she mumbles to herself, and then, triumphantly, raises her hand up, a white stylus pen in hand. I notice, absently, that she's not wearing a wedding ring. "Kidding, found it!" She sets it at the top of the tablet, where it stays in place with what I'm assuming is a magnet, unlocking the screen.

I try not to stare, but when the screen lights up, it opens to a clearly in-progress design of a pale blue negligee. Noticing my observation, she navigates away quickly, opening a note-taking app and starting to pack her bag back up.

I watch as she grabs things, throwing them absently in the abyss, before spotting the small, white and purple box among the Target receipts and containers of chapstick.

A vibrator. An unopened, bullet vibrator, sitting on the dark wood of the desk.

"Sample from work," she says to herself, as if it's the most normal thing in the world, and I fight the stunned look that threatens to spread across my face. My cock gives an involuntary twitch at the sight. Piper makes a small sound in the back of her throat, but collects herself quickly and grabs it, along with the last of the debris, save a large, yellow tape measure, and haphazardly throws it in her bag before setting it on the floor in front of the desk. She picks up her tablet, hugging it to her chest, and reaches around her back, hitching the tape measure to her waistband like a handyman "Shall we?" Without waiting for my response, she stomps towards the open door like she's leading a tour. I can't do anything but follow.

The Pine is a rustic space, a large barn-style venue hiding on a few acres behind the neighborhoods where most of us grew up. From my understanding, we hadn't done a lot after the acquisition several years before - mostly focused on upgrading the catering kitchen to full services, sprucing up the suites, and adding a covered outdoor ceremony option that was much-needed for sunny Texas days.

"Will we have access to the full space?" Piper asks. She steps into the echoing room, which is bustling with decorators adjusting tablecloths and florists placing hanging greenery over the edges of the large, stone mantle of the fireplace at one end of the room. On the opposite side, a DJ is loading in large speakers, talking to Claudia, while next to him, a group of gruff looking men sit around one of the round tables, pouring over a laptop.

"Absolutely," I answer, trying to keep up with her quick, purposeful steps.

"I'll need specs for the digital signage." She points to the TVs above the built-in bar and next to the buffet area. Realizing I didn't grab anything to take notes, I pull out my phone.

I'm off my game.

A text appears across the screen.

SAVANNAH BURROUGHS
What was that about?

I don't have the time or energy to respond to her question. We weren't attached. I didn't owe her an explanation as to why I hadn't wanted her to give me a kiss before she left, like a doting girlfriend.

Digital signage specs, I type into the notes app.

"I think Jackie mentioned something about a volunteer DJ, we'll have to make sure that they have a screen so we can play the stupid slideshow Carla and Fallon want to do." She rolls her eyes, and I have to agree. It is a stupid idea. But I was just here to provide the venue and the things that came with it. Not my circus, not my monkeys.

She looks over the room, making a few more notes on her tablet before walking over to the bar area and unhooking the measuring tape from her belt. "Can you?" She extends the base to me, and points to the side of the bar near where I'm standing. She takes the metal tabbed end, walking to the other side of the bartop and placing it on the end.

"72 inches," I say flatly. She lets go of the end, the tape flying back into the base in my hand, and she gives me an apologetic smile.

"I want to get a few more while we're still here." She walks back towards me, putting her tablet down on the bar to mark the measurement. She holds out her hand for the tape measure.

"I got it." She looks up at me - it's not a huge height gap, especially in her heels. Through her long lashes, her blue eyes are narrowed in question. I just stare back. After a long second, she looks away, and then quickly down to her tablet, busying herself.

From the corner, I hear the front door opening, a gust of wind ruffling the long, ivory curtains on one wall.

"Whoo-wee, look what we have here."

I watch as Piper's entire body stiffens at the voice coming from behind us,

CHAPTER 5

and when I turn, very, very slowly, I pray silently it's not the person I think it is standing in the doorway. But it is.

It's Andy, toothpick hanging out of his mouth, framed by a smattering of dark facial hair, a huge, black cowboy hat on his head. He holds a dry cleaning bag over one shoulder, and he wipes his camo boots on the carpet before making his way over to me. Piper, I notice, stays turned around, but her hands are clenched into white-knuckled fists on the bartop.

"Andy," I say, not able to help the tone of surprise in my voice. He crosses the distance between us, reaching his hand out for a shake, which I give coldly.

"What's it been, Fitzy, five years?" I cringe at his use of my childhood nickname, at the familiarity.

"Six," I correct.

"That's right." He takes the toothpick out of his mouth, flicking it lazily towards a trashcan in the corner, missing. "What are you doing here?"

"WHG bought The Pine," I answer quietly, my gaze shifting back to Piper, where she's pretending to be interested in something on her screen.

"Right," Andy says in a drawn-out drawl, and waves over my shoulder at the group of men huddled at the table. "I work for TanTex," he adds in explanation, lifting the suit on his shoulder slightly. "Have to give some bogus award or something." His eyes scan across the room, taking it in, before settling on Piper's back. "Did I interrupt?"

"No," I reply quickly, but Piper chooses that moment to turn, slowly. Her blue eyes are steely, and I look between the two of them. Andy's face searches hers, confused, but then recognition flashes and his eyes widen.

"P-Piper?" He stumbles on his word, and takes a step towards her. She steps back into the bar, and panic floods her eyes for a moment, clearly feeling cornered.

"Andy," she says, giving a curt nod. "We were just finishing up. I can leave you two-"

"No," I repeat my earlier answer, again, all too quickly. "We have some items we need to finish." I turn back to Andy. "Good seeing you, man." I tack on the end, trying to add some familiarity back to the conversation - like I'd seen him since my awful wedding to Olivia all those years ago, where he'd been so hammered by the time we cut the cake that my sister had to call him an Uber.

"You too." He nods, apparently understanding that it's the end of the conversation, and I reach out to Piper, putting a hand on her elbow. She stares down at the contact, and then up at my face. Just for a miniscule moment. And then she turns around, grabbing her tablet wordlessly. I lead her back towards the office.

"Piper?" We both turn at Andy's voice, a question in his tone, and he takes a few steps towards us, his face now more sincere. "For what it's worth," he starts, his mouth twisting in what's clearly an uncomfortable expression, "I'm sorry for your loss." We both stare at him.

Jesus. Did everyone know but me? Had I been living under a rock that our entire graduating class knew that Piper Delmonico had loved and lost, but I didn't?

Not a rock, I realize. Just a miserable marriage and a career that's probably going to give me high blood pressure in the coming years.

"Uh," she stammers, and her grip on her tablet tightens. "Thanks." And without another word, she turns back around, hurrying toward the office in her wide-heeled boots while I try to keep up. I follow her past Tif's desk, and close the door to the office behind me as she practically collapses in the chair in front of the desk, sinking low. She slaps her tablet on the desktop, and her hands cover her face. I slide into the chair across from her, leaning back and crossing my arms. I hear her take a deep, shallow breath.

"Do you need anything?" I ask quietly. She freezes, as if realizing for the first time I'm in the room with her, and lowers her hands to look at me. "Water? Coke?" I gesture to the small bar cart in the corner. "A shot?" A small smile plays at her lips, and I notice her hands are shaking a little bit.

"Did you just make a joke?"

"It's been known to happen," I protest, pulling off my jacket and draping it over the chair back behind me. "But it wasn't entirely a joke." She lowers her hands completely, shaking her head in answer. "Was that the first time you've seen Andy since...?"

"Graduation, yeah." Piper closes eyes and takes another deep breath. When she opens them again, she looks at me. "Has it really been six years since you've seen each other?"

"It has." I absently log into the computer in front of me, opening up my email. "Since my wedding." Her eyes shoot down to my hand on the keyboard in front of me. "Olivia and I are divorced," I answer without making her voice the question.

"I'm sorry," she says in a small voice, the smallest it's been since she stepped into the office earlier, and I give a small shrug.

"Shit happens." There's a pregnant pause as she looks over me. "I'm sorry, too." She grimaces. "What?"

"I hate it when people say that." She looks down at her hands, splayed across her legs. "It makes me feel...fragile."

"I don't think you're fragile."

Fuck. I said it out loud.

"You don't know me," she responds almost immediately. It's true. I don't. I

CHAPTER 5

barely knew her ten years ago, and I feel like I know her even less now. "This is the most you've spoken to me in one day in the twenty-plus years I've known you." Also true. "And you have no idea what I've been through-

"I know a little," I interrupt, and I realize it's the absolute wrong move. Her eyes, which had been sad and big, narrowed, and steeled again. "I read some after the meeting last weekend."

"Oh, you read some?" Her voice has a snide tone to it I haven't heard before. "Let me guess, you Googled me?" I blink at her. "And what did you find, Fitz? Please, enlighten me." I shift in my seat, feeling like I've bitten off more than I can chew. But it's the first time I've ever heard her say my name, and it stirs something in me.

"Well," I start, fidgeting. "Not much. I saw the obituary, and a few articles. An event." Her eyebrows raise, and she crosses her arms, her fingers flexing involuntarily.

"The baseball tournament?" I give a small nod. "Did you read all about how the funds go to some poor soul fighting cancer in shithole, Kansas?" She laughs, and it's almost villainous as she continues without waiting to respond. "What they don't mention is that the first year, they tried to say the money went to pay for his family's expenses." She tips her head down, giving me a pointed look. "They had *zero* expenses. They didn't pay for jack shit. My family paid for living expenses, upfront medical costs, hell, it took me a year to pay my aunt back for his funeral, while his family sat and jeered at me with their cozy little community of supporters three states away." I try to keep my face neutral. "My mom, my sister, my aunt, my friends, they spent more time with Mickey than his own family did in the end.

"I can't believe they didn't help you." It comes out as a statement, and my tone is more accusatory than the disbelief I feel.

"They did nothing. They and their friends spent months making my life hell from Kansas while I was Mickey's full time caregiver. And, when he died, they sued me for the life insurance to add insult to injury."

I'm floored. What kind of people would do something like that? Abandon their child and then reap the benefits of his death?

"So no, Fitz, I'm not fragile." She stands quickly, and my response is immediate, standing with her as she leans over to pick up her purse, clearly over the conversation. "And I don't need pity from you of all people, because what happened to me is just another prime fucking example of people sitting by while a living, breathing human being gets treated like absolute shit."

Her comment hits me in the chest like I've been punched. Me. She was talking about me. And the times I'd sat by while Andy and Olivia teased and taunted her, about the times growing up when she was made to feel inadequate. And it had happened all over again just years later.

"People like Andy," she says, pulling her bag onto the desk and stuffing her tablet inside, "People like my former in-laws - fuck, people like my late husband - they made me small."

"People like me," I breathe. She stops, looking back up at me. "Can I ask you something?" I keep my voice even, trying not to display my interest, but my curiosity at this situation is clearly visible to her, because she nods, resigned. "What about his daughter?" She sucks in a quick breath. "It's OK if you don't want to tell me, I just-"

"No," she says, and her hands, which had been perched on the table tightly, relax slightly. "I didn't know Kayla existed until months before Mickey died."

"How long were you together?" The question is personal, but at this point, I've laid my cards out on the table.

"Four years total," she answers, her mouth twisting slightly at the corner. "But no one even mentioned her, or her mother, until I found out about them. And then even a DNA test couldn't convince his family that she wasn't his." At what I'm sure was a shocked look on my usually passive face, she adds "It's a long story."

"You don't have to get into it." I look down at my desk. "I'm sure it's a lot."

"It is a lot." She smiles sadly, and then, without warning, reaches her hand up to hold the side of my face, the cold metal of her rings against my cheek. The touch nearly makes me flinch - it's soft, but the look on her face isn't affectionate. It's determined. "You can actually be a pretty good conversationalist when you're not putting up a front. I don't know that I've ever seen you without chronic RBF."

I can't help the huff of laughter that bubbles up, still trying to recover from her touch. Her smile widens slightly.

"But I stopped making myself small for people a long time ago. I'm not about to do it again." She takes her hand back, and my cheek feels cold. She hikes her bag on her shoulder and turns, crossing to the door before turning back to where I stand, still slightly stunned. "I'll have to come back another day to take measurements, I need to go." Piper gives me one last smile, this time brighter, before heading out the door, her mess of curls bouncing behind her as I watch her go.

As soon as the door clicks closed behind her, I fall into my seat, groaning.

I had completely and totally misjudged the situation she was in, and it was my own damn fault. Making assumptions about things I didn't truly understand. Trying to riddle them out before I really knew what was going on. Deep diving into things that weren't my business in the first place, making an ass of myself in the process.

CHAPTER 5

Piper had come in here ready and willing to help us do something for the people we'd graduated with, even those who had treated her like shit - like me - and I'd basically told her that I'd believed every word I'd read on the internet about her like some conspiracy theory nutbag.

I lean forward in my chair, cradling my head in my hands. Her tape measure sits on the desk next to my elbow.

There was something about her I never noticed all those years ago, even after her near-complete transformation later in school. She treated me like everyone else. Despite the shit Andy had thrown at her, despite what I'd let happen to her, despite what had happened to her in the time since we'd last seen each other; she talked to me like I hadn't been a part of the cause of her pain. She smiled at me, though it was heartbreaking and even a little cold. But for all the shit she went through, when I probed, she answered. I accused, she explained. And she was kind, kinder than I deserved. That piece of her she'd held onto, through it all.

I fucked up. This woman, the one I'd just let leave my office without so much as an apology, was something else. I couldn't deny anymore what I'd been thinking since returning to my office weeks ago, hours after seeing her for the first time in a decade. I overlooked her, not due to any fault of her own, but because I was so wrapped up in my shit that I couldn't see through the walls I'd built to keep my emotions in check. I was too busy pretending I didn't care about anyone else to actually care about anyone else.

I groan to myself again. There was no denying she was attractive. She was, even in high school, if not a little more quirky. But she had morphed into this curvy, confident woman that designed lingerie, for Christ's sake.

And the way my fucking heart lept into my throat seeing that vibrator.

I can't help the mental image that seeps into my brain. Watching her slip off that blue negligee from her drawing, crawling on top of my duvet and leaning herself up against my headboard, that purple bullet in hand. Spreading her legs, lowering the vibrator down...

I shake my head. Stop it. I need to apologize. Anything else would require showing that I cared. And after years of refusing to share that side of myself with anyone but one person, and that one person betraying that trust, I'm not sure I can do that again.

A part of my brain, feral and hormone riddled, says that I don't need to show I care in an emotional sense to put my head between her legs and make her moan until she forgets who she is, much less what she's been through - what I helped put her through.

Logic tells me, though, that I don't deserve for her to even give me the time of day.

CHAPTER 6

Piper

I stare at the email open on one side of my screen, rereading it for probably the tenth time today. It's been 72 hours since I opened it.

Where the hell do I even start responding to this?

> Piper,
>
> Please see below for all relevant measurements at The Pine. I've included a tech spec sheet from our AV consultant.
>
> Should you need anything further, please don't hesitate to reach out via email or text.
>
> **Fitz Westfall**
> Chief Operating Officer | Westfall Hospitality Group

I felt dumb the first time I read it. Fitz doesn't just work at WHG. WHG is Westfall Hospitality Group. It's his *family's* company. And I was too busy holding my resentments to put two and two together.

But more than that, the content of the email surprised me. Not only was the tech sheet thorough, but he included measurements for practically every surface in the venue, down to the width of the bathroom stalls. I'm not sure if I'll need to use that one, but it's nice to know they're A.D.A. compliant.

I wonder if he had someone else take the measurements? Or if he took them himself? Part of me enjoyed the mental picture of him taking that tape measure around the venue early one morning, noting all the different numbers in his phone. Bending over in those well-fitted pants...

CHAPTER 6

"You good?"

Kyle's voice snaps me out of my thoughts, and I blink at the screen. What was I doing?

Oh, right, invitations.

"Sorry," I mutter. I pull up the message from Jackie with the details we'd hammered out on our last call. I had stayed mostly silent, listening to them go back and forth on start times while I worked on my latest sketch for work, this one of an ivory set with large, sparkly snowflakes front and center. It wasn't my finest work, but it was something I felt Brianna would like.

"She's read that email, like, fifteen times," Carla says from her desk, and I glare at her over my shoulder. We're gathered in the office Carla and I share, scrolling through my inspiration sites for ideas on eye-catching print and digital designs. Carla is taking the opportunity to cyber-stalk people to add to the contact list she's maintaining with Fallon, the screen on her neat desk in the corner split between a digital copy of our yearbook and Facebook.

"I can see why," Kyle responds, stretching in his seat. "He sounds accommodating. Not a word I'd use to describe Fitz."

He leans back in his padded chair from our dining table, looking around the room. My desk is surrounded by designs, like my cubicle at work, but these pieces are different. Unlike the office, here, I keep my personal designs showcased. Commissions, creative pieces, projects I'd like to complete one day, all scattered across the walls. There's a small space cleared around my keyboard and mouse for use, but the rest of my L-shaped desk is littered with crafting supplies. Hole punches, rhinestones, the overflowing drawers spill into my workspace, leaving my bookshelf the only organized area in the entire room.

"Are these all yours?" Kyle asks, and points to the drawings on the wall. I nod. "I've been working on my stuff too, it's not particularly good, but it's fun when I've got time to kill before a dinner rush." He pulls his phone up from the desk, scrolling for a second, and then shows me his screen.

It's a beautiful hand-drawn landscape of a field, tall yellowing grass topped by a bright, burning sun.

"Is that behind the rec center?" I ask. He seems surprised.

"Yeah, it was kind of a hang-out spot for all the neighborhood guys growing up. How'd you know?"

"No reason," I say, a bit too quickly. Carla looks at me from her desk. She knows what I'm thinking - about the time that Andy and I layed out in that field, on top of his letterman jacket and a blanket he had stashed in his backseat. "That's gorgeous," I add, pointing to his phone. He grins, his sandy hair falling lazily into his face. He turns again, peering at the viking armor designs in front of me. "Those are commission pieces from Greensleeves last year." He nods appreciatively.

"Paid for this dumb bitch's eye surgery," Carla jeers, looking pointedly at Bex, who's curled up in one of her many dog beds, losing her absolute mind over a silent squeaker toy.

"I haven't been to Greensleeves since I was a kid."

"I think we went together once," I ponder, and he seems to think on it for a second. I have vague memories of our parents packing us up in a car one weekend and driving to the local renaissance festival, letting us run wild with padded swords and bags of kettle corn.

"I'm pretty sure you're right." He laughs, probably remembering the same thing I am. "Our parents probably hoped we'd start a budding romance." I hear Carla's chair whirl at his words, but he laughs again. "Like that was ever going to happen." Normally I would let a comment like that hurt, but I know where he's coming from. Kyle and I were opposites, and had always been, finding camaraderie in seeing each other sneak out of our respective houses for years without really saying anything to each other.

"Hate to break it to you," I say, reaching over and patting his knee, "but you're not really my type."

"What, I'm not tall, red haired and wearing a suit from somewhere other than Men's Wearhouse?" I snort.

"As if. Fitz isn't my type, either."

"Well, he's definitely mine, but there's no chance he bats for my team." It goes so quiet you could hear a pin drop. And then, noticing my shock, Kyle laughs. "You didn't know?"

"Didn't know what?" Carla says, and I give her a pitying look.

"Kyle is trying to say that Fitz is the type of guy he goes for." Her head bobs back, eyebrows furrowed, confused. And then her mouth makes an "o." I turn back to him, making a note to confer with her on this later. Her teenage crush just shattered into a million pieces. "That explains so much." It really did. Kyle fell into an artsy crowd, just like Alex, but he was always too quiet and aloof to really spend time with us.

"My parents probably think I'm this huge failure," Kyle says, "They expected grandbabies by now."

"Welcome to the disappointment club," I say, laughing. "Party of 2."

"You have an excuse," Kyle replies, knocking his knee against mine with a sad smile.

"Dead husband is more of a bad *Lifetime* movie than an excuse," I muse, and he seems a little too stunned to speak. On my phone, a notification from our camera chimes to tell me someone is at the front door.

"Don't mind her." Carla rolls her eyes at me. "Piper forgets sometimes that we don't all make dead husband jokes with a straight face."

The doorbell rings, and Bex immediately starts barking.

"Jesus Fuck," Carla swears. "I'll get it." She jogs out of the room, Bex scurrying after her.

"You would think the sign that says 'Do not knock or ring doorbell' would have been a good indicator not to do it," I say sarcastically to Kyle. I hear the door open, and a few muttered words, before it closes again, and Carla's feet pad across the living room floor.

She comes into the doorframe slowly, a confused look on her face. In her hands is a dark wicker basket, a bottle of champagne on one side, chocolates on the other. There's a card in the front.

"Secret admirer for Valentine's day?" Kyle asks Carla, and she shakes her head, her eyebrows knit together.

"It's for you." I lean back in my chair.

What? Who would send me something like this? All of our friends know we're sober. My birthday isn't for another few weeks. And as great as my boobs had looked, I don't think I made that much of an impression on the firefighter to warrant this.

Besides, I fully intend to spend Valentine's Day taking advantage of steep chocolate discounts before binging both versions of *My Bloody Valentine*. It's a personal tradition.

"Holy shit," Kyle breathes suddenly, standing and taking the champagne out of the basket as Carla sets it on the corner of my desk. "This is a $300 bottle of champagne."

"You can have it," I say absently, reaching for the card. He stares at me. "What? We're both sober." He gives me an appreciative smile.

"There goes my plan to get you plastered at the reunion so you can tell me all the salacious details of your tryst with Andy senior year." I give him a sardonic look, my finger sliding under the seal of the small envelope and slipping out the plain white notecard with the WHG logo on the front.

> *You deserved better than what the people like us gave you. Please accept my sincerest apologies.*
> *— FNW*

I stare at the notecard in my hand, reading it several more times to make sure I wasn't making shit up in my head. Carla moves to stand behind me, reading over my head, and Kyle leans close to me, his cheek practically resting on my shoulder.

He lets out a low, long whistle.

"What the fuck is that supposed to mean?" Carla asks, and I shake my head absently.

"I told him that I let people like Andy make me small, after we ran into him."

"You saw Andy?" Kyle asks, sitting back to look at me. I nod. "How'd that go?"

"Nothing anxiety meds and silent meditation couldn't fix," I reply with a shrug, setting the notecard down on my desk. I had, indeed, come home to sit in front of my bed on a yoga mat, completing an hour-long meditation before heading out for the evening. I look up at Carla. "Though I'm pretty sure I have some resentments against Fitz I need to noodle out."

"Don't we all?" Kyle adds with a sideways grin, and he bumps me with his knee again. "Marble Man Fitz is cracking for you."

"That sentence makes zero sense to me," I say honestly, quirking my head to the side.

"I heard Ryan call him that one time. I think that was their nickname for him." He looks between us. "You know, 'Marble Man'." He straightens his face stoically, and I laugh at his serious expression.

"Got it." I touch the edge of the notecard, my eyes following the jagged cursive of Fitz's writing. "I don't know about cracking. I think I made him feel bad."

"Good!" Carla humphs. "Douche sat by while Andy beat on you and Vic."

"That's what I said."

"And what did he say?" Kyle asks, and they both look at me. I hold my hands up, feeling cornered. I hadn't told Carla the complete details of our conversation - part of me is still trying to figure out how the number of words Fitz has spoken to me in more than two decades basically tripled in a matter of minutes.

"I think this is his response." I lift the card at the corner, and then turn around to look at Carla. "What the fuck do I do?"

"Well, what the fuck do you *feel?*" Her question stumps me. Feel? What do I feel?

In the years since high school, I honestly haven't given Fitz a passing thought until recently. He was so far off my radar, a blip in the memories I'd long since hoped to forget with each passing day and therapy visit.

But truth be told, even between the last two times I'd seen him, something had changed. Whatever he'd found, whatever he'd read, made him question me so personally - made him seem...interested? A way I don't think I ever would have described him before. Sure, he was a man on a mission, running for class office and organizing committees, but interested in a person? On a human level? That required showing emotion, feelings, which, up until that day in the office with him, I have never really seen Fitz show, even in the years I saw him with

CHAPTER 6

Olivia.

My brain is flashing big, red warning lights, a "Do Not Enter" biohazard sign plastered across the thoughts like an impending zombie apocalypse.

"I don't think you're fragile."

Had he seen me all those years ago? Did he see me now? Me, not the shell of good looks and a career in a tantalizing field that left most men panting?

And did I want him to see me? See me in a way that wasn't more than the girl tasked with making things look pretty at this god-forsaken reunion that I don't think either of us are looking forward to?

It's a scary thought. Someone who knew me before the trauma that changed the course of my life, someone who had seen what I used to be, what I became in high school, and what I am now.

I'm reading too much into this.

I give a sideways glance at the bookshelf behind me, stuffed with stories of redeeming relationships and war-torn love. What I'd buried myself in for years, finding solace in fantasy worlds built with purpose, with meaning; with a clean wrap-up and often, a happy ending.

I sigh to myself. No, Fitz was just feeling guilty after I told my truth and he realized he was a part of it.

"I feel like I need to thank him and move on," I reply finally, and Carla rolls her eyes before sitting back in her seat. From in front of Kyle, I pick up my phone, opening my text thread with just Fitz.

PIPER DELMONICO
I appreciate the gifts. You really didn't have to. Thank you.

In only a few seconds, the dots indicating his typing pop up, and I suck in a breath. Kyle leans over again, and at this point, I don't blame him for practically cuddling my shoulder.

FITZ WESTFALL
It's the least I can do. I meant my apology. Hindsight is 20-20.

"What does *that* mean?" Carla asks, and I feel her cross her arms behind me.

"He's got some serious regrets if he's willing to say something like that." Kyle blinks, leaning back in his chair and shaking his head.

"He regrets that it's impacting my ability to help with the reunion," I lie. Both of them give me pointed looks before Carla speaks.

"If you think that man gives a flying fuck about the reunion beyond his potential obligation as a class officer, I'm going to have to do a sobriety check." I snort. "It's been a decade. Did you ever stop to think that maybe he's changed just as much as you have?"

Her words stop my racing brain. She's right. Absolutely right. I'm not the same people-pleasing good girl I had been long before Andy and I got involved. I'm certainly not the wounded flower I'd turned into to hide the absolute shame I was feeling during my trauma.

So why have I, from the get go, assumed that Marble Man Fitz had changed just as little on the inside as he had on the outside?

CHAPTER 7

Fitz

Piper doesn't text me back. For days, I check my phone out of habit, just to make sure I don't miss a notification on my watch.

Nothing.

The champagne and chocolates had been my sister Frannie's suggestion - I told her I needed to apologize to someone, and that someone was female, and no, it wasn't someone I was romantically involved with.

Yet.

Yet? Romantic involvement was the last thing I needed right now, smack dab in the middle of our busiest season of the year, fresh - kind of - out of a nasty divorce, and the fact that she doesn't particularly like me is also problematic.

I sit back in my desk chair, my hands cradling the back of my neck. Maybe I'm projecting my cynicism a bit?

OK. A lot.

I can practically feel her hand on my face from that day in the office. A light touch I didn't deserve after jumping down her throat - assuming the worst and then telling her as much. I can see her eyes burning into mine, bright and blue and swimming with compassion I didn't deserve. There was a good chance I was letting the feeling inside of me - guilt, maybe? - cloud my perception of whatever that moment had been.

But after Olivia, the string of one night stands and less-than-friends with benefits has been a bit...extreme. Being with one woman for your entire adult life, your entire sexual life, and then losing that partnership, can be hard. Especially when it's made abundantly clear that the same exclusivity wasn't honored for you.

Sex no longer carried the intimacy it once had - really, hadn't had in a long, long time. Long before I found out about Olivia and Ryan. But when I think about Piper, despite the near-feral thoughts I'd been left with after seeing that purple device on the desk, I can't help but wonder if that deep interest could spark something more.

Fuck. What am I saying? I've seen her twice in the last few weeks, including one time where she heavily implied I was a pain point for her. Now I'm hoping for hearts and flowers?

I glance at the tape measure that's been sitting on the corner of my desk, taunting me.

A constant reminder that I'm a fucking chickenshit, who shouldn't be this high up in a company that makes this much money, if I can't talk to one girl. One woman.

Then, an idea strikes me. I fish my phone out of my pocket, snapping a picture of the tool and sending it to her.

> **FITZ WESTFALL**
> You left this at my office.

Moments later, the three dots appear.

> **PIPER DELMONICO**
> LOL Carla was asking about that yesterday, I thought I'd left it in my trunk. Oops.

I'm surprised by the casual tone of her text, but even more surprised that the three dots appear again.

> **PIPER DELMONICO**
> I'll have you know I thoroughly enjoyed the chocolates, as did Carla. We may have had the majority of them last night during movie night.

I feel a small swell of pride in my purchase and stare at the screen, pondering my response.

> **FITZ WESTFALL**
> What did you watch?

Smooth, Westfall. Fucking smooth. But then she responds almost immediately.

PIPER DELMONICO
Is Fitz Westfall asking me a personal question?

FITZ WESTFALL
I mean, I feel like I kind of crossed that line the other day.

PIPER DELMONICO
True chainz.

I fight the laugh that threatens to come up, but feel my lips turn up at the corners.

FITZ WESTFALL
Color me intrigued.

PIPER DELMONICO
Color me suspicious.

"What are you smiling at?" I look up to see Frannie standing in the doorway to my office. Hadn't that been closed? I must have been distracted.

Quickly, I lock my phone and set it face-down on my desk.

"Nothing, what's up?" I ask. She cocks her head to the side, her deep red hair, the same color as mine, falling over her shoulders, hazel eyes scanning me.

"Something's different about you." She closes the door behind her, crosses the distance to my desk, and falls into the padded armchair in front of it. "I haven't seen a real smile out of you in a while." Her tone says what her mouth doesn't. Since Olivia. Since before then, really.

"Are you here to question me about my facial expressions?" I ask, giving the stack of papers in her hand a pointed look. She rolls her eyes, tucking her hair behind her ear.

"Just trying to make conversation. We haven't talked in a bit." It's true, we haven't. Not entirely my fault - the marketing department is chaotic all the time, but with wedding season in full swing, spring break promotions running, and summer specials in the works, it's a special kind of hell that only Fran loves. More power to her. "I heard you were at The Pine the other day with someone. I'm guessing that's who the gifts were for." She gives me a knowing smile. "That who you're texting?"

"No."

Frannie cackles. Actually cackles.

"That face doesn't work on me, Will." I feel my nostrils flare at her using my family nickname in the office. "Oh, don't do that."

"Do what?"

"Pretend like affection is an inconvenience."

"It is." She lowers her head, looking at me through her lashes like I'm the dumbest person in the world. Maybe I am.

"Whoever she is, she's pretty," she says offhandedly, finally leaning back in her chair and adjusting the papers in her hands. I raise an eyebrow at her. "I have eyes everywhere." Tif. Tif must have told her. I'm pretty sure the two of them are college friends. She hands me the stack of papers, seemingly moving on with a hefty breath. "I need some opinions on these that aren't from our team. We're starting to go cross-eyed."

I spread the stack out on my desk, looking at the draft marketing materials for Cosette for the next calendar year.

"What's wrong with them?" She humphs, looking frustrated.

"Nothing's *wrong* with them," Frannie says, her voice sad. "I don't know, they're just...missing something."

"You came to the wrong Westfall." I push them back together, trying to slide them across my desk. She stops me, a manicured hand forcing them back.

"I'm not bothering Dad with this."

"But you're bothering me with it?" My phone buzzes on the desk, and we both glance at it before she responds.

"I'm asking for your opinion because I value it. But if helping me is an inconvenience, too..." She moves to grab at the papers, and the stab of guilt in my chest moves my hand for me, covering them so they stay right where they are.

"You're a shitty manipulator, anyone ever tell you that?" Her face immediately splits into a grin - her plan, the entire time.

"It's one of the many reasons you love me," she says as she stands. I look up at her, rolling my eyes and placing the stack of papers on the corner of my desk. "I think you'll be able to add some perspective my team can't. After all, you used

CHAPTER 7

to be boots on the ground."

It's true, I was. Long before I worked in this office, just a few hundred yards from our father's, I managed several of our venues - what he had called "a thorough education on the family business." In reality, I think he was worried I didn't have what he believed it took to help run this company, and was stalling until he could make that decision. But something, probably my increased dedication thanks to my seemingly doomed marriage, changed his mind.

So unlike a lot of the leadership on this floor, I have seen the ins and outs of the spaces we offered to clients each day. I ordered linens, maintained decor inventory. I organized menu tastings with happy couples and sat with sobbing families while they planned a wake. I inspected overnight rooms and watched José pull off a four course meal with a delayed supply shipment and a skeleton crew. Which is why I still find myself on site most weekends, if not to help out, then just to observe. And it was what let me know exactly what the people at this company are capable of, which was more than my father gave them credit for.

"I'll take a look at them," I tell her finally.

"Good. And do me a favor, Will." I quirk an eyebrow at her as she throws me a final glance over her shoulder in the doorway. "Don't pretend she's an inconvenience, too, because no woman who makes you smile like that can be."

And I'm left staring at the doorway again, my mind whirring. Smiling like what?

Like you like her, you fucking dipshit.

I bring my hand to my face, rubbing my brow and looking at my phone screen.

PIPER DELMONICO
We watched Hell House, for the record. Shitty horror movie. You've probably never heard of it.

I bite my lip. *Shit.*

FITZ WESTFALL
Original or director's cut?

The three dots appear, and then disappear, and then there's a few agonizing minutes where she doesn't respond.

PIPER DELMONICO
Color me surprised.
Director's cut, obviously.

OK. If I wasn't interested before, I definitely am now. Andy and Ryan used to give me mountains of shit about my horror movie collection growing up, and Olivia found it distasteful, especially since she couldn't handle blood.

FITZ WESTFALL
Color me disappointed. Original is far superior.

And when the three dots immediately appear, I know I made the right decision in texting her.

CHAPTER 8

Piper

A steady stream of texts from Fitz continues over the next few days, and I feel guilty knowing there was a constant nagging in the back of my head. I'm waiting for the conversation to turn dirty, to inevitably take a 180 all the way out of whatever we have going.

And what is it we have going? I have no fucking clue. But some of his texts have made me laugh more than I have in a long, long time. Unlike in-person Fitz, *texting* Fitz is sarcastic and very vocal in his opinions, especially about horror movies. Not something I had expected from Mr. Buttoned-up, but I couldn't complain about anything except some of his increasingly unhinged thoughts on a few of my cult favorites. And I do mean cult favorites.

The first picture comes through while I'm at my desk one morning, reading my emails. Not a dick pic, thank God. A photo of the tape measure I'd left at The Pine, thoroughly chilling on top of a cardboard box labeled "Clarified Butter."

FITZ WESTFALL
Buttering up for a good week.

PIPER DELMONICO
That was the worst. Solid D- if I'm feeling generous.

He takes it like a challenge. The next comes when I'm at home, curled up on the couch with Bex and my iPad, trying to perfect a piece for the winter collection, a black bustier covered with cabochons that looked like chunks of black ice. Snow falls outside the window of the apartment, providing more than enough inspiration for what I'm working on.

The tape measure is on a bar I don't recognize, an out of focus bartender mixing drinks in the background. A pink paper umbrella is nestled on top of it.

My sobriety hasn't been broached, and honestly, while I'm not embarrassed about it, it isn't exactly a shining beacon of my strong comeback from the last several years. And the stories to tell that accompany that side of my life aren't things I want to text anyone about, even someone who continued to surprise me like this.

PIPER DELMONICO
What, no pun?

FITZ WESTFALL
No, I'm waiting for the party to be-gin.

PIPER DELMONICO
F. Just straight F. Next.

FITZ WESTFALL
Come on, that was a solid C at least.

PIPER DELMONICO
This is feeling increasingly roaming-gnome-y.

FITZ WESTFALL
I've been everywhere, man.

I snort, and Bex nuzzles up from her place under the blanket, staring at me curiously.

"You'd laugh too if you could read." She cocks her head at me, and I give her good girl scritches. Bex was one of my saving graces during the worst time of my life - a constant source of affection when I felt like the world around me was crumbling. Mostly, because it was. And she had seen me through it all. The cheating. The lying. The horseshit with Mickey's family, and his inevitable passing that left me hollow and broken. Even in my fight for sobriety, she was a reminder that no matter how much I fucked up, she loved me. The closest thing Mickey and I had to a child, and I love her with my whole heart.

On Friday, I'm getting ready to leave for the weekend when my phone buzzes.

"Ooh, another message from loverboy?" Vic asks. I roll my eyes while he comes to stand behind me, looking over my shoulder as I unlock my screen, still seated at my desk.

FITZ WESTFALL
Holy cannoli, that's a lot of dessert.

The accompanying photo is of a dessert spread that is, in fact, a lot. Cupcakes and mini pastries, even, yes, cannolis. Nestled in the middle of the table is the tape measure, sitting on a doily like a sweet treat.

PIPER DELMONICO
C+, only because those look like my Nona's cannolis.

He responds almost immediately.

FITZ WESTFALL
Showing signs of improvement. And they're amazing. If they weren't being fed to 400 drunk Red Raiders, I'd snag a few for myself.

"Gross," Vic says over my shoulder. I have to agree. 400 drunk Texas Tech grads sounds like a nightmare. We didn't even go to a college with a decent sports program, but even we heard how wild they party, only rivaled by Aggies at weddings and similar celebrations.

PIPER DELMONICO
That sounds like a horrible way to spend a Friday night.

FITZ WESTFALL
I like watching my team pull stuff like this off. It's a big event and they've got it in the bag.

My fingers freeze mid-thought. His team? That sounded so...proud? Like they were his kids winning a state championship. Marble Man, huh? Maybe to the people I knew. But this different side to Marble Man Fitz was very much not made of stone.

The next morning, I sit on my usual bench at the dog park down the street from our apartment, sipping a hot tea and bundling further in my layers. It's a bristling March morning - we managed to escape the end of February's short snow storm with only a few days stuck in place. The infrastructure in Texas for winter weather is minimal, despite some sort of storm happening nearly every year. I couldn't imagine what it was like for Fitz, with events rescheduling left and right as people couldn't drive on the roads to get anywhere.

Just as that thought crosses my mind, my phone buzzes in the pocket of my plaid pullover. I fish it out, watching Bex run like a fucking psycho across the mulch, no particular aim in sight.

FITZ WESTFALL
Having a ball.

Long fingers hold the tape measure in front of a tan-face doberman, whose mouth is full with a bright tennis ball.

PIPER DELMONICO
What a cutie. Solid A for doggo.

I send it, and hear a ping from somewhere behind me. Weird. The three dots immediately appear.

FITZ WESTFALL
I know I am. Color me flattered.

Fitz Westfall is flirting. That was flirting, right?

PIPER DELMONICO
In your dreams, Marble Man. Also, rude of you to assume I'm up this early.

I hear the ping behind me again, and swivel in my seat. There's no way. As I scan the dog park, I don't really know what I'm looking for. I haven't seen Fitz outside of a suit since high school, I'm not entirely sure what he looks like in normal clothes.

PIPER DELMONICO
Where are you this morning with that handsome boy? Assuming boy, but that could be entirely sexist of me.

Ping.

FITZ WESTFALL
Dog park. Yes, boy, Roscoe. Why? Care to join?

Fuck. I stare at my phone. *Now or never, Delmonico.* My heart beating faster, I press the dial button, and the phone rings once.

"Uh, hello?" Fitz's gruff voice answers, and I hear it twice - once real time, and then delayed over the phone. I turn my head, trying to figure out where it's coming from.

"Hey, what dog park are you at?" I try to keep my voice casual as I stand, gripping my tea tighter in my other hand. Bex stops running at my movement, but promptly resumes as a chihuahua saunters by her.

"One over by my house." I spot him. Or rather, I spot his hair from behind, his elbow outstretched as he holds his phone to his ear. Even from this far, I can see his bicep is tight against the gray sport-tek jacket he's wearing. I quietly make my way that direction.

"I was serious, if you want to -"

"Join you?" I slide onto the bench next to Fitz, whose normally blank expression is very much colored with shock. His eyes flit between the phone to his ear and me, and then, at the same time, we both put them down. "Swear, I'm not stalking."

My instinct is to reach out and hug him - this man that's made me laugh more than a few times recently. But I restrain my overly-affectionate urges and settle on a wide smile. To my surprise, he smiles back. It catches me off-guard, the flash of white teeth, the crinkles at the corners of his green eyes.

"Hey, what are you doing here?" He holds a coffee cup in one hand over the side of the bench, the other putting his phone into the pocket of his joggers. He gives me an appraising look, and I can't help but flush, thankful I at least ensured my hair wasn't a rat's nest before leaving.

"I live down the street. Couldn't sleep." I shrug, taking a sip of my tea and leaning over on the bench, watching Bex sidle up to a group of dogs. I spot, almost immediately, the Doberman from Fitz's picture.

"Everything alright?" I turn my head to look at him, and his expression is hard to read. Not surprising. But it looks like a flash of concern crosses his eyes.

"Too much going on up here." I tap the side of my head with one finger. "We have a big deadline coming up this week and I'm starting to feel the pressure a little bit."

"Where do you work again?"

"AllHearts," I respond.

"And you design..." he trails off, and I swear his neck flushes as he brings his drink towards his face.

"Apparel," I answer, and his eyebrows lift. "Which is a fancy word for lingerie."

"That's what I thought I heard at our first meeting, but I couldn't be sure." He gives me an appraising look. "Big deadline in the lingerie business?" Before I can react the way I want to - mildly affronted - he course corrects. "Shit, sorry, that sounded dismissive." He pauses, and I want to laugh at the way he's stumbling on his words. "It's hard to find information on you."

"You mean aside from my dirty laundry splattered all over the internet?" His mouth lifts at one side, and his shoulders shake in a small laugh.

"AllHearts," he repeats. His hand finds the back of his neck. "That would explain the samples."

"Samples?" And then, my mind flashes back to that day in the office - my mortification when I realized I'd pulled out the bullet vibrator our toy department gave out at our last staff retreat. AllHearts was one of the leading adult companies in the world, and in the business of pleasure, we pretty regularly had items from different departments available for us to take. Overstock. Discontinued products. Samples.

Don't get me wrong, I'm pretty confident in my sexuality - after years of pent up frustration and trying to regain some semblance of decency after being publicly humiliated by Andy, I'd finally resigned myself to owning it. Owning my curves. Owning who I am.

CHAPTER 8

That's how Mickey and I met - a dating app hookup that turned into much, much more. And at first, he seemed invigorated by my confidence. Turned on, even. I was the life of the parties he brought me to, the bringer of the hot, single friends, which is how Alex and Nolan met. Even Brett, who, at that point, was getting ready to marry my sister, vouched for the affection Mickey felt for me - Brett and Nolan played college ball together, and long before that, Mickey and Nolan owned the field in Paulsville. Brett told me Mickey was looking for someone that could hold her own, and I was just that. Until I wasn't.

Unable to stop myself, I burst out laughing at Fitz's clear embarrassment.

"Right, samples." I watch Bex separate from the group, looking around, and when she spots me, she runs at top speed to the bench, her little black legs taking her as fast as they can. She practically barrels into my lap, and I laugh again, letting her nuzzle into my chest. "This little devil ate my last bullet, didn't we?" I pet her face and watch out of the corner of my eye as Fitz's own eyes widen slightly. "Fitz," I start, saving him, "This is Bex. Bex," I turn to the man next to me, and present him with the dog in my arms, "Give Fitz some snugs."

"Oh," he says, still seemingly shocked, but he takes her from my outstretched arms, holding her a foot away from his face. She gives him a few sniffs before launching herself at him. And like I've shattered whatever glass wall was up, he lets out a loud laugh, low and gravely, and something inside me melts.

I take a sip of my tea, watching them as Bex tries to lick every square inch of exposed skin. That laugh made me want to do the same.

Stop it. Jesus Christ. *Licking him?* A month ago he was just a name on my list of resentments, long since tucked away in the stepwork I'd completed in my first year of sobriety. But now, *now*, sitting next to him, that list is nearly forgotten.

Still watching Bex and Fitz, I see the Doberman notice us all together, and he bounds towards us, coming to a screeching halt in front of the bench, nearly knocking into our legs.

"Roscoe," Fitz chastises, trying to pry Bex away from his chest, which probably smells like the dog in front of us. Roscoe looks at the two of them, heartbreak in his eyes, and I make a small cry.

"Oh, baby." I lean forward, scratching the top of his head, and his big, brown eyes immediately go molten. "Is your mean daddy ignoring you for a beautiful girl?" I nod my head towards Bex.

"Two," Fitz says offhandedly, and he finally wrangles Bex down to the ground, where she makes a frustrated noise before turning her attention to Roscoe. I look at Fitz, confused.

"Two what?"

"Two beautiful girls." He says it with a completely straight face, draining what looks like the last of his coffee. It's good, because while he's leaning back it gives me a chance to completely fall apart. "Was that too forward?"

"Are you asking for permission to hit on me?" I ask, mostly to clarify for my own sake. Fitz glances at me out of the corner of his eyes, which are still mostly trained on the dogs in front of us. They sniff at each other.

"Maybe."

I pause. My next words could open or shut a floodgate. Betray what I'm feeling or hide it far, far away under a mountain of past regrets and preconceived notions. Let me open myself up to something more than a bad date or one night stand for the first time in years.

"Permission granted."

CHAPTER 9

Fitz

I swear silently to myself as I follow Shelley down the concrete hallways leading to what they call the suites of this tiny stadium.

I'm going to murder my sister. All Frannie had to do was email this woman and tell her she'd have to reschedule.

"But it's the third time I'll have done that," she whined to me this morning. I was out for a morning walk with Roscoe when she'd called, making her scheduling problem my problem.

"You're the VP of Marketing," I reminded her, pausing to let Roscoe sniff around and pressing my earbud further into my ear.

"And you're my favorite brother," she said sweetly.

"That's a low bar, you've only got two, and the other one is usually too stoned or hyper-focused to be anyone's favorite." She laughed on the other side of the call.

"Pleeeeeease." She drew out the word, sounding like her toddler, Greta. "We got the final sponsorship proposal weeks ago and I just haven't had a chance to make a visit." What was left unsaid was the reason why - my niece fell off a swing in early February, leaving her a little worse for wear and Frannie hovering like a helicopter mom. I pulled my phone out of my pocket, and sighed when I saw that I had no meetings after three.

"Fine." The squeal on the other side had me pressing the end call button, and even Roscoe was startled in the middle of his early morning business.

"Your sister is so sweet, I'm so sorry she couldn't join us," Shelley says, her heels clicking on the unfinished concrete.

"She wishes she could be here." I adjust my jacket, glad she's also in a suit - I don't feel so out of place amongst the crowd of t-shirts and short shorts the fans are wearing, taking advantage of the beautiful March evening.

"So this hall is where your suite would be located, the one in the proposal we sent over is actually getting the floors refinished, but I'm going to show you one that's identical." Her brown bob sways with her quick steps, and we round a corner. Outside of one room, a man stands, headphones in, clipboard in hand. "It's currently occupied with some of our player family and friends, but I let the main points of contact know that we would be stopping by for a quick peek." She smiles as we approach the door, and the attendant grins at her, just as the overhead announcer calls out the guest team. "Filipe," she says to him, and they fist-bump. She pulls a retractable badge towards the door and swipes it, and Filipe opens it as we walk in.

"Enjoy yourselves," he says.

"Right this way, Mr. Westfall." I trail in behind Shelley, who, this close, I realize I dwarf. I nod my thanks to Filipe and turn to look at the suite.

Much of the buzz happening inside dies the second we walk in the room, and I look at Shelley as she calls "Hailey!"

"Oh, good," a dark haired woman says from the far side of the room, and comes towards us, passing a group of still people standing around a table, all staring at me.

I freeze.

Alex Barton has changed, but not enough to be unrecognizable. Her blonde hair is swept into a high ponytail, and a dark jersey stretches over what's clearly a pregnant belly. And she's glaring daggers at me.

And then my eyes trail to the people standing next to her, holding each of her hands as she stands from her chair.

On one side is Carla Montgomery, a blue Alamos jersey on. She eyes me suspiciously. And on the other side is...oh fuck.

I haven't had much of a chance to talk with Piper since seeing her last weekend, but that doesn't mean my head isn't reeling. That short conversation had left me with more questions than answers - namely, what in the actual fuck I was going to do now that those feelings were out in the open.

I mean, sure, I had a reputation for being a little closed-off.

OK, a lot.

But that didn't mean that I didn't have feelings in the first place - and those feelings were now muddled and confused and unclear. But I knew I had them. Maybe I'd always had them, somewhere deep down - and that was why I was so frustrated by Andy's actions all those years ago. And cold, calculating Olivia was the antithesis to Piper, who radiated humility and light.

Was comparing Olivia and Piper fair? Probably not. One woman I'd known most of my life, and had fucked me over in the culmination of 10+ year relationship. The other, I've known the same amount of time, but had spoken to more in the last several weeks than in the previous twenty years combined.

But in the days we'd spent going back and forth with my bad puns and horror movie critiques, it felt like we'd built a rapport. When the words "two beautiful girls" came out of my mouth, it really was a gamble. I had nothing to lose at this point, though.

I know I don't deserve her grace. She knows I don't deserve her grace. And she's giving it to me anyway.

And when I look at her now, her dark curls tied back from her face by her baseball cap, wearing a jersey-style dress, all I want to do is make her let me apologize to her over and over again, to let me hear her story, to let me get to know this person that was still smiling despite the things she had endured. Or, at least, she was normally smiling, but now she just looks shocked.

"Mr. Westfall, this is Hailey Gibbons, her husband Luke is on the team." Shelley looks between the two of us as I extend my hand to the dark haired woman in front of me. "Hailey, this is-"

"Fitz." It's not a question as it comes out of Alex's mouth, and she lets go of the hands holding her own, making a slow pace towards us. Hailey turns around to look at her as she steps up. "What are you doing here?"

"Oh," Shelley says, surprised. Behind Hailey and Alex I see Carla, Piper and who I'm pretty sure is Penny, her older sister, fall into a hushed conversation. Piper throws up her hands like she's defending herself. "You know each other?"

"You could say that," Alex answers, her hands falling on her lower back. "We went to school together."

"How wonderful!" Shelley says with a small clap. Even Hailey winces slightly when she does it, and I silently guess that Alex has told Hailey about me, and my recent intrusion into Piper's life, based on the way Hailey takes a protective step towards her friends when she hears my name. The walkie talkie on Shelley's hip beeps, and she pushes the earbud coming out of the back of her jacket further into her ear, leaning away from our group.

I turn to Alex while I have a chance.

"Look, I didn't know-"

"Are you stalking us now?" Carla comes up behind Hailey and Alex, but her expression is more friendly.

"I was just telling them that I didn't know you were going to be here," I try to explain, but my tone is tight and I see Alex furrow her brow.

"So it was just coincidence that you -"

"I'm so sorry," Shelley interrupts, "but I'm getting called away on an emergency."

"He can stay here with us," Alex says. All of us look at her, I think equally shocked; there's a glint in her eye that worries me.

"Are you sure?" Shelley asks, but she's clearly relieved.

"We're sure," Piper answers as she and her sister step up next to Alex, who looks at her friend with a maternal fury I've seen Frannie exude around Greta.

"Oh, you're a Godsend," Shelley says lightly, and then reaches out, squeezing Hailey's shoulder. "Quite a gang you've got here." She turns to me. "You'll let me know if you need anything."

"Absolutely," I say quickly, wanting her to get out before Alex has my balls in a vice and I'm left explaining to Fran why the Alamos don't want us to sponsor them anymore. She scuttles back through the door, and I look at the group of women in front of me, swallowing.

"Alex's husband, Nolan, is on the team," Piper explains. Her fingers toy nervously with the hem of her dress, an elongated version of the one Alex is wearing, I realize.

Piper's best friend purses her lips, clearly unhappy, despite her insistence that I stay.

What do I need to do to get back in her good graces? I make a mental note to ask Piper when an ebony-skinned man walks up next to Penny, looking vaguely familiar.

"Hey babe, who's this?" he asks. He holds a plate of food out to her, but before she can answer, Vic walks up next to Alex, also holding out a plate, and looks at me, startled.

Jesus. This might as well be our high school reunion, right here.

"Fitz, hey, man," he says, and surprises me by holding out his hand. I shake it, and then offer it to the other man.

"Fitz Westfall."

His eyes dart to Penny, but he takes my hand.

"Brett Robinson. I think you know my wife, Penny." When he smiles, I realize where I know him from.

That day at the dog park, Brett was the one with his arms around Piper. Internally, I feel myself relax a little. So this wasn't her boyfriend. This was her brother-in-law. If I was a betting man outside of our regular poker games, I'd wager the other man was probably Alex's husband. Piper mentioned in passing that Alex's husband and her brother-in-law were close.

"I see daddy!" a voice calls from the corner of the room near the glass doors to the stadium seats, and Hailey turns back. From this far, I can only see a tiny mop of dark hair, like hers.

The announcer welcomes the home team to the dugout, and there's a smattering of applause from around the suite.

"Coming, Luke," she says, and then peers at Alex. Noticing her unwavering eye contact with me, Piper reaches out and squeezes Alex's arm. That seems to knock her friend back to earth, because she looks at Piper, who gives her a reassuring smile, nodding back to me.

Alex sighs, a resigned, frustrated sound, and then shoots me one last glance before turning around to waddle off. The rest of the group follows her, leaving Piper and me alone.

Piper

"Hi."

That's the best I can do? *Hi?* I stare at my feet, clad in hand-painted Alamos Vans from two seasons ago.

"Uh, hi," Fitz replies, and his hand moves to the back of his neck. Am I making him nervous? I've never seen him nervous before. "WHG is sponsoring the Alamos, my sister was supposed to come tour but her kid is sick," he explains.

I didn't know he had a sister. Truth be told, I don't know a lot about the man in front of me. His calm, measured demeanor has kept me from knowing how he felt about anything. I had seen his parents a few times - graduation, a pep rally or two when the lacrosse team was in finals - but beyond the fact that they owned WHG, I was clueless.

"That's too bad," I say, trying to impress empathy in my voice as I look up at him, but fail miserably. I was surprised when he came through the door, but if the last three years in A.A. have taught me anything, it was that everything happens for a reason.

"Do you mind?" He nods towards the bar, and I shake my head, shrugging.

"I'll be here," I say, and point to the table a few inches away. He nods, and pulls his jacket off, hanging it over the back of one of the chairs before stiffly walking towards the bar. I watch him go. His pants have got to be custom, with how tall he is. The way they fall in all the right places.

I pull out my phone for the first time since arriving.

DYLAN ANTON (1)

GROUP TEXT (3) *Alex, Carla, Penny, Vic*

VIC MONTERO
OMG

ALEX CALLOWAY
Stalker

PENNY ROBINSON
Let us know if you need rescue service.

I swipe away the group message, and open Dylan's.
He's sitting twenty feet away, probably the closest we've been in months, and he can't even come talk to me in person?

DYLAN ANTON
Who is that?

Jesus, how do I even answer that? To Dylan, of all people. I spotted him in the stadium seats at the front of the suite when Vic and I arrived fashionably late, as always, fighting Dallas traffic to get here after work. Dylan gave me an awkward wave when we walked in, returning to his conversation with Carla - before she realized Alex and Penny were about to waterboard me for information about Fitz, because Carla's loose lips could quite literally sink ships.
I sigh as I respond to Dylan.

PIPER DELMONICO
We went to school with him, small world.

Why did I downplay it? To Dylan? Dylan, whose decade of sobriety was the only reason I had found my way to my first meeting. Dylan, whose brother had been playing on the Alamos as long as Nolan had. Dylan, who, at one point, I was sleeping with more than without.
That was long-since over, especially since resigning myself to dating again after a New Year's Eve spent alone with Bex, a spicy werewolf novel, and a bowl of cookie dough, which realistically, is how I plan to spend my birthday in just a few days.
"Everything ok?" I nearly jump as Fitz steps up to the table next to me, a clear drink in his cup. He takes a sip, and then sets it on the table.
"Oh, yeah." I lock my phone and put it face-up on the table. "Just some family stuff." So much for my rigorous honesty. He nods, and stretches his arms out in front of him. With one hand, he unbuttons the sleeve of his dress shirt, rolling it up slowly before doing the same to the other. And I watch. Every. Agonizing. Moment.
Like a surge of heat, I feel my face flush, and I'm forced to look away. I'm

practically salivating.

Maybe it's just been too long since I've done anything. Maybe I'm getting a PMS hormone rush. Or maybe, without the immediate wall I've had up around Fitz, once always accompanied by Andy, I'm realizing just how much I'm attracted to him.

It's all three. All three things are probably true.

His burgundy curls. His deep green eyes. Even the smooth, hard planes of his face, devoid of any emotion.

"Piper?" Shit. I shake my head. He must have said something and I wasn't paying attention.

"Sorry, what?"

"I was asking how the rest of your week went," he repeats, taking another sip of his drink. His arm tightens as he brings it to his mouth. Pulling it away, he licks his lips.

"Oh, good," I breathe out, and realize that I don't have a drink to distract myself with, having left my Dr. Pepper on the other table. "We made our deadline yesterday." I hitch my thumb back at Vic, who's holding a plate up next to Alex while she surveys the two of us from across the room. Fitz's eyebrows raise in confusion, and I realize why. "Vic and I work together at AllHearts." Understanding flashes on his face, and he gives Vic a sideways glance before looking back at me.

"I'm glad the two of you have stayed friends. You seemed pretty tight back at Southwest." I nod. If he only knew what the years after that brought us.

"We still are," I reply, shrugging. "Nothing like going through massive amounts of trauma together to instill a long-lasting friendship." He winces ever so slightly, I think because he assumes I'm talking about what happened between Andy, Vic and I all those years ago, but that was only the tip of the iceberg. "What about your friends?" I ask, genuinely curious. "I mean, clearly, you and Andy haven't talked. What about you and Ryan?"

Beneath the passive face, I see him blanche, and his hand finds his collar, trailing down to the top of his tie, which he loosens uncomfortably.

"Uh, no," he answers, sounding unsure. "Ryan and I haven't talked in a while." He swallows slowly before averting eye contact, downing the rest of his drink in one go. Well, shit, I seem to have touched a nerve. "He and Olivia are actually together." Somewhere in the back of my head, it registered that I did know that - Carla, or maybe Alex, had mentioned it at Brett's last jazz show.

"Talk about a downgrade." If I didn't currently have a sobriety chip stashed in my wallet, I would have sworn the words that just came out of my mouth were from drunk Piper. But it was. So that wasn't even an excuse. I just let my loose lips fucking fly.

But it was so, so worth it, because Fitz's head snaps back and he barks out a loud laugh that makes me grin, even though I can feel the pointed stares of my friends around us. Before he can recover, my phone buzzes on the table, and I see that it's a text from Carla.

"I'm glad someone feels that way," Fitz finally says, and then completely abandons his tie, stuffing it in the pocket of his suit jacket. He undoes the top button of his blue dress shirt. "Especially since she'll probably have their kid on her hip at the reunion." It's my turn to be shocked this time - ok, that part, my friends had left out. I cringed. "Yeah. Tell me about it."

"Were they - I mean..." I trail off, not wanting to pry, especially in such a public space, but he just shrugs, his normal unreadable face returning.

"Oh yeah, they were fucking long before the divorce. Probably for years." He pushes the cup on the table back and forth a few inches between his hands.

"I know how you feel," I say honestly, and he looks back up at me. "Mickey cheated on me, too." Surprise crosses his face, and I toy with the edge of my watch band as my phone buzzes again.

"You get that," Fitz finally says, pointing to my phone, and I watch as he reaches to put his empty cup on the bar's corner with his long arm. "I'm gonna run to the restroom." He gestures to the hallway behind me, where a "restroom" sign sits above the doorway. Then, he gives me a small smile, his head nodding towards the stadium seats at the front of the suite. "Save me a seat?"

I nod, unsure what to say after my confession, and watch as he passes me. I pick up my phone.

CARLA MONTGOMERY
You good?
Holy fuck, did Marble Man just LAUGH?

CHAPTER 10

Fitz

Two Years Ago

A perfectly-decorated tree glittered in the fading light of the evening across my living room, just two weeks before Christmas. Liv's voice was just loud enough that I could hear it, still on the video call about some sort of presentation for her executive meeting the next day. She ran to her office to take it the second she got home.

I wanted to continue with my night as normal. I really did. But on the counter, her phone was buzzing. And my gut was telling me something is wrong.

Slowly, I pushed myself up from the armchair I was perched in, and made my way to the counter. If it was nothing, I'd ignore it. But I was betting it wasn't.

The last several months, hell, several years, hadn't been the best. Distance is a good word - separate worlds was better. Like we were roommates, clinical and unfeeling, sharing a home, a bed.

We'd never been the most passionate couple, even after this many years. But we fit together like two ambitious, emotionally stunted people did. Pushing each other to be better in our careers, our networking. Never really personally.

When I flipped over the phone, I read the screen, and when I saw the name, I felt my stomach drop.

Ryan.

A missed call and two texts.

My heart thudded faster in my chest as I unlocked her phone - the password still the same as always. Our anniversary. The one thing we had in common those days, it seemed.

There were only three text messages in the thread between Liv and Ryan.

RYAN TRINH
We need to tell him. Soon.

OLIVIA WESTFALL
I know. I just don't want to blow things up. We have to get through the holidays and then I'll talk to him about it.

RYAN TRINH
Is that fair to him? He deserves to know the truth. I love you.

My stomach lurcheed, and I had to fight the bile rising in my throat as I reread the messages.
I love you.
I love you.
I love you.
My best friend and my wife. What a fucking cliche. I wanted to throw the phone against the wall. I wanted to storm into her office, through those frosted double doors, and confront her in front of whoever she's on her video call with.
But quick reaction has never been my style. So, I locked her phone, putting it back where I found it, and walked over to the minibar in the corner, pouring myself three fingers from the expensive whiskey her father got us for our anniversary last year.
When she came out of her office a while later, her usually perfect, expensively highlighted hair was disheveled, like she was running her hands through it. One of the few signs she was feeling anything other than the viper-like cunning she's had as her default nearly as long as I'd known her.
In some ways, I knew that wasn't totally her doing. Like me, she had a tough relationship with her parents growing up, which left her second-guessing and then completely not trusting everyone around her. That cunning was her mask, as much as my lack of outward emotion was mine. It was part of why we worked. Until it didn't.
She noticed me, settled back into my chair, and squinted at the glass of whiskey in my hand, which was still mostly full.
"Starting early?" Her voice dripped with sarcasm. It was early, since we

CHAPTER 10

came home a few hours before normal to get ready for dinner with Paula, my step-mother, and her parents, as they'll be in Florida over Christmas. She made her way to the wine fridge built into the bar, and poured herself a glass of what I assumed was her go-to, sauvignon blanc.

I didn't mince my words when I answered her.

"Do you want to tell me what's going on with you and Ryan?"

She froze, her glass halfway to her face, and closed her eyes. I took a deep sip of my whiskey, trying to steel myself for her response.

"I'm not sorry," she said. I know I must have startled, because she let out a bark of laughter, dry and humorless, before taking a deep gulp of her wine and turning to face me fully, leaning against the bar. "I'm not. It's about damn time you noticed."

"Noticed?"

"You've been all but physically absent for a long time," she said. My eyebrows nearly reached my forehead, and I opened my mouth to argue, but she pressed on. "Look, I'm not saying I'm a fucking saint, but you had to see this coming."

"See you and my best friend sleeping together coming?" She narrowed her eyes at me, and then took another sip of her drink.

"I love him, Fitz. In a way I'm not sure I ever loved you." The words hit below the belt. Loved. Past tense. I let it ruminate, like a bad taste in my mouth,

There was a burn in my throat, due to a lot more than the drink I've been nursing. Ten years. Ten *years* of time together, and that was the way we had to end? Not even with a bit of respect, like I would hope I'd be due after this much time together.

As much as I wanted to get up and scream, to tell her the ten thousand ways she's wrong, I didn't. There was a part of me, deep down, that knew we were never really made for each other. That we were the same side of the same coin, never a balance, always cold and unaffected by the world. At least, that's what I thought.

I can't say that I've been a saint either. Late nights at the office, weekends spent at venues, all to push towards the ever-present goals my father kept scrawled on that damn whiteboard of his like a war plan.

But the idea of being alone, truly alone, after that long with the same person - the only person I'd ever been with, was enough to make me nearly lose my lunch as she tipped back her glass. So I did the same, hoping the burn down my throat would settle the unease of the conversation we were about to have.

I'm drying off my hands as I step out of the bathroom door, ready to head back to sit down next to Piper, when I turn the corner and see the one person I was hoping to avoid tonight.

Alex leans against the wall, arms crossed over her belly, with a fierce look on her face that says I'm in for it.

"Westfall," she says evenly, and pops a bubble with the gum in her mouth. I swallow.

"Alex," I reply, giving her a nod. "Good to see you."

"Cut the shit, Fitz." Jesus. Ok. Here we fucking go. Her nostrils flare as she takes a tentative push off the wall, making a measured step towards me. "What are you really doing here?"

"I told you," I start, but she cuts me off.

"There's no such thing as coincidences." She pops another angry bubble. "And frankly, as much as Piper wants to believe in a higher power or whatever, the only fate happening here is the fate of me kicking your ass for sending that shit to her."

"I have no idea what you're talking about," I respond, trying to wrap my head around everything she'd just said. Higher power? What did I send to Piper that warranted this kind of response? Alex lets out a dark laugh.

"You really don't know her at all, do you?" she asks.

"No, I don't." I cross my arms, too, feeling defensive as she glares up at me. "But I'm trying, here."

"Then fucking try harder." She takes another step towards me, and steadies herself on the wall again. "You sent champagne to a recovering alcoholic, you complete and utter dipshit."

The silence that follows is long as I process what she said. Piper? An alcoholic? *Fuck.*

"I didn't know," I finally say in a quiet voice I'm not even sure she hears. But she does, and her response is another laugh.

"You wouldn't, because up until the last few weeks, you've said a total of ten words to any of us." She gestures back to the suite, indicating her friends - Piper's friends. And she's right. I'd interacted the most with Carla in school, mostly because she dated a teammate of mine senior year and attended several parties with him. But Vic? Alex? "You have no idea what she's been through - what we've all been through - and-"

"That's what I'm trying to figure out!" I interrupt, and then realize my voice is raised. Her eyes widen, and she's momentarily silenced. I take advantage of it. "Alex, I know I fucked up. I know, I sat on the sidelines and watched Andy - watched everyone - treat her - treat you all - like shit."

"Damn straight," she says in a flat voice, nodding.

CHAPTER 10

"But I've been getting to know her the last couple of weeks, and I want nothing more than to make that up to her. To you all." She eyes me suspiciously, her arms tightening over her chest.

"I have a hard time imagining you two having much to talk about."

"You'd be surprised," I manage, attempting to keep the smile from playing on my face. "We've got a fair amount of shared horror movie knowledge." She makes a disgusted face.

"My God, that's terrifying." She looks me over, as if appraising me. "I don't trust you."

"I don't blame you." I give a small shrug. "I was an idiot."

"Was?"

"Am." There's a moment of silence before I get the courage to ask what I want to. "She's been through a lot since high school, hasn't she?" Alex looks up at me again, and then blinks. Suddenly, her eyes are shining, and she looks away.

"We all have," she says quietly, dabbing at the corner of her eye. "Mickey and his family put her - put us - through the ringer," she continues. "It's not my story to tell, though." She glances over her shoulder, where the national anthem starts to play. Feeling awkward, I look around for tissues, but there's nothing in the hall. Without thinking, I hold out the paper towel in my hand, and she laughs, taking it and using it to mop up the tears coming out in droves now. "Sorry, pregnancy hormones."

"Don't worry about it." She reminds me of Frannie, hormones raging and ready to fight anyone, regardless of size, and I can't help but smile.

"This is the most I've seen your face move, like, ever." She laughs again, and then blows her nose unceremoniously into the paper towel. "Come on," she says finally, nodding her head back to the suite. "We'll miss first pitch."

Piper

Carla knocks my shoulder from her seat next to me, and nods her head behind us. When I turn, I see Alex, face stained with tears, coming out of the bathroom hallway behind the glass separating the stadium seats from the air-conditioned suite, followed by Fitz.

Oh shit.

I give Carla a concerned look before watching as Alex makes her way to the stairs, where Vic helps her down to the front row, and she plops into a seat next to Penny. I lean forward next to her ear.

"What did you do?"

"Nothing," she says sweetly, but it comes out as a little bit of a gurgle. I humph, leaning back in my chair and taking a long sip of Dr. Pepper as Fitz comes up next to me.

"This seat taken?" he asks, but it's half-hearted. His jacket is on the back of the chair he points to, next to me, and sits down before I can answer.

"Maybe I was saving it for someone," I joke, and he gives me a sideways glance before leaning close.

"Someone tall, dark, and handsome?" I can't help the unladylike snort, but before I can reply, we're interrupted.

"Dylan Anton," I hear from behind me. I turn to see Dylan reaching his hand out to Fitz, who looks at me, confused, before shaking it. "My brother is that asshole, next to her asshole." He points to Greyson and Nolan, then Alex in front of him. On cue, Greyson is first to bat and headed towards home plate, swinging his bat and dancing to his 80's walk-on song. Deep in conversation at the pitcher's mound with the catcher behind his glove, the pitcher turns to watch Greyson walk up, and the catcher returns to his spot.

"Asshole is an understatement right now," Alex growls under her breath, sinking further into her seat. "Bastard can't even pick up his own dirty socks." Literally anything anyone does is likely to tick her off at this point. She's perpetually in the overly-hormonal stage of pregnancy that left us all on edge.

"Nice to meet you, man," says Fitz. "What do you do?" A curt question that got straight to the point - typical Fitz. Dylan chuckles.

"I'm at Southern Star Mutual," he answers, taking a swig of the Corona in his hand. "Mostly underwriting, a little reviewing." He looks at me, and then over my head to see his brother at the mound, and the first pitch thrown. "Well, shit," he adds. Ball 1.

"Dylan is the youngest supervisor in his division," Carla says next to me, and I look at her, then back up to Dylan.

"When did that happen?" He had been angling for a promotion for the better part of a year, but it had been a while since I'd checked in with him - a while since we'd spent any time together, really.

Second pitch. Ball 2. The pitcher and the catcher converse again, and Greyson kicks dirt off the base, apparently waiting for them to get their shit together.

"A few months ago," Dylan answers, taking another drink. "They finally-"

But I don't hear the end of his sentence. The catcher resumes his place behind Greyson. The pitcher winds up. The third ball of the game makes contact with Greyson's bat, and with a bang it flies off as Greyson heads for first.

What I don't see is that the ball is coming directly at me. Before I know what's happening, it collides with the side of my head.

I hear a sickening crack as my eyes fade to red, then black, and I'm pretty sure I hear Dylan say "Oh fuck, P," before I lose consciousness.

CHAPTER 11

Piper

Five Years Ago

"Shit," Alex murmured, and I heard her chair whine as she pushed it back. The alarm on the oxygen monitor was going off again, and there were a couple of beeps before it quieted again, returning to the slowing beep of the heart monitor next to it.

I couldn't see anything. I had my face pressed into the blankets on the bed, my quiet sobs muffled as I held Mickey's hand, which was growing steadily colder in my own. Melissa, his mother, sniffled quietly from her spot on the opposite side of the bed.

Beep. Beep. Beep.

Every minute, the time between the rhythm became longer and longer. The music from Melissa's phone hummed softly - some country song that she'd been playing on repeat since Mickey had pushed away his oxygen mask for a final time. He was done. He was done with all of it.

It was just the four of us, now, Oscar, Melissa, Alex, and me - the rest of Mickey's family went back to their hotel after a particularly bad day with his oxygen levels. And when they'd dropped again, and I had rushed to find a respiratory tech, Mickey shook his head - he didn't want to be strapped to machines to stay alive, whether conscious or not. It was a discussion we had long, long before this day.

Back before I knew about Kelsie and Kayla. Back before we'd tied the knot in that tiny hospital chapel. Back before we'd sat in a quiet room and heard a doctor tell us that the cancer had spread to his brain stem - which was causing all of these problems now.

"Are you sure?" Melissa had asked, and he nodded - still coherent enough to make his own decisions, but even if he wasn't, I would never force him into something he didn't want. A life, or lack thereof, that he didn't want.

The alarm sounded again, blaring against the otherwise quiet of the room, and again, Alex silenced it.

I thought of Mickey's sister, back at their hotel with her kids and husband. The youngest of which is, I believed, one of the reasons Mickey had made it as long as he did. Determined to meet his new nephew, who would likely be as stubborn as his namesake.

His brother, with his pent up frustration and a knack for taking it out on others - I imagined him pacing around the hotel room, knowing his parents sat here while Mickey drifted away.

I even thought of Kayla - was she nearby? Staying in the same hotel as his family, maybe? Mickey had made it very clear to his family from his last diagnosis that he wanted - needed - to focus on trying to make it to meet his newest family member. He said he had let the story Kelsie had woven live on for too long, he'd given too much energy to it, and it was time to focus on the few options that he had left to try and win this battle.

I knew in my heart there was always a chance that Kayla was his - that, DNA or not, they look alike. That the DNA test could have been faked all those years ago, in that tiny lab in that tiny town. That the supposed daughter he hid for years, while secretly spending time with her behind my back, could legitimately be his. But when it had all come to light, when he had other people telling him just how strange it was that Kelsie had chosen to re-emerge when he was nearing the end of his life, it seemed to knock some sense into him.

My heart ached for them. For the little girl who believed her father was dying that night. For her mother, who was either trying to do something right by her little girl and find a man who would step up when her real father wouldn't; or was actually telling the truth, and had been railroaded by the same man who lied to me - cheated on me - and his family, whose wrongs I couldn't even begin to list.

My heart ached for the truth I wish I'd been told from the start. The memories we all could have made together, if Kayla was his, if it had all just been one misunderstanding and Mickey had told me he had a daughter-figure he wanted to keep in his life. But those possibilities died long before this day.

"Piper?" I felt Alex's hand on my back, and I opened my eyes, glancing at her. She was standing next to the alarm, which she must have gotten to before it went off again. I looked at the numbers.

His oxygen level was below 10%. My eyes slowly slid to the man in front of me. His eyes were closed. His chest made shallow attempts to rise and fall with the little breath he had left. His face was pale.

We'd long since said our goodbyes - tearful and love-filled as we waited for his family to arrive from Kansas for the first time in months, watching our favorite movie in his tiny bed together. But knowing it's coming and seeing it happen are two different things.

I heard a strangled sound come out of my own throat as I stood from my chair, still holding Mickey's hand. Melissa and Oscar, huddled together, watched when I perched myself on the edge of the bed, holding his hand in my lap and squeezing it.

Beep. Beep. Beep.

"It's ok," I choked out, tears streaming down my face. I fought a sob. "You go." I reached out, stroking his scruffy face, unshaven from months in and out of hospital beds. "We'll be ok." I glanced back at his parents, who nodded, even though Mickey couldn't see them. Oscar gave his son's other hand a squeeze over his wife's delicate fingers.

"We'll see you soon, bud." Lips trembling, his own tears freely falling, he leaned down and placed a gentle kiss on Mickey's wrist. Melissa crumpled into his side, her shoulders shaking with sobs.

I couldn't look at them. I couldn't watch their sorrow, couldn't let my head get muddled with the hate my heart held for them, for all of the things they'd done, said, in the last several months, so I turned back to my husband.

And as we sat there in that cold hospital room, Alex by my side, the oxygen level slowly reached zero percent, and the heart monitor flatlined.

Melissa let out a choking wail, and Alex stood from her chair, fumbling with the machines by Mickey's bed, which were all whirring furiously to alert staff of what was happening.

Of what had happened.

Of my husband's death.

Finally, after muttering under her breath, Alex pulled the cord out from the wall completely to silence the machines.

I couldn't move. I couldn't think. I sat there, staring at Mickey's face. I knew that behind those eyelids were beautiful blue eyes that I'd been captivated by the day he first walked into my life.

Blue. His lips were blue.

Noticing this seemed to snap me out of whatever trance I was in, and slowly, I stood from my perch. My body moved without even thinking, and I stepped towards him, leaning over and placing a soft kiss on his cold lips.

"Piper," Alex said again, but I just turned, making my way towards the door - aiming for the family room down the hall where I could escape the horror in this room.

Melissa let out another wail, and Oscar was talking under his breath, sobbing.

And hearing that, I stopped in my tracks. I reached my hand out, finding the arm of the fold-out couch in the corner, and tried to steady myself. But I failed.

My knees went out from under me, and I fell to the floor, landing on the backs of my feet and cradling my head in my hands, letting the sobs fall freely. I let out sounds I didn't know I could make, wailing noises I thought only existed in dramatic movies.

I'd been mourning for a long time. In reality, since the minute of Mickey's diagnosis. Mourning what could have - should have - been. Recently, mourning the relationships I'd had with his family and friends before the events of the last few months. The solidarity I thought we would share after this moment. The way we'd be able to lean on each other in our grief.

In that moment, I mourned it all. I let it all wash through me, as Alex's arms wrapped around me, holding me while I let out screams that bring staff running to the room.

And as they hoisted me up from the floor, I couldn't stomach looking behind me. I wanted to remember Mickey as the man who walked through my front door years ago, holding a motorcycle helmet in one hand and smelling like gasoline. Remember the moments before our lives went to shit, and the times between those terrible days when even in the midst of crisis, we managed to find reasons to smile.

CHAPTER 12

Piper

Beep. Beep. Beep.
I have that dream a lot. It's a frequent one when I've been thinking about the past, or worrying about the future.
But I've never had the sounds continue in my head after waking up.
I'm sure I'm awake. I flex my fingers, my eyes still closed. I can feel a rough blanket. I wiggle my toes. I have socks on - weird, I don't normally sleep with socks.
Beep. Beep. Beep.
I feel my heartbeat quicken as my eyes flutter open.
"Fuck, she's awake," I vaguely hear someone say, but my eyes are flying wildly around the room. I know this room. I've been in this room before.
And my brain whirs, flashing back to hours spent in this very hospital with Mickey, hearing bad news after bad news.
Beep. Beep. Beep.
What am I doing here? Why -
I look down, and instead of sitting in the chair I was so familiar with, perched at the side of the bed, I was in the bed. The rough blanket over my body is a hospital blanket, and the socks, I have no doubt, are yellow and grippy and ten sizes too big for me.
I try to take a deep, meditating breath - but instead, short, shallow ones come out as I stare at my hand. An IV is taped in place on the back, a clear liquid pumping in at a steady pace. I can feel the cold as it snakes through my veins. My eyes follow the IV line up, up to a bag on a stand.
Beep. Beep. Beep.
Fuck. My head pounds, and I move my other hand to touch the side, where I feel a huge knot. One of my fingers is covered with a taped pulse oximeter, the cord leading to another machine on my side.

I try to take another breath, but it's just as shallow as the first. My heart is pounding, and I feel the first beads of sweat on the back of my neck.

"Piper?" I try to follow Alex's voice, but all it does is take my brain right back in a room floors above us, where she said my name over and over to check on me on the worst day of my life. "Piper." It's a statement this time, and a hand waves in front of my face, then stops.

Beep. Beep. Beep.

"Fuck," I say to myself, and I move the hand with the IV to try and rip off the pulse oximeter taped to my finger.

I need to get out of here. I need to get away from that sound, from this familiar room, this familiar hospital. This hospital I spent months in, got married in, lost my husband in.

"Piper, no!" Before whoever is talking can get the words out, I have the tape off, and an alarm sounds, loud and familiar.

I keel over in the bed, my hands over my ears, and my breaths come out as gasping sobs.

"What are you doing in here?" I hear Alex say.

"Stop it, stop it!" I cry over the wailing alarm, and somewhere in my periferie I see bodies rushing into the room. Someone tries to pull one of my hands away from my ears, but I grip them harder and can barely hear someone say "Don't, she's panicking because of the sound."

I feel a hand on my back as I nearly bend in half, burrowing my face in the blanket and pushing my hands further into my ears. People mill around the room, and I feel bile rising in my throat, my chest heaving.

Suddenly a bedpan slides onto the blanket next to my face, and there's an eerie silence as the alarm stops and I hurl my guts out into the pink plastic bin, spluttering and coughing, my hands still over my ears.

All the while, a hand circles on my back, soothing me through the wave of panic and nausea as I slowly release the vice grip on my head, finally looking around the room.

They've pulled extra chairs into the ER suite - Carla and Penny stand in front of their low seats next to my bed, concern etched across both of their faces.

Beside me, one hand on my back, stands Alex, eyes wide with panic, holding the cord for the monitor next to my bedside.

And in the doorway stands a stunned looking Fitz.

Fitz

A woman in a white coat hurries past me, a nurse behind her, and she walks quickly up to Piper's bedside. I stand in the doorframe, dumbstruck, heart racing.

Sheer terror. That's what stares back at me from Piper's normally sparkling blue eyes. That gaze that's usually so joyful, so happy, is distraught and scared, and now, I think a little embarrassment crosses her face as she sees me in the doorway.

God, embarrassment? Aside from the wild expression and the obvious location, she doesn't look like she just took a fly ball to the head. She looks like Piper.

My Piper.

Clenching and unclenching my fist at my side, I try to give her the best smile I can. It seems to catch Alex off guard, because for a second, she blinks at me from next to her friend, mouth opening and closing.

"Piper, how are you feeling?" the doctor asks, and leans over to look into Piper's eyes. She pulls a light pen out of a pocket and points it at her, and Piper blinks a few times before following the light with her gaze.

"My head hurts," she says quietly, and her eyes flit back to me. The doctor turns, gazing around to all the people in the room.

"I've got this," Alex says shortly, dropping the cord still in her hand and striding towards me with more force than I'd been expecting. Carla teeters behind her.

"Where are you -" Piper starts.

"We'll be right back, sweetie," Carla says over her shoulder, and Penny sits next to her sister in the bed as Alex grips my arm firmly and leads me out of the room.

"What the fuck, dude?" she seethes when we're out of earshot, but she doesn't stop moving. She just drags me through the hallway until we're pushing through the door back to the waiting room that I'd barely registered on my way in, running on adrenaline and fear and my own sense of terror.

For the first time, I notice a jersey-clad group sitting in the corner, and they all stand when they see Alex and Carla, the man from the field running to embrace who I can only assume is his wife. Alex nearly collapses into his arms.

"She's awake," she says, and a collective sigh of relief falls over the group. The other guy from the field - the one who hit the fly ball, Greyson, I think - falls back into his seat, burying his head in his hands.

Brett pats his shoulder, relief flooding his face, as Carla releases her hug from Vic and flies into Dylan's arms, letting out a shuddered sob. Dylan grasps her, hard, holding her head to his chest as she cries.

"She was so panicked," Alex breathes, letting go of her husband and looking around the group. Dylan raises an eyebrow at her over Carla's head. "The heart monitor started going off and she just fucking lost it." Tears stream down her face for at least the second time today, and Vic leans over, grabbing tissues out of the box on the table next to him and handing them to her. She takes one, and then turns to me. "You shouldn't have been in there."

"Dude just ran right past us," Dylan says, nodding at me, and I fight the urge to glare at him.

It was obvious, watching the short interaction he had with Piper in front of me at the game, that something had happened between the two of them. The tone he's using now is indignant, and implies I have no right to be here.

I guess, really, I don't.

"I'm sorry," I reply sincerely, and then sit in one of the nearby seats, scrubbing my face. "I was so worried, and-"

"We're all fucking worried, man," Vic counters, but his voice is soft. He turns back to Alex. "How is she, otherwise?"

"Doctor was looking at her when we left," Carla says, sniffling as she pulls away from Dylan. "Her neck is fine, they did an immediate read on the scans to check. She'll probably have a nasty concussion."

One minute, she was sitting, talking, the next, keeled over on the ground in front of me. And my heart felt like it was in my throat.

"Do you need anything?" Alex's husband says to her, wrapping an arm around her again. "I know that must have been triggering for you, too." She sniffles.

"It was, but I'm just glad she's awake, I was-"

Mid-sentence, she snaps her mouth shuts, and looks down as a trickle of water hits the floor underneath her. Alex looks up at her husband as we all stare. Slowly, she leans her head back into his chest as he stares down at her, shocked. Her shoulders shake in what I think is sobs at first, but turns out to be laughter.

"Of-fucking-course," she mutters, and then her eyes find his again. "Well, looks like we're having a baby."

CHAPTER 13

Piper

Nope. Nope. Absolutely not. I am not staying at this hospital. It may damn well be one in the morning, but I don't fucking care.

And I tell my mother and Penny as much as I try to force myself out of bed. Wordlessly, my father puts a hand on my shoulder, and looks down at me, pleading in his eyes.

"Please, love," he starts, and I cross my arms in resignation, trying not to tangle up all of the lines still attached to my hands. "Just for the rest of the night, the doctor said if you're looking OK we can take you home tomorrow afternoon."

"I can't be here, Papa," I breathe out, falling back on my pillow and closing my eyes. I'm in a regular room now, staring at the same four walls I looked at on my wedding night, where I'd slept on the pullout couch listening to Mickey snore in the bed across the room. "It's just...it's too much."

"I know." He leans over and kisses the top of my head. I feel like a child, being told what I can and can't do. And deep down, I know it's because I'm angry. I'm frustrated that I'm here, that this happened, that I can't even think straight, much less get up and walk out of here. Then, he looks at his watch, and shares a glance with my mom and Penny.

"Surprise, bitch," I hear from the door, and my head snaps so fast at Alex's voice that my neck gives a satisfying pop. Immediately, my family rushes to my side, but I laugh, rubbing at the side, and that seems to tell them I'm ok. I'm more than OK - I'm grinning as Nolan wheels Alex into the room in a clunky wheelchair. She's dressed in the same disgusting plaid hospital gown as me, her sweaty blonde hair pulled up in a high bun on top of her head. Wrapped tightly in a white blanket, a little pink hat on her head, is my Goddaughter.

Wordlessly, I hold out my arms, already feeling the tears streaming down my face.

"Gimme, gimme, gimme," I sob, and Alex grins as she hands over her daughter delicately. My father comes around and claps Nolan on the back as they observe us - he walked Alex down the aisle when her own father hadn't bothered to come to their wedding. He was the closest thing Nolan had to a father in law, but I don't think either of them were complaining. Nolan and Brett already came as an inseparable pair. Having them with two women he cared deeply about was just icing on the cake.

Silently, I stare down at the sweet face in my arms. Pink cheeks, a button nose, just like Alex had in all the pictures I've seen of her as a baby.

"I had to promise Amy box Cowboy's tickets," my mom explains, gesturing to Alex and Nolan, who I know shouldn't be out of their part of the hospital. But Amy, one of the nursing supervisors, had helped arrange Mickey exiting his designated area for something other than testing when we'd married at the chapel downstairs.

"Worth it." Papa slides an arm over my mom's shoulder, kissing her temple.

"We haven't told anyone besides a few people the name," Nolan says gruffly, and gives a slight nod towards my parents, who clearly have been playing double duty supporting all of us. I know his mom is probably breaking every speed limit between here and Kansas trying to get here to see her first grandbaby.

"Spit it out, then," I choke, trying not to lose my absolute shit for the umpteenth time today. I look back up at my best friend, and she's grinning too.

"Mikayla Grace Calloway." My eyes find my Goddaughter's face again, still so serene and wide-eyed as she takes in the new world around her. Then, Alex adds, "Mickie."

And I fucking lose it. Tears start streaming down my face harder, and Nolan, clearly concerned that I'm going to drown his daughter, reaches for her. I hug her closer to my chest.

"Don't even think about it, Calloway." I sniffle, and then look up at him. He's smiling, if not still concerned, and I can't help but smile through my tears back at the man who has my best friend's heart.

Nolan wouldn't have been someone I'd chosen for Alex, not by a long shot. She'd always gone for the bad boy - the black leather jacket, motorcycle type. But when they'd met long ago at a party Penny hosted for one of their baseball wins in college, it was clear to everyone but her there was a spark there. He was a golden retriever of a guy, despite dominating on the field, and I think she was a little scared of being too wild for him.

Boy, had that changed fast. Their domestication now was bordering on HGTV levels, when they actually got to home-make between baseball seasons.

When I'd managed to match with Mickey online, it had been sheer coincidence - I didn't even notice that we had mutual friends until we were days deep into an intense conversation about vintage cars, something my dad taught me about growing up. It had taken Mickey mentioning something to Nolan, who mentioned something to Brett, who mentioned something to Penny, for me to even realize that Mickey was the friend of Nolan's that had recently moved to DFW for work.

On our first date - first hangout, really, since he just came over and we talked until three in the morning - he told me all about the mischief he and Nolan caused in club baseball growing up, and then on school teams. When Nolan left for his college scholarship, and Mickey was left behind to go to school there, it had pulled them apart.

But within months, it was like they'd never been separated. Nolan, Brett and Mickey fell into an easy friendship - the happy-go-lucky best friend, the soulful artist dating my sister, and the man who settled for a career he didn't love halfway across the country to get out of his tiny hometown.

Losing Mickey - loving Mickey - had broken me in ways very few people would ever understand. But his death also broke Nolan, broke all of my family and friends - our friends - in some ways. And it was what kept us together, kept us close, and kept us fighting for moments like this, when joy shoved shadows aside and made us all forget, however temporarily, of the horrors we endured together.

When I finally settle in my own bed the next night, I'm frazzled and frustrated.

"Stop fussing over me," I whine, ripping the comforter Penny was adjusting away from her. She purses her lips, looking back down at me, and then to my mother in the corner, who's tossing laundry into a long-forgotten basket. "I'm f-" Carla's glare from the door cuts me off. "I don't need all this." I gesture around the room, the last light of Friday filtering in through my curtains. There's a stash of snacks sitting on my side table, along with a newly-purchased gallon size water bottle with a long straw and half a dozen get well soon cards mixed with a few birthday ones. At least three blankets cover my bed, and Bex is patiently waiting for my sister to stop moving them so she can climb in next to my legs.

"No phone," Mom says, and I roll my eyes - which hurts, just a little bit.

"The doctor said no excessive screen time for the first 24 hours. It's been…" I look around, and then realize I don't have a clock in my room, since I just used my phone and my watch, which are on the side table. Penny's eyebrows, now raised, tell me not to look at it.

"Just over 24 hours," Carla supplies, but then bites her lip when my mom and sister look at her.

"See!" I laugh, trying to adjust myself on the over-fluffed pillows, which were waiting for me, freshly laundered, when I'd walked into the apartment. "Mama, I'll be ok. I just need rest." Her nostrils flare, dark hair, just like mine, swishing over her shoulder, her Yale sweatshirt pushed up at the sleeves. She shares a look with Penny. "Seriously. Pen, go give the kids my love. You've been away from them for, like, a day."

"Brett's got it," Penny says dismissively, waving her hands, but I press on.

"Y'all." All three of them look at me, then. Mom looks like she's about to smack me for trading my colloquial Italian terms for something so southern, but I needed to get their attention. "Go. Please." I give them all a pleading look. "Carla will be right down the hall. If anything happens, I'll get her." Mom and Penny look at her, and she nods, though concern still etches her face. I think if it were up to her, she, like everyone else, would have rather seen me trapped in the hospital bed for at least another day. But I needed to get the hell out of there, and despite their protests, they understood.

Finally, I'm able to convince them to leave me, and I shuffle down in my covers, taking a deep breath as Bex hops up, snuggling next to me. Reluctantly, I pick up my phone from the side table, turning it on for the first time since it was plugged in to charge when we got home.

The notifications are jarring. Consistent buzzing in my hand, a flurry of drop-downs and pop-ups that I try to dismiss, wading into my texts. (68) Messages.

Jesus. I pick up my gigantic water bottle with both hands, taking a long sip before I try to tackle any of these.

BRIANNA VILLAREAL
Vic just told me what happened. Let me know what your PTO plan is.

I roll my eyes - I'll deal with that one tomorrow.

Group Text (5) *Alex, Carla, Penny, Vic*

CARLA MONTGOMERY
All comf at home.

CHAPTER 13

PENNY ROBINSON
After kicking us out.

ALEX CALLOWAY
You're welcome to come help with the literal baby instead of the functioning adult.
JK Nolan might murder the next person to walk in the door, she's been crying non-stop and the nurses keep waking us up.

VIC MONTERRO
Hope that's not an indicator for the next 18 years.

I bite my cheek. Vic was playing with fire - but he wasn't wrong. Nolan may be a golden retriever, but his parenting skills were close to zip as an only child. The only interaction he has with kids were Brett and Penny's.

In a separate text with just Penny and me, Alex informs us her milk has come in. As much as Carla is a stronghold in our friend group, especially in more recent years, Alex is closer to our third sister than our friend. I have my own, sobriety-forged sisterhood with Carla that they would never understand, and everyone seemed to be OK with it.

I smile to myself as Penny sends congratulatory .gifs to the group chat, and continue sifting through my messages.

DYLAN ANTON
Hope you're doing ok, P. I didn't want to overstay at the hospital. Let me know if you need anything.

Dylan. Oh Dylan. We had left things in a weird place, the last time we were together - New Year's last year, my wedding anniversary, and I'd promptly broken out into sobs when, after fucking at midnight, I looked at the clock to see what time it was. What *day* it was. New Year's Day – my wedding anniversary.

Anniversaries were hard - unlike A.A. anniversaries, which I celebrated - the ones that involved Mickey and the trauma surrounding us left me empty on those days, which often involved taking PTO and a morning yoga class. The pain eased as time passed, but the closer we got to May, the anniversary of Mickey's passing, and his birthday just a few days later, our entire group felt the collective dread.

I'd managed to avoid a ton of interaction with Dylan since the last time we were together, but we almost always saw each other in a group setting when cheering on the Alamos.

Most of these messages I don't even know how to respond to, so I just leave them on read and keep scrolling.

Nothing. Not a single text from Fitz.

Something in my chest pangs uncomfortably, and I pull Bex closer. Had I scared him, just like I scared Dylan? The physical manifestations of my internal scars just too much?

I make it until Monday before I feel like I'm going to tear my hair out. The last of my Happy Birthday texts from Sunday have come and gone - with a promise from my friends and family to celebrate once I'm feeling better. The last several birthdays have been ghostly reminders of the one spent in the hospital with Mickey, and I haven't pressed making anything special for this year.

I've gone to three virtual meetings in less than 48 hours, watched an entire season of *Outlander*, started the same load of laundry four times and when I finally sit down on the couch with the last of the cupcakes Carla brought home yesterday, tempted to text Vic to check in on our recently submitted project, I'm starting to get angry.

What was I thinking? Assuming that Fitz was any different than what I'd imagined all those years ago. Cold. Unfeeling. What else would explain his sudden complete silence after days of back and forth, after something like Friday?

No, I tell myself. Hold on. There was a reason I was starting to let my guard down. Fitz was putting in the effort, more effort than even Mickey had in our beginning, trying to get to know me instead of love-bombing and an endless sea of information on himself only. He was trying.

The silence still hurts.

Carla's out at a newcomer's meeting, and I stare around the apartment, contemplating what to eat for dinner. I have a playlist going through the speaker in my bedroom, the door open to play through the limited space we share.

Just text him.

The thought drifts to my head, and I try to shake it away. No. Texting first makes me look clingy.

Jesus. What was I, 19? No, texting first isn't clingy - it's assertive. It's dominant. It's...necessary.

PIPER DELMONICO
Do we need to alert the media that Jigsaw is back? Seems like a plausible explanation for your disappearance.

CHAPTER 13

The second I send it, I nearly facepalm. A *Saw* joke? Seriously?

The three dots appear, and I suck in a breath. Then, they disappear. And for a solid minute, there's no response. Then five. And by ten minutes, I'm pacing around my bedroom, Bex watching me worriedly from her perch at the end of my bed.

My phone buzzes, and I nearly run to it on my side table.

BRIANNA VILLAREAL
Your PTO is approved through next Monday. Please enjoy your time off.

Time off. I roll my eyes. That's what she's calling this? Like it's a vacation, not recovering from a near traumatic brain injury.

The phone buzzes again in my hand, and I click the notification that slides down from the top before it's completely visible.

FITZ WESTFALL
I didn't want to bother you. You should be recovering.

I snort. Was I a China doll? The doctor wouldn't have let me come home if they didn't believe it was safe. So why was everyone acting like I was going to break any minute?

Maybe because I had. Because, even without permanent physical damage, I had cracked momentarily, and shown everyone just how not-ok I was sometimes.

PIPER DELMONICO
Not fragile.

I left it at that, and got up to attend to the load of laundry that had just buzzed, letting my frustration fuel the focus on getting at least one load actually washed and dried. When I came back, he'd responded.

FITZ WESTFALL
You took a fly ball to the head and lived to tell the tale. You're anything but fragile.

I can't help the small smile that comes to my face. I had, hadn't I? Another incredible thing in my life - another trauma that could have killed me, but it didn't.

PIPER DELMONICO
It feels like I scared you off with

I ponder how to finish the sentence. What do I call it? Episode? Attack? Moment? None of it feels right.

PIPER DELMONICO
It feels like I scared you off with my reaction to being in the hospital. I wouldn't blame you if I did.

I press send, and let out a shuddering breath.

And I wait. For fifteen minutes I wait. And then, I'm done waiting. I put my phone on the TV stand at the foot of my bed, switching back on Outlander and hiding myself under my blankets, feeling exhausted and slightly humiliated.

CHAPTER 14

Fitz

When I make it to the second floor, I look up and down the cold hallway of the apartment building I'm in, trying to look at the door numbers. 2225. Ok. I turn to my left and see 2220, and stride that direction, reading each number as I pass. 2215. 2210. Finally, I'm in front of 2205.

I put the bag in my hand on the ground in front of the door, and try to adjust myself. In my haste to get over here, I'd thrown on the first clean shirt I could find, not even looking in the mirror. Now, I regret that choice - I'm sure I'd made a complete mess of my hair running my hands through it, reading Piper's text messages.

Scared of her? No. Worried for her? Most definitely. In awe of her? Absolutely.

As soon as she sent that last text, I texted Carla and asked for their address. I knew she lived nearby, given the fact that we both went to the same dog park in a city full of other options, but when I finally coaxed it out of Carla after promising she could personally kick me in the nuts if I did anything to upset Piper, I wasn't wrong. She lives less than ten minutes away, and truly, I could have just walked here.

I pull my phone out of my pocket, and text Piper.

FITZ WESTFALL
Come open your door.

There's no response - no indication she's seen it.

Had I scared her off this time?

My mind has been racing since Thursday night - sleep was minimal, and my brain kept replaying that sound, the horrible crack as the ball slammed into her head. Frannie tried to talk to me about it this morning, when I was clearly distracted in our leadership meeting, but I'd just locked myself in my office, sure most people would just write it off as my normal, brooding personality. But she could tell.

Piper hadn't scared me off reacting poorly to being in the hospital, though I wasn't entirely sure what she was reacting to specifically. She had reminded me what the years of trauma she'd been through could do to people, and the role I'd played in hers. I wanted to give her space to figure out if I was worth her time, knowing that some of that pain had returned in full force with me right there to witness it.

So when she texted me - a joke, at that - I couldn't help but feel relieved. And then frustration gave into impulse, which is how I find myself in my current position. Outside her door, with a bag of food, waiting for her.

When she doesn't text back, after a few minutes, I ring the doorbell, and immediately regret it. The sound of the electronic chime echoes through the space behind the door, and I hear her dog barking and someone cursing at top volume in a different language, footsteps thudding. The door flies open.

"There's a sign, you-"

Piper freezes, her hand pointed to small white writing on their black door. I run my eyes over her. Her normally immaculate curly hair is pulled into a thick, rumpled pile on the top of her head, curls framing her pink cheeks. She's wearing a pair of tight black leggings and a long sleeve sweatshirt with what looks like some sort of Tarot card on it.

It's the first time I've seen her in something even mildly unkempt that I can remember, and I feel something stir inside of me.

"Fitz?" Her eyes scan me, my face, my messy clothes, and her eyebrows knit together. "What are you doing here?" She pauses. "How do you know where I live?"

"I have my sources," I say flatly, and don't wait for her to invite me in as I pick up the bag and push past her, into the small apartment.

An open living room and kitchen is decorated with stacked bookshelves and hanging plants, a large, hand-woven white tapestry over the back of their blue tweed couch. Nothing matches, there are clothes and plates and cans of soda everywhere, and a part of me internally cringes. Compared to my home, which is all metallics and clean lines, this feels lived in. Maybe that wasn't a cringe at this, I think. Maybe it was a cringe at my clinical living situation.

"Hey!" she protests, though her voice has some humor in it as she closes the door and follows me to where I clear off a corner of the counter from unopened mail and set the bag down. "You can't just barge in here, what if I'd been indecent or something?" I don't turn to face her as she talks, but smirk to myself.

CHAPTER 14

If only. Bex, her tiny dog, scampers around my feet, sniffing at me to figure out, I'm sure, where Roscoe is.

"Carla told me you hadn't eaten yet," I say, ignoring her protests and unpacking the contents of the paper bag. Two containers of the meal José was prepping at Cosette for a tasting today, which he'd sent back with Frannie for me. "I hope you like pasta." Instantly, I realize it's a dumb statement. There's a pause.

"I'm Italian," Piper says in a dry voice, but I can hear the smile. "Of course I like pasta."

"Good." I keep working, popping the lid open on one of the containers and moving to the microwave above their small stove. When I get it started, I turn, leaning against the oven door handle, crossing my arms. She's got one hand on the counter near where I was standing, the other on her hip, and she has her eyes narrowed at me. Her rings clink on the marble as she nervously taps her fingers.

"Remind me to kick Carla's ass later," she says, and I nod.

"Noted. Now go back to bed." Her eyes widen, and then her brows rise.

"Fitz, I-"

"You should be in bed, resting. I brought dinner, and popcorn, and…" She tilts her head, and I reach forward, pulling a container of microwave popcorn out of the bag. She makes a face and I try not to be offended. Bex sits statue-still at my feet, laser focused on the crinkling plastic. "What, don't like popcorn?"

"No, I do," she says, shaking her head, her hands reaching up to adjust her hair, her shirt riding up to show a thin strip of skin above the hem of her tight pants. I note that the bellybutton piercing from high school is gone. "Microwave popcorn just tastes like shit compared to what you get from the theater." She seems to consider her words for a moment, and then looks apologetic as I slide the container back in my bag. "Sorry." Looking frustrated, she lets her hair out of the bun, a silky hair tie still in her hand, and shakes it out, leaning to one side to massage her scalp.

I notice, rather suddenly, that her shirt is a Tarot card, but not a normal one. What I think would normally be the depiction of some sort of wizard, mountain, blade, whatever, is replaced with the outline of a woman, kneeling, facing away with only a pair of black panties on. Above her head is the card number, "XXX," and across her back is the phrase "Yes, Sir" in swirling writing. The name of the card, at the bottom, reads "The Good Girl."

I swallow hard, and press myself further into the counter in front of me to hide the immediate rise of my cock at the thought of Piper in that same position.

"Noted," I repeat, and it comes out in a hoarse, throaty sound that leaves her pausing again, head tilted at a weird angle. I point vaguely to the only hall in the apartment. "Bed." She narrows her eyes at me, but I see something in them, just for a second, that makes me even more uncomfortable against the handle of whatever drawer I'm about to smash my full hard-on into.

"Bossy. Only because you brought food." Finally, with an eye roll, followed by a wince, she turns and walks slowly towards the hall, a final glance back at me over her shoulder.

I watch her long legs go, and when she and Bex are finally out of sight, I let out the breath I'd been holding in, taking a step away and looking at the bulge between my legs.

Get with the program, man.

I will myself to relax, trying to shake the thoughts out of my head as the microwave goes off behind me, and I turn to find silverware while the rest of the food heats up.

Five minutes later, I'm walking down the hallway balancing two glasses of water and the two containers, searching for her room. I pass a few doors - one looks like a shared office, and the other is closed with a C, woven out of thick gold wire and pearls, hanging on the door. Directly across the hall, I head into the only open door and find Piper sitting atop a canopy bed, draped in a purple, gauzy fabric.

I pause in the doorway, taking it all in. The room is lit by two gold lamps on either side of the bed, and strings of lights that weave in and out of the fabric above her. The walls, painted what I think is a light gray, are covered in posters and paintings and tall bookshelves. Each shelf is arranged artfully, like displays at a bookstore, with candles, art, and what looks like memorabilia.

"I take it you read a lot," I muse as I make my way into the room, and she looks up from her phone. Smiling at me, she sets her phone on the side table and turns back.

"You could say that," she replies, and then holds out her hands to take one of the glasses of water and a container of food from me. She sets the water down on her side table, the food in front of her, and then she looks at me where I stand on the side of the bed.

There's nowhere else to sit, but I don't want to invite myself into bed with her.

I don't have to - she gives me a sheepish smile, patting the spot next to her on her deep green sheets, a pile of blankets rolled down at the foot of the bed. Gingerly, I slide off one of my tennis shoes, then the other, and slowly sit down, pivoting to put my long legs out. Bex barely registers my movement from her place by Piper's feet, which, I notice, are covered in thick, fuzzy blue socks.

"What are we watching?" I ask, setting my water down and gesturing to the TV, which is displaying a screensaver slideshow of photos, mostly of Piper and her friends, the ones I'd either already known, or met recently. As she holds a small remote up and points it to the screen, I see a quick flash of a photo of

CHAPTER 14

Alex, Penny, Nolan, Brett, Piper, and who I think is Mickey. But he looks so different from the photo I'd seen of the two of them - his face was full, his eyes were bright, his hair longer.

"I was watching Outlander." She seems a little embarrassed to admit it, so I hide my smile. She would absolutely be friends with Frannie, especially given the number of familiar titles I'd seen on the shelves in the living room that I know she has sitting in her home office. "We can watch something else." I watch her as her eyes flit across the screen, scrolling and settling on one of the *V/H/S* movies, something I know we've both watched. She turns to me, then, and catches my eye. I don't look away. "What?"

"I'm glad you're ok," I answer, and then take a bite of my food, because I don't know what else to say.

Well, I do.

I want to say, "Piper, I'm so sorry I was such a shitbag, and I can't believe you didn't kick me in the balls that day in the office at the Pine, because I definitely deserved it." And also, maybe, "If you keep looking at me with those giant blue eyes I'm not going to be able to sit comfortably, much less *watch* anything."

But both of those don't seem like options at the moment.

Finally, she sighs, and picks at her food with her fork.

"I'm not really totally ok," she admits, and I stare down at my own food. For me, it's easier to talk when I'm not being stared at, when I'm not being watched. Maybe it's the same for her. "Physically, yeah. But otherwise…" She trails off, shrugging, and then takes a bite of the gnocchi. She chews, slowly, before a satisfied smile slides across her face and she lets out a low moan of approval.

I force my eyes shut, crossing my legs over each other.

"Who made this?"

"One of our chefs," I simplify when I'm finally able to speak, because calling José anything else would likely lead to probing questions, and this wasn't about me. I wasn't about to stear this conversation, our first conversation in person, out of earshot of spectators, towards myself and my drama.

"Well you can tell them that as a full-blooded Italian, I approve." She takes another bite, settling herself back on her pillows and wiggling her shoulders in what I think is a little happy dance. I can feel the smile on my face, and her head tilts slightly as she chews, like she's not sure what to make of it.

We sit there for a few minutes in silence, panic-filled screams filling the room from the TV, eating the food I'd brought. When she puts her container down on her bedside table, taking a long sip of water, she lets out a big sigh and lifts up her shirt, moving her hand over her stomach appreciatively. I feel myself swallow hard again, finishing the last few bites of my food.

"I definitely needed that," she finally says, closing her eyes and leaning back against the wall behind her bed. "I've been snacking all day." Without looking, she tilts her head towards a mountain of packages on the TV stand.

"Sugar all day after a concussion? Sounds like a great idea." She peeks out of one eye at me and then closes them again, but I can see her rolling them behind her lids, and she winces again. "Does it hurt when you do that?"

"A little." She reaches behind her head, eyes still closed, and pulls her curls out over her shoulder. "The doctor gave me pain meds, but I'm trying not to use them too much if I don't have to. Tylenol is working for the most part."

"Masochist?" I ask sarcastically, and she snorts.

"No, alcoholics try to avoid swapping one addiction for another." She pauses for a second, peeking out at me again. "I don't like the idea of being dependent on something again."

For a minute, it's quiet, as I'm at a loss for what to say. It's not something I'd ever considered, that slippery slope from one substance, one addiction, to another. But she had an absolutely fair point.

"You can ask me about it, you know," she says softly, and I look back to see she has both eyes open. She tilts her body to the side, curling her long legs up closer to her chest and leaning the side of her head - the non-injured side - against the wall to face me. "About the drinking. I know Alex told you." I nod, taking another sip of water to give myself time to think.

"I didn't know when I sent you the champagne."

"I know." She gave me a wide smile that made me relax a little bit. "You had no reason to. Most of us don't go walking around with a pin that says 'I'm Sober!'" She glances around the room. "Though, I'm pretty sure I have one here, somewhere." My shoulders shake with a small laugh as I sit up, pushing myself closer to the opposite end of the bed and crossing my legs to give us both room. My bed at home is a King, but this definitely is not. She turns her head to face me, using the remote to pause the movie still rolling on the TV behind me.

"Did it start after your..." I trail off, unsure of how to finish my sentence.

"After my husband died?" I nod, and she does too. "Yeah. I mean, I never really even touched alcohol when we were younger. Alex was the wild one, I just-" She pauses, seeming to catch herself in whatever she was about to say. "I didn't drink, and then suddenly I did. And it was easier to numb the pain than to actually face it."

I lean back on one hand, using the other to give Bex a couple of scratches down her back. She looks up from the toy she's chewing on, just long enough to give a satisfied "humph," before going back to it.

"It seems like you've faced it since then." I try to make it a statement, but it comes out as a question, and she smiles.

"I'm trying. Trying to figure out who I am after everything." She gestures around her room. "You should have seen what my house looked like when Mickey and I were together. This is me. This is my safe space, my sanctuary. That was what I told myself I should be..." She shudders. "The best thing I could have done for myself was walk into my first A.A. meeting. The second was moving out of that place and here with Carla."

"Is she sober too?" I ask, because I'm genuinely curious. She nods.

"Almost five years. She's been through some shit too." Piper pauses, and then stretches out one of her legs, nudging Bex with one of her sock-covered feet. Bex doesn't even look up, and Piper purses her lips. "I guess we all have. Even this one." She smiles down at her dog, and for a second, I swear tears welled in the bottom of her eyes, and then they were gone in an instant.

"I'm sorry for my part in that." I look down at Bex, avoiding Piper's eyes as she takes in my words. This conversation was turning deep, and when things turn deep, I curl into myself. I reinforce that shield with ice and pikes and don't want anyone to make eye contact with me because I risk showing what I'm feeling. I'm not sure how she handles tough conversations.

"I don't blame you." Her voice is quiet, and I give a small nod, still not looking at her. "Hey." I see her move out of the corner of my eye, and she's sitting up, crossing her legs in front of her and leaning towards me. "Look at me."

I feel my heart pound in my chest as I finally do what she asks, and her eyes are steel. Cold, blue steel as she wills me to listen to whatever she has to say.

And I'll do it. For that look of determination, the strength, I'd do just about anything, I realize.

"I don't blame you," she repeats, tossing her hair over her back and raking her hands over her face before continuing. "And I want you to look at my face when I say this, because I want you to know that I mean it."

I'm sure my mouth hangs open a bit at her words - like she'd read my fucking mind, and wanted the exact opposite of what I was thinking. Of what I would have wanted in the situation.

"You are not my trauma - you're not to blame for it, you're not the cause of it." She gives a small smile. "Was whatever Andy and I were back then traumatic in the end? *Fuck yeah.* And did it lead to me throwing myself into something more traumatic with another down-home country boy baseball player with a tendency to cheat on fabulous women? Probably." I chuckle as she gestures up and down to herself. "I mean, who does that? I'm amazing."

I want to agree with her, but I don't interrupt.

"I had resentments towards you, yeah. Probably still do. But I'm noodling those out, I'm going to meetings, I'm working with my sponsor." I tilt my head, trying to make sense of that last sentence. "But this brooding, can't tell whether you're constipated or happy thing has gotta stop."

A shocked sound comes out of the back of my throat, but I try to hold in the laugh that bubbles up.

"That!" she exclaims, hands both pointing at me like I'm the letters on a Wheel of Fortune board, surprising both me and Bex, who looks back at her with wide eyes. "That's what I'm talking about!" She pulls herself up on her knees and wades over the sheets towards me, settling back down on her heels right next to my legs. "That was funny, and you wanted to laugh, but that stick is shoved so far up your ass you're not sure whether you're smiling or grimacing."

A bark of laughter falls out of me, and her grin widens.

"I do *not* grimace," I correct, one hand on my chest, offended.

"That," she repeats, ignoring my interruption and pointing to my face. "That's what I want. That's what I need from you, if you're really sorry." She puts a hand on my knee, and I'm frozen momentarily, watching her as her thumb strokes a lazy circle over my bare skin. "You've gotta stop treating me like you did all those years ago, with that mask. I don't think you're the same person - you wouldn't be here if you were." She gestures to me, in her bed, sitting next to her dog, having just shown up unannounced with food and telling her forcefully to go to bed in a non-sexual way.

Piper gives my knee a squeeze. "I'm not the same person, either, but I'm also not the person I was between then and now. Not always, at least." In that second, her confidence falters, and then she says, almost as if to herself, "I'm not fragile."

Before I register what I'm doing, I push myself up on the bed, sitting up on my knees and reaching my hand out to grasp the back of her neck, my fingers lacing through her curls. Trying to be gentle with her already aching head, I guide her to sit back up on her knees with my other hand on her lower back, head tilting so she's looking me in the eyes.

There's panic in them, but also, as they search my face, something else. That same thing from the kitchen.

"You are *not* fragile." Her eyes dart away, and I pull her hair, just slightly, so she's looking at me again. She bites her lip, eyes wide, and I have to steel myself before I continue, praying that she doesn't feel my immediate reaction against her stomach.

"You want me to look at you, I'm looking at you. You keep saying you're not fragile, like you're trying to convince yourself, but you know it. I know it." Her eyes are as wide as saucers as she stares up at me.

Lust. That other thing in her eyes is lust.

And before I can overthink what I've just said, how fucking sappy it sounded, I crush my lips down to hers in a hard kiss, something I've been thinking about since that day in the office at The Pine.

CHAPTER 15

Fitz

I pour everything I haven't said, everything I want to say, into that kiss, as my free hand wraps around her waist and pulls her closer to me. She lets out a squeak of surprise and I smile against her mouth, trying not to let the ache I'm feeling take over entirely.

Her hands land in my hair, holding me tight against her as her mouth moves over mine, hungry, like she'd been waiting for this as long as I have.

It's everything I hoped it would be, and so much more, as I finally pull back, my chest heaving, my heart thumping wildly.

"You fucking terrified me last week," I breathe out, and lean my forehead against hers, closing my eyes and trying to relish in the feeling of her body still pressed into mine. Her hands wander down, over my arms, and touch them almost reassuringly. "I was so worried that just when I was getting to know you, I'd lost you. I feel like I'm just scratching the surface of what I missed a decade ago."

And as the words come out of my mouth, low and raw in a way I haven't been for a long time, I realize how true they are. That the panic I'd felt was fear - fear of the idea that I'd just about resigned myself to even considering the possibility of something more, only to have it ripped away.

Piper's quiet for a moment, still breathing deeply, before I feel her sigh against me.

"Not fragile," she repeats, and my chest rumbles in disagreement with the phrase. She laughs, tilting her head back to look at me, and her gentle hand swipes at what I'm sure is a stray curl falling into my face. I need a haircut. "I'm too hard-headed to let something like a little fly ball take me out."

"Hard headed, you say?" I let go of her neck, my hand finding the line of her jaw and moving my thumb across her lip, now swollen and red. The sight takes my mind to places I'm not sure I can commit to, not in this moment. "Well, that might be a problem." She tilts her head, still smiling. "I think anyone who knows me well would agree that being hard-headed is one of my top-five strengths."

She doesn't miss a beat.

"So what you're saying is that we'll make quite the pair?" I can't help the grin across my face as I lean down and press another, more gentle kiss on her lips. "What are your other strengths?" she asks coyly, and I press my lips together. I don't know if I have the willpower to keep myself from doing all the things with her that I want to - not if she keeps talking like that.

"Well," I start, and then, with one gentle push, she falls back into her pillows with a huff, clearly not interested in putting up much of a fight. Bex jumps off the bed at the sudden movement. Piper's hair is splayed out behind her, wild curls everywhere, her sweatshirt riding up. I crawl on top of her, surprising even myself.

Like her words, her orders to drop my mask, snapped something in me. Like saying what she needed from me gave me permission to let down some of my walls.

"I've been told I'm quite...strategic," I say, and then plant a leg on either side of hers, leaning down to kiss her again, savoring it. She lets out a musical laugh, her hand finding its way into my hair again.

"Tell me how that works for you," she asks, and I brace myself on either side of her head, questioning. "I want to get inside your head. Past this." Her free hand strokes my cheek, and I lean into it momentarily.

"Are you sure about that?" I dip down, so my mouth is right next to her ear. "It's not a pleasant place." She shudders below me, and I'm pretty sure all pretense of hiding my growing erection goes right out the window.

"I don't believe that for a second," she breathes as I push myself back up to look at her. Her face is resigned, determined again, so I relent.

"I'm strategic about what I want, how I want to do it. I like plans and paths to make things happen." I lean down, kissing her deep again. "I'm consistent, though I think that one is faltering lately." She smiles up at me lazily, understanding that I mean breaking my consistency with her.

"I think my team would say I'm an activator."

"Team," she repeats, and I don't press on as I go to continue. But, before I can say anything else, she hooks her legs up and pulls me to the side by my shirt. I nearly flail off the bed, and with a laugh she lands on top of me.

"That was, uh..." I look up at her, her grinning face, wild hair. "Impressive."

"Go on," she soothes, and runs a finger down the line of my chest. "Activator, you were saying." I clear my throat.

"Yeah, uhm, activator." I swallow. "I know what motivates people, and can use that to push them to succeed."

"Must make you a great boss," she mutters, and then leans over, hair falling around us as she kisses me deeply, her hips moving at just the right angle to make me go rock hard. When she sits back up, she's chuckling.

"I'm responsible," I choke out, though I feel far from responsible in this moment, with a recently concussed woman straddling me, doing things that can't be good for her healing process.

"I know that one." She pulls her hair to one side, sitting back to watch me. "You've always been responsible, since we were kids." I stare up at her, and feel the urge to ask her how much she remembers from when we were kids - long before we both became a sliver of the people we are today - but decide against it. "And five?" she asks.

"I said I was hard-headed," I reply, trying and failing to keep my face straight as she moves above me. She tips her head back, laughing, and the sight makes me want to do all sorts of things.

"That's not a strength, that's a character defect."

"I'm not sure whether I should be insulted or not," I say honestly, and she smirks down at me. "Analytical," I finally answer. Without waiting for my explanation, she hums.

"Not a one relationship building," she says in a musing voice, and I feel myself sit up slightly, nearly knocking her off balance. I grab her hips, and her eyes go glazed, just momentarily, as she stares at me. "What?" she asks, and puts her hands on my chest, feeling my heartbeat thumping. "You think just because I make pretty things for a living, I've never taken a strengths test?" Piper gives a sly smile as I splutter.

"What? No. I just didn't realize-"

"You forget," she interrupts, and holds onto my shoulders as she leans back to look at me. "While you were Mr. Class VP, I was winning my own scholarships and competitions." The proud look on her face tells me that she's just teasing, that she's not offended by my surprise, but I still have to ask.

"So what are yours? Your strengths, I mean," I clarify when she looks confused.

"I'm mostly strategic thinking and relationship building," she says plainly, and then rocks her hips again. I fight the hiss at the back of my throat as my fingers dig into her, just barely skimming the skin above her waistband. Then, she touches her nose to mine. "But that's to discuss another day." Before I can protest, her lips are back on mine, and this time, it's not a delicate, light kiss.

Her hands grip both sides of my neck where it connects to my shoulders as my hands hold her firmly in place. Her tongue darts out, just slightly, and that's all it takes for me to lose the last of my self control.

Still holding her hips, I rock against her, and she moans as she wraps her arms around my neck. I shift myself further up against the headboard, and don't let my mouth leave hers as everything goes quiet around me, my blood pumping too loud to allow for anything else. Her kiss is furious and I feel the same emotions pouring out of me again, holding her close.

The way I want this woman is consuming. What started out as an ember that day in the office at The Pine became a smoldering flame as we got to know each other. Nearly losing her was like throwing gasoline on the fire.

I feel her hips move in circles above me, and when I meet her rhythm, only a few flimsy layers of fabric separating us, she hums against my lips, nails working into my scalp.

It tells me what I need to know.

She wants this too.

There's a natural break, and before I get too carried away, I pull back, panting.

"Piper," I groan, and she smiles, ducking her head back in. "Piper," I repeat, and hold the side of her face, my thumb finding her pink cheek. I hear a gurgle, and think for a second that it's Bex, somewhere on the floor, before I hear it again and realize it's coming from Piper's stomach. She flushes, face redder than it already is, and her eyes widen before she grimaces.

"Hold that thought," she says, and gives me a last quick kiss before climbing off of me and heading towards what I assume is an en-suite bathroom, closing the door behind her. I sit back against the headboard, closing my eyes and trying to steady my breathing.

Did that just happen? Or was I just having a really, really good dream.

"You're lucky it's just me," a voice says, and my eyes snap open to see Carla standing in the doorway, leaning against the frame with her arms crossed, eyebrows raised. Her blonde hair is pulled into a slick bun, the first time I've seen her in professional clothes. "And not Penny or Alex, or God forbid one of the guys." She gives me a pointed nod, and then glances down. I follow her gaze.

"Fuck." I scramble to pull blankets up over my lap. She laughs, light and amused, before nodding towards the bathroom door.

"She ok?" I don't know how to answer her, but she continues without waiting. "Hottest girls have the worst stomach problems," she supplies, before glancing around the room. "She eat?" I nod. "Good, that's a start." She twirls her keys around her finger as running water sounds, followed by the door opening. Piper looks straight at me, but when she realizes I'm looking elsewhere, she sees Carla and nearly jumps.

"Jesus," she says, putting a hand to her chest. "Give a girl a little warning next time." I cross my legs, trying to will my boner to subside so I can get up and interact like a normal person.

"I'll be in my bedroom," Carla announces, and then gives me a death glare.

"Don't be too loud."

"You say that like I'm the loud one in this group," I retort, gesturing among the three of us.

"I don't know," Piper says quizzically, and sits on the bed near my feet. I can still hear her stomach gurgling. "Gentleman in the streets-"

"Freak in the sheets," Carla finishes, and then walks around the corner without so much as a glance back. I shake my head, trying to pretend like she didn't just say that, and Piper laughs, falling back across the bed and putting her hands on her stomach.

"I hate to be the bearer of bad news," she says, turning her head to look at me, "but I've got some fierce cramps going on and it's a bit of a mood killer." Piper pauses, closing her eyes and shaking her head like she regrets the overshare of information. I just find it endearing, but that may be my receding boner speaking for me. "I think we might have to press pause on whatever that was." She waves her hand between us, wiggling her eyebrows suggestively. I smirk at her.

"I was just about to suggest a pause also." She narrows her eyes. "Not permanently," I add quickly, because I can see her mind whirring, plain as day on her face - so opposite from my own functions. "I don't want to hurt that pretty head of yours." I lean forward, and give her arm a playful tug towards me. She sighs in resignation, and then works her way up the bed, crawling under the covers and sitting up next to me. Then, playfully, she pulls the blankets up, inspecting the pitched tent still waiting below, and she lets out a snort of laughter.

"Stop it," I mutter, and wrap an arm around her waist, pulling her into my chest and scooting down into the bed. With another deep sigh, she settles her head in the crook of my arm and chest, and my hand finds her hair - soft and wild from our activities. "Besides," I say, and then kiss the top of her head, "I don't want to rush this. I don't want to fuck this up." Again, I add silently to myself.

"Me either," she says quietly, and re-starts the movie. I sit there, holding her, my brain racing.

What the fuck? What in the *actual fuck*, Fitz? I'm not sure if the question is more because I'm shocked, or because I'm disappointed in my lack of restraint, or both. And this affection - this softness. It's not a side of me that I'm used to showing. Frankly, I'd forgotten it existed.

But before I can think on it too much, I hear a gentle mumbling and realize that Piper, in just a few minutes, has completely passed out on my chest, and all I can do is smile the shit-eating grin I've been hiding since her lips first met mine.

CHAPTER 16

Piper

I wake up on my own the next morning, blinking several times at the canopy above my bed, trying to let the memories of last night trickle back, rather than hit me like a tidal wave.

Bex is curled up next to me under the blankets, snoring loudly, and when I shift, she rustles, popping her head out to say hello and blinking her weary eyes.

I realize, with a jolt, that Fitz isn't in the bed next to me - and he definitely had been when I'd fallen asleep. Hadn't he? Or was that a post-concussion fever dream?

I grope under the covers for my phone, scratching under Bex's chin, and finally locate it on the side table, plugged into the charger. I have several messages waiting for me, but open his first.

> **FITZ WESTFALL**
> Had to head out early for work and didn't want to wake you.
> I walked and fed Bex. Hope you feel better today.

Though the words are plain, my heart patters a little bit. He walked and fed my dog. He didn't want to wake me.

"I was wondering when you were going to emerge from the land of the dead," Carla's voice drawls, and I look towards my open bedroom door to see her leaning against the frame, a large coffee cup in hand. An admin at a physical therapy office, she's dressed for work in dark blue scrubs, her short blond hair straight against her cheeks. She smirks at me from over her cup. "He left at about 6." I glance down at my phone. 7:15 a.m.

"I must have fallen asleep during the movie," I admit, pushing myself up against my headboard and letting Bex cuddle into my lap.

CHAPTER 16

"You did," she muses, taking a drink. "I went out to the living room at about midnight and he was out there, he made sure you took your meds, too." My eyes widen at her words, and I let my head fall back against the wall, mortified.

Memories from the night before flood me, a vague whisper of someone shaking me awake, shoving my daily pill container and a glass of water in my hand before letting me fall back asleep.

"What was he doing in the living room?" I ask finally, and she smirks again.

"Come see for yourself." She nods towards the hall, and I pull myself out of bed to follow her.

It's spotless. The entire living area, kitchen, even our small breakfast nook with a two-person table, all spotless. The cans and food containers that had littered the counters are gone, the mail stacked in neat piles by recipient on one corner. I shudder to think what clothes were littered around the room as I see them piled in a laundry basket under the bar. The blankets on the back of the couch are folded into neat little rectangles, and even the TV remotes are lined up on the coffee table next to a straight stack of trashy magazines we'd discarded at our yearly vision board party.

"Uh," is all I can manage, and Carla nods appreciatively next to me, drinking her coffee.

"He cleaned, he walked the dog, he brought you food..." She runs her eyes over me, still clad in my sweatshirt and leggings, my hair a rumpled mess. "Did you swear allegiance with unlimited head or something in those texts?"

I snort, my fingers reaching out to touch the tv stand near the hallway entrance, which has clearly been wiped down.

"It's been very PG-13," I admit, and don't add *as much as I wish otherwise*. "With the exception," I say after a moment, "of my accidentally throwing a vibrator on his desk at The Pine." Her horrified look tells me I'm not going to get out of this conversation without telling her details, so I move to get coffee from the half-empty pot on the counter.

By the time I'm ready to head out the door, I've penned a response to Fitz and wait to press send until I'm locking up, Carla right behind me.

PIPER DELMONICO
Were there woodland creatures in here last night or did you clean my apartment?

I close the phone, throwing it back in my purse and walking out to my car, where I pause, watching my roommate throw her big bag in the backseat. She stands up and catches me looking at her, arms crossed, and raises an eyebrow.

"I have a tendency to run head-first into things," I say quietly, thinking back to a conversation I'd had with Penny and Alex when I first got to the game last week.

They'd pressed me for information on my interactions with a certain redhead, and after sharing a look that told me they'd talked outside of our normal group chats about their concerns, Penny reminded me that I sometimes *ready-fire-aim*.

"You do," Carla agrees with a nod, and I roll my eyes at her. The dull thud of pain is still present, though less than yesterday.

"Do you think I'm running head-first into this?"

Of all of my friends, I've been close with Carla the shortest amount of time. We ran in completely different circles in school, and really the only time we ever crossed paths was during the occasional fitting when Vic and I were helping with costuming for their productions. She went to college out of state, I stayed local. But in the last several years, as Alex fell into domesticated life, traveling with Nolan and Haley and their baseball family, Carla has helped me pick up the pieces of my broken life. She saw me at rock bottom, at a time when my friends and family had no idea how to help me, and didn't judge, didn't make me feel like an addict. She was my friend, and sobriety just compounded that.

Needless to say, I trusted her opinion. It wasn't colored by seeing first hand what Andy, what Mickey, had done day-to-day, like Alex or Penny.

"I think you're being appropriately cautious," she says without hesitation, and then continues. "How long has it been since someone has been to the apartment?"

I pause. Dylan. Since Dylan. She doesn't wait for my answer, because she knows it.

"Exactly."

"I didn't invite him over," I half-argue, but she rolls her eyes, popping on her oversized sunglasses and opening her front door.

"You didn't kick him out, either." Ok. She has a point. "P, clearly you don't think he's the devil incarnate, or he wouldn't have been as hot and bothered as he was last night." I see her eyebrows raise behind her glasses, and she gives a sly smile. "From my forty-thousand-foot view, it looks like he's changed too, for the better."

"I think he has," I reply with a shrug, and then look up at the bright, cloudless sky. "I guess we'll see."

"Don't overthink it." She smacks my side, between my hip and my butt, and I flinch away. "Go to your meeting, tell Lisa I said hi." And with that, she slides into her car, leaving me contemplating that still-thrumming buzz all over my body that I've felt since Fitz laced his hands in my hair.

There are a lot of misconceptions about alcoholics.

We drink because we're weak.

We're weak because we're lesser.

We're lesser because we all come from low income, tortured households with battered childhoods and addictions passed down from our parents.

My mother may have her single glass of red wine before bed every night, but that does not, an alcoholic, make.

Probably one of the worst preconceived notions is what meetings are like. There's no forced share, no making people stand to talk about their demons. No one forces you to find a sponsor, to find your higher power, whatever that may be. It's your choice.

My choice, walking into my first meeting years ago, was one of the best things I could have done for myself.

And sure, the coffee sucks. The walls of my home group are littered with motivational posters like a middle school guidance office. The chairs are worse for wear and the carpet is stained from years of use. But it became my safe space outside of my home, to share my feelings and my wrongs with people who have been through similar struggles.

No judgment. Just a group of drunks who've done the same stupid shit you have, some worse, sharing their strength and providing their guidance.

Which is why, the second I step foot inside, immediate relief washes over me.

I spot Lisa across the room, talking to a group of older women, and beeline to her, pausing to say hello to a few friends along the way.

Lisa, my sponsor, is only a few years older than me - but sometimes, it feels like she could be my mom's age, with all her wisdom. That's what ten+ years of sobriety will do for you. When I met her at only my second meeting, Carla had introduced us, suggesting that we go for coffee, and in the first ten minutes she dropped an F bomb and the fact that she was drowning it in a long list of fantasy novels to read. It was pretty easy to do anything she said after that, including working the steps.

"Hey, girl," she says when she notices me approaching, reaching out and giving my arm a gentle squeeze. The women with her, Diane and Sophie, I notice, give wide smiles. "How are you feeling?" She touches the side of my head lightly.

"Doing better," I answer, my hand meeting hers and then giving it a squeeze. "Glad to be back in person." I haven't been to an in-person meeting since the

Wednesday before, which for me, was weird, as I usually try to attend at least three a week on the light side. When things get busy, I can substitute in-person for virtual, but it's not the same. I feel recharged every time I leave a meeting here, my social battery full and ready to rock and roll.

"We missed you," Diane adds, and then squeezes my arm too. "That video just killed me."

I cringe. A video of my untimely fate at the game has been making the rounds on the internet - luckily, my avoidance of social media left me somewhat in the dark to the commentary, but I'd received a couple of emails to my business account, the one tied with my commissions, after someone did some next-level research.

I made it to the meeting just in time - behind the ladies, Greg, who's chairing, steps up to the podium at the front of the room, and we find seats in the first couple of rows.

Greg welcomes everyone, and asks for a moment of silence followed by the serenity prayer. I use the moment to look around the room - spotting some familiar faces, as well as a few new ones. I make it a point to go speak to one of the girls in the back row, who looks nervous as hell.

"God," Greg starts, and we follow along.

"Grant me the serenity to accept the things I can not change, the courage to change the things I can, and the wisdom to know the difference."

This was the easiest prayer for me to get behind - after years spent trying to fit the mold of a good Catholic girl, something really even my parents never expected of me. A big part of working the steps is accepting a higher power - whatever that power is to you - and how it can work in your life.

For a long time, my higher power was just affectionately known as my H.P. Alex laughed the first time I told her, calling it my *Daniel Radcliffe* in jest. But that H.P. slowly transitioned into a general belief in a force, unnamed for me, controlling the universe. And that had - *has* - worked for me. Even in the unknown, I find comfort in the idea that there is a guiding hand at work. I've seen too many strange things happen to simply believe in coincidence anymore, especially after the last several weeks.

So, as Greg works through the introductory part of the meeting, has Diane read How it Works, a quick overview of the program meant to summarize the meaning of the twelve steps and the work we do inside and outside of this room, I find myself zoning out a bit. Lulled by the comfort I find in this space, I let my brain wander.

Last night felt like a hazy memory of a TV show I'd watched a long time ago. The details were there, but they felt clouded by too-good-to-be-true feelings.

I made out with Fitz.

CHAPTER 16

Fitz Westfall.
In my bed.
After he *brought me dinner.*
And then he tucked me into said bed, cleaned my living room, made me take my meds and then walked my dog before he left.
Too good to be true feels like an understatement.
And given my time in this exact room, I try my damnedest not to think the next thoughts that flash through my head. But they do, anyway.
When does the shoe drop? Something this insanely positive in my life, where is the overwhelming negative that typically accompanies it?
As I slide into a booth across from Lisa at our go-to diner after the meeting, and Rose, who's a member of the same group as us, wastes no time in bringing over two cups of coffee with all the fixings. I make my usual - three creams, one sugar - as Lisa scowls at it.
"You would think after three years you'd be used to my milk-coffee." I take a long sip, sighing.
"You would think after three years you'd text me when big shit is happening." I look at her over my cup, raising my eyebrows, and she stares right back. "Don't give me that look, you know what I'm talking about."
Carla is *so dead.*
"He stayed over last night," I said finally, setting my cup down on the worn black table and crossing my legs on the torn booth. I had managed to change out of my outfit from the night before, and am wearing an appropriate (for me) pair of stretchy black pants that let me fold up easily underneath myself. Lisa at least has the gall to wait a few seconds before smirking at me.
"And how was that?" She sips at her coffee, black, and looks at me over her white glasses, a stark contrast to her deep skin and beautiful brown eyes.
"Surprisingly wholesome." Lisa gives me an appraising look. "My stomach started acting up." Her eyes flit down to the coffee in front of me. I know what she's thinking - that it'll irritate my stomach further. She's not wrong. "This is about fifteen percent coffee. Let me enjoy the little things while you press me about my non-existent sex life." She holds up her hands defensively
"I wasn't going to say anything." I fix her with my stare. "Ok, I was, but mostly just say you seem...happy?" The last part is a question, but before I can question, her phone rings on the table. She flips it over, looks at it, and then says "Shit, be right back, Bridezilla calling."
I roll my eyes as she jumps out of the booth, answering the phone with her best customer service voice and stepping outside the glass double doors.
Lisa Kate, everyone, florist extraordinaire.
I realize for the first time that I never looked to see if Fitz responded this

morning, and dig in my purse. His response was a .gif of woodland creatures cleaning in Enchanted.

> **PIPER DELMONICO**
> Clearly underrated Disney movie.

Immediately, three dots appear.
Jesus, was he waiting for me to text back?

> **FITZ WESTFALL**
> Absolutely. Prince McSteamy is the internal monologue I have every time I watch a romance movie.

Oh boy. Well. He's trying.

CHAPTER 17

Fitz

My eyelids feel heavy as I stare at my phone screen, watching the three little dots whir as Piper responds.

PIPER DELMONICO
Close, but no cigar. McDreamy, not McSteamy.

And then she adds a .gif of Patrick Dempsey for good measure, and I die a little on the inside. That's what I get for trying to make a reference to a TV show I've only seen in passing when either Olivia or Frannie were binging.

FITZ WESTFALL
I take it you're a fan, then?

PIPER DELMONICO
I mean, it's hard not to be when Meredith Grey is one of the few examples of thriving widows in modern media.

And then I die a little more. Shit, I was not trying to bring up hard topics over and over again, but here I am, putting my foot in my mouth. Before I can apologize, she responds again.

PIPER DELMONICO
Besides, Patrick Dempsey is a powerhouse. He has a non-

profit that helps support cancer caregivers, which hits close to home.

So, hard topic, but also something she seems invested in.

FITZ WESTFALL
Is that what you were? A caregiver?
You don't have to answer that if it's too much.

The three dots appear, then disappear a few seconds later, and by the time my door swings open, it's been five minutes and I keep glancing between my phone and my computer screen like a lunatic.

"Christ, man." I don't even have to look up to know who it is. "You look like shit." Now I look up, and fit my brother, Freddy, with the worst look I can muster in my current exhaustion.

"Can I help you?" I say, though the iciness is half-assed. There are very few people who get even a sliver of reaction from me - Freddy and Frannie are two of them. Piper is quickly becoming one as well.

"Oh, fuck off," he says lightly, flopping into one of the armchairs in front of my desk and setting his feet up on the edge, his checkered Vans well-worn and way too dirty to be sitting on furniture this expensive. I eye him warily - his hair, the same color as mine, is far too long, nearly touching the bottom of his ears with ringlets. He pushes up the sleeves of his blue sweatshirt, which sports the LSSU knight astride a black horse, displaying the tattoos he's been slowly adding to since the day he turned 17. "I came to see if you wanted to go get lunch downstairs, but clearly you need a nap."

My phone buzzes, and I quickly - too quickly - grab for it. But Freddy is too fast for me, leaning forward and snatching it out from in front of me.

A rumble leaves my chest as he reads over the screen, where I'm sure he can't read the text, but can at least see who it's from.

"Ooh, who's Piper?" I reach across the desk and try to get it, but he holds it up, peering at the screen feet away from his face and typing on the screen. To my horror, I hear the unlocking sound.

"What the *fuck*?" I jump to my feet as he does the same, backing towards the door and scrolling up in my messages with Piper. Panic shifts through me, and I take several long strides to where he's standing, his fingers on the door handle.

"You should have changed your password, dude, it's still your anniversary with Liv." As he reads, his eyes widen. "Holy shitballs, you slept at someone's house last night?" In a flash of red hair, the door opens and he flies out of it, walking backwards down the hall as I stalk after him. I try to avoid the confused looks of Georgia and the surrounding staff, because I probably look like I'm about to commit cold-blooded murder. "Oh my God, Will, this is disgusting. Are you talking about Paranormal Activity?"

Hell, murder actually sounds appealing at this point.

I want to correct him - technically, I didn't really sleep last night. But that would mean admitting that I was there in the first place, which would result in the interrogation from hell.

Once Piper fell asleep, I let her lounge until I had to slip out to the restroom, where I noticed a daily pill box with the night's medicine still in it. When I knocked on Carla's door and asked her about it, she blanched and then said that it was unlike Piper to fall asleep without taking them.

Based on the box, she hadn't missed any in the last few days, so I chalked it up to the distraction of our activities and gently woke her up with a glass of water and the pills in hand. Then, when I went to take the glass to the kitchen, I stood there, staring at the disaster of a living room for so long that it started to make my eyes hurt.

So, I put on a true crime podcast and got to work.

It wasn't until I looked at the clock - four a.m. - that I realized how long I'd been at it. I snuck back into bed with Piper, who was, at that point, face down on the pillows and breathing heavily, and spent a few hours just enjoying being with her before I had to head home to let Roscoe out and get ready for work.

"Fred?" Frannie peers out from her office just a few doors down, and Freddy, still walking backwards, tosses my phone over his shoulder at our sister, who flinches, barely catching it in time before looking between the two of us. "What's going on?" She retreats back into her office, my phone in hand, and I nearly body-check Freddy as I push past him to get to my sister.

"Will's got a girlfriend." He doesn't even try to hide the absolute mirth in his voice as I lunge for the phone in Frannie's hand, which she holds back, pursing her lips at me. I still. She knows I won't go after her physically like I would Freddy, but I'm not above the death glare I give her.

"She's not my girlfriend," I snarl, and then instantly regret the words as her eyes widen and she looks down at the phone in front of her. I've basically just admitted the truth to her. She scrolls for a second, her eyes going even wider, before she seems to come to her senses and locks it, handing it back over to me.

"Is Piper the girl you had at The Pine the other day? And the champagne?" Frannie asks, and I feel my nostrils flare, crossing my arms. "She is, oh my God."

"Fitzwilliam Nicholas Westfall," Freddy says snidely, and I whir on him. He just smirks. "Where'd you find this one?"

"Nowhere," I mutter, and stuff my phone back into my pocket before either of them manage to get it unlocked again.

I make a mental note to change the password to something neither of them can guess.

"Hold on. *Piper.*" Frannie sits down in her deep green velvet office chair. "Not...*Piper Delmonico?*" I start, staring at her. "Oh *God*, Will." She stares back, blinking. "You sent her *champagne.*"

"Why is that a big deal?" Freddy asks, and sits down in one of the chairs across from Frannie, resuming his earlier position with his feet up on her desk.

She gives him a disgusted look, but answers. "She's sober."

"Jesus Christ," I manage, and sit down next to my brother, rubbing my temples. "Does everyone fucking know her life story?" Frannie snorts.

"No, Chloe's sister is her roommate."

Carla. Carla's sister was one of Frannie's friends from high school. And also an employee of WHG.

I guess I'm lucky that she hadn't found out earlier.

"Champagne, dude?" Freddy asks, and I shoot him a glare.

"I don't think he knew that when he sent it," Frannie responds, sitting back in her chair and touching the tips of her fingers together in a way that looks very much like our father. I shake my head, agree with her defense of me. "And I didn't know that's who he was sending it to."

"With good reason." I swallow, and then pull my phone back out. I hadn't even looked at how she'd responded.

PIPER DELMONICO
I mean, yeah. I was Mickey's full-time caregiver for like, six months.

Jesus. I try to hide the way my lips thin at that thought, but clearly not well enough.

"Is that why you look like you slept under a bridge last night?" Frannie says quietly, but I can hear the smile in her voice before I look back up at her.

My next words make the smile stop.

"She nearly died on Thursday."

"Excuse me?" Freddy leans forward in his seat, his long hair falling around his face, his hands clasped in front of him, clearly invested in whatever I'm about to say.

"Did you see that video going around from the Alamo's game?"

Frannie sucks in a breath. "Fuck, that was Piper? That got hit in the head with the fly ball?"

CHAPTER 17

I nod as Freddy lets out a low whistle. "Were you there?"

I nod again, and scrub my hand over my face.

"Yeah, and then Alex Barton - er, Calloway's - water broke about three feet from my shoes."

Frannie's head bobs back, making a face, and Freddy, ever the mature one, shudders. "At the stadium?" he asks.

"No, at the hospital."

Frannie blinks at me. I rub my temples again, thinking about walking in on Piper in a panic. Maybe I do need a nap.

"You went to the hospital?" I look up at her, my face passive, still dipped to rub at my temples.

"Shit, dude."

"Yeah," is all I can come up with in response to my brother.

"She ok?" he presses. I shrug, and then lean back in my chair, letting my head fall back.

I weigh my next words - they might be assholes, but they're assholes that know more about me than anyone else in my life, have seen more than anyone else in my life.

"She's been through a lot," I start.

"Her husband died," Frannie says to Freddy, and I peer at her over my nose. She at least has the decency to flush.

"I think being in the hospital was triggering for her, or something."

"No, shit," Freddy snorts, as if it's the most obvious thing in the world, and we both look at him. "What? I'm getting a psychology degree, fuckwads. I may look dumb but I know what trauma is."

He's not dumb - we both know that. If our father had his way, Freddy would have gone down the same business-degree path as Frannie and I. But he didn't show any particular talents for any of the areas WHG touched on, and when he'd earned a full ride to LSSU to study psych instead of UT's McCombs Business School, like me, it took Dad a full year to get on the bandwagon.

"She's got it in spades," Frannie says warily, and a part of me regrets not talking to her sooner. I didn't think about the fact that Frannie was a Sophomore when I was a senior - she may have even known Piper at one point.

Both of them look at me, then, and I can see their eyes scanning me, like they always do when they're trying to get a good read on where my head is at.

I've always been in a different place than them mentally. Part of it, I think, is because I'm their half brother - our several years of separation was due to the fact that our father remarried after my mother's death. And while Paula, their biological mother, has been in my life basically from day one, there's a piece of my brain that never really settled into this perfect happy family frame that Dad so desperately wanted.

We all have the same fiery hair, eyes only a few shades different, but that's where the similarities stop. I've got my mother's coloring, tan and freckled, and tower over both of them. They look like twins sometimes, with their pale complexions and shorter frames that are more athletic, like Paula.

Paula is a good woman. The only mother I've ever known. But that piece that never fell into place is the same piece that questioned the situation Piper was in with Mickey and his supposed child.

Freddy and Frannie have always been filled with something I envied - warmth. It was like whatever combination my parents created when they had me was the wrong recipe, and just one tweak - Paula - made all the difference. Where most people couldn't tell what was going on in my head until I spelled it out, both of their emotions were either on their sleeves, or their faces. Both utterly unable to hide any moniker of emotions they felt.

"So how was last night?" Freddy asks slyly after a long pause, and I reach out to shove him.

"What happened last night?" The three of us turn towards the voice behind us, and in the doorway stands the Armani-clad, stone-faced Chris Westfall - our father.

"I was working on some budget report charts," I answer coolly.

The literal last thing I need is either of my siblings blabbing Piper's name for him to hear.

"Late, clearly," he remarks, gesturing to my face. Fuck, obviously I underestimated how rough I looked this morning when I left Piper's. "I came to see if you were going to the Women in Business luncheon tomorrow, Francesca, or if I needed to send someone else so you can focus on outstanding items."

"I'm sending Courtney for me," Frannie says, answering Dad's measured tone with a similar one of her own. "Greta has a parent lunch tomorrow and Jason can't make it."

I think all three Westfall men scowl at the sound of Jason's name - Frannie's fuckwad of an ex husband who was sleeping with not one, but three other women when their relationship fell apart, just a few months after my niece was born.

"Alright. Send her my love." The words are tender, but his eyes don't look it, as he turns to me. "I'm meeting Ethan and a few others for a round this afternoon, can you make sure nothing goes upside down while I'm gone?" Well, there goes my secret plan to sneak home and try to catch up on the sleep I haven't been getting.

"If this place can't operate without you when you're off golfing, I don't know how it's as successful as it is." Freddy's comment is meant more light-hearted than it comes across, I can tell, but Dad purses his lips anyways. "I'm sure Will has this covered."

Dad looks between the two of us, probably debating whether it's worth it or not to make any additional commentary, before deciding against it and giving a curt nod.

"Okay," he says, and then fixes me with a stare. "Let me know if you need anything." He turns and walks out of the room, and I see Frannie's shoulders visibly relax.

Of the three of us, she has the best relationship with our father, so for her to be so wound up around him tells me I'm not the only one who's felt the pressure the last several months as we push for record-breaking profits. Again.

Couple the work pressure with a divorce right after my own, and a sick kid, I can only imagine the pressure she's under without adding Dad's watchful eye and never-enough attitude to it.

"So," she says, and then leans forward in her chair, shaking her head like she's trying to forget the interaction we just had. "Tell us everything."

CHAPTER 18

Piper

PIPER DELMONICO
Ok, but have you SEEN Fear Street?

FITZ WESTFALL
No, it's a show about teenagers. Why would I watch that?

PIPER DELMONICO
You like Scream which is literally Degrassi but a horror movie. This opinion is invalid.

FITZ WESTFALL
I think I'm missing something. Zombies? Of all the horror tropes?

CHAPTER 18

PIPER DELMONICO
Judge away, Westfall. It's my comfort genre.

FITZ WESTFALL
Not even scary vampires? Come on, I never pegged you for a zombie girl.

PIPER DELMONICO
*Zombie Woman. Edward ruined vampires for me. Sparklyedward.gif

FITZ WESTFALL
I'm just saying that if you gave it a chance, you'd probably like it. I saw all of those fantasy books on your shelves.

PIPER DELMONICO
You want me to give a Russian mermaid horror movie a chance because I read high fantasy romance books?

FITZ WESTFALL
I'm not saying they're the same, but...

PIPER DELMONICO
As fun as that sounds, I don't think anyone in The Mermaid is going to tell someone they want to lay them out on a table like their own personal feast.

FITZ WESTFALL
???

I can't help the smile that spreads across my face reading Fitz's response to my reference.

"Can you come take a look at this?" Vic's voice chimes over the cubicle wall separating us, and I sigh, moving to roll out my chair and stand up when I back into something. Someone, rather.

"Oh, crap," I call, and turn to see Brianna wiping at her jacket with a tissue in her hand, where coffee has spilled down the front. I wince. "I'm so sorry."

"No, no, I snuck up on you." She makes an effort to smile warmly but it still comes across as cold, and she sets her cup on the corner of my desk. "I wanted to come talk to you about the winter collection." Her face tells me it's not good news, and Vic, like the nosy bitch he is, rolls out from behind the wall. Luckily, Brianna doesn't seem to notice.

"Everything ok?" I ask, and slide my phone into the pocket of my dress.

I wrapped up my week of PTO without seeing Fitz again - we texted back and forth, but between commission pieces, meetings, and then added Auntie Piper duties while Brett was out of town for a work conference, I've been crashing hard every night.

It also felt like Fitz was staying true to his word about not wanting to rush things. My spicy book reference was, so far, the only dirty text to pass between us, and he didn't push to come back over.

For now, we were getting to know each other, while we both barreled through what felt like busy times for each of us. Going back to the office was heaven, something I never thought I would say, but I'm dreading the impending doom of my birthday dinner this weekend.

"Oh, yes, it's fine," she answers cooly, still dabbing at her lapel. "We need to pivot for this collection, I'm afraid. Something more...mainstream." My brows furrow. "Your designs are beautiful, Piper, but I want a few more that are in-line with the rest of the team. More subtle." I bite the inside of my cheek. Subtle.

From a lingerie collection that she originally wanted to be Elsa themed.

"Alright," I reply, trying to keep my tone even. "What did you have in mind?" If she was going to come back with critiques, I needed specific feedback.

"Subtle," she repeats, and I fight the urge to tell her that's not helpful. "You know what the brand is."

"I do," I start, swallowing hard, "but I also know that our more daring pieces have been pretty successful in previous collections." She pushes back with a hard look down at me, and I do my best not to wilt. "If I remember correctly."

"With numbers the way they were last year, we can't afford daring." She picks her coffee back up and takes a long draw before continuing. "I'm sorry, Piper. I'll need at least five more designs by next Friday." She doesn't even wait for me to respond before she paces away, and I turn to look at Vic, who's staring at me with raised eyebrows.

"Breathe," he says, and I shoot him a glare.

"Simple." I turn back to my desk and pull my tablet towards me, huffing. "Fucking great."

"Simple is Brianna's middle name." I feel Vic's hand on my shoulder, and calm a little bit. "Do you need help coming up with anything?"

"No," I sigh. "I have some extras from the last batch. They're just boring as hell." It's an understatement. Compared to what I love doing, these are practically off-the-rack department store designs.

But, if that's what Brianna wants, that's what she'll get.

When I finally pull into a parking spot at the front of our building, Carla is outside with Bex in a grassy area, talking and scrolling on her phone. She looks up when she hears me, and the glint in her eye makes warning bells go off in my head. This bitch is up to something.

"Did Vic beat me here?" I ask, but already know the answer. He left at least twenty minutes before me - I was too focused on the rage shading I was doing to notice the time.

"He and Kyle are already upstairs." Her answer is clipped, but there's something else behind it, and I narrow my eyes at her. Vic was coming over for movie night, but Kyle was popping by to work on a few things before his double header serving gig this weekend.

"And?"

"Nothing," she says with a sly smile, and that does nothing to set me at ease. Bex jumps at my ankles as we make our way up the stairs, and I push the door open while digging in my purse for my phone, which I haven't checked since before my conversation with Brianna. When I finally look up, I see Kyle and Vic sitting at the bar in the middle of what looks like an animated conversation.

And Fitz sitting on my couch, holding a bouquet of white roses. No, not roses.

Tulips.

I freeze mid-step, and Vic and Kyle quiet as they observe me - probably waiting for my reaction. Carla doesn't even try to hide her amusement as she finds a corner in the kitchen and leans against the counter.

"Uh, hi."

Again. Breaking hearts with my charming intros.

"Hi." He stands from the couch, and I notice he's still clearly dressed from work, in a white button up and gray dress pants. Wordlessly, he crosses the room, and holds the flowers out to me.

And then, in one swift movement, bends down and brushes his lips across mine in a quick kiss.

If I wasn't still before, I'm stone now as he looks down at me, one hand on either one of my arms.

"I, uh..." Words. What are words?

The doorbell rings, and I let out a stuttered breath, able to use the momentary distraction to try and regain my composure.

Fitz just kissed me. In front of all of them. And he was smiling.

Fitz

The sound of the doorbell seems to knock some wind back into Piper as she sets the flowers down gingerly on the counter next to her bag, and turns to open the door. Dylan stands on the other side, wringing his hands anxiously.

I haven't asked Piper about Dylan, haven't probed her about much beyond what she's given freely in conversation, but there was something in the way that he was quick to introduce himself at the game. And then, the way he spoke in the lobby at the hospital.

Sure, Carla had basically clung to him like an injured puppy, but she always had a flare for the dramatic.

Maybe it was the raging, possessive caveman piece of my brain that had been so quick to judge that first day at the dog park.

"Dylan, what are you..." Before she can finish her sentence, Dylan looks past her and sees Vic, Kyle and me. Carla pushes off her perch in the corner of the kitchen, eyebrows knit, and comes to stand behind her friend.

"Sorry," Dylan mumbles. "I didn't realize I was going to be interrupting a party."

"What are you doing here?" Carla finishes for Piper.

"I can come back another time," he replies, shoving his hands in his pockets and turning to leave.

CHAPTER 18

"No!" Piper says, and then steps aside, pushing Carla away to make room for him to enter the apartment. I feel my chest tighten at the eagerness of her voice. "You're already here."

"Thanks," he says quietly, and then weaves through the doorway, giving me a confused look as he makes his way to the living room. He turns back, and looks pointedly at Piper. "Can we talk?" His eyes flit to the flowers on the counter.

Good. I'm even more glad I brought them now.

"Sure." Her voice is gentle, and she gives a small smile. "Give me a minute to change, I literally just got home." Piper turns back to me and gives me a similar smile, though part of me wants to think it's a little brighter, before walking towards her room, Bex at her feet, clicking the door closed quietly.

Kyle lets out a low chuckle.

"I think she feels ambushed, dude," he says to me, and I know he's right. Just like the last time I'd been here, I came over unannounced, and to add to it, so had Dylan.

I hadn't started out the day planning to go to Piper's after work. But I had back to back meetings, a stressful lunch with my father and several of our business associates, and an email from Olivia that raised my hackles.

It's a simple email - something about taxes and trying to wrap up an audit on her finances from when we were married - but it left me simmering and trying not to take out my frustration on an undeserving Georgia.

I need a dose of something. Of warmth. A particular person's warmth.

"Is everything alright?" Carla asks Dylan, and he nods, sitting down on the couch with a huff while keeping an eye on Vic and Kyle. Something is going on, obviously. Before Carla can protest, I turn on my heels and make my way towards Piper's room and knock on the door.

"Come in," she says quietly, and I pause for a moment - surely she's decent if she's telling anyone who may be at the door to come in.

I realize, when I look up from closing the door behind me, that I'm wrong.

She's got pants on, at least, yellow and wide legged and flowing. But above the waistband, which is tight around the drop of her waist, she's wearing nothing but a light purple bra that I can just make out from beneath her dark curls, tied back with a green bow.

She looks over her shoulder when she hears the door close, and a moment of surprise floods her face, followed by a sly smile as she turns back and continues sifting through a pile of laundry on her bed. When she turns, I notice a tattoo weaving its way up her right side - a sentence written in script font, bordered by flowers similar to the ones on her bag from that day in The Pine. I feel a rumble in my chest as I cross the space between us, coming to stand behind her, and she pauses what she's doing, leaning her body back into my chest and looking up at me.

I would be lying if I said I hadn't felt more relaxed in the last several weeks, talking to her, than I have in years. It would be a bigger lie to say I haven't thought about doing what I'm doing now, reaching out my hands and wrapping my fingers around her hips. I watch her eyes close momentarily, like she's steeling herself, and she reaches up one hand to come and settle on the back of my neck, the other gripping my hand on her hip.

"Thank you for the flowers," she breathes, and then looks back up at me.

With those wide eyes staring at me, I want nothing more than to lay her down on the bed and lose myself in her. But I settle for moving my hands forward, wrapping my arms around her midsection and resting my chin on her shoulder.

"You're welcome," I sigh, and breathe in whatever it is that she's wearing that makes my mind wander to the night spent in this bed. Shampoo? Perfume? "Vic said you'd had a bad day."

I hadn't pressed him on it when I'd arrived at the apartment, flowers in hand like a dope. I also hadn't heard from her since earlier in the afternoon, but her last text left me reeling.

That text. I didn't have any idea what it meant until I searched the phrase and the immediate results were some not-safe-for-work fan art involving paint and references to "big wingspan energy." I had absolutely no idea what I was looking at, but it was enough to raise my blood pressure. That was the kind of stuff she was reading? It made my Tom Clancy look G-rated.

"You talked to Vic?" She sounds surprised, and I feel a rumble of laughter in my chest.

"Well, no, he said that before you got here. I already had the flowers at that point." She smiles, her thumb running along the edge of my hairline. "You've got quite the band of suitors here for you."

She snorts.

"Vic and Kyle are more apt to court you than they are me." I think on that. Vic, I suspected. Kyle, not so much.

"And Dylan?" Almost imperceptibly, she freezes, and then lets out a long sigh, twisting so she's facing me. Before I can stop myself, I get a full view of her chest, encased in that light purple bra that's embellished with gold embroidery along the edges. I have to force myself to look at her face, which is crinkled in thought.

"Dylan and I..." She pauses. So there was a Dylan and her. "Are not like that. Not anymore." She watches my face as my eyebrows shoot up, and almost immediately she grins, laughing. "You don't have anything to worry about, Fitz. That ship sailed a long time ago."

"But there was a ship?" Her head bobs back as she looks up at me, nodding. "How long ago?"

CHAPTER 18

"Does it matter?"

Does it? I mean, to me, yes. Probably some latent knee-jerk reaction to the flaming ending of my last relationship. But this wasn't a relationship, was it?

I step back, giving her space as I answer. "I don't know." The words are meant as an answer for myself, too, but they're the wrong ones to say, because hurt flashes in her eyes and she lets out a shallow breath before turning back to the bed, searching again in the clothes.

"It clearly does, or you wouldn't be asking," she says without looking back at me. Piper seems to find what she's looking for, because she throws a long sleeve sweater over her head before turning around, not making eye contact as she strides towards the bathroom. "For your information, anything Dylan and I had ended with a post-coital emotional breakdown on my wedding anniversary last year." I recoil at both her honesty, and the mental picture it paints as she flips the light on aggressively, and leans forward over the counter, rubbing at her eyes in the mirror.

"I'm sorry," I say, meaning it, but her head snaps towards me, and her face tells me she's not convinced. This conversation turned very, very quickly.

"Are you, though?" She turns back to the mirror, observing herself. "I mean, Fitz, we're not even dating." Her words make my chest pang, but she continues. "I talk to you more than I talk to Alex, but you can't even trust me when I say there's nothing to worry about." She flips the light off and emerges from the restroom, closing the door behind her and leaning against it, watching me. I cross my arms, more out of discomfort than anything, and she raises her eyebrows at the motion.

"I appreciate you stopping by, but even you said that you didn't want to rush things. I think this," she gestures between us, "is the definition of rushing things." I gather that she means more than just me seeing her half naked, and watch as she steps towards the bedroom door. "I'm not about to define the relationship with someone I haven't even been on a date with."

Her hand turns the doorknob, and I know the conversation is over. I stuff my hands in my pockets and walk towards her, stopping just short of the door and looking her in the eye.

"I do trust you, Piper." I mean it. In the short time that I've been getting to know her, I trust her eons more than I think I ever trusted Olivia. Piper wears her heart on her sleeve, like Frannie and Freddy, and that openness puts me at ease around her in the same way it does around them.

I lean down and press my lips to hers in a hard kiss, which I'm thankful she returns, her soft mouth moving against mine. I hope that kiss says everything I need it to as I walk out of her apartment, eyes on me the entire way.

CHAPTER 19

Piper

Five Years Ago

I stared down at my ripped cuticles, hands spread on my thighs as somewhere off in the distance, I heard the latest *Mission Impossible* movie coming from the TV.

Shelby, my favorite nurse on this extended hospital visit, shuffled into the room, and I looked up to see her pale eyes scanning the faces around me.

Melissa and Zander were planted firmly in uncomfortable chairs on the other side of Mickey's bed - Melissa with her head close to Mickey's, where she was undoubtedly whispering sweet nothings about his daughter and her mother.

Penny, in the seat next to me, pretended to read on her tablet, but was really watching the other two like a fucking hawk.

And me, zoning off and looking at my hands, because I didn't sleep a minute the night before, knowing that Melissa and Zander were coming back from their hotel first thing and I'd have to endure their company. Endure this.

On my birthday, no less.

No warning, they just texted when they were halfway here from Paulsville, saying they were coming to see Mickey (for the first time in months). Maybe his recent seizure had scared Melissa. It scared me, driving to his chemo appointment when he started convulsing in my front passenger seat.

We had plans for the night - even though Mickey was half out of it, he had enough wherewithal to agree with my mother in bringing a cake up to the hospital and enjoying dinner here, like we had on our wedding night. Making another memory surrounded by the smell of disinfectant and scrambling to find enough places for all of us to sit. I realized in the last few days that it was likely

CHAPTER 19

the last birthday I'd get to share with Mickey, with his health rapidly declining. The thought made my bones ache.

I noticed, now, what Shelby had in her hands - a new brief, wipes, and a catheter kit. Penny seemed to notice as well.

"Let's go get some coffee," she said to Melissa and Zander, putting her tablet on the table next to her and standing.

"I'm not going anywhere," Melissa half-seethed, and Penny just raised her eyebrows.

"I think everyone would be more comfortable if we had some privacy," Shelby said in a soft voice, setting her supplies down on the rolling table between myself and Mickey's bedside.

Melissa eyed me, and then glanced at the items Shelby set down. "I changed his diapers, I can be in the room."

Shelby's face matched Penny's, brows to her forehead. "He's an adult, ma'am."

"You're not making her leave."

It wasn't a question, it was an accusation, pointed directly at me.

Zander looked a little green around the gills as he tried to pretend like this confrontation wasn't happening, staring at the phone in his hands, his long dark hair, the same as Mickey's used to be, falling around his face. Penny opened her mouth to respond, but Shelby was quicker.

"Mrs. Davis has been doing this for Mickey for months." I didn't miss the emphasis on the word Mrs. I was sure Shelby had overheard Penny and I discussing the fact that the Davis' refused to even acknowledge the fact that we were married. And she wasn't wrong.

Since the cancer started affecting his mobility, my status was upgraded from wife to nurse. Medication management. Brief changes. Catheterizations. The seizure and his subsequent hospitalization was the first reprieve I'd had from my duties in weeks.

As if sensing the tension, Mickey, half asleep, reached his hand out off the side of the bed - towards me. I jumped up, my heart beating faster in my chest, taking his cold fingers in my own and rubbing them in an attempt to warm him up.

"Well," Shelby said. "I think that settles that."

All I want to do is text Fitz. The second he walks out my door, I want to pick up my phone and apologize.

But I don't. I know I don't have anything to apologize for. And I also know that if we were taking things slow, the last thing I needed was to pour my heart out and tell him the real reason I froze - the fear that ran through my body when I opened the door to find Dylan, knowing that Fitz was right behind me. The fear that felt confirmed when he questioned me about Dylan, as I expected he would.

Jealousy wasn't a pretty shade on Fitz. But neither was distrust.

"Happy Birthday to youuuuuu!" Everyone drags out the last word, and I fight the urge to roll my eyes as Penny shoves a cake in front of me - red velvet with cream cheese icing, the words "Happy Birthday Piper!" Scrawled across the top in purple lettering.

When they finish singing, I lean forward and blow out the single, sparkling candle at the top, and everyone cheers.

"Happy Birthday, *passerotto mio*," my father mutters, leaning down and placing a kiss on the top of my head. I smile to myself, and reach my hand up to pat his on my shoulder, which he's been squeezing since they brought out the cake. He knows birthdays make me uncomfortable - especially this one. Officially older than Mickey will ever be. A year I've been dreading.

But I let Penny pick up a cake, and Mom plan a family dinner with my friends, mostly to pacify her and her need to keep calm and carry on.

"What'd you wish for?" Vic asks, sliding into a seat next to me and helping my mother dish out slices of cake, handing me a corner piece - extra icing.

Shit. I didn't wish for anything.

What was there to wish for? I look around the table, at Alex and Nolan, enjoying their first night out as parents while his mother watches their newborn, at Vic and Carla, on the verge of throwing cake at each other over something he'd said, at Penny and Brett, and my niece and nephew, Hunter and Aria, patiently waiting for their own slices. My family - the people who have been with me through the worst of the worst - related both by blood, and by trauma. I'm surrounded by the people I love most in the world.

But there's a pang in my chest as Alex and Nolan lean in for a quick kiss. As I spot Brett's hand give Penny's a squeeze. The could-have-beens, should-have-beens, hit me, and suddenly my eyes well.

Mickey should be here.

No. *Fitz* should be here.

Mickey isn't coming back. But Fitz, Fitz could. Would, probably, if I had the ladyballs to text him.

And then guilt, cold and palpable, washes over me. Truth be told, that's what left me so wound up when Fitz came into my room days before. Not just the fact that he didn't trust me when I told him there was nothing left between Dylan and me - because there wasn't. It was the guilt that resonated through me feeling so fucking comfortable in his arms. Like we'd been there a thousand times before, even though this was all so new.

The guilt at the idea of moving on. The guilt directly tied to the stigma of relationships after loss. The guilt that I'm feeling right now, wishing Fitz were here to be a part of this group, even though we haven't even ventured into the light of day together.

No, I tell myself. Don't jump too fast. Don't swim out too far. So I answer Vic.

"Nothing. I've got everything I need right here."

CHAPTER 20

Fitz

Sunday night, I'm back at Cosette, and José is practically buzzing as he flits around the kitchen, tasting pans of sauce and tossing instructions at his staff. Frannie and I watch, amused, from our perch next to the swinging double doors, where servers are already pacing in and out with the pre-plated salads.

Frannie's team is on site taking photos of the event happening tonight - an over-the-top 50th Anniversary celebration that rivals most of the weddings we do. Old Dallas money at its best. I agreed to tag along, both needing the distraction and also wanting to get a better feel of what she was hoping to express in the marketing materials she had me reviewing for her.

I've barely spoken to Piper since Friday - I let things simmer before texting her a short apology yesterday morning, but her response had been curt and there hadn't been much since then.

Were we talking a lot? Sure. Especially for me. But the near-stop on talking all together gave me a sort of whiplash I wasn't expecting. Like I was missing something.

"If José would just agree to be the star of this campaign, I'd be done," Frannie whines, picking up a piece of toasted baguette from the plate next to us and dipping it in whatever red sauce José's made for the night.

"I told you, mija, this face doesn't do cameras," he replies, making a circle around his face and then breaking out into a grin. "Let this place shine, not me. I won't be here forever." I shudder at the thought, but know he's right - he's teetering on the edge of breaking into the retirement I knew he'd been stocking for the last several decades. He deserves it.

"Nope, not allowed," Frannie says simply. "I can't put up with this one and his emotional shitshow by myself." She hitches a thumb at me, and I scowl. "You can't say I'm not right."

"Oh, you're right." I shoot the same look at José.

"Gang up on me, why don't you."

"Not like you don't deserve it," Frannie mutters, and then scoops a heaping dollop of sauce into her mouth. "You've been a fucking roller coaster of emotions for the last couple of weeks, and I don't like it. It's weird."

"It's a girl." José points his tasting spoon at me, and I'm vaguely reminded of the night after seeing Piper again for the first time. "And he won't tell me anything."

Frannie looks between the two of us, clearly confused. José knows more about me, about my life, than most people outside of her and our brother - and Olivia, at one point. Growing up, I'd gravitated towards the warmth and personality José exudes, rather than the cool one my father gives, and Frannie knows that. She knows why - she and Freddy have their own issues with Dad, but they understand that as the oldest and the outlier, it had the most emotional effect on me.

"There's nothing to tell."

"Bullshit," Frannie coughs, mostly to cover the word. "Oh, I'm sorry. I mean, of course, nothing to tell, that's why you haven't stopped checking your phone every five minutes." I cringe, phone in hand, and stuff it back into my pocket. "What did you do this time?"

I glance around the kitchen - most of the staff isn't paying attention, just following José's rapid instructions, mostly in Spanish, but I still hesitate at answering.

"I may have said something stupid about her ex," I say cautiously.

"Her ex?" Frannie asks, but continues, "Or her dead husband?" There's a clatter as whatever utensil José's holding clatters to the counter, and I turn to see him staring blankly at us.

"Way to be subtle, Fran." She smirks. "Her ex, who is very much alive." And sleeping with her roommate, I want to add, but don't. Chloe, Carla's sister, and Frannie are still pretty good friends, and I don't want to put her in that position.

I'd suspected something after the baseball game and hospital, but Carla's tone of surprise when he showed up at the apartment, coupled with the fact that they quickly pulled out of an intense conversation when I left Piper's room the other day, confirmed my suspicions. It wasn't any of my business, but it did ease my mind a bit.

"You've lost me," José says, and leans forward on the metal countertop, hands pressed flat.

"Cliffs Notes?" Frannie asks, and José nods. I just sit back and watch as Frannie tries to summarize. "Will is talking to someone he knew from high school who's since lost her husband." José blinks at her, and then looks at me, but Frannie continues. "And as his opening act, he sent her a bottle of champagne, which she couldn't drink, because she's a recovering alcoholic."

"For the record," I retort, "that last one was your idea."

"Dead husband," José breathes. "Dios Mio, what did you get yourself into?" I pause a beat before responding.

"I have no fucking idea." I scrub my hand across my face. "I swung by her place this week with flowers, and her ex showed up wanting to talk to her, and I may have indicated that I didn't trust her to tell me the truth about him."

"Yikes on a bike," Frannie says, wide-eyed, and José scowls. Someone from the other side of the kitchen yells a question towards him, and he answers, before picking up a big spoon and a pot from in front of him.

"Trust is a big deal, especially starting out a new relationship." I nod, leaning back into the counter behind me. "And especially for sober people." My eyebrows knit. He sounds like he's speaking from experience, but running down the list of people I know in José's tight-knit family, I can't think of anyone he's ever mentioned as being sober.

"Did you just show up to her place unannounced?" Frannie asks, and I nod. "Jesus, Will. No wonder it didn't go well. You show up, he shows up - she probably felt cornered, and you added insult to injury." I scowl back at her as she adds "You've gotta consult me on these things."

"I don't need your advice for everything woman-related." I lean my head back, staring at the white tiled ceiling - noting that it probably needs to be cleaned, or replaced, soon, and adding it to the mental checklist I have going from this site visit.

"No," José adds, but when I look up at him, the smile on his face isn't reassuring. "But I think I know who you should talk to."

"This? *This* is your brilliant idea?"

I try to steel my expression over my sunglasses as I stare at the idea Frannie said was "genius." She and José had looked at each other in the kitchen like they knew exactly what to do, and the idea of the two of them working together on something made me uneasy. This confirmed my suspicions.

Saoirse Bradley is not exactly someone I would consider a paragon of good advice. Hell, she's not even someone I would consider, period. As one of Frannie's college friends, and now an employee of WHG, I think I've barely spoken thirty sentences to her since we met.

But apparently, she's my saving grace.

Or, at least, that's what José says as he gives me a look that pointedly tells me to shut up, and Seer stares down at us from where she stands in front of our table, arms crossed.

"This is what you brought me to work for on my day off?" She gives José and Frannie a look that could kill, her brown eyes narrowed. She tightens her arms over the black, oversized tee shirt she's wearing, which hits nearly her knees, given how short she is. The cream colored hat she has on her head is nearly half her size.

"Sit down," Frannie says forcefully, and pulls the chair next to her out. I can't see Seer's eyes rolling when she slides her sunglasses back over her face, but I can practically feel it.

"No one is forcing you to be here," I say coolly.

"I am." Frannie looks at her friend, meeting a cold stare with a grin as the waitress comes up to take Seer's drink order. "On us," Frannie says to Seer, as if she needs reminding that we're technically her bosses, and she's at a WHG property - the Monarch, which is next door to our office. The restaurant on the bottom floor has a covered patio, so the three of us found a table outside while we waited for whatever Frannie and José had planned. This is not what I was expecting.

"We thought Seer could help in your current predicament," José says warmly, gesturing to the girl across the table from me with his coffee cup. He's driven a while to be here, too - and I'm grateful that he's looking out for me by orchestrating whatever he has. I'm just doubtful it'll do anything.

"Which is?" Seer asks, unwrapping her straw and shoving it aggressively in the glass of Diet Coke she ordered.

"You know what, this isn't a good idea," I start, and move to back my chair up. Frannie gives me a look that tells me if I move, she'll cut something off, so I pause. "I'm just not sure-"

"That I'm useful?"

"That's not what I said, and you know it." It comes out more clipped than I intend, but Seer smiles.

"There's the Fitz Westfall we all know." She turns to Frannie. "And you said he was a lovesick puppy." Frannie scoffs and smacks her friend on the arm, but Seer doesn't even flinch.

"The girl he likes is sober, too," José says to Seer, and my eyebrows furl.

"You're sober?" I ask, and Frannie looks at me like I'm dumb.

"Almost two years." Seer takes a long draw through her straw. "Figured Frannie would have mentioned something since she basically had to pick me up from rock bottom."

"I did," Frannie mumbles. Almost two years - that would have put me smack dab in the middle of my divorce, and just shortly before Frannie's. Jesus, and she'd still been there for Seer. Frannie just looks at me, though, and the pity in her eyes tells me we'd both been thinking the same thing. The memories were rough for both of us. I realize, now, that Seer and Frannie must be closer than I thought. And I feel like an ass for not knowing, so wrapped up in my own stuff that I didn't even notice.

"It's cool, you've had other shit going on." Seer shrugs, putting her drink down as the waitress comes back with a charcuterie board. Seer greets her by name this time - and I realize that she probably knows more people here than I do, since she works on site. "How long has she been sober?"

"Three years," I answer confidently - that much I'd managed to extract.

"And how long was she drinking before that?" I falter. "Don't know?"

"It, uh, hasn't come up." Seer nods, her expression appraising, and I can feel her eyes on me from behind the sunglasses that hide a third of her face. "Her husband died, I know it got bad after that."

"Jesus, Fran," Seer mutters. "You didn't say that."

"Well you know now." I lean forward, trying to busy myself with picking at some of the local selections in front of us. Finally, after I chew and swallow a piece of Manchego, I add "Look, I'm way out of my depth here. I need help."

Seer's smile is feline as she says "Thought you'd never ask." It's not particularly reassuring, but I realize I don't really have a whole lot of options for people to turn to about this. Outside of my brother and sister, Todd, José's son Mateo, and a few old frat friends from college, I keep to myself.

So, I fill in the blanks I'm sure Frannie didn't - and they listen. I talk about seeing Piper for the first time, about looking into what had happened since the time we'd last seen each other. About her coming to The Pine (leaving out the vibrator), and the texts since. I even tell them about the stupid pictures of the tape measure, which is still sitting on the dresser in my bedroom, taunting me. I talk about showing up to her house with food, and then the other day.

By the time I'm done, Frannie and José are staring - Frannie with her mouth partly-open.

"Fuck," she says finally. "Who are you and what have you done with my brother?" I groan, leaning forward in my seat and rubbing the heels of my palms into my eyes.

"Shut up, Fran." I swallow hard, and then look up at Seer. "So?"

"Well," she starts. "I think you definitely overwhelmed her." I look at her over my sunglasses with a face that clearly says "no shit." "Don't look at me like that, boss man. If you knew as much you wouldn't have done it." She sighs, scooping up a piece of pork butt on a slice of bread and topping it with fresh honeycomb.

Ok. I may need to try that one. She takes a bite and chews, seemingly pondering her next response. "If she's been through that much, she probably has a pretty close knit group of friends, yeah?"

"I think so," I answer, though it doesn't sound as sure as I wish it had. I copy her movements on the board, and she eyes me while I take a bite. It melts in my mouth, and I have to keep myself from groaning out loud. She must be able to read my face, because she smiles.

"That honey is from a bee sanctuary down the street from us in Lawrence. We got it sourced a few months ago, haven't looked back since." I think she and José can sense my confusion, because she continues. "I developed half the current menus here with this one." She points to José, who nods appreciatively.

Hm. That one, I didn't expect. I mean, sure, Seer was one of Frannie's friends, but not all of her personal referrals turned out to be rockstars. Case and point - Savannah. But as far as I was aware, Seer was a bartender on-site at one of our restaurants. Occasionally, I think she subbed as a line cook.

"My little protege," José says with a shove of Seer's shoulder. And suddenly, I feel like I've been living under a rock, unaware of anything going on in the lives of the people I care about.

"Don't let your son hear you say that." Seer clears her throat, looking around anxiously, as if Mateo may show up at any moment. He's not working today - I asked before heading this way this morning. "Back to the issue at hand. If she has a tight friend group, they've probably been with her through the worst of it. That's a tough barrier to crack."

"I'm working on it," I retort, adjusting in my seat. "I think Carla, her roommate, and I, have at least an amicable relationship." Seer snorts, and then pauses, looking at Frannie.

"Carla, as in Chloe's Carla?" Frannie nods. "Hm, small world." She turns back to me. "Carla is a good start, and will be a good ally in understanding Piper's particular brand of sobriety."

"Brand of sobriety?" I echo.

"Everyone's different," Seer explains, sipping on her drink. "Paths are different, sponsors are different. And if you're in the program, the higher power you believe in tends to influence what that looks like. Did she give an indication as to what that might be?" I try to think about anything I've seen, or heard, about Piper and religion, but nothing comes to mind other than...

"She's catholic, I think. Though, I don't think she practices."

"Religion is different from a higher power," she says, and all three of us look at her then. She holds her hands up defensively. "Don't shoot the messenger, man. Not all of us are religious. You can be spiritual without picking an organized group to associate that faith with."

This is the most I've talked about religion or spirituality in years - and the conversation is starting to make me feel uneasy. I didn't think it's come up mostly because Olivia was never particularly interested in anything, and we didn't grow up in a household that believed in anything besides the Westfall name.

"Did you notice anything at her place? Books, posters - inspirational quotes or anything?"

Her shirt.

"Her what?" Frannie asks, and I blanche, realizing I said it out loud.

"Nothing, never mind."

"Well now I need to know," Seer says, half-grinning. I stay quiet.

"Come on, Will. Can't be that bad." José smiles encouragingly, but I feel color slowly creeping back into my face as I picture the design on her shirt the other night, and can't possibly bring myself to describe that. Not in front of him. Not in front of Frannie.

"Spit it out, or I'm not helping." Seer's face is serious, and I look between the three of them before pressing my eyes closed and sighing.

"She had this shirt on the other night at her place. It's the most casual I've ever seen her." I look up at Seer. "Most of the time she's dressed up, but she was wearing this sweatshirt that had some sort of...tarot card I think. Or something like it."

"What did it look like?" She asks.

"Uh," I stutter, and slide down further in my seat. "Well, where it would normally have like a symbol or drawing or whatever, it was an outline of a person - a woman - wearing just underwear."

José chokes on the sip of coffee he's just taken, and Frannie's eyebrows shoot up, but Seer's face is unreadable.

"And it said 'good girl.'" Frannie lets out a snort, and Seer, to my surprise, doubles over, her shoulders shaking in laughter for a solid thirty seconds before she sits back up and pulls her sunglasses off, wiping below her eyes.

"Shit, it's a good thing I'm not wearing makeup." Seer looks at Frannie, who I can tell is trying really hard not to laugh, but she lets out a cackle that has me wincing. Clearly I'm missing something. "That's not an A.A. Thing," Seer says, still laughing. "That's a kink reading thing."

"Saoirse," José chastises, horrified. I have to say, I agree with him, glancing around to make sure no one is paying attention. Sure, in the privacy of my bedroom, I can do with a little kink. But in front of my employees?

Kink. It was a kink thing. And she'd been wearing it on her shirt. Piper, who at one point, wore a purity ring like a badge of honor.

"Does she have a lot of books?" Frannie asks pensively, and I nod.

"Tons."

"That answers that, then," Seer says, as if it's the most obvious thing in the world. "My guess is she enjoys a good steamy romance novel."

"I like her already," Frannie says, popping a grape into her mouth and nodding in approval. "I would guess not super into organized religion, either, but you never know." She and Frannie both eye me.

"You should ask her out on an actual date." José still looks horrified. "None of this 'talking' nonsense."

"I've been trying to get to know her," I defend. "This recent interaction just put a damper on those plans."

"Get to know her in person." His tone is firm, but I can see his eyes soften as he looks at me. "It's one thing to type words behind a screen. It's another to see how they react - to watch how they light up or dim based on what you say."

"When will you see her next?" Frannie questions, and I shrug.

"We have a call about the reunion on Sunday."

"Don't wait that long," Seer urges, sliding her sunglasses back on. "If she's being cagey over text, be straight up and ask her to dinner or something. Or, better yet," she pauses, "bring her to Menagerie."

"Ooh, yes! If she's as retro as you say she is, she'd probably love it." Frannie's excitement is almost enough to sway me. Almost.

"I don't want to bring her where I work."

"All the more reason," José adds. "I'll be there Saturday for a show, why don't you invite her to come out for that."

"I'll be working too," Seer says.

"Well clearly I need to get a job at Menagerie so I can creep." I give Frannie a look, and she laughs.

It's not a horrible idea - I think being around José may set me at ease, though Seer knows how to press my buttons, so I'm not sure how I feel about having her there.

"I'll think about it," I say finally, loading up another piece of bread and chewing on it to give myself a distraction while I ponder the idea of taking Piper out on a date.

CHAPTER 21

Fitz

Come on. Where are they? I scan the shelves in front of me, sure I'm overlooking what I came here to get.

Ah. Got 'em. I reach my hand out towards the bottom row, when another hand nearly collides with mine. Green nails. Gold rings.

"Oh, I'm so-".

The voice stops short, and I look up at the body connected to the hand, and nearly fall backwards.

"Fitz?" Piper gapes at me, her arm still outstretched towards the container of pickles we were both reaching for.

"Uhm, hi," I manage, crossing my arms and offering a weak smile. She's still dressed from work, I would guess - in dark pants and a soft looking sweater with a string of pearls around her neck. She brings her hand back to the handle of the cart in front of her, which is littered with premade meals from another shelf nearby. "Grillo's, huh?" Her eyebrows furrow, and I nod my head towards the container we were both going for.

"Oh, yeah," she says, recognition flashing on her face. "They're my favorite. Most of the time I eat them straight out of the container." I do the same, though I'm not quick to offer that information like she is. Her eyebrows stay furrowed. "What are you doing here?"

"I was craving pickles," I reply, finally picking up one of the containers and handing it to her, then getting my own. "Figured I'd walk here and come pick up a few things. I'm just down the street."

"You weren't kidding when you said you were close." She appraises me, her eyebrows finally relaxing. "Look, I-"

"Listen, I-"

We both start at the same time, and then stop, and she smiles sheepishly, tucking her hair behind her ear. Oh, shit. Did I make her nervous?

CHAPTER 21

"You go," I tell her, trying to be a gentleman. In reality, I want to spill all of the words stuck in my brain for the last few days - but I'm interested in what she has to say first.

"I'm sorry," she finally says, and I tilt my head in confusion.

"You have nothing to be sorry for." I pick at the edge of the container in my hands. "You had every right to be defensive."

"I wasn't being defensive," she argues half-heartedly, laughing, but when I fix her with a look, she practically rolls her eyes. "Ok, maybe a little bit. But really, you don't have anything to worry about with Dylan." She swallows, hard, and looks down at her hands on the cart. For a second, I swear she wiggles her right hand, rings glistening the fluorescent lights overhead. "If I'm being honest, I'm feeling..." She glances around at the mostly empty store, which is small and situated below some of the apartments near hers. "Guilty."

"What do you have to feel guilty about?" I ask, still confused.

"This." She gestures between us, and gives a small shrug. "It has nothing to do with you, and everything with me getting in my own head." She sighs, and then leans down against the handle of the cart. The V of her sweater falls to the point where I can see straight down her shirt, and I try my best to keep my attention on her face. "There's this whole thing about widows, and their chapter two..." She trails off, examining her hands again.

It's the first time I've heard her refer to herself as a widow, and it kicks something into place for me. Widow. Piper was a widow. She hadn't just loved and lost. She wasn't just a recovering alcoholic. And maybe it was hearing it come out of her mouth, but even reading that obituary, seeing those comments, it didn't make me understand like hearing her say it did.

She's scared. Probably more scared than I am at whatever this is. Because as much as I don't like feelings, as much as I try to mask mine, Piper wore hers on her sleeve, and based on what she'd told me, those feelings were very much trampled into the ground.

And as much as I'm physically attracted to this woman in front of me, as much as my entire body wants to be in contact with her, it's the conversations that matter. It's the way she talks to me like I'm not made of stone - of marble.

"Hey," I start, and take a step towards her. She doesn't recoil, which I take as a good sign. I reach my free hand out to grip her forearm lightly. "Whatever you're feeling, we can work through." I pause, squeezing her arm. "Together." Her mouth tips up at the corner, eyes shining slightly. "This doesn't feel like-"

Before I can finish my thought, someone says "Piper?" And we both turn to see where the voice is coming from.

Piper

Six Years Ago

"So close!" Ken's voice rang across the small yard, and a chorus of laughter followed as another one of his friends tried, and failed, miserably, I might add, to affix the small paper in his hand to the drawing taped up on the window.

"Clearly he's not that bad at landing on the target in real life," Bethani taunted, sipping at the fruity drink in her hand - something virgin that their bartender friend had whipped up and passed to the mother-to-be as she waddled around the patio. Ken and Mickey's coworker rolled his eyes as he handed the blindfold back to Bethani, returning to his also pregnant girlfriend.

Bethani wasn't kidding. The dude was horrible at pin the sperm on the uterus, the outrageous party game we were playing, but obviously it wasn't an indication of actual skill. I hid my smirk behind the Mike's Hard in my hand - the same one I'd been sipping on for half an hour while all of the guys from Ken and Mickey's team attempted their own...implantation? I cringed to myself.

Wordlessly, Bethani held out the blindfold and another little paper sperm to the next victim: Mickey. His blue eyes brightened as he laughed, his face creasing, tighter in the last few months than before.

When he looked at me, taking the blindfold, I felt the words he was saying without actually speaking. Without hearing the country twang, the midwestern boy charm that firmly had my heart from the day he walked in my front door.

We hadn't had the foresight to think about our future - future lives, future children - when he'd hastily started chemo at the beginning of this journey. And as his body became frailer, his hair ever disappearing and his soft features melting into jutting angles masked by now too-large clothes that we couldn't afford to keep replacing, the chance that we would ever get a day like that, baby shower and all, became slim.

So I tipped my bottle to him, and watched Ken clap at Mickey's shoulder, probably a little harder than he intended, because he was celebrating, didn't you know? He was going to be a dad. So he'd said eight thousand times on that bittersweet day.

I stared at my hand in my lap, my angry, red cuticles nearly the same color as the itchy folding chair I was perched in. Another coworker helped tie the blindfold over Mickey's eyes, and his laugh was bright again as he was spun, around and around, stopped and swaying right in front of the crudely drawn female anatomy.

CHAPTER 21

Blindly, he reached out, sperm in hand.

"Cold!" someone called, and he moved to his right.

"Warmer!" another said. He kept going. "Warmer!"

"Red hot!" Bethani giggled, and without any effort at all, Mickey reached forward and stuck the tiny black figure in his hand smack dab in the middle of the uterus.

As everyone around us howled, he slid the blindfold off and doubled over, shaking his head as he laughed.

Effortless. He made most things look effortless. The way he'd kissed me the first time, soft and slow. How he'd introduced me as his girlfriend to these very people, years before. Effortless, like the way he covered up the other girls he'd talked to in the months leading up to his diagnosis.

I saw the wave of nausea hit him as he sat back up - but Ken didn't notice. He kept laughing, handing Mickey a small brown bag topped with tissue paper.

I sipped on my drink, trying to steel myself for all the comments we're in for. I felt like the partner of the girl who catches the bouquet at a wedding.

Mickey pulled out the tissue paper, and then his prize at the bottom of the bag. I watched the way his face folded again into a light smile as he held up a box containing - I shook my head, trying not to cringe visibly - two toilet seat shaped shot glasses.

A prize for the couple containing a girl who could barely finish one drink in a four hour period, and a guy who would likely never drink socially again.

I stare at Bethani where she stands next to a display of tortillas. She's got a package of corn ones in her hand, and her eyes are firmly planted on the hand Fitz has on me.

As soon as Fitz notices, he moves his hand away, and turns to face Bethani, though I can tell he's watching me out of the corner of his eye.

"Bethani," I say, my voice strangled, and she tosses the tortillas in the basket slung over her arm, taking a few steps towards us and then, to my surprise, reaching out and pulling me into a forceful hug that has me stiffening. Her long, cherry-red hair flies out around us.

"It's so good to see you!" She exclaims, letting me go and holding me at an arm's length, looking over me. "It feels like it's been forever."

"Yeah," I agree, because it has. Literal years since I've seen or spoken to this woman. Next to me Fitz clears his throat, and I shake my head, trying to clear it of the memories. "Bethani, this is my...friend, Fitz." Her thin eyebrows shoot up at the word friend, but she take's Fitz's hand and shakes it, lips pursing almost unseen.

"So nice to meet you," she says, but her tone is clipped.

"Bethani," I start to explain, "is Mickey's boss' wife." I look up, using my finger to run over the words mid-air, making sure I've gotten the correlation correct. Fitz nods in understanding as she turns back to me. "How have you been? How's work?"

Work. She's asking about the marketing job I had for years before I made the switch to AllHearts.

"Good," I answer. "I've been at a different company for a few years now."

"Oh? Where are you now?" I swallow and glance at Fitz before answering.

"AllHearts. I'm on their apparel design team." Her eyes widen as she more than likely waits for me to yell "gotcha!"

"Oh," she repeats, clearly trying to save face. "That's great." Her tone says anything but great. I'm not surprised by her reaction, in fact, when anyone who was close to Mickey hears what I do now, I expect worse. Because Mickey was conservative. Because he was old-fashioned. Because he would have let me work at a company like AllHearts over his dead body. And that's what it, unfortunately, took for me to get out from under that stigma and do something that I truly enjoy.

"I really love it," I explain. "You remember all those commission pieces I used to do? Well, I kind of get to do that full time now." She nods, like she's trying to piece together old memories she probably didn't even care to store anywhere.

Because Bethani and I weren't really close. We hung out because Ken and Mickey were friends. We attended their annual parties, watched their dogs, but Bethani and I were on two separate planets most of the time. She was a party girl, who, with Ken, had to pound shots before Mickey's funeral just to get through the day.

The ironic part is that if I had really started drinking before I did, I probably would have been taking shots with them.

But Ken and Bethani stuck by me through the funeral, through the days after when I was fighting the Davis family to dig myself out of the financial hole I'd landed in while caring for Mickey. Until they didn't stick by me - until they made their allegiance very, very clear.

"Well, I won't keep you two," she says, and I can sense that she's gathered the wall that immediately sprung up when she approached isn't coming down any time soon. She looks at Fitz, and gives him a tight smile, then reaches out to give my arm another squeeze. "Let's get drinks soon," And without waiting for my reply, she turns and walks away, pulling out her phone from her back pocket.

I close my eyes, letting out a deep, settling breath before looking back at Fitz. His face is hard to read, but his eyebrows are raised like he's waiting for me to explain.

"That was...uncomfortable." I laugh to try and lighten the mood, but he puts the pickles into the basket of my cart and crosses his arms. "It's a long story."

"I've got time." I had a sneaking suspicion he was going to say something like that.

"Fine, but not here." I glance around - while there's not many people in here, there's a very real possibility that Bethani is waiting around a corner to report back on my movements. Fitz glances pointedly between the contents of my cart and my face before he responds.

"I'll help you carry these back up." And that offer, I won't refuse. That is, after I grab a second container of pickles for Fitz.

By the time I'm all checked out, Fitz has both of my pretty, flowery reusable grocery bags hiked onto one of his shoulders, and motions for me to lead the way out of the store and into the beautiful night air. It's a perfect spring night - cool, but not cold, and I'm thankful I wore my sweater from work.

"I take it the two of you haven't talked in a while," Fitz says cooly as we head up the sidewalk. "Given the drinks comment."

"You would be correct." I sling my purse over my chest, slipping my wallet back in. "It's been a few years."

"But you were close?"

"I wouldn't say close." I bite the inside of my cheek, glancing behind me. "Mickey and her husband were close, they transferred from a different company together. Bethani is..."

"Not you." I look at his face, and he's got a small smile playing on his lips. He means it as a compliment.

"Absolutely not. But they were there through a lot of the shit. Came and visited in the hospital, drove all the way to Kansas for the funeral. Ken was a pallbearer and Bethani cursed the whole way through the visitation when-" I pause, stopping myself. That's a story for a different time. Preferably with a weighted blanket and some sort of sugary treat. "When things got nasty. I thought they were behind me, 100 percent."

"But?" Clearly I am not hiding my distaste well. We pass a small, fenced-in yard outside one of the apartments where a big Goldendoodle is sitting up on its front paws. I fight the urge to give it scratches, and look at him. Despite moving up the steep hill gracefully, his eyes haven't left my face. When we turn into my complex, I cross my arms - as if the action will physically guard me from the feelings I'm having.

"But, they weren't. They got distant, but they invited me to one of their regular get togethers and I thought everything was good. Until I showed up with a guy, and I thought Ken was going to murder him."

"Dylan?" I let out a snort.

"No, Dylan and I didn't ever really go on dates." I catch a flash of distaste, and laugh again. "Dylan isn't the only person I've been with in the last few years, Fitz. He's just the one you've met."

"I didn't say anything," Fitz protests, holding his arms up, and I roll my eyes.

"You didn't have to." I sigh. "Bethani read me the riot act about making Ken uncomfortable, how he just wasn't ready to see me with anyone else. At first I tried to understand, but after a while it pissed me off."

"Understandably," he mutters, and then seems to catch himself, shooting me a sheepish glance as we approach my building.

"I found out a few weeks later that they were still friends with most of Mickey's family, and were basically taking any information they could get back to them. We only realized because his mom made a new Facebook page and wasn't smart enough to block Alex before she popped up in 'people you may know,' could see all of Melissa's friends, which happened to include Ken and Bethani."

This time, distaste really does flash across Fitz's face, and something inside me is incredibly satisfied that the story is as gross to him as it was to me in real time. We climb the stairs up to my door, and as I fish out my keys, I continue.

"None of us really put up with that shit anymore." I unlock the door, pushing it open, and hold it to the side for Fitz to filter in. I realize, to my embarrassment, that the apartment is almost back to the state it was in before Fitz went full maid mode. But he doesn't seem to notice as he pushes aside a pot of pasta from our dinner and places the bags he's holding on the counter. My mind flashes back to the night he showed up with dinner. "They're fucking dumb if they think that the Davis' have any loyalty towards them."

There's the sound of a door swinging down the hall, before Bex's tiny nails skitter across the floor, and Carla's voice sounds in the open space.

"Who's fucking dumb?"

CHAPTER 22

Fitz

Carla rounds the corner as she speaks, and then freezes when she sees me standing in her kitchen. Bex continues walking, settling at my feet, where I bend down to pick her up, giving her neck a few scratches as she nuzzles into my chest. I can't blame Carla. Last time she checked, I was probably still on Piper's list of people not to let into the house for the time being. Truthfully, I'm surprised I'm here, myself.

"Bethani and Ken," Piper says simply, and comes around to where the bags are, unloading the packaged meals onto the counter. "We ran into Bethani at the store." Carla makes a face. "Yes, exactly that face."

"Bitches," Carla says, like she's observing the worst kind of demon making a human sacrifice, and then walks up, taking the container of pickles in her hands. "I'll be in my room if you need me!" She turns to walk away, and Piper lets out a strangled noise.

"If you eat all of those, I'll smother you in your sleep."

"Love you too!" Carla calls over her shoulder as she disappears around the corner. Bex stares after her momentarily, before turning back into my chest.

"Asshole," Piper says under her breath, and then seems to remember that I'm there. "Sorry, she's a pain sometimes." She turns to the fridge and starts moving things around. Wordlessly, I set down Bex, who seems to be getting restless. I pull out my own container of pickles and reach over her shoulder, setting them on the shelf of the fridge in front of her. She pauses momentarily, but then continues. "You didn't have to do that."

"I know. I wanted to. She seems like a good friend," I muse.

"She is, I'm lucky we connected." Piper looks over her shoulder, her face framed by those dark curls. "I need to do a few things in here, then if you want, we can hang out for a little bit?" My heart soars as I nod.

"Absolutely. I'm going to run to pee really quick." I cringe internally, but she just nods and turns back to her task in the open fridge. Before I can say anything else embarrassing, I make my way towards Piper's bedroom. When I push open the door, a familiar smell hits me, and I try to look for the source. I spot it in one of the bookshelves, a wax warmer shaped like a lantern, with golden, molten wax atop. It smells buttery, like baked goods - the same way it has the last two times I've been over.

Her room is surprisingly clean compared to when I've been over - no laundry in sight, though her vanity in the corner is strewn with makeup. I start when I see, on her bedside table, that purple vibrator from the day at The Pine is plugged in. I had no plans of trying anything, but now, swallowing hard and adjusting the front of my pants, I have other thoughts.

I make my way into the restroom, and by the time I'm done, drying my hands on a fluffy purple towel on the towel rack, I've taken in the gold accents everywhere, her counter covered in Bobby pins and hair ties and enough curly hair products to stock a salon.

I've never been particularly good about caring for my curls - they just kind of do their own thing, and so far it's worked out pretty well. I wonder what they would look like if I took a fraction of the care Piper seemed to with hers, given the transformation they've taken in the last decade?

I hear Piper humming to herself, the faint sound of music coming from her phone in the corner of the kitchen, so I don't bother her. Instead, I cross the hall into the office she and Carla seem to share, where the light is on. It's apparent which desk is Piper's from the start. Carla's, in one corner, is neat and only has a big all-in-one computer with a few piles of papers. If I remembered correctly, Carla was in some sort of medical profession - she probably didn't need a whole lot of space to do anything at home.

Piper's, on the other hand, is a reflection of her other spaces in the house. The kind of chaos I expect from her, at this point. The L-shaped desk is nearly covered in sewing and crafting supplies, with scraps of leather, lace, metal tools, all scattered over cutting boards and sheets of vinyl. Her sleek Mac is surrounded by half a dozen different cups, with varying levels of emptiness.

The bookshelf in this office is, compared to the one in her bedroom, neatly stacked with spines from edge to edge, like they were trying to cram as many into the space as possible. The ones in her bedroom looked mostly like fantasy, with crowns and swords and vines on the covers. In the living room, the shelves were filled with nonfiction titles about fashion, culture - even a few car ones, I'd noticed the night I stayed over. It looked more like my own shelves, littered with introspective titles on leadership, historical pieces on various wars.

But as I trail my fingers over the spines on this shelf, they're all so incredibly different. Some dark, with skulls and weapons. Others, bright and cheerful with little cartoons on the front. I pick one at random - something orange and about bodyguards.

The uncomfortableness I'm feeling below the belt instantly becomes a raging hard-on as I sift through the pages I randomly opened to, where not two, but at least four people are engaged in things that involve moaning and licking and coming. Heat rises in my cheeks as I flip to the next page.

"A far cry from Twilight, huh?"

Piper

Fitz nearly jumps a foot in the air when I speak, leaning against the doorframe, and the look on his face when he whirls around to see me, slamming the book in his hands closed, is priceless. Flushed skin, wide eyes. And as I scan over his body, which is covered in a somewhat tight gray tee shirt and black sweatpants, I can't help but notice the bulge between his legs. I feel the smirk on my face as he speaks.

"Uh, yeah," he starts, holding the book up a few inches. "What's this?" I snort.

"Why choose romance with a bodyguard trope." His eyebrows knit together in confusion, and I watch him swallow, Adam's apple bobbing. "A girl with multiple guys, in this case, her bodyguards."

"You couldn't just watch porn?" he asks, and I can't help but to laugh again, coming forward and taking the book from his hands.

"I don't watch porn," I explain, and then hold the book up. "I read it like a fucking lady." I pause as Fitz lets out a surprised laugh. "I think I have that on a shirt somewhere." He takes the book back, and gingerly places it on the shelf where he pulled it from, and I notice him adjust himself in the process. He scans over more of the books on the shelf.

I nearly bite my cheek to keep myself from saying what I want to say. But damn, an embarrassed Fitz? A turned on Fitz?

The power that courses through my veins is the same as the time he spent the night. Knowing that you are, partially at least, the cause of some else's arousal?

"If you think that's spicy," I start, trying to keep the other thoughts from coming out of my mouth. "There are some dark fae fantasies in my room that would probably turn your hair white." He freezes, hand on the spine of a particularly fun hockey romance. "But if you want real-world spice, might I suggest that white one on the bottom shelf?"

He is, as I guessed, as curious as I am power hungry today, because even as I say the words I'd been biting back, he shoots me a glance, and then promptly picks out the book I mentioned. This time, he starts at the beginning, and with his body turned halfway towards me, I can watch as he flips through the pages.

First, confusion. Then, shock. And I swear I see his cock twitch as he finds some of the more scandalous pictures.

"I did that last year, mostly to model some of my own pieces," I muse, crossing my arms over my chest and peering at him over the glasses I'd thrown on when I changed. Finally, he closes the book, and sets it on the corner of the desk. Maybe so he can steal it? One can hope. Smiling lazily down at me, his eyes nearly glazed over, he slips his hands over my hips, touching the soft fabric of the leggings I changed into.

"I never pegged you for someone who would do boudoir," he says softly, and reaches one hand up to touch the string of pearls around my neck. My Nona's pearls. The same woman whose ring I wear, that Mickey proposed to me with in that dreary hospital.

I shake the memories out of my mind, and wrap my arms around Fitz's neck.

"I don't think you would have pegged me for a woman you would have talked to, much less anything else."

"I would have talked to you," he says, his voice small, and I realize I've hurt him, just a little, as he stares down at me, his brow furrowed.

"We've probably passed each other a dozen times on the street, at the store, the dog park." I shrug, playing with the collar of his shirt. "I don't know what changed, but I'm not complaining."

"I've changed." His voice is still soft, but his gaze is fierce as he brings that hand up, under my chin, and tilts my head up. "As much as you've changed in the last ten years, so have I." He tucks a stray curl behind my ear, and if he wasn't holding me up, I'd probably buckle to the floor.

"I believe you." I reach up, pressing my lips to his in a chaste kiss - though the feeling of his still present hard-on is anything but chaste. It makes me smile against his mouth, and when I pull back, he's smiling faintly too.

"GooutwithmeSaturday." It all comes out as one word, but I'm pretty sure I understand what he says.

"Like, a date?" He nods, flushing slightly, and absently plays with the end of the strand of hair he's holding. His eyes slide over the shirt I'm wearing, which says "Sober AF," and I swear, his lips turn up at the corners.

"Yes, like a date. I want to take you out, before this goes too far." He gives a pointed glance between us, where he's still pressed against my stomach, and I choke out a laugh.

"That's fair, I guess. Though, I thought you might want to have your wicked way with me after seeing those pictures." He lets out a soft groan, and presses a kiss to my forehead.

"Trust me, I do. But, I'm trying to have more self-restraint than that." He leans back, and holds my head between both of his hands. In this moment, with the way he's looking at me, I feel precious. Not in a cute, baby precious kind of way. A cherished, wanted kind of precious. Important. Seen. "Besides, when I have my wicked way with you, I want you in the privacy of my home." He brushes a kiss along my cheek, his mouth close to my ear. "And I want to peel you out of something you designed, if that's possible." I shudder as his breath caresses my ear, and when he faces me again, I can feel the flush in my face as I nod. It's in agreement to a lot of things - the date, the outfit, the idea of sleeping with Fitz, which truthfully, has been on my mind for a while.

But the feral look that washed over his face, flipping through that book of my boudoir photos, where I was someone very different from the girl who stood before him - I like that look. And I also worry about that look. That girl was boob taped and professionally made up and, while, I'm confident that I can do a pretty good job of those two things myself - is that what he's expecting? The girl who managed to bag his douche of a playboy best friend?

Or did he see past all of that, all the way to the glasses and the sassy shirts and the shelves of worlds I like to slip into?

CHAPTER 23

Piper

"Piper, can I see you for a second in my office?" I barely register Brianna's voice over the music in my headphones, but when Vic reaches around our partition and kicks the leg of my chair, I pull an earbud out.

"Be right there!" I manage, and roll out to wind around the gray cubicles and into her office towards the end of our hall.

You would think, as the type of company we are, that AllHearts would be more boisterous. Bright colors and fun, sexy offices that evoke the same kind of vibe as our website - our marketing. But I learned my first week here that the creative energy was mostly saved for the products, something I was completely ok with if it meant getting me out of the house.

"You called?" I swing into the doorway of Brianna's office, which is just as drab as the rest of our spaces - no artwork, just her M.B.A. diploma and a family picture on the wall behind her.

"Close the door for me, will you?" She gestures to the seat in front of her desk with a hand sticking out of a black blouse, holding onto a pile of papers on the other, and immediately my heart rate skyrockets. I can feel it in my chest as I turn to close the door behind me, and I try to take a deep, steadying breath before I turn back around.

I do not do well with authority. In general, I am a people pleaser - always have been. Penny and I joke regularly that I got all the oldest daughter traits, and she doesn't mind one bit. She's always been the carefree one, the one who fit in easily, who found a place in any social setting, who didn't automatically assume her ass was grass when a supervisor wants to talk behind closed doors.

I try to find an ounce of grace in my bones as I slide into the seat, careful not to trip, and Brianna sets down the papers in her hands with a sigh. My throat closes when I realize they're printouts of my last batch of designs.

"Is something wrong?" I stutter out, and immediately curse myself. It's obvious from my tone that I'm nervous as hell, but she's oblivious as she laces her hands together in front of her.

"You're incredibly talented, Piper," she begins, and I immediately sense the *but* I know is about to rear its ugly head. "But..." I see her eyes flit to the drawings in front of her. "Piper, I know you have a better grasp on our brand than this."

I don't get angry often. Truly. Maybe it's the run in with Bethani. Maybe it's the lack of sleep, looking forward to my date with Fitz.

Maybe it's just my patience finally wearing thin after years of making my ideas dull - making my ideas small - for this company.

But I feel my jaw clench, and in my lap, away from her eyes, my fingers immediately find a cuticle and start picking.

The pain sears through me because, fuck, I realize with a start - it's been years since I've done that. Years since I've been pushed to the point of self-sabotage to keep my mouth from saying what my brain is screaming.

And, yet, I still don't say it.

I don't say what's floating through my head - that my most outlandish ideas have been the ones to get customers in the virtual doors in the last few low-performing seasons. That my marketing degreed ass knows what their brand is backwards and forwards.

Instead, I say, "I'm sorry you feel that they're not on brand." I splay my hands out on my knees, letting the tips of my acrylic nails dig into my plaid pants. The one thing I splurged on, my nails, to keep myself from doing exactly what I'd just tried to do.

Brianna takes her glasses off, her dark brows furrowing in a tight line. I glance from her face to the picture behind her - her daughter has the same dark hair, the same tight smile.

"Is something going on?" she asks quietly, setting the glasses on her desk and fixing me with a stare. I feel myself shift - in all my time here, I've never been called to the carpet like this. "It feels like something has changed in the last few months."

"I mean, the incident at the game- "

"No," she interrupts. "Before that. You just haven't seemed..." She pauses, worrying at her bottom lip like she doesn't want to say what she has to. "You haven't seemed yourself."

I'm not sure how to answer her.

Myself? I haven't seemed myself?

Was something going on? Had something happened in the last few months to make her think things were different.

"I've had a lot going on," I hum out, my nails digging further into my knees.

"Is it your reunion?" she asks plainly, and then rolls her eyes. "I heard you and Vic discussing it the other day. If other creative projects are taking your attention-"

"It's got nothing to do with my attention." She looks taken aback that I would interrupt her, but I press on, trying to get the words out before I stop myself. "My creative projects outside of work will not impact my results here. I'll take some time to review the rest of the team's greenlit designs and see what I can come up with to fit with them."

I will not apologize. I will not back down. And, assuming that's where this conversation was headed, I won't be told I'm not allowed to have other things going on outside of work.

Brianna blinks at me, and then, silently, she hands over the pile of papers she was looking at, along with a manila folder.

"These are the ones we decided to move forward with." She eyes the folder, and then looks up at me, her shoulders rolling back. "We need to get this season wrapped and to production in the next few weeks, Piper." I nod, taking the papers from her and pressing them to my chest, which feels warm and protected under the thick, cable-knit purple sweater I'd thrown on this morning to beat one of the last cool early spring mornings. I rise, doing my best not to teeter as I look at her.

"I'll let you know if I have any questions?" I ask. Brianna nods, once, slowly, like she's not sure who's standing in front of her. And frankly, I'm not sure, either, as I turn on my heels and walk out of her office, tossing the paperwork down on my desk. I pull my purse out, take a deep, steadying breath, and look at a confused Vic for just a moment before I mutter "I'm heading to a meeting," and stomp out of the office like there's a fire behind my ass.

"If your goal is to give the man an aneurysm, I think this'll do it," Carla says cheekily, staring down at the outfit laid across my bed.

I reach out, feeling the sheer fabric of the underbust corset I've picked. Black, with pink peonies stitched into the mesh. It's not sturdy or boned with steel - it's meant to be an accessory, not an undergarment. But that's what I'm going for, when paired with the black dress next to it, to go underneath.

To the side is a black lace set I designed with AllHearts several seasons ago. The bra clasps in the front, with a delicate, black bow, and has crossing strips of lace above the cups. The panties, simple and lacy, have a matching garter belt with black bows. I have a pair of mauve thigh-highs, which match the florals on the corset, rolled up next to my black Mary Jane heels.

"He said retro, right?" Carla asks, and I nod. "Well, this is definitely retro." She lifts the corset, holding it in the air. "You kept saying you were going to make me one of these." I roll my eyes.

"Sure, let me add it to the list after the other fifteen things you..."

My watch vibrates against my wrist.

FITZ WESTFALL
I'm leaving the house shortly, are you almost ready?

My heart thumps in my chest as I respond.

PIPER DELMONICO
Yep, let me know when you're here and I'll meet you outside.

Did I want him to be a gentleman and come to my door? Yes. Did I want to let Carla give him a lecture on treating me like a lady, which she'd no-doubt sworn to do under threat from Alex? No.

I turn to my vanity, giving myself a once-over. My black robe tied over my chest, I scrunch at my curls, freshly washed and styled, moving pieces one way and another across the top of my head. I swipe under my eyes - lined with my signature cat-eye. I left my lips plain, with the dramatic eye. Pearl studs match my pearl necklace, layered with a few other gold chains.

Silently, I run my hands down my sides. It's been a long time since I got this dressed up for a date. It's been a long time since I felt this way about a date, truth be told. And while I'm feeling myself in this sexy makeup look, in the outfit I'm about to put on, there's this little nagging voice in the back of my head telling me one word. No.

No. Wear something less outlandish. No. You shouldn't accentuate your curves. No. He's only going out with you for one thing.

I shake the thoughts from my head. Fitz asked me out. Me. It wasn't an accident, or a cruel joke, he was getting to know me and wanted to go out on a proper date.

And that fact has me terrified.

Because despite everything, despite that little voice in the back of my head that's been there since I was old enough to be body-conscious about my curves next to the tall, toned sister I grew up with, I'm proud. Proud of what this body has been through with me. Proud that I'm still standing. And proud that I'm willing to even put my heart on the line like I am now.

And am I looking forward to seeing Fitz out of his clothes as much as I'm looking forward to seeing his reaction to this particular lingerie set? Absolutely.

I stare down at my rings momentarily, as Carla watches. Most of them are decorative - but one, on my right ring finger, is important. My wedding ring. My grandmother's before me. The one Mickey proposed with. The one I've worn every day since then, for better or for worse, even without him here. Partially because it meant a lot to me, as something of my grandmother's. But part of me, however small, is considering taking it off for the night, thinking back to the day I made promises over it in a hospital chapel.

Five Years Ago

"You look beautiful," Penny cooed, brushing my hair over my shoulder to expose the skinny collarbone, framed by a pale floral neckline. I smiled at her in the mirror - a sad tilt that doesn't meet my eyes.

"You about ready?" My mother appeared in the doorway behind us, and immediately, her eyes welled with tears. I stared at the three of us in the mirror - the same dark eyes, hair - the only resemblance to my father is my rounded jawline and the natural curl pattern to my hair. "Oh, passerotto mio," she mumbled. *My little sparrow.* She moved forward quickly, crushing me in a tight hug.

"Mama, you're going to make me cry," I choked out, and she pulled back quickly, blotting at her own eyes.

"I know this isn't the way you wanted to do it, but you do look beautiful," Penny repeated, her hand on my arm.

My wedding day. It's true, it wasn't the way I'd wanted to do it. In the years Mickey and I had been together, I'd imagined our wedding a million ways. A big, beautiful chapel, filled with our closest friends and family. My parents' backyard, string lights above us. Never this - never getting ready in his hospital room to meet him and Vic down in the hospital chapel.

But it was perfect nonetheless.

The clock ticked ever so loudly in the back of my mind each day, and after his last scan's we'd made the decision - no matter what, we were tying the knot. He wanted to have his wife by his side, and I knew that I wanted to be just that, despite our troubles.

"I wish you all could come down with me." I swallowed the tears that pricked at the corner of my eyes. Hastily, Penny bent down, pulling a tissue out of the front of the built-in vanity and handing it to me.

"I know, but this is how you wanted to do it, and we will respect that." My mother touched her hand to my face, and I closed my eyes, nuzzling into the warmth.

I would've given anything to have them - all of them - with me. To have my father walk me down the aisle. To let my niece and nephew be the flower girl and ring bearer, running up to Mickey to hand him the simple band we'd ordered and had express shipped last week. To have our friends and family give us their blessing, in person, for our union.

But after the constant harassment from Mickey's family - the texts, the passive aggressive social media posts - I just couldn't stomach the idea of more shit for them to hold over my head, if my family came and his wasn't even aware we were doing it. So we decided, together, to make it intimate. Vic would marry us. My friend Jasmine would take pictures, so we could share when we were ready. The idea made my heart hurt, but I knew, deep down, it was the right call.

I followed my mother out of the restroom, and she handed me a simple, white bouquet that matched the flower pattern on my dress. I'd picked out my clothes in just a few minutes, stopping into an off-the-rack formal store between running to see Bex for the first time in weeks and going to the courthouse to file the more complicated paperwork for obtaining a marriage license without Mickey appearing in the office.

Outside the door of the hospital room, several staff members from the floor lined the wall. In the weeks we'd been here, off and on, we'd grown close. They knew that outside of that hospital, I was the one doing what they're doing here. Changing his briefs. Catheterizing him. Managing his medications. All of the unromantic things that come with being a caregiver.

But they also saw our movie nights, cuddled up in the hospital bed with a bag of microwave popcorn. They heard my sobs through the bathroom door when we got bad news from the latest oncology fellow to visit. They felt my silent, steely frustration when messages from Melissa or Oscar rolled in, not-so-subtly implying that I was holding him hostage when in reality, he wanted nothing more than to continue fighting, to meet the goal he'd had for the last several months - to meet his new nephew, due in the spring.

"Piper." I turned, and at one side of the door was my father. His graying beard was trimmed short, his tan skin crinkling into a smile across his face. His eyes welled with tears as he pulled me close, whispering in Italian, "I'm so proud of you." I let out a choked sob, trying to hold back my own tears as he pulled back, holding out his arm. "You ready?" I nodded, using the tissue in my hand to swipe at my eyes.

I laced my arm through his, my bouquet in my other hand, and we walked towards the elevators together, the line of hospital staff grinning as we go. No, this wasn't the fairytale I'd hoped for. But the love I felt for Mickey was something real - something tangible. I knew we deserved this step in the journey we share. And as my father kissed me on the cheek and I stepped into the elevator, watching the doors slide close on his tear-stained face, I felt a bubble of happiness well up in my chest. The first one I'd felt in a long, long time.

"You don't have to take it if you don't want to," Carla says after a minute. I glance up at her, and she's giving me a small smile, likely knowing exactly where my head was at. "But I've never seen you take that thing off when you go out."

"This feels...different," I respond, twirling the ring on my finger, a set of welded gold bands with a single diamond.

"Different how?" she asks. I purse my lips, trying to find the words.

"Everyone else I've gone out with, slept with, since Mickey...I don't know. They didn't know me before, right?" I pause. "Somehow it feels more intimate, going out with Fitz." She seems to think on that for a second before responding.

"You don't need me to tell you what to do. But you've said enough times that he wouldn't have wanted you to spend your whole life alone." I do know that, because Mickey said it, point blank, in the days leading up to his death. In that cold hospital room, while we watched the in-room entertainment on his TV, he told me through struggling breaths to be happy. We both knew what was coming, at that point.

I stare at the rings again, and close my eyes, taking a deep, steadying breath before opening them again, looking right at my own reflection.

"This is a part of me," I say finally, holding my hand up. "It's a part of who I am. I'm not going to change that for Fitz. Or for anyone, really." Carla gives me a small smile in the reflection of my mirror. "Now, you can leave or you can watch me get naked," I add confidently, and Carla turns on her heel as I slide off my robe, nearly hitting Bex in the face with it as I toss it in the corner and miss the laundry basket by a few feet. She starts, darting out of the room after Carla.

CHAPTER 23

By the time I'm sliding on my heels, my phone buzzes again.

FITZ WESTFALL
Your carriage awaits. If you have a hair scarf, I would bring it.

I smile at my screen, replying with a quick *Be down momentarily*, grabbing a silk scarf from my closet. Leave it to Fitz Westfall to know what a hair scarf is.

When I step out of my room, Carla lets out a low whistle from her perch on the couch. I flip her the bird.

"Don't shoot the messenger, bitch. You look hot as hell." Nervously, I grin and pop my heel out behind me, tiling my head back and letting my curls fall. She claps excitedly. "How do you feel?"

"Nervous?" It comes out as a question, but she nods.

"It's ok to be nervous. But I think it will be great." She pushes up from the couch, crossing the space between us and gripping at my arms with her hands. She's dressed for a night in - sweatpants and a tank top - but her eyes, brown and magnetic, bore into me. "Don't psych yourself out. Do you have everything you need?" She peers at my tiny purse slung over my shoulder. "And by everything, I mean, did you pack condoms and your meds?" I don't even fight the eye roll. I've had an IUD for a while, but my better-safe-than-sorry mentality left me wanting to be sure.

"Yes, you presumptuous mother hen." I open the bag to show her. "Look, I even packed a little face wipe so I'm not sleeping in my makeup."

"If you do any sleeping," she says, and then pets my head like I'm Bex. "I've taught you well, Padawan."

"I'm leaving," I reply, laughing, and she looks between me and the door.

"Is he not..." She points at the door behind me, and I shake my head.

"I'm meeting him at the car downstairs." Carla crosses her arms. "Don't give me that look. I know you and Alex will rip him limb from limb if he hurts me - he knows it, too. We don't need you to remind us." She narrows her eyes at me.

"Fine." I raise my brows at her use of the word. "Text me if you need me to come get you, bring you more rubbers, anything." I close my eyes, shaking my head at the mental image of Carla making an emergency condom run. "Bex and I will be here, just chilling. We're gonna have a girls night in, right, Bexy?" She turns back to the dog on the couch, who completely ignores her. I make my way to the door while she's distracted. I almost make it out before she screams "MAKE GOOD CHOICES." And I slam the door before she can say anything else embarrassing.

CHAPTER 24

Fitz

I lean against the passenger side of the car, which I've pulled up just out front of the entrance to Piper's building. Shifting nervously, I cross my arms.

No. You look like a douche.

I put my elbows back, and they drop - I forgot I have the top down.

Finally, I settle on putting my hands in my pockets, peering out at the over-watered grass surrounding her apartments. They tried to keep this place looking nice, but even in the limited time I'd been inside, I'd noticed the lines cracking across the ceiling. The floorboards warping in certain spots.

Then again, I'm driving around in a car worth more than most people make in a year. I can't exactly judge from my pedestal.

I notice movement out of the doorway, and when I see Piper take the final steps downstairs, I blink several times, swallowing hard.

How did I never notice this woman before? If we did cross paths outside of the context of the reunion - or even before then, all those years ago. Sure, the red hair was something else. But she'd always had this natural swagger. And I was too busy reinforcing my own walls to even look her direction.

Flipping through that photo book in her office, I learned something about the woman in front of me - she was fearless. Maybe not all the time, but when she was comfortable, which she clearly was with whoever was shooting those pictures (I hadn't asked, but hoped it was a girlfriend), she shone.

Like a star. Like a fucking diamond.

I notice her stop halfway to me, and I think she's eying me, but I realize quickly she's looking at the car behind me.

"Is that a MK III?" she asks, and I nearly fall over.

"Uh, yeah," I stammer, and she steps up next to me, peering inside of the open interior. Blue leather. Manual shift. The Austin-Healey is in great shape. "1964." Her hands slide over the cream exterior, just above the passenger door handle.

"It's beautiful." She eyes me, giving me a head-to-toe glance that has me feeling self conscious. "Did you restore this?"

"My brother and I did," I answer honestly, unable to keep my eyes off of her. The lacy corset covering her midsection is giving me a clear outline of her full chest and hourglass figure. "It's not my daily driver or anything. But it's fun for stuff like this." I reach in front of her, pulling the door open and holding out my hand, which she takes gingerly as she steps up, sliding into the seat with more grace than I'd expect with heels that tall. Before I let go of her hand, I bring it to my lips and give it a light kiss. Her sheepish smile is incredibly satisfying as she folds her feet into the car, adjusting the full skirt of her black dress.

"I feel overdressed." She pulls a purple silk scarf from her bag as I make my way to the driver's side, sliding in next to her.

"You look perfect." I look at her when I say it, so she knows I'm being serious.

"I look like a bum in comparison." A bum in $800 shoes, but I don't need to elaborate on that. She gives me another nervous smile before using a clip to hold back her curls at the nape of her neck, and then tying the scarf over her hair. The wind was already blowing at a mild rate - I didn't want her to feel like she was caught in a tornado on the way to dinner.

"I think you could wear a potato sack and not look like a bum," she says as I start the car, and I smile to myself when the engine purrs. I reach out a hand and give her knee a squeeze while she buckles her seatbelt.

"The feeling is mutual." I put a hand on the gear shift, and turn to her. "You ready?" She nods, but even under the sunglasses she's slid on, large and in charge, I can tell she's nervous. "Hey," I give her knee another squeeze. "You look beautiful." She smiles.

"The feeling is mutual." Beautiful, eh? I take that as a sign, and shift the car into gear, driving away from her apartment.

Piper

We're on the road for a few minutes before I get up the nerve to speak. Why I'm so jittery and anxious, I don't know. Hadn't we been talking for weeks? But I think, deep down, a part of me, that small bit left from high school Piper, is freaking out a little bit.

I was on a date with Fitz Westfall. *Fitz Westfall.* Me. If you'd told me this was going to happen even a year ago, I probably would have laughed you back to whatever bar you came out of. But it's reality, and I'm losing my shit.

"I don't know all that much about you," I finally say, resting my arm on the top of the door frame and watching the trees as we zoom away. We're heading towards downtown, that much is obvious, as he turns onto the access road. But instead of merging onto the highway, he stays in the right lane. The long way to wherever we were going, I guess.

"I feel like that's the point of tonight," he responds, his hand shifting the gear in between us. "And any dates that may or may not follow." He's wearing sunglasses, but when he looks at me, I can almost feel the hopeful look in his eyes. "What do you want to know?"

Everything is my real answer. But I go with "You said your brother and you rebuilt this car?" He nods, his hand coming to rest back on the wheel. I watch the way his crisp white button up tugs at his forearm, where it's rolled up. Paired with gray slacks, he looks like he just walked out of an Armani ad. Then again, I'm pretty sure his shoes actually are Armani.

"Technically my half-brother, but yeah." I watch him as we cruise down the road. I didn't know his parents weren't together anymore, or that they had remarried. "It was something we could do together. He's a science guy, and I've never really been into anything else he likes - but this, this we could compromise on."

"Older or younger?"

"Younger." He lets someone in a white truck merge in front of us. "He graduates from LSSU in May. We've got Frannie, my sister, between us, though. She's got a daughter, Greta."

"Right." Something in my memory goes off - I had briefly met his sister when we were in school together, she was a Sophomore our senior year. But if I remember the right person, she looked very, very different from her brother - same red hair. That's where the similarities ended, with her pale complexion, narrow nose, only having gotten close enough to see during one of the student fashion shows we ran and the few trips we may have been on together in large groups of rowdy kids for our *Marketing Student Organization* competitions. "Is she your half-sister?" Another nod. I wonder to myself which parents I'd seen at our school functions, the few times I remembered seeing any at all. Was that his mom and stepdad? Or his father and stepmother?

"She went to LSSU, too."

"Ah, so you're the lone Longhorn." I give a pointed nod to the gigantic ring on his right hand, now gripping the steering wheel.

"Not completely lone," he says, a small smile on his lips. "My mom went to UT, too." His hands tighten on the steering wheel. Before I can press, he offers "She passed when I was a baby."

"I'm sorry." My voice is quieter than normal, and that makes him look at me, just slightly, before his hand reaches out and gives my knee a squeeze.

"It was a long time ago." His hand doesn't linger, finding its way back to

CHAPTER 24

the wheel. "What about you? Any other siblings?" I shake my head, and then, remembering he's driving, respond.

"No, just Penny. Though, we consider a lot of our friends, family at this point." He nods. "I've known Vic pretty much my entire life, so he's the closest thing I have to a brother, not including Brett and Nolan."

"Your entire life?"

"Our families went to the same church growing up." His head tilts towards me, just slightly, and I laugh. "I haven't been involved with the church in a long time. But he was probably the best thing to come out of that time." I twirl one of the rings on my fingers absently.

"What do they do? Your family?" The question brings me back to the day at the baseball game, and I smile to myself.

"Is work all you think about?" He shrugs, but smirks. "My mom's an attorney, mostly contract litigation. My dad is a textile dealer, he has a warehouse in Shopper's Alley. He's the one that taught me about cars." I run my hand along the pristine interior of the door next to me. "Penny and Brett both work for a payment processing company in Fort Worth."

"Carla does something medical, right?" I knit my brows, but answer.

"Yeah, admin at a physical therapy office. How'd you know?"

"I mean, Facebook," he says, as if it's obvious. Ah. "Also, I picked up, like, four pairs of scrubs the other night in your living room. Do either of you ever get changed in your bedrooms?" I snort. I hadn't thought about what all he'd picked up in our living room the night he stayed over - and silently, I pray to myself that I didn't have any of my embarrassing giant granny briefs from my own personal shark week lying about. "What about Alex?"

"She works for a marketing firm from home. Same one I used to."

"What made you leave?" We stop at a red light, and he looks at me.

"Sobriety," I say, honestly. "And I was sick of staring at my wall, by myself, all day." I shrug, fidgeting with the hem of my dress, noting that part of it is starting to fray. Internally, I note to add it to my fix pile.

"I get that." He's still looking at me, and suddenly I feel a swoop in my stomach. "Actually, that's a lie. I could probably work at home all day, but I also dislike people." I laugh at his admission.

"Clearly not all people." Fitz smiles, genuine and bright, and that swoop hits harder.

"No, not all people." He turns back to the road as we enter the winding streets of downtown, where traffic is buzzing as people get to their first destinations of the night.

"You never said where we're going," I muse.

"You'll see." The teasing tone in his voice takes me by surprise, but I take it as an answer as I watch the people stare at the gorgeous car we're in - and probably, the gorgeous man next to me, as well. I'd never really taken any time to appreciate how attractive he was until the last few weeks. Probably because, way back when, I would have never even given him a second glance. In the same way I never gave Andy a second glance, I was never a ladder-climber - I didn't yearn for men that I felt were totally out of my league. But as the years passed and my confidence grew, I realized, apprehensively, that men like Andy were lucky to have someone like me even give them the time of day. Because behind all the bravado and womanizing tendencies, he was scared shitless of someone like me. An open book. Someone who knows what she wants and goes for it. No games. No bullshit.

But Fitz, I ponder as we pull into a valet line in front of the Monarch Hotel, feels different. Based on the conversations we've had - he knows, or at least somewhat understands, what he's getting himself into.

And aside from that stoic stare from those piercing green eyes, there was so much else that drew me to him physically - those deep auburn curls, waiting to be tamed. That dimple in his chin, which always looked freshly shaven. Lashes that had me jealous. Fitz could probably have any woman he wanted, and yet I'm here with him. And I drank in that power, however much a part of my brain reminded me that he was lucky to be here with me, too.

Once we're in park, I pull my hair out of the clip and take off the scarf, shaking it loose around my shoulders, stuffing both items in the glovebox in front of me. I swear he watches, until one valet comes up and opens my door, and another meets him at his.

"Mr. Westfall," the valet on his side says with a little nod.

"Mike," Fitz responds, and then stands, leaving the car running. As I amble out, careful not to catch my tights on anything, I hear him say "none of the kids driving this one, ok? Just you or Aaron." Mike nods his head in understanding, tearing off the bottom of a valet ticket and handing it to Fitz, who stuffs it into his pants pocket and then turns to me. I realize that all three of them are eying me - Fitz, Mike, and whoever the third valet is.

Because I'm staring. I'm staring at Fitz and when I realize it, I blush furiously and turn around, stuffing my purse under my arm and wait for him to come around to my side. When he does, his face is unreadable, but he touches my arm lightly and leads me through the front door, which a uniformed man is holding with a smile on his face.

"Evening, Mr. Westfall," the doorman says.

"Edgar," Fitz responds with another nod.

"Do you know everyone by name?" I ask under my breath as I stop, momentarily, in my tracks to appreciate the gorgeous art deco lobby in front of me.

CHAPTER 24

I've only been here once before - senior year, prom. And from what I could remember, it hasn't changed much.

"I try to," Fitz answers coolly, waiting for me to take everything in. The mirrored walls, deep brass of the fixtures. The old-Hollywood era furniture and decor. "Our office is next door, so I'm here quite a bit. We do a lot of meetings in the conference space." I look back at him, and he tilts his head toward the bank of elevators across the red carpet of the lobby, which reads *The Monarch* in thick script font. His hand still touching my arm, I follow him as he presses the down button. Down?

"Where are we going?" I repeat my question, hoping that this time, he'll actually give me an answer, but the corners of his mouth turn up as he gives my elbow a squeeze.

"Someone's impatient," he teases, and his eyes are nearly burning with intensity. "You'll see soon, I promise." I take a deep breath as the elevator dings and the doors slide open. I follow him in, my heels clicking on the tile floor, and lean against the railing on the back wall, steadying myself.

Why the hell am I so nervous? It's a date. I've been on dozens - hundreds, maybe - of dates.

But none of them were with him. I chastise myself - the only reason this feels different is because he's known me for a long time. But has he really? Did the last ten years, where we never saw each other, not really, even count towards that clock? Did any of the time before, when I felt like completely different people compared to who I am today?

Fitz presses the button marked LC - lower conference, I read next to it - and when the door slides shut, he turns to me, ducking his head to look me in the eyes where I'm perched.

"You ok?" He asks, and I give a small nod and try to smile. His face tells me he's not convinced.

"I feel like you're taking me to a secret sex dungeon or something." His head falls back in a silent laugh, and he looks at me again, eyes crinkling.

"Not a sex dungeon, promise." At arm's length, he can eye me from head to foot, and he does just that, one hand running down my arm as the elevator crawls downward. Then, he rests his hand against the elevator wall above my head, and my breath hitches.

"You sure about that?" I feel myself swallow, and he tucks my hair behind my ear with his other hand, leaning forward to give my forehead a small kiss. The elevator dings, and he smoothly stands back up, adjusting his sleeve like he wasn't just being intimate. *Wall, back up.* When I follow him out of the elevator into the hallway outside, it looks like a normal conference center. Intricately patterned carpets, neutral wallpapers. Framed photos of different spots in DFW line the walls. We pass huge depictions of the Stockyards, Reunion Tower, coming to a stop in front of a picture of the glittering Dallas skyline at the end of the hallway that's at least five feet tall. Absently, Fitz reaches out to a tan phone that blends into the wall so well, I didn't notice it until his long fingers started pressing buttons.

Then, I watch as the frame swings open, and a soft lull of jazz music escapes the dark doorway hidden behind it.

"What in the Hogwarts..." I say, mostly to myself, but Fitz lets out a little snort next to me, and then holds out a hand. Gingerly, I take it, and let him lead me towards the doorway, where he climbs in, holding my hand up to help me step over the boundary.

Because it's me, my shoe catches on the top of the door, and I barrel forward, crashing hard into Fitz's chest.

"Whoa," he breathes as I nearly knock the wind out of him. His arms wrap around my shoulders, and I look dumbly up at him as I orient myself.

"Not a sex dungeon?" I repeat, because being pressed up against him, breathing in the smell of his freshly laundered shirt and whatever aftershave he's wearing, I don't know that I'd be entirely opposed to the idea.

I realize how tall he is, this close to me - even in my heels I'm bending my head back to look up at him, and my mind immediately wonders where he shops for clothes, because he can't just get shirts with his arm length at Nordstrom. His eyes flash with something lustful, and his mouth turns up again as he whispers, somewhat horsley, "Not a sex dungeon." I laugh half-heartedly, separating myself from him. He gives me another look, one I can't read, before grabbing my hand and leading me towards the source of the music, down a dark hallway lit by green bulbs.

We emerge on the other side of the hall into the room where the music is coming from, and I stop in my tracks, floored.

CHAPTER 25

Piper

I feel like I've stepped into a Gatsby-era nightclub, the extreme of the same decor littered across the hotel above. My eyes scan over the dark room, the black, wainscot walls, the plush, velvet couches and chairs, the brass light fixtures of all shapes and sizes that droop down from a ceiling covered in tarnished mirrors. I stare up, into my own reflection, and Fitz gives my hand a squeeze.

"What is this place?" I breathe, and turn to see that he's staring at me. I blink, but he doesn't flinch as he answers.

"The Menagerie. It's a speakeasy." He gestures forward, toward the ornate, upholstered bar, where a blonde woman is mixing drinks in front of a wall of bottles. She holds the cocktail shaker in her hands up above her shoulders, and looks around the room as she mixes the drink, her eyes landing on the stage across the room where a musical act is setting up.

I follow Fitz to the far side of the bar, where the curve of one end meets the wall, and see that there's a *Reserved* sign in front of two blue velvet barstools. He pulls one out for me, and I climb on, careful not to repeat my fall from earlier. I'm pleasantly surprised to feel that there's a purse hanger under the bar top.

Fitz sits gracefully in the chair between the wall and me. He picks up the reserved sign, folds it, and sets it on the other side of the bartop.

"Fitz, this is gorgeous." I run my hands over the cool black quartz in front of me.

"Appropriate, for a gorgeous date." He's staring again, and I roll my eyes.

"Hey." Under the bar, he puts one hand on my knee. "I'm serious."

"You're surprisingly corny," I counter, and settle my hand on top of his. His eyes flicker down, and then he turns his hand upside down, letting our fingers lace together. My heart pounds.

"Well, look what the cat dragged in." We break eye contact to look up towards the bar, where the blonde, who's shorter than I first thought, stands placing cocktail napkins in front of us. She reaches towards a pile of long cards, and when she puts twos in front of us, I realize it's the menu. And it's just as pretty as the rest of the room around us.

"Seer," Fitz says, inclining his head towards the bartender as her eyes scan over both of us. She's wearing a pair of crepe black joggers, with a short sleeved red lace top tucked in, showing off the full sleeve of intricate tattoos on her left arm. Her almost white-blonde hair is cropped at her shoulders, and it reminds me of Carla's. And I can't help but feel like I've seen her before, but I can't place where. "Piper," Fitz starts, and looks at me, then the woman in front of us. "This is Seer."

She holds her hand out towards me - her fingernails are painted black, and silver rings, much like my gold ones, glitter on her fingers. I take it, and her deep brown eyes crinkle as she gives a small smile.

"Nice to finally meet you, Piper. I've heard a lot about you." Startled, my head whips towards Fitz, and he's giving Seer a look that would kill if it could. "Oh, don't give me that look, boss-man." She rolls her eyes towards the mirror ceiling, and then nods down towards the menu. "I'll give you a minute to look that over."

Seer busies herself making two glasses of water, and I whisper under my breath "You've been talking about me to people at work?" Fitz squeezes my hand.

"Seer is my sister's friend."

"You've been talking about me to your sister?" He smiles.

"Most of my friends are bachelors, and I wanted to do this right." Fitz nods towards me, and I can't help the smile as I look down, scanning the menu in front of me.

"They have mocktails!" I manage after a moment, my fingers sliding along the names of all the delicious sounding drinks. He gives me a satisfied smile as Seer sets down the glasses in front of us.

"Damn right we do." She tilts her head towards the menu. "Crafted by yours truly."

"Seer is also sober," Fitz explains, and I try to hide the startled look at the woman behind the bar as she gives him a reproachful look.

"Tell the world, why don't you." But then she smiles, and looks at me. "Two years in, a lifetime to go." Seer taps on the menu in front of me. "See anything you like?"

"Coconut mojito," I answer without hesitation, and she nods in approval.

"Good choice." She turns to Fitz, who looks at me like he's asking permission.

"You can drink around me." I shrug, picking the menu back up and looking over the food options.

"Blue Moon," Fitz finally says, and Seer paces away to start making the drinks.

"Sorry, I wasn't sure..."

"I'm not going to take your beer and chug it or anything," I mutter, half-laughing. Even in my worst binges, I didn't touch beer with a ten foot pole. He just looks at me, a line between his brows, and I reach forward, pushing my fingertip into it. "It's weird seeing you emote so much." His eyes tip towards the ceiling.

"You just surprise me," he says quietly, and gives my hand another squeeze. Not sure how to respond, I take a sip of my water. As I watch Seer muddling mint in front of me, I try to place where I recognize her from. It can't be from here, and I don't think she went to school at Southwest. College, maybe?

A loud whistle breaks me out of my thoughts, and we all turn towards the sound, which came from the bustle near the stage. A latino man with a black hat tilts his head at Fitz, gesturing for him to come over, and Fitz lets go of my hand. Instantly, I feel cold at the loss of his touch.

Fitz stands from his chair just as Seer comes up, placing our drinks in front of us, and he leans down until his mouth is right next to my ear.

"I'll be right back, ok?" I nod dumbly, because the feeling of his breath on my ear sends a literal chill down my spine.

Get a fucking grip, Delmonico.

Then, with absolutely zero shame, I watch him walk towards the stage, where the man, standing behind a sound board, pulls Fitz into a half-hug. *Those pants.*

"Dude's got it bad," Seer says, and I turn to see her standing with one hand on her hip, looking between Fitz and I with raised brows.

I swear, I know this woman.

"What do you mean?" I ask, and she fits me with a look that tells me she sees right through my placating response.

"The Westfall men are notoriously hard to crack," she replies simply, putting a lime slice around the rim of the glass in front of me. "He's basically humpty dumpty around you." I snort, and pick up the drink, taking a tentative sip.

The moan I emit is near-sexual, and Seer gives a satisfied shoulder shake. That's when I realize where I recognize her from.

"Have you ever been to Greensleeves? The renaissance festival?" I narrow my eyes at her, trying to picture the woman in front of me, with her sleeve tattoo and nose piercing, in garb. But the shoulder shake reminds me of the court dances that the noble characters do from time to time, all stately and beautiful. To my surprise, she grins.

"You're presently speaking," Seer starts, and her voice slides into a thick Irish accent like it's nothing, "to Lady Serena O'Neill, niece to the Earl of Tyrone." I stare as it clicks.

"Celtic Court. You're on the Celtic Court." She nods, pushing a blonde curl out of her face. I knew I'd seen her somewhere, though her appearance behind the bar couldn't be anything further than what I remember her looking like last fall.

"Home away from home," Seer muses, still with the accent, and then sighs wistfully, her eyes looking a bit distant. When they settle on me, she narrows her eyes at the bodice I'm wearing. "You get that there?"

"I made it, actually." My hand settles across the boning in the front as her eyes widen.

"You made it? It looks a lot like my friend-"

Before she can finish her sentence, a tall brunette comes out of the nearly hidden doorway behind Seer, and stops in her tracks.

"Piper?"

"Chloe?" I look at Carla's sister, surprised. "What are you doing here?"

"I work here," she supplies, and then gestures to the bar around her. I realize she's dressed fairly similarly to Seer, in black pants and a red top.

"I thought you worked at a salon?" She laughs, shaking her head and setting down the tray of glasses she's holding in front of Seer, reaching over to give my arm a squeeze.

"Doesn't pay enough by itself, not while I'm still in school." She smiles, her eyes the exact same shade of icy blue as Carla's. Seer looks between us.

"Perfect timing," she starts. "I was just saying how Piper's bodice looks like that one you wore to your birthday last year."

"That's because she made it," Chloe explains, tilting her head towards me. Seer raises her eyebrows, crossing her arms and giving me an appraising, impressed look.

"Designing was my manic sobriety skill," I say with a shrug, taking another drink. "I did it for fun a lot, but once I stopped drinking, I needed to channel my energy into something else."

"So you picked lingerie?" Seer's voice isn't judgemental. Surprised, maybe. I give another shrug, and then feel someone pass behind me, realizing Fitz is sliding back into his chair.

"What did I miss?" he asks, looking between the three of us, and panic flashes over his face momentarily.

"Let me guess." Seer narrows her eyes, brows scrunching together, and tilts her head at an angle. It feels like she can see into my soul, and I want to squirm. "Pisces." I fit her with a confused look, my head bobbing back.

"How did you know?"

"It's a gift," Chloe quips, and starts putting the glasses she brought away under the bar where she's standing.

"And a curse," Seer adds, and then looks at Fitz. "This one has Virgo written

CHAPTER 25   175

all over him, even if I didn't know his birthday, because his sister is a sap and goes all-out for any excuse to celebrate."

"She does," he agrees, and then holds up his beer in an imaginary toast, taking a deep gulp while still eying us.

"Happy belated birthday, by the way." Chloe gives me a warm smile as she puts the last of the glasses away.

"Wait, what?" Fitz sets his beer down a little too hard, and some of it sloshes over the edge. Automatically, I reach over, using one of the napkins to clean it up.

"Pisces," Seer repeats, with an eye roll this time.

"When was your birthday?" His voice is quieter than normal, and suddenly I feel like I've done something wrong. Seer, sensing the discomfort, slides towards the other end of the bar to take care of another customer with Chloe. Behind us, the band on stage is starting to gear up.

"Uh, a few weeks ago." I swear hurt flashes in his eyes as his hand finds a place on my knee again.

"Why didn't you tell me?"

"I don't really do birthdays," I manage, putting my hand on his. "Or, at least, my birthday." His eyes narrow, but I think he senses that I don't want to be pushed on the topic, because he just nods, and then jerks his head towards the menu in front of me.

"Did you find something you want to eat?" I give him my best knowing look, licking my lips and not breaking eye contact. He wants to play hard ball with the pretty words and whispers against my ear? Two can play at that game.

"I mean, yes, but it's not on the menu." I think I hear Seer laughing from her perch a few feet away, but Fitz shifts uncomfortably before rolling his eyes and lacing his fingers with mine again, effectively ending any further humiliation I had considered.

CHAPTER 26

Fitz

If she keeps making sounds like this every time she eats something good, we're going to have a problem.

That's all I can think as Piper takes one bite of the French Dip in her hands and lets out a guttural moan.

"First the drink, now the food," Seer observes, crossing her arms in front of us. "She sure knows how to flatter a girl."

"Speaking of," Piper says, completely ignoring the fact that I haven't touched the plate of Mediterranean chicken in front of me. She holds up her empty glass.

"Another of the same?" Seer asks, and Piper shakes her head.

"Whatever you think will go best with this." She points down to the sandwich in front of her, and Seer tilts her head.

"Any hard no's?"

"Pineapple," Piper replies, and I know there's confusion on my face, as well as Seer's, when she says "Allergic."

"Noted." And Seer steps away, pulling several things in front of her and working on a drink to go with Piper's meal.

"I like her," Piper muses, looking at me and grinning. "I mean, I know she's your sister's friend, but I may claim her too if she comes up with things like this." She gestures down to the food and empty glass in front of her.

"Frannie will probably fight you for her." She snorts, taking another bite of her food, and I finally dig into my own.

It's refreshing, seeing her enjoying herself. Probably because, for the better part of a decade, I've been watching Olivia half-heartedly pick at kale salads and plain chicken. And don't get me wrong, that fact is one of the only reasons I'm still in decent shape after this long, having shared in a lot of similar meals, but if growing up around José has taught me anything, it's that sometimes the best things in life happen around a good meal and better company.

CHAPTER 26

"I'll be right back," Piper says suddenly, breaking me out of my thoughts long enough to see her hop off her stool, grabbing her purse. She gives my shoulder a gentle squeeze before heading in the general direction of the restroom.

"You hurt her," Seer mumbles as she sets down Piper's drink and another Blue Moon in front of us, "and I'll murder you myself."

"Ditto, I'll help Carla hide your body," Chloe calls from her spot wiping down the bartop a few feet away. I fix them both with a look that I'm hoping portrays my 0% intention on ever hurting the woman with me, but Seer just raises her eyebrows.

"Need I remind you that she isn't the first person we know that you've hooked up with?"

"We aren't hooking up," I choke out, having just taken a sip of my beer. It spills down my chin and I pick up a napkin, trying to mop up the mess.

"You and Savannah are - or, were," Chloe says plainly, and my stunned silence makes her laugh. "You think she wouldn't tell us?"

"I, uh," is all I can manage.

"Shit." Seer throws the rag she's holding down on her workstation. "Speak of the fucking devil." She's peering over my shoulder, towards the staff entrance by the kitchen, and when I swivel in my seat, I see Savannah standing against the wall, arms crossed, craning her neck to see over the crowd starting to gather as José's band finishes their first set. As fast as I turned, I'm back facing Seer in a second.

"Did you call her?" It comes out more accusatory than I mean, and she crosses her arms, too, raising her brows at me.

"No, *Fitzwilliam*, I didn't call Savannah to tattle on you."

"One of the girls up front may have called her," Chloe offers. "She's still pretty tight with most of them."

I hadn't considered that when we'd made it through the lobby, not a care in the world, earlier this evening. But the last thing I need on my first date with Piper is my sometimes-hookup making a scene. Sure, we'd set some boundaries from day one. But in this moment, I'm realizing I probably should have actually verbalized that we weren't seeing each other any more - even if it was over text.

I move to get up from my seat, but Seer lunges forward and puts her hand on my forearm.

"Don't," she says, and tucks her hair behind her ear, looking genuinely concerned.

This close up, I notice something I hadn't before. Nestled inside her ear is a hearing aid, nearly the exact color of her skin, so small I wouldn't have seen it normally, but in this corner of the bar, the light is just right. Before I can ask her about it, she puts her bar key down on top of her rag.

"I'll deal with this." She turns on her heel and goes through the back of the bar, appearing a moment later near the staff entrance. I watch with Chloe as she approaches Savannah, who's dressed like she just came from a much wilder night out than anyone would have in the chill vibe here.

Piper chooses that moment to emerge from the restroom hallway, and as she passes Seer and Savannah, I'm reminded just how short Seer is - it's easy to forget, because honestly, she's kind of terrifying. I've seen enough clips of her swinging a sword in a full renaissance gown to know not to fuck with the tiny bartender.

As Piper slides into the seat next to me, she looks between me and where the other two women stand on the other side of the room.

"Everything alright?" she asks, taking another bite of her sandwich and narrowing her eyes at me. I feel heat creeping up my cheeks, trying to determine how to proceed.

"All good," Chloe answers without waiting for me. "One of our friends just came in." Chewing, Piper looks between us and them, and when her eyes narrow again while looking at them, realization hits me. She's seen Savannah. That day, at The Pine, Savannah had been in the office with me. And...oh, God.

It's obvious when Piper realizes what's happening, watching Savannah gesturing at us while Seer stands in front of her, clearly trying to calm her friend down. Mateo, José's son, appears in the doorway next to them a second later, wearing a kitchen uniform. Piper freezes, only momentarily, and then reaches out for her water, taking a long sip before fixing me with a serious look.

"I think you better go talk to her," she says, jerking her head towards the door. "Looks like she's real upset over that business proposal." And then, she gives a small smile that tells me *she's* not upset, not mad, or even concerned that another woman just showed up on our date to try to talk to me.

And I'm not sure whether to be thankful for that smile, or worried that something like this, which would normally concern most women, doesn't phase her.

"Looks like you don't have to," Chloe cuts in, and we all look to see Savannah giving us one final glance, before turning on her heel and stomping back through the entrance. Mateo follows after her, and Seer makes her way through the crowd, back to the side entrance of the bar, just in time to meet José at the doorway. When they both emerge behind the counter, I take a steadying breath. Part of me has always relaxed with him around - and if anyone can charm Piper, it's him.

"All good, Mateo's talking her down," Seer says, throwing her rag back over her shoulder and leaning against the workstation in front of her. "You may get a nasty text, later, though." She gives me a small, sad smile, but under the bar, Piper sets her hand on my knee and gives it a squeeze, like she's reassuring me without saying a word.

"*Mija*, what did I tell you," José says disapprovingly, looking at the drink in front of Piper's plate. "The orange slices are just fine, you don't have to do the little twirlies."

"I *like* the little twirlies," she replies, rolling her eyes and flaring her nostrils in a way that tells me they've had this discussion several times before.

"I like the little twirlies, too." Piper says it without a hint of hesitation, and we all look to see her holding up the coiling, thin orange rind in her fingers, letting it bounce like a piece of curled ribbon.

"See," Seer says, like that's proof her opinion is correct. "The customer is always right."

"I don't know that I'd consider us customers," I cut in, and Seer's look tells me clearly to shut the fuck up.

"You're not." José points to me, then Piper next to me. "But she is." He steps towards us both, holding out a weathered hand to the woman next to me. "You must be Piper, I'm José." Piper looks between him and I, and then gives his hand a firm shake. "We've heard so much about you."

"As everyone keeps saying," she mutters with a smile that borders on shy. I don't know that I've ever seen her shy about anything in the 20 years I've known her. Granted, most of those, I was too oblivious to notice *anything* about her.

"They're a bunch of gossips," José says conspiratorially, gesturing to Seer and Chloe behind him.

"I heard that," Seer yells, not looking up from her motion of pouring a shot of Patron.

"Good," is José's response.

"Does everyone who works here know you?" Piper asks me, and then takes a sip of her drink before moaning. I shift in my seat uncomfortably, and catch Chloe giving me an amused look out of the corner of her eye. I take a drink instead of shooting her a glare.

The few times I'd been to the Menagerie by myself had been when José was still managing the kitchens at the Monarch, which included here. His son Mateo was bartending back then. Seer had been there once, maybe, but this week was the most time we'd spent together in the years of friendship she'd had with my sister.

Then again, the same could be said for my time with Piper.

And as I watch her get dragged into a conversation about the merits of Mocktails vs. Non-Alcoholic beverages, I can't help but appreciate how easily she finds herself talking to José, to Seer and Chloe even. Like she could find a home anywhere. Her hands switch between holding up her sandwich and waving about with the animated conversation, and at one point, she throws her head back to laugh, her mouth wide and eyes crinkling, and something pangs in my chest.

I missed what could have been years of this. And sure, I didn't exactly drag Olivia out to do things - if I could avoid interacting with most people, I did. But José, he was as good as family to me, and the way Piper fell into step with him only makes me appreciate her more.

"So when you're not trying to pull conversation out of this one," I hear José start, and it pulls me out of my thoughts, "what do you do for a living?" I watch the moment of panic pass over her face and she picks up the drink in front of her, stalling for time.

"Mmm," she says dramatically, peering over José's shoulder and making eye contact with Seer. "Watermelon and...ginger?" Seer touches her nose and then points at Piper as an answer. "I work here in downtown, actually." Drink still in hand, she absently adjusts the napkin in front of her. "For AllHearts."

I count the beats, watching José's face. One. Two.

There it is.

His thick eyebrows nearly hit his hairline as he looks over Piper. If it weren't for the corset over her dress, she could have passed for a fashionable 50's school teacher.

Except I knew that more than likely, what she had on underneath was anything but matronly. And I do my best not to think about that as José finally regains his ability to speak.

"And what do you do there?"

"I'm on the apparel team." The same half-answer she'd given me. Except at least, for me, it had been coy for a different reason. More for effect than true shyness. I assume this evasion is because it's clear that José is a figure of authority among us.

"She designs lingerie, José," Chloe deadpans, and I can just barely make out the blush on his face through the low lighting. Piper hides her face behind her glass as she takes another sip of her drink.

"You act like he doesn't know where kids come from." Seer leans close to us, and I brace myself for whatever she's about to add to that sentence. "He's Catholic, not a priest, Fitzwilliam."

There's a sputtering sound and then I feel liquid hit my hand as Piper chokes on her drink, doing an actual spit-take across the bartop in front of me.

"Oh," she coughs, "G-god." She hits her chest, and my hand finds her shoulder as she shakes her head, trying to clear her throat. She pulls napkins towards her, trying to clean up the mess as she splutters more. "I'm sorry. F-*Fitzwilliam*?" Seer doesn't even look kind of embarrassed as she smiles back at us.

"Fitzwilliam I-don't-know-or-care-what-your-middle-name-is Westfall."

CHAPTER 26

José's chest shakes as Seer punctuates her answers with shakes of cinnamon on what looks to be the top of an espresso martini.

"My mom was a big Jane Austen fan," I try to explain, just loud enough that Piper can hear me.

"It's still better than Frederick," Chloe argues. "Poor boy is doomed."

"I don't know, I think Francesca takes the win on this one." Seer shrugs, carrying the martini down to whoever ordered it. Piper looks between everyone like she's not quite sure if we're being serious or not.

"Fitzwilliam," she repeats, looking at me and narrowing her eyes. "Well, clearly that's all I'm going to call you from now on."

"Don't," I plead, less than playful but not serious enough to be demanding. One of her eyebrows shoots up.

"Bet."

"I like this one." José points at her. "You're welcome back any time."

"Because this is your place," Chloe says with an eye roll. "Last time I checked, it was his name on the building." I grimace, hiding my face in my drink. Shit. Piper was right. I do that a lot.

"His name might as well be on there with it for this one." I gesture around the room, and when Piper looks confused, I explain. "José helped come up with this place. He and my dad went to hospitality school together."

"When was that again?" Seer asks, stepping back up to her spot next to José.

"Back before landline phones?" Piper snorts into her drink as José takes the rag off Seer's shoulder and bops her with it, then turns and gestures towards the plates in front of us.

"You kids done?"

CHAPTER 27

Piper

"You don't even work here," a voice calls, and the guy who had ushered away Fitz's unknown "business meeting" friend comes through the back door of the bar.

It had taken me a minute, but I did recognize her - and then very quickly realized that what I'd walked in on weeks before was not, in fact, a business meeting. And the idea that they'd been messing around moments before we'd open the door made my face flush.

I swallow hard, nodding as José takes my plate and hands it to him.

"No, but my children do." José ruffles the man's short black hair, and in return, he makes a face, deep brown eyes crinkling, before arguing.

"Not all of us."

"Half of us." Seer shrugs, and I look from her to the man in front of me. While the man who's just joined the conversation looks the spitting image of the one in front of us, minus twenty years or so, Seer looks nothing like José. They must all sense my confusion, because Seer adds "Not by blood, obviously."

"You're too pasty to be his kid," Chloe calls from where she's pouring a beer from a tap, the glass angled to let the foam level out.

"You're one to talk," Seer argues. "You and Fran practically glow in the dark, you're so white."

"Jesus," the newcomer says, adjusting the plates in his arms and extending a tan hand to me. "Sorry about them, I'm Mateo."

"Piper," I reply, and I can't help my smile at the banter around me. I turn to Fitz. "I didn't realize you had such charismatic friends."

"I don't know that I'd call them friends," he mutters, emptying the last of his drink and setting the glass on the bar in front of him. Mateo plays outraged, settling a hand over his heart. "Ok, maybe you," Fitz resigns with a slight roll of his eyes.

CHAPTER 27

Interesting. Tattooed and dangerous with the kitchen apron doesn't strike me as the kind of person Fitz would spend time with on the regular, but maybe that's just my bias of knowing who his friends used to be.

Clearly, he knows José well enough to come here tonight. If I had to guess, he picked this place knowing he would be surrounded by people he could lean on. The idea is both heart-warming and a little terrifying. He cares that much?

"I'll have to remember that I'm not your friend the next time I think about letting your ass win a hand of Blackjack." Mateo purses his lips as he takes the empty glass in his free hand, and then gives me a nod. "Nice to meet you, Piper. Hope to see you around." He tilts his head to Fitz, who nods back, and then he disappears back into the dark hallway behind the bar.

"Sorry," Fitz mumbles, his fingers toying with the bar napkin in front of him. "I didn't consider the amount of shit they'd all give us. I assumed they'd behave." He says the last part just loud enough for José and Seer to hear him.

"You know what happens when you assume, Will." My ears perk up at José's nickname for Fitz, but I don't pry. "I'll let you two kids get back to it." He leans over the bar, putting a hand over mine and giving me a warm smile almost identical to his son's, tipping his hat off his head. The gesture reminds me of Brett in so many ways, and I make a mental note to ask him if he or any of his band members have ever been here. It seems like just the place they'd like to play at. "It was nice to finally meet you."

"Likewise." I give his hand a squeeze, and he does the same before turning and heading into the dark doorway.

It felt, for a moment, like we knew what the other was thinking. He was, I think, silently thanking me for being here, a part of this place, with Fitz. I was thanking him for whatever affection had helped carve the increasingly-less-marble man next to me.

As we're getting ready to leave, a thrum of excitement starts to fill me. We'd foregone dessert, though I told Fitz I one thousand percent intended to come back to try the sticky toffee pudding that seemed to be a house specialty. I was already full, and truth be told, too excited to see what the rest of the evening had in store.

"Here," Seer says, pulling my bar napkin towards her, snagging a pen from her workstation and writing down a string of numbers. "I may not be tall," she starts, "or ginger, but I'm good for other things." She gives me a playful wink and I give a dramatic wink back.

"And you know how to wield a sword." She nods pridefully.

"There is a zero percent chance you're going anywhere near a sword," Fitz says in a low voice. I snort.

"Bet, *Fitzwilliam*." I drag the name out, and as I watch his face, something sparks behind his eyes. The same something that was in them that night in my bedroom.

Fuck. I have been doing my absolute damned-est to not think back to that night. To not think about the way my entire body curled towards his as I breathed him in, felt the way I affected him.

That's a lie. I thought about it a lot. Especially testing out that purple vibrator.

But this look is something I've been trying to keep out of my head for fear of exactly what it's doing now.

As if on cue, my watch buzzes against my wrist - it's detected a sudden jump in my heart rate while I'm inactive.

No shit.

"No swords, got it." Seer's voice snaps me out of my thoughts. "We could see if one of the fire jugglers has a quick lesson they can teach you."

"Absolutely fucking not," Fitz says, standing from his barstool, at the same time Chloe snorts.

"Piper needs to play with fire less than anyone I know. She will burn that whole tinderbox to the ground." I fit her with a glare and take the hand Fitz offers me, climbing out of my stool. As if a sign from the gods, I trip over the strap of my purse and into the bar top - and try my best to hide it as I stuff the bar napkin into my bag. Chloe howls with laughter, and even Seer smirks. Fitz just gives me an "I told you so" look.

"You don't get to pass judgment," I whine, reaching up and patting the side of his face, which has just a hint of stubble that catches me by surprise. "Give it a few more months, then maybe you can make jokes like that." As if it's instinctual, he leans against my hand, and then seems to catch himself, stilling.

"Ok," is his only response, and yet it makes my stomach swoop.

I don't trip through the portrait hole on the way back out, which I count as a personal win, but when we make it to the elevator, I nearly fall as Fitz grabs my hand and yanks me into his chest. My fingers find the smooth, warm fabric of his dress shirt and I lean back to see his face, which looks almost boyish.

"You have fun?" he asks, and there's a hint of wistfulness in his voice. I nod. "Good. I didn't mean to overwhelm you with everyone, I didn't realize Chloe and Mateo would also be here."

"It's alright." I blink up at him. "José is important to you, hm?" He nods back, and something in his jaw ticks, but he doesn't look away. "Well then. I'm glad I got to meet him, *Fitzwilliam*."

Fitz's eyes glint again before he reaches to press the elevator button. Before I have time to pull away, he pulls my waist closer to him and gives me a searing kiss. I can hear the blood pumping through my brain as his lips work against mine, slow and drowsy like we have all the time in the world, instead of the seconds it's going to take to be right back in the lobby of this hotel where he knows everyone.

I lean into him, kissing him back just as fully, and feel one of my feet leave the ground in a move of sheer giddiness. Oh, mercy. A foot popping kiss.

Before I can stop myself, a giggle bubbles up and through my lips, and Fitz pulls back. His eyebrows knit together just in time for the elevator to ding. He pulls away completely, but one hand stays on my arm as I find my balance back on two feet.

"I'll tell you later," I half-whisper, giggling again. I doubt he'll understand, unless he was forced to watch Princess Diaries with his little sister growing up. But at least it will give him an idea of how my scattered brain sometimes works.

I don't realize it's raining until we make it to the front door and see the pounding drops hitting the pavement like a tidal wave. Fitz pulls out his phone and looks at it.

"Should be pulling up in..." He looks back out the door just in time for his shiny car to pull into the circle drive in front of the hotel, reaching a break in the rain provided by the covered space. The top has been pulled up, and when the valet steps out, he gives Fitz a thumbs up. Fitz gives a small nod back, and then looks at me. "You ready?" He holds out his hand for me to take, and as if I'm the shy one, I glance around the lobby. It's all but emptied, with only a few people behind the front desk and concierge area.

I look down at his hand, lacing my fingers between his, and giving it a squeeze before letting him lead me towards the car. He lets another valet open the door for me this time, and then I watch him slip the one driving a $50 before sliding into the front seat next to me. The radio is already on, and when both doors close, he gives me a sidelong glance before shifting the car into gear and pulling forward. The loud rain surrounds us the second we leave the cover of the front drive.

"I'm gonna take the back way home, too, if that's ok." His grip on the steering wheel is tight as he looks out into the road, squinting.

"More time with you?" I deadpan. "Oh no, I'm devastated." He fits me with an exasperated look, but leans over and puts a hand on my thigh briefly before taking a slow turn.

Fitz is mostly quiet the whole way, the music on the radio serving as the only sound aside from the rain and the occasional far-away horn honk as we take the access road back. He's not wrong to take the side streets - Texan drivers are bad on normal days. In the rain, it's like putting a fawn on an ice rink.

It's not until we're at the light just a few streets down from where we both live that he pauses to look at me. Immediately, I feel my heart lurch as I realize where we are.

"I, uh," he starts, and then lets one hand leave the steering wheel to grab the back of his neck, rubbing nervously. "I can take you to yours." It doesn't make sense - he's already taking me to mine. It's not like he was going to leave me out in the rain. But I tilt my head, fixing him with wide eyes and a small smile that makes him gulp almost audibly.

"Or?" I ask. He blinks, and then a slow smile spreads across his lips.

"Or, you can come back to mine."

"And you can peel me out of what I'm wearing underneath this." I gesture down to my torso, and his eyes follow my hands. He bites his lips together as if he's trying to keep a shit-eating grin from his face, but his hand tightening on the steering wheel tells me all I need to know.

"Among other things," he agrees with a nod, meeting my eyes. His hand goes back down to the steering wheel and I let my own replace it, feeling my fingers lace into the hair at the nape of his neck. For just a second, his eyes close.

Then, a horn honks behind us, and we both jump.

"I think you've seen my place enough," I supply, turning back towards the road. "Let's see what Casa de Westfall looks like." He hastily looks back at the road and signals before turning right from the one lane road into one with a few lanes. The angry mom in a mini van speeds past us, laying on her horn, and I snort, my hand not leaving the back of Fitz's neck.

CHAPTER 28

Piper

We inch towards the entrance to the nicer neighborhood on this street, and I'm not surprised when Fitz takes a turn in, slowing down when we reach a white stone house with black detailing. It's modern and kind of brutal - and it definitely fits what I'd imagined a house bought with Olivia would look like.

Don't get me wrong, Olivia wasn't my favorite person in the world growing up. But she certainly wasn't the worst of my tormentors. No, Olivia was too cool and aloof for that. If she noticed me it was because I was either directly in her way in the hall, or one of her Pom Squad friends needed their uniform stitched up from making one too many high kicks.

But she's clearly wounded the man next to me - this man that I've come to care about, to my own surprise. Which, to me, might as well make her the gum on the bottom of my vintage shoe.

"Fuck," Fitz mumbles, and I realize he's digging around in the center console before reaching in front of me and pulling the glove compartment open. "Damn it."

"What?" I reach and grab my scarf and hair clip before I forget them.

"I left my garage door opener inside. I grabbed it since we weren't driving that." He gestures to the car outside my window, next to us in the driveway, a blue sedan. "I must have left it on the counter."

"Nervous amnesia?" I ask playfully, and he scowls. "Jesus, I'm kidding, Fitz."

"Sorry." He steadies himself with a deep breath. "I just wanted tonight to be-"

"It doesn't have to be anything," I counter. "Just let it be what it is. Do we need to make a run for the front door?" He eyes me before nodding slowly. "Ok, let's do it." He seems surprised, but I reach back and put my fingers around the silver handle, my purse grasped in the other hand.

"Ready?" he asks, and before either of us can second guess it, I'm yanking open the door and slipping out. I feel the cold rain seeping through my stockings the second my legs are outside, but I don't stop as the door slams behind me and I make my way across the driveway and up the brick path to the front door. Fitz is just in front of me and keeps looking back like he's expecting me to fall flat on my face going for the door.

In his defense, it's a totally legitimate concern.

His keys jingle as we make it under the small awning over the front door, providing some cover from the rain as it pours around us. His key clicks in the black door and he pushes it open, ushering me inside before following and closing the door with a thud that echoes in the room we've entered.

I laugh, feeling the way my hair is plastered to my cheeks and neck in places, and try to pull it away from my pearl necklace delicately. Fitz looks as soaked as I feel, his hair dark with the water and his usual curls straightened out as they hang around his face. He shakes his head slightly, and water droplets hit me.

"Jesus, down, boy," I shriek, trying to cover myself. And then I hear a distant jingle and the click-clack of paws on the tile floor. When I turn, I have only a second to glance around the house before Roscoe comes bounding out of what looks like it may be the kitchen. Before he can knock me over, I kick off my heels and do my best to clamber down to the ground and sit, just in time for him to nuzzle up against my face.

"Roscoe," Fitz chastises, shaking his head again.

"Would you stop that? Go get a towel, you mongrel." He smiles as he slips his shoes off and puts them on a neat rack near the door, doing the same with mine, like it was second nature. I watch him pad across the entryway, which is cavernous and white with very little decor on the walls, until he disappears into another hall.

Roscoe takes that opportunity to lick up the edge of my cheek.

"Roscoe," Fitz says again, and drops a fluffy gray towel in my lap as he grabs his dog's collar to pull him away. "Let's go outside." The word seems to be the only thing that can distract the dog from his mission of completely clearing my face of makeup, and he follows Fitz back down the hall. Another door opens and closes, and Fitz returns, another towel in hand. I try to dry off the top of my head, my arms, as best I can, and Fitz's gaze doesn't leave me as he towels dry his hair.

After a moment, he reaches out his hand for the towel, and before I can move to get up, he's back down the hall and opening that door again. Roscoe comes back with full force but Fitz calls his name from another room, and I hear the tell-tale sound of dinner being served as the dog diverts from his mission.

Interested, I pull myself to my feet and slowly step down the hallway, moving towards where I think the sound came from. When I turn into the room at the end of the hall, a chrome and gray kitchen stares back. In one corner, Roscoe is face-deep in a bowl of kibble. In the other, Fitz is standing with his back towards me.

"I'll be right back," he says loudly, like he thinks I'm still in the hall. I move towards him, and when my hand reaches out to make contact with his side, he jumps. "Fuck!"

"No need to scream." I laugh as he turns to face me, and I get a look at what's in front of him. Laid out on the counter is a tablet, a remote control, and a box of chocolates. I glance back at his face, and his eyebrows are scrunched again in concentration as he clicks at the tablet.

"Stupid fucking sound system never works when I need it to," he mutters, glancing at me and then back to the task at hand.

Suddenly, from all corners of the house, some sort of fast-paced orchestral music vibrates around us, and I lurch, mockingly covering my ears and looking at him in surprise.

"God, damn, son of a-"

"Language!" I snort at his eye roll as he grabs the remote and points it vaguely above him, rapidly clicking a button as the sound lessens.

"Sorry." He clicks at the tablet again, and the music switches to something a little softer. "This thing never cooperates when I need it to. You'd think, after how expensive it was..." he trails off, watching my face, and then he cringes a little bit.

"It's ok," I say conspiratorially. "I'm clearly only dating you for the money." I gesture down to myself, soaking wet in all the wrong ways, and he laughs, the tension in his shoulders seeming to melt away. "I like that sound." He quirks an eyebrow, leaning his side against the counter.

"Yeah?" I nod, and he reaches his hand out, brushing a strand of hair that's stuck to my face away with his fingers. "I like making you laugh, too." He smiles, but it turns a little wicked as he leans forward. "I think I'll also like making you scream."

I start, and involuntarily, a cackle slips past my lips. His eyes widen, horrified, and my hand clamps over my mouth.

"I'm so sorry," I breathe from between my fingers, my body still shaking with laughter. "That just...God, it sounded like something a secret serial killer would say right before they, like, pull the knife out from behind their back." His face melts, his head snapping back in a deep laugh, and he runs his hand through his rain-darkened hair.

"I guess I set myself up for that. I was trying to be..." His lips thin, and he swallows. "I don't know what I was trying to be." He eyes me, and then holds out his hand for mine. I remove the one covering my mouth and place it in his. "What were you laughing about in the elevator?"

"We had a foot-popping kiss," I say dumbly. His head tilts to one side, and I use his hand holding mine to balance as I kick my stocking-clad foot out behind me. I know instantly that he has no idea what I'm talking about, and I look like a complete lunatic making a Princess Diaries reference that absolutely doesn't land. "Ok, welp, I'm going to go die now." I try to pull away, to turn towards the front door, but he yanks my hand again, pulling me back so that I land against his chest with an oomph. I look up at him, and those green eyes stare back, searching my face for something.

"You know, you don't have to try to be anything," I tell him. I let my hand come up between us, toying with the point of his collar. "You won me over by being yourself - your real self. Don't start trying to cover that up again, *with innuendo*, this time." His eyebrows come together, and instinctively, I reach up and poke my finger at the line it makes above his nose. "That's what I want."

His mouth opens to say something back, but I cut him off by pushing myself up on my toes, my mouth meeting his in another kiss that has my blood pumping, my heart thudding against my chest and my watch vibrating to let me know it's not just in my head.

"Do you need to get that?" Fitz separates from me long enough to ask, and I shake my head, pulling the watch off my wrist and setting it down on the counter.

"Consider that 'do not disturb' mode." He gives me a wicked grin, reaching out and pulling me back against him by the waist. Instead of kissing me, his nose nuzzles into the side of my neck, where he inhales deeply.

"Does that mean you're mine for the evening?" he asks against my skin. I use my fingers already on his chest to stroke, right over his heart, and he leans back up, looking at me.

"Only if you want." The hesitation in my own voice catches me off guard, like I'd voiced a concern I didn't know I had. His brows furrow, just slightly, and I continue. "I mean, sure, I'm here, but you could have your wicked way with me and-"

He cuts me off by pressing his lips against mine again, and this time, I don't pull back. I don't lean away to make sure that I'm not reading too much into this.

I let his tongue trace along my bottom lip, and give him entry to push further, one hand still at my waist, gripping the edge of my bodice. His free fingers lace in my hair, and before I can let out the moan muffled by the kiss, always a sucker for that intimate touch, I'm being backed into the kitchen counter.

Fitz

This evening had not quite gone according to plan. But here, with my body pressed against Piper, pulling her to me like she's a lifeline, all of that melts away.

The rain. The music. The goddamn comment I had to open my stupid fucking mouth and say.

I don't even like to talk, but it was like my brain was mush, looking at her with her waist so defined, her hair plastered to the side of her face from the rain, those big eyes staring up at me like she still can't believe she's here.

Like she's the one who's shocked I gave her the time of day, and not the other way around.

"Is the screaming still an option?" she says against my lips, and I pull back to look at her, not quite sure I've heard her correctly. But when I can see her face, her bottom lip is tugged between her teeth, and she's waiting for my answer. Wordlessly, I hold my hand out to her, and pull her down the hall and into my bedroom.

It hits me when we walk in how sterile my room is compared to hers. My whole house, really. Her space is flooded with memories and reminders of the people and things she loves. Mine is accented with chrome and full of white space. I can tell that she notices, too, as she toggles her head from side to side, taking in the lack of personal touches and abundance of square, clean lines.

"Big fan of monochrome, I see?" she asks, the fingers of her hand not held by mine brushing the edge of the entry table, which houses just my charging station for my phone. It used to sit there at night - until I went to bed texting the woman holding my hand. She looks around at the gray upholstered bed, the deep charcoal curtains, the white square side tables with matching chrome lamps. Comparatively, my home looks like it's staged and ready to sell. I close the door softly behind us. Then, her eyes zero in on the pop of yellow sitting on the dresser on the wall, feet away from the end of my bed.

"Is that..." She lets go of my hand, which almost makes me scowl, and takes a tentative step towards the space, her stocking clad feet barely making a sound across the dark wood. She picks up the tape measure in her hand, and turns it over, no doubt seeing Carla's name written in permanent marker. Slowly, her lips turn up in a mischievous smile. "Is this what you look at before you go to sleep?" she asks quietly, and then looks up just in time to see heat flaring into my face.

"I've been meaning to give it back."

"She got a new one to hang some art last week," Piper answers with a shrug, setting the tool back down on the dresser. She turns back towards me, sidling up to my chest and placing both her hands on the smooth fabric of my shirt, running her fingers over it as she looks up at me. "But *Fitzwilliam*," she starts, and a sound involuntarily leaves the back of my throat. Even I can't tell whether it's because I hate hearing her call me that - or because I love it. "I never pegged you for the romantic."

"There we go assuming again." I let my hands fall to her hips, accentuated by the corset or whatever this is she's wearing over her dress, and her eyes flit down for just a moment before she turns in my arms. When she pulls her hair off to one shoulder, she looks at me over the other, batting her long lashes in a way I know is immediately for my benefit.

Alright, so we were playing that game. She wasn't going to hear me complain.

"Can you help me?" She nods down to the lacing across her back.

"How did you get into it?" I ask. She blinks up at me as if to say *don't ask stupid questions*. "Uh, right, shutting up and undressing you." I bite my lips and close my eyes momentarily, wishing I could take back that last bit, but my hands slide up from her hips to tangle in the black silken ribbon lacing up her spine. With one pull on the end of the ribbon and a yank of the middle apart, it loosens. She sighs.

"Much better." I hold her arm to help her balance while she shimmies it down over her hips to the floor, but when she moves to stand and turn, I find her waist and hold her back to my chest. Her head turns towards me, just slightly, but I don't give her the chance to ask what I'm doing before I brush her hair back over one shoulder and lean down, brushing a kiss along the exposed skin.

When she shudders against me, I know I'm a goner.

CHAPTER 29

Fitz

One hand around her waist, I lace the other under her arm and grip her shoulder from the front, holding her against me tightly while I nip at her neck. Her fingers wrap around my own in both spots, squeezing as if it's the only way she can communicate.

The little moan she makes when I reach the spot just behind her earlobe makes my cock twitch against her, and I know she's felt it because her jaw moves as she smiles broadly.

"Do you like feeling what you do to me?" I ask in a low whisper, and she nods wordlessly, using one hand to pull my face down until her lips meet mine. I step forward and she moves with me, pushing the front of her hips into the dresser and letting my arousal grind against her ass while our lips tangle and her hand pulls at the hair at the base of my neck.

After a minute she manages to twist in my arms, and, mouth still on mine, she clumsily undoes the buttons on my shirt, laughing against me as she fumbles. She throws it open and I let it fall to the floor, letting go of her for just a moment to pull my undershirt over my head too.

She freezes momentarily, taking in my naked torso, her eyes stopping for a millisecond on the bulge very, very visible through my pants, and her mouth tilts up again. Turning half way, Piper lifts her hair up, and my fingers find her zipper and pull, carefully watching every inch of skin that becomes exposed down her back, paying special attention to the black lace bra peeking out.

When she turns back around to wiggle out of the dress, I step back, not noticing when I've gone too far until my legs hit the back of the bed. At the same time her dress falls to the floor, I lose my balance, stumbling back onto the end of my bed with a thud.

I feel my breath hitch, less than hear it, because my blood is pumping so loudly through my head I don't hear anything else. My eyes scan from her face, where something apprehensive flashes across her features, and then down her long neck, to the pearls she's still wearing. Her tan skin is interrupted only by the black lace bra that hugs at the swell of her breasts. It fits her perfectly, but I'd expected no less. That tattoo I'd glimpsed the other day has several friends, I discover, one at her bra line on the other side of her stomach that says something I can't make out from here, and another floral piece peeking from the top of her underwear on the other side.

Black and lacy too, they stretch across her hips and hug every curve just right. And fucking hell, she's wearing a garter belt, matching the rest of the set, that's holding up the pair of pink tights I've been trying to keep my eyes off of all night. Where they attach to the top of the tights, there are little black bows that match the one perfectly nestled between her breasts.

Like a present. A Piper present, wrapped in black lace and trying to kill me, because she is doing just that. Trying to kill me.

Killing me with her long legs as she stretches one out in front of her, leaning against the dresser and putting her hands on the edge to steady herself, eying me right back. Killing me with the way her cleavage pushes together as she puts her weight on her arms, shoulders jutting towards her ears. Killing me with the way her teeth tug at her lip again, and her nostrils flair, just slightly, as her quick breaths make the tendrils of hair falling across her chest shake.

She is breathtakingly gorgeous, and I wish I could snap a mental photo of her just to remind myself how incredibly fucking stupid I was to let anyone treat this woman like anything less than she deserved. Like anything less than perfect.

Piper

I give it a few seconds before finally trying to regain Fitz's attention, nodding towards where he fell at the end of the bed.

"Is my lack of coordination finally rubbing off on you?" I realize what I've said the second it leaves my mouth, and I close my eyes momentarily in embarrassment. I hear the breath of his short laugh, and when I open them again, the look on his face has stayed the same, unfazed.

For a second, I really think he's going to leap across the room and ruin my favorite set of lingerie. I'm not sure, at this point, with the way heat is pooling between my legs and my heart is thudding in my chest, that I would be entirely opposed to the idea. I can make more, right?

No. I shake the idea out of my head. This is not a smutty scene in some dark fantasy romance where the beastly hunk of a love interest rips off yet another good pair of underthings. This is real life, and in real life my ass and my boobs are being held up by $75 worth of lace and spandex that I will be incredibly upset if damaged. It just wouldn't be the end of the world, is all I'm saying.

Wordlessly, Fitz leans back on one hand, bringing the other up to gesture for me to come to him in a move that makes my mouth dry. Ok, it's been a while, but it hasn't been that long.

Ok, it has. I try to make my deep breath as unnoticeable as possible as I push off the edge of the dresser I'd been perched on and slowly step towards him, doing my damndest not to slip in these tights. I keep my eyes on his face, his green eyes watching each move I make until I'm standing a few inches in front of him, unsure of how great I look at this angle.

"You seem nervous," he observes, finally breaking that hungry gaze to sit back completely on both hands and scan me up and down. Unconsciously, I cross my arms over my chest, and he zeroes in on the way my breasts push together further. I have to fight back a laugh.

"If you had told me a decade ago we would be here, doing this-

"I would have said I was incredibly lucky." He says it without hesitation, his eyes not leaving my face. I give a half laugh - I'd meant the comment as a note to the absolute insanity of this situation, but his look is serious.

"Back then? Would you really?" I cross my arms tighter and look down at him. I can feel my eyebrows knitting together. "I didn't think you really paid me much attention, aside from hindsight now." With another look up at me, he leans forward, and his hands finally touch my skin - just a graze right above the line of my underwear, but it sends heat across my body, to my core, so fast I suck in a breath. Then, he leans forward, the side of his face pressing into my soft stomach, hands wrapping around my hips.

"I wanted to knock Andy's teeth out at several points," he replies plainly, and plants a kiss just to one side of my belly button. I press my lips together to keep the shit-eating grin suppressed, lacing my fingers through his hair. Normally, I'd try not to fuck with beautiful curls like his, but at this point, I don't think either of us are going anywhere any time soon.

"Oh, really?" I feel him nod against me, and then he plants another kiss on the opposite side, letting his hands trail back until they're brushing over my ass. They keep going down, down, until each hand reaches the spot where the garter ties connect with my stockings.

"Really," he breathes, and then deftly pinches the clips. I feel the stockings sag in the back, and he runs his fingers over the place they'd been covering. A shiver zips up my spine, and I arch into him. "There were days when I'd look across the room at you and wonder what he ever did to deserve you."

"Nothing." He looks up at me, then, eyes narrowed slightly, and his hands trace the tops of the stockings until he's reached the same clips on the front. "He didn't do anything to deserve me." Without breaking my gaze, he unclips the fronts, and they both fall to my knees. "Truth?"

His hand reaches down to grab one of my ankles, and I nearly lose my balance when he starts to pull one of my legs up into his lap. I lean forward, resting one hand on his shoulder, and he does the same, but instead of kissing me, which is what I think he's going to do, he keeps bending until his nose nuzzles the inside of my thigh. I feel my supporting knee buckle, and he smiles against me. "Yes, please." Inch by inch, Fitz rolls down the pink stocking, letting his hands smooth over my freshly-shaved calves.

"Back then, I was so shocked that Andy gave me any attention at all that I probably would have agreed to just about anything." His hands freeze with the stocking around my ankle, and I know instantly it was probably the wrong thing to say. But he continues, lifting my foot up to take off the last of the fabric and tossing it into the pile with my other discarded clothes, letting it back down to the ground and then gesturing for the other leg. This time, I put it in his lap myself, to save myself the chance of falling on my ass.

"Piper," he starts, and his voice isn't breathy or husky anymore. It's clear as day. He takes this stocking off more quickly, peeling it down to my ankle before he looks up at me again. "He didn't deserve even a second glance from you." I smile down at him, and let my hand drift up from his shoulder to cup his cheek, which he turns into like he has before. He slides the second stocking off my foot, and it joins the first, but instead of dropping this foot to the ground, he slides his hand back up behind my knee and yanks it, letting me fall forward into him.

My knees find a spot on either side of his firm thighs, and when my legs spread and my hands fumble for the back of his neck, I realize just how exposed I am - how I'm laid bare for this man who's known me for more than half my life. For this man I feel like I barely understand, but want to let do dirty, wicked things with me until both of us are complete puddles. I swallow, trying to breathe deep as I look down at him, those green eyes staring up at me with so much intensity it makes my insides clench. Except, it's not just lust there. It's not just passion or Fitz being horny as hell, though I think both of us are at this point. It looks like admiration.

"He didn't deserve anything from me," I finally answer, and his hands run up and down my back, making me shiver again.

"Neither do I," he murmurs, and I feel my eyebrows shoot up.

"Is that what you think?" I ask, sitting back to look down at him. He doesn't answer - just runs his eyes over my nearly-naked torso, landing on the swirling ink on my side.

"What does it mean?"

He's avoiding my question.

CHAPTER 29

"Is that what you think?" I repeat, and graze his ear with my thumb. Underneath me, something twitches, and I nearly smile to myself, but I'm trying to hold his gaze with the same serious face he's making at my stomach. "You think you don't deserve me?" His fingers trace where his eyes look.

"*We delight...*" he reads the script aloud. I use one hand to grip his chin, forcing him to look up at me. At this angle, I'm probably all neck folds, but I really don't care.

"Quit being evasive, *Fitzwilliam*." Finally, he smiles, and it's dazzling. Like calling him that has knocked him out of wherever his brain went. I swallow, trying not to let that smile take me for all I'm worth, and trail my fingers up the side of his face until they reach his ear, and it's like I've found his weakness. I finally smile to myself, and he looks curious, just for a second, before I lean forward and let my lips barely touch his ear.

"Do you think you don't deserve all the things I want to do with you?" I ask. Again, there's movement below me, and I brush a kiss along his clearly sensitive skin. "Do you think I'd be here if I didn't believe you deserved me? If I didn't want this just as badly as you?" I sit back up, and his eyes follow my face intently, long fingers gripping my waist. I'm thankful for the secure feeling, because when I take my hands from his neck, his own arms tighten around me. I feel my hands tremble as I reach for the center clasp on my bra and pinch it open, letting my heaving chest fall free. Fitz lets out a strangled sound, somewhere between a moan and a choke, and the corner of my lips tip up as I shift one side of the straps off.

"Fuck," he says quietly. And those eyes, so filled with admiration just a moment ago, turn dark and hungry.

CHAPTER 30

Fitz

I don't even give Piper time to process my standing, gripping her thighs up and feeling her flail against me. I just turn us both around and half-toss her on the bed, where she lands with a surprised "oof."

Predatory heat surges through my body watching her chest shake with the movement - her nipples are dark and hard with whatever tension she's feeling too. And she's still wearing those God damn pearls.

"I don't think I deserve you," I say, my voice still just as clear as moments before, and I find the button on my jeans, working them open until I can slide them down, standing at the foot of the bed in just my boxers. Piper bites her lip, squirming slightly when she sees the way my cock is straining against them.

I climb onto the bed until I'm sitting at her feet, where her legs are splayed open, and use my hands under each knee to pull her towards me, her chest bouncing. One hand above her head on the pillows, I lean down, letting my lips hover above hers. "But I'm willing to do whatever it takes to make sure you know exactly how I feel."

"Fitz?" she says, and I lean back, just enough to see her face and the sultry smile she's making, those giant blue eyes staring up at me. "I never thought this would be a problem for you, but please, shut the fuck up and kiss me."

I don't hesitate to do exactly as she asks, taking her lips in mine - hungrily, ferociously, because having her pressed up against me, chest to chest, while she wraps her long legs around me, has my heart pounding and my head spinning like I could just float away. The feeling of her fingers tangled in my hair, her calves pressing into my ass, feels ten times better knowing that she thinks I deserve a second of her time.

My lips trail down the side of her jaw, finding the hollow of her collar and letting myself burrow into her neck, just for a moment. She lets out a contented sigh. Finally, after breathing her in, the way she smells like her room somehow, rich and smooth and sweet, I keep moving down, kissing across her collarbone and to the place where her breasts fall apart. When I run my nose down the spot, I feel her swallow hard, and glance up to see her closing her eyes, head tipping back and arching her chest towards me.

I take that as my cue, sucking one of her nipples into my mouth and taking the other breast in my hand, rolling my thumb over the top. She lifts further, like she's trying to give me more access, and while one hand finds my hair, the other finds the waistband of my boxers.

"We're still wearing too much clo-clothing," she manages, voice cracking on the last word when I graze her nipple with my teeth. I smile, reveling in the fact that I'm driving her just as crazy as she's making me. "Don't be a tease."

"I have no intention of leaving you hanging." I keep kissing down her stomach, until I reach the tattoo on the opposite side of her stomach from the big floral piece, my fingers running across similar patterns. My eyes find the words again.

"*We delight in the beauty of the butterfly,*" she says breathily, looking down at me. "*But rarely admit to the changes it has gone through to achieve that beauty.*" I hum in satisfaction - I'd been wondering what those words, so important to her that she had them inked into her soft skin, had meant. I note to ask her about it later - but this, with her naked in my bed and practically writhing, isn't the time or place.

When I hitch a finger beneath the hem of her underwear, she lifts her hips, watching me, and I pull them down in one swift motion. She moves to lift her legs to let me slide them off - and then her knee collides directly with my cheekbone.

I hiss automatically, and she mirrors my actions when my hand flies to my face.

"Oh my fucking God," she cries, and reaches out to assess me with her free hand. "I'm so sorry."

"I'm alright." I press on the spot where her knee made impact. "You didn't get me that bad." She groans, rolling her head into the pillow and splaying her fingers across her face.

"Ok, I'm dead. Goodbye. Please tell everyone I died embarrassed and horny." I can't help the deep laugh that rumbles from my chest as I lean forward, grabbing her wrists and pulling them away from her face.

"I'm sorry, but there's no way I'm having that conversation with Alex." She snorts, and the way her face crinkles makes me feel better, despite the sting in my cheek. "Besides." I pull both her wrists into one hand, and press them into the pillow above her head, feeling satisfied when her eyes widen. "I can't let you die embarrassed *and* horny. It would be a failure on my part."

Before she can talk, because I know she's going to, I press my lips to hers and run my hand down her soft stomach, until my fingers reach the patch of dark curls right above her pussy. I can't see it, but I can feel the way her knees clench together, and I reach out, knocking her knees apart with one hand while our tongues tangle and she squirms beneath me. When I find her just as wet as I'd hoped, I let loose a groan against her mouth.

She responds by pressing herself into my hand, and when the tips of my fingers find her clit, she jolts, mumbling something against my lips. When I pull back, gasping, still working at her, this close I can see that the makeup on her nose and forehead has smeared, revealing her flushed skin beneath. That makeup is probably on me, now, but I couldn't care less.

"Fitz," she moans, and the word, the way she says it, makes my body melt into hers, cock instantly becoming completely hard against her side. I lick my bottom lip as I stare at her face, the glazed look in her eyes. She bucks against my hand. "I have condoms in my purse." I can feel her hard nipple rubbing against my skin with each deep breath she takes.

"Don't get ahead of yourself," I reply, and touch my nose to hers in a way I think would make me nauseated if I saw anyone else do it. But to her - with her - it feels like a way to reassure her I'm here for this moment. I'm here for her, for her pleasure, as much, if not more, than mine. When her eyebrows knit together, I answer by slipping a finger inside her and her hips lift again.

"I want to come with you." She swallows as she looks at my face, her flush deepening with every crook of my finger, every circle my thumb makes on her swollen clit.

"You can come more than once." Piper gives another breathtaking smile, though it falters for a second when I add a second finger, letting go of her hands above her head, her eyes fluttering shut.

"I know I can, I do all the time." I pause for a heartbeat, a vision of Piper in that canopy bed, legs spread, using that stupid little vibrator, dances across my brain. "I just don't normally with someone else." I resume what I was doing and she hums in approval, her eyes sliding closed.

"I think by the time I'm done with you, you'll stop thinking that's acceptable."

"Where did this come from?" she asks, one hand gripping the duvet beneath her like a lifeline.

"What do you mean?" I mutter against her breast as I run my lips across it.

"Have you always been this aggressive?"

"Do you really need the answer to that right now?" To punctuate my question, I graze my teeth across her nipple again, and she whimpers. "That's what I thought."

"Fuck off," she breathes.

"Later, right now, be a good girl and let me make you come."

Piper

If I hadn't been edging towards an orgasm before, I am now, hearing Fitz's voice, husky with need, asking me to let him make me come.

Who could say no to that?

He fucking called me a *good girl* and if I was still wearing my panties, they'd have dropped.

I've never been one to come from penetration alone, but the feeling of his long fingers inside of me is enough to make my insides clench. I know myself well enough, though, that I reach out towards the side table where I'd thrown my purse, snapping it open.

"Hey, I said don't get ahead of yourself," he says against my ear when he sees the flash of foil from a condom wrapper as the purse tips over. I roll my eyes, my hands digging until I find what I'm looking for. Triumphant, I pull the small, black velvet bag out and hand it to him, just as a particularly strong wave of pleasure hits me and I arch against him. "What's this?"

"A friend," I answer, a little more coyly than I mean to, but he takes the hint and pulls his hand back. Immediately, I feel cold and empty, and regret all of my life choices leading up to that moment. But the look of shock on his face when he pulls the purple bullet out of the bag, one hand still slightly damp with the wetness he was causing, is worth that feeling.

"Fuck yeah." His exclamation makes me bark out a laugh, and I run one hand down my face, rings grazing the tip of my nose.

"Do you want to use it?" I ask him, and feel the flush of embarrassment sliding up my cheeks. He nods, turning it over in the hand that was inside me moments ago.

Suddenly, he pushes himself up and leans against the headboard next to me, bringing me towards him with one hand under each of my arms. "Jesus Christ, Fitz." He laughs, pulling me tight against his chest, right between his legs, pushing my hair to one shoulder, leaning into the other.

"I want you to show me how you use it," he says into my ear, and the shiver that runs down my body is completely involuntary as he holds the vibrator out in front of me. I take it, and he pulls my legs over each of his until I'm leaning back against him, totally spread out. His lips find that soft spot behind my ear that he whispered over earlier, and I melt into him.

Making myself come in front of someone else isn't particularly new to me. It's something most men enjoy, and honestly, when they don't know what the fuck they're doing, it's nice to get off before my entire lower half goes numb from friction burn. But this feels different. Tight against Fitz's chest, he can feel every movement, every twitch of my body, and I can feel the way he's reacting when I hold the vibrator in front of me. I'm about to bring it down between my legs when his hand stops me.

"Wait." His fingers on my wrist direct my hand upwards, and when the vibrator is right in front of his face, he leans forward, taking it into his mouth and wetting it. I feel my breath hitch when it leaves his mouth with a "pop."

"There." And then he leans down, capturing my mouth with his and pushing my hand back down towards my soaking center.

The second I feel the vibrations against my skin, I buck up, already sensitive from all the heavy petting. When I reach my clit, I moan against Fitz. One of his hands holds the side of my face, the other weaving around my front and toying with one of my nipples.

He alternates between letting our tongues tangle and looking down over my heaving chest, kissing my neck as he watches how I move the vibrator against myself, until his hand reaches down and wraps over my own. I let him take it from me, and when he pushes it down against my clit, I writhe, laughing. "Not that hard," I half-whisper, my head falling back over his shoulder as he finds the right pressure, circling with the tip until I'm trembling against him. My hand finds the back of his neck, and when I look at him again through my near-orgasm fog, he's got that same look of admiration, if not a little determination, on his face.

"You're so fucking beautiful, Piper," he says into my ear, "and I want to feel this gorgeous body of yours come undone against me."

I feel my orgasm crest a few shaking moments later, and I pull his head towards me until I can crash my mouth into his, burying my near-feral scream against him. But he pulls back, mid-kiss.

"Don't stifle yourself." I let out a guttural moan as wave after wave hits me, gripping at his neck and one of his thighs hard enough that it'll probably bruise, but he doesn't even blink as I writhe against him, completely aware that just behind my ass is his cock, long-since hard and begging to be set free. When I finally come down from the last jolt of pleasure, Fitz clicks the vibrator off.

It's been a long time since I came that hard from anything other than my own conviction and a steamy eBook.

I sigh, feeling like jelly and painfully aware of the layer of sweat between us. When I sit up slightly, it makes a sound, and I wince.

"You ok?" he asks, and I laugh, running a hand through my hair, mostly out of nervous habit at this point, shaking my head.

"Ok is one word for it." Fitz smiles, leaning down to kiss me again before crawling out from behind me. I sit back against the headboard, watching him stand to set the vibrator on the side table, still close enough to reach, and walk into what looks like a bathroom, water running for a few moments, before coming back with a box that he sets next to my new favorite toy.

"Is that brand ok?" he asks casually, like he hadn't just set a jumbo box of condoms on the table. I nod, trying to hide my smile as he leans back against the dresser, crossing his arms over his bare chest, seeming to enjoy the view of me naked against his headboard as much as I'm enjoying the view of his lean muscle and the clearly pitched tent he's sporting. "I liked feeling you come against me."

"The next one you can feel around your cock." I match his casual tone, shrugging, and he quirks an eyebrow. "Or not, I mean -

He shuts me up by putting his thumbs over his waistband and pulling his boxers down to his ankle in one fluid movement, and the painful looking way he's standing to attention makes my mouth dry.

"I got tested last week," he says, still casually. "All clear." I nod. I know he's been with at least one other person recently - or at least, I can assume, based on the way his not-business-meeting had been adjusting herself that day at the Pine. But Fitz has been honest with me - painfully honest - from day one, so to believe he would lie about something like this, something so serious, would be hard. We hadn't exactly had the "are we exclusive" discussion yet - just hours after our first actual date, despite weeks of talking. Modern problems for a modern situationship. Relationship? Gah.

"They ran a full panel when I was in the hospital." He winces, almost imperceptibly, but I still catch it. "I'm good." I pause. "And I have an IUD, for the record. But..."

"Better to be safe." He smiles, and with one hand, he gives himself a lazy stroke, gripping the edge of the dresser with white knuckles. "You have no idea how long I've been thinking about this, Piper," Fitz says, nostrils flaring slightly. I swallow.

"How long?" It can't be that long, surely.

"Truth?" I nod as he echoes my question from before. "Since that day in Calhoun's class. The way you stood up for yourself..." He closes his eyes, like he's picturing us that day, more than a decade ago, and when he opens them again, the smile that crosses his face is feline. "And now you're mine."

CHAPTER 31

Fitz

Mine. The word bounces around in my head, in the room, like a caged bird set free.

Mine.

But instead of the panic, the uncomfortable look I'd been expecting from this woman in front of me, Piper's smile echoes mine as she glances towards the box on the side table, then the tape measure behind me, and then finally, at my face.

"Yours." I cross the room and join her on the bed so fast that when I kiss her, fully, deeply, and my cock nudges against her warm skin, it feels like only a second has passed. I feel her smile against my lips, and when I sit up, reaching for the box of condoms, she traces a nail down my chest.

We delight in the beauty of the butterfly, but rarely admit to the changes it has gone through to achieve that beauty.

A butterfly. Beautiful, transformed.

That's what Piper was. Not just physically, but the woman that laid beneath me, that was running her hands over me like the touch could reach my fucking soul, was a different person than the one I knew ten years ago.

The way she takes the condom out of my hand, ripping it half-open with her teeth and rolling the rubber onto me, not breaking eye contact, isn't something I could have ever really imagined for us, as much as I'd wanted it back then. So when I nestle myself between her legs, putting my weight on a forearm by her head and brushing a curl out of her face, I have to remind myself that this is all real.

That the first opportunity at something serious, post-Olivia, post the cataclysmic end of the longest relationship in my life, is with someone who's mere fingers in my hair makes a shiver run down my spine.

I position myself at her entrance, and when I meet her gaze again, she gives me a small nod, her nails dancing up my back while I push into her, kissing her deeply. While Piper gasps into my lips, I groan at the instant warmth, the incredible feeling of being nestled inside her, inching forward until I'm buried all the way. When our lips break apart, both gasping, she smiles up at me, eyes shining in the light from the lamp on the side table. She wraps her legs around me and trails a finger lazily up one of my arms.

"We can go fast and hard later," I manage, a shaky hand raking down her side and gripping her hip, pulling her even tighter against me. "Right now, I want to savor this." Piper nods up at me, her thumb brushing my temple as I pull out, almost all the way, and then slide back in.

I almost come on the spot when her eyes roll back in her head, mouth going slack. I pump in and out a few times, slowly, just watching her face for a moment, so expressive, a reaction to every small movement. It's a sight that has my chest constricting, knowing it's satisfying her. I lean forward, running my nose up the side of her neck, breathing her in as we find a steady rhythm.

Piper's hands grab at me - my hair, my arms, even my ass at one point, which makes my cock twitch inside her and elicits a wicked grin that makes me want to speed up and take her much more quickly than she deserves.

But I'm determined to do better. Hitching a hand under each of her knees, I pull her down on the bed with me, and her eyes fly open.

"What are you..." I grab a pillow from the other side of the bed, yanking her hips up and sliding it under her without ever pulling out. "That was impressive." I fight the urge to roll my eyes, sitting all the way up on my knees and pulling her legs up until I'm holding her calves against my hips. Slowly, I pull out, and then pump back in.

She moans, long and loud, and I know I've made the right move. When I shift to reach over to the side table, her eyebrows knit together again. I hand her the vibrator.

"I want to feel you come around me. I'm going to hold these," I explain, squeezing her shins for emphasis. She flushes, and damn it, it's fucking adorable, but she doesn't hesitate in switching the vibrator on and bringing it between her legs while I find a steady rhythm that seems to hit the spot for both of us.

I feel the vibrations immediately, and it sends a thrum of pleasure through my entire body. Fuck, if that's what the residual feels like, I can't imagine how she must be feeling right now. I want her - both of us, selfishly - to feel like this all the time.

It only takes a few seconds for a small jolt of pleasure to work through her, and when she clenches around me, I throw my head back, biting my lip to keep a moan from escaping.

"Don't stifle yourself." She echoes the words back at me, and when I look down at her, that wicked grin is back.

She's fucking testing me.

"I'm not great at expressing my emotions," I say simply, and her chest shakes with laughter, breasts bouncing.

"You're not marble, Fitz." She pauses, and then glances down between us. "Ok, not all of you." The joke is bad, but it's enough to make me laugh, deep and hearty, but when her pussy squeezes my cock, it cuts short. "I don't want you to pretend you don't feel this." And when it happens again, I realize that she's doing it intentionally.

Fuck. I thought I was a goner before.

"Come around my cock," I start, and push a little harder this time as I pump into her. "And we'll see if I can hide anything from you."

"I'm already close." Her eyes close again, head leaning back like she's concentrating.

"Good." I run my hands up and down her calves, which are toned from what I assume is years of those punishing heels. "I want at least one more from you before we come together." She hums in approval, and grinds her hips towards me as I thrust, until she's cursing under her breath in what sounds like Italian.

I feel her orgasm before she even has a chance to tell me she's coming, and it nearly knocks the wind out of me to feel her both all around my cock and to watch her writhing beneath me. And when she's coming down, her lip trapped so tight between her teeth I think she's going to draw blood, I lean forward, nipping at the lip myself so she lets it go.

"Don't stop," I say into her ear, and she nods against my neck, her lips placing a gentle kiss on my shoulder that leaves me shivering. When I sit up, her entire body is quivering with aftershocks, but to give her credit, she doesn't once stop moving that damn vibrator between her legs, the strokes in time with my own. "Fuck, Piper." I feel myself getting close to my own release, that glorious peak in sight as she presses her legs into my hips like a vice.

It isn't until she's muttering again that I realize we're both on the edge together.

"*Fitz*," she moans, and when she starts convulsing around me again, it's all I can do to stay upright as my own orgasm wracks my body, leaving me twitching and panting and watching the last of her waves wash over her. I push forward, my mouth crashing into hers in a hard kiss as she lifts up to meet me. With a soft laugh, she collapses back onto the pillow, one hand coming to her forehead as her eyes rake over my face.

"Fuck," I murmur, nuzzling against her again and trailing lazy kisses up the space where her shoulder meets her neck. Her nails drift down my back, and for a second, I just breathe her in.

Goner. I'm an absolute goner.

CHAPTER 32

Piper

As soon as I'm able to roll out from underneath Fitz, I do. Heart racing, I sit at the edge of the bed, painfully aware of the way my stomach folds, my hair sits on end in places - all sense of confidence washed away after that look Fitz gave me. The one that says "this is more than just a fuck."

Granted, I knew that. I knew that going into this; into this bed, into this date, hell, into this relation- uh, whatever this is.

But seeing that look on his face made my stomach do a somersault in a way it hasn't in a long, long time. If we're honest, since Mickey.

And my heart, like my stomach, does a fuckin' summersault too.

Grace is not my strong suit - so somersaults need to stop.

"Can you find me something to wear?" I throw over my shoulder, and when I look back, he's leaning on one side, but he's pulled the duvet over the lower half of his body. That line has returned between his eyebrows, but he reaches out, his fingers trailing down the lower half of my spine in a delicate way that makes my stomach clench.

"Sure." He pauses. "Is everything ok?" It takes a heartbeat for me to plaster a smile on my face, trying to ignore the panic rising in my chest, and I lean back, pressing a kiss to his lips.

"That was wonderful." Not a lie. The sex was wonderful. Too wonderful.

I haven't come that hard in a long time - haven't felt someone so frenzied with me that I could tell they were holding back, though I guess with Fitz, I was used to him holding back.

I push myself to stand, and immediately feel the slick between my thighs, satisfying but also a stark reminder of the reason my heart was beating out of my chest. I take the few strides towards the bathroom and step in without looking back.

I stare at myself in the mirror as I wash my hands a few moments later. Hair a mess, both from the sex and the rain. Literally stark ass naked, save my jewelry, with red splotches all over my chest, my neck, even my thighs. My makeup is mostly gone, both on Fitz's face and the pillow I'd turned my cheek into out of habit to muffle my cries.

This is bad. This is very, very bad.

When I step out a few minutes later, there's a tee shirt laying across the edge of the bed. Oversized, just the way I like it. I ignore the shorts sitting next to it, and move to sit down when I see a glass of water sitting next to my purse.

Well, fuck. He got me water.

With a deep sigh, I dig in my bag, pulling out the individually wrapped makeup wipe I packed - horrible for your skin, but I wasn't about to pull out a ten step skincare routine here. At least, not from this Barbie purse. I'm wiping my face off when Fitz slips through the door, Roscoe jingling behind him. He's got a pair of basketball shorts slung around his hips, riding so low I can tell he doesn't have underwear on.

I swallow, trying to look away as he leans against the wall next to the bathroom door. Once I finish with my wipe, I offer it to him, and he smiles, pushing off the wall to come sit in front of me. Concentrating, I wipe the cold cloth across his face, managing to remove the majority of the foundation on his nose and forehead.

Before I can lower my hand completely, he lifts his fingers to my wrist.

"Hey," he says, and his voice is gentle as he searches my face. I give a smile, but he purses his lips. "What happened there?"

"What do you mean?" He gives me a look that very clearly says *cut the bullshit*, and I sigh again. "I'm just in my own head." With my other hand, I reach up to touch his face, brushing my thumb along his cheek. Instead of nuzzling into it, he leans sideways, brushing a kiss across my palm. It's surprisingly tender, even for today.

"Do you want to talk about it?" I rub at the back of my neck, pulling the last of my hair out from under the tee shirt I'd thrown on - a burnt orange monstrosity with a *UT Athletics* logo across the chest.

"Can I say no?" I laugh, trying to lighten the mood, and reach into my purse, retrieving the small pillbox I'd brought with me. When I dump the pile into my hands, his gaze lands on them. "Behold, my normal person potion." He smiles, but it doesn't quite touch his eyes as he pivots, pulling his long legs underneath him on the bed. Roscoe climbs up on the other side, curling up next to him.

"Normal is overrated." He sounds matter of fact, but looking around his room, his life - it's so normal. So orderly. And I'm a big whopping mess with a pile of happy pills in my hand, having a near panic attack after fantastic sex because I'm catching feelings for someone I'm actually allowed to catch feelings for.

I'm allowed to catch feelings for Fitz, right?

Conspiratorially, I lean forward, crossing my legs like him and holding up the smallest of the pills between my fingers.

"Anxiety." I pinch it between my palm and my other fingers and grab the next biggest. "Migraines." It joins the first. "ADHD - or, whatever they're calling it now." A larger one goes into my palm. "Depression." I palm the two largest and grab the last one, round and white. "Sleep." I put that one back into the container, and take a deep gulp from the cup on the side table before swallowing down the stack of pills.

He watches me, unfazed, like it doesn't bother him one bit that I only function because my chemical imbalances are managed by my psychiatrist of eight years and freaking *Walmart pharmacy*.

"Do you want to see all of mine?" he asks, and I freeze with the glass halfway to my mouth, ready to take another sip. He hitches a thumb towards the bathroom. "Anxiety, allergies, digestive problems, take your pick." I quirk a brow, returning the glass to the table.

"Digestive problems?" I lean forward, resting my elbow on my knee and my chin in my hand. "Does Fitzwilliam get an upset tummy?"

He makes a disgusted face.

"Please don't ever say that sentence again," he pleads. I laugh, falling back onto the pillows behind me. "You didn't take the sleeping pill," he says after a moment, and I glance down at him.

"I wasn't sure if I was sleeping here," I say honestly, and wave a hand in front of my face. "You may get sick of looking at all this before it's time to hit the hay." For emphasis, I fold my chin down, giving him a serious look with emphasized neck rolls and wheezy breathing that borders on physical comedy.

To my surprise, he lets out a sigh, and then yanks one of my feet out from underneath me, pulling it into his lap and working his thumb into the arch with surprising vigor. I close my eyes, unintentionally letting out a little moan.

"Stop that," he says, tapping at the top of my foot as if in warning, "or I'm going to fuck you to kingdom come." My eyes snap open, but when I look at him, he's just focusing on my foot, his thumbs kneading back and forth.

"Who are you and what have you done with Fitz Westfall?"

Without looking up, he responds "Who are you and what have you done with Piper D-"

He stops himself, and I realize when he doesn't look up, heat suddenly flaring on his cheeks, that he doesn't know what my last name is. I sigh back at him. It's valid.

"Legally, Davis." I monitor his face, but nothing changes. "For the most part,

I still go by Delmonico." There's a momentary silence where Roscoe scratches at his ear, and I take a deep, steadying breath, staring at the smooth white ceiling. "I'm not good with intimacy anymore."

He glances up at me, just for a second, before returning his attention to the task at hand. I continue, only seeing him out of the corner of my eye.

"I used to be really good at this - dating. I think everything with-" I pause, "I think everything that's happened over the last few years has made me wary."

"Wary of me?" I look down at him, but his fingers are still working, massaging into the balls of my feet where I'd been putting all my pressure in my heels.

"No," I breathe, half out of desperation and half trying to stifle the groan his hands elicit. "Wary of this." I gesture between us. He pauses, and then presses harder into my foot. I grit my teeth, but through the pressure, it feels amazing. "Fitz, I'm sorry - we've been on one date and-"

"Don't," he says, and stops completely. Part of me is concerned - the other part wants to beg him to keep going. "Don't apologize for panicking because you felt something." Looking down, with the palm of his hand, he pushes on the top of my foot, where my toes end, and the stretch up my calf makes me wince, but then my entire leg relaxes. Not looking at me at all, he continues. "Because I did too."

"Did?" He smiles to himself.

"Do." He pulls out my other foot and starts the process all over again, digging into the arch. "I do feel something."

"Marble Man Fitz feels something?" I ask with a smirk. Here we go again, always trying to make other people feel comfortable by compensating with humor.

"Don't," he says again, and glances up at me. "I've always felt something. I just don't let people see it." The way he clenches his jaw makes my heart break into a million little pieces, watching him work his hands into my bare feet like it's the only thing keeping him from falling apart in front of me.

"Oh, sweetheart." At my words, he looks up, and I see something flash in those deep eyes of his. I'm not sure what the look is, but I pocket it. He avoids my gaze, focusing on a spot behind me, as I continue, "Who made you feel like you couldn't show your feelings?"

Fitz pushes down on the top of this foot, same as the other, and then lets it rest in his lap, fingers working idly across my calf. I push myself up against the headboard, losing contact with him, and he grimaces, finally meeting my gaze. Gone is any glimmer of the time we've just shared, of the way we'd been pressed together moments before. The look on his face is cold, so much so that tears prick in the back of my eyes.

"Fitz." I hold my hand out to him, and when he takes it, lips pressed together

CHAPTER 32

in a thin line, I pull him up to me. His head rests in the crook of my arm where I sit up against the upholstery, his ear against my chest, and run my fingers through his hair, pressing a kiss to the top of his head. A shiver runs down my back when a slight breeze hits me, and before I can even ask, he's helping me bring the duvet up over us until we're nestled underneath.

For a minute, he just sits there, and I listen to his breathing. His hand wraps around my waist, and I'm thrown back to that night in my bedroom all those weeks ago. When his fingers tighten on the shirt I'm wearing, it feels like he's gripping me for support.

"How much do you know about my dad?"

CHAPTER 33

Fitz

"Not a lot," Piper says quietly, and I pause, unsure of what to say next.

My heart may be beating faster now than it was minutes ago, coming down from that delicious high while still inside Piper. But that's only because I don't talk about this, not with anyone, really.

Not even Olivia, because, while she's known me since kindergarten, she didn't *really* know me until we were much, much older, and now I question whether she ever did at all.

"I'm surprised you didn't look us up." I run my thumb over the smooth imprint on the shirt she's wearing, one of my favorites that I've kept with the intention of having it turned into a pillow or something for the media room upstairs, where Longhorn football games are a regular occurrence. Right now, though, the idea of the shirt anywhere but on Piper's body makes me itchy.

"That's your thing." I can hear the smile behind her voice, and press a kiss to her orange-covered chest before sitting back to look up at her. "I want you to tell me what you want me to know. I've worked on my ability to trust people for a long time, I wasn't about to start whatever this is by not letting you tell your own story."

Whatever this is.

"Shit," she mumbles, and I realize what else she's said at the same time she does. "I didn't mean you, Fitz, doing that." I swallow as she stumbles for words, her face tightening in concentration, and I give my head a shake.

"I know." I try to inject as much softness as I can without letting my voice break, because she's completely right, even though she didn't mean it. I had cyber-stalked her before I'd even taken a moment to let what I was doing wash over me, gathering information without knowing why and without realizing the effect it would have on my opinion of her.

She's always been smarter than me, but in this instance, I'm incredibly grateful

for the grace she continues to give.
So, I take a deep breath, and let it all spill out.

Fifteen Years Ago

"Chris, that is absolutely not an option," Paula's voice wafted through the open door to the bedroom she shared with my father, and I sat at the bottom of the staircase, my arms wrapped around my knees, the cold marble pressing into me.

Beside me, Freddy tapped his well-worn Nike cleat, which he didn't even get a chance to change out of before all hell broke loose.

"He can't do this," Freddy said, mostly to himself, balling his fists up tight and flexing his hands like he's trying not to hit something.

"Not worth it," I murmured back, closing a hand around his, and his foot stopped moving. He looked at me, eyes narrowed. He knew it was bad if I was the one initiating physical contact. I gave him a squeeze, more for myself, and let go.

"He can't keep getting himself into situations like this, Paula," Dad said, a little louder than she was. "We said last time if we had to bail him out again, this is what we'd do."

"We didn't have to bail him out," Paula countered. "He's twelve, Chris, not nineteen."

"He's old enough to know not to get into fights."

I sucked in a breath. If only he knew what the fight had been about. Some kid at the mall, making a comment about Ryan's older sister, who was picking us up from the movies. When I'd squared up to him, with a few inches on him, even though it was clear he was way older, he tried to land a "yo-mama" joke spat in my face like it was the funniest thing in the world.

The second he'd said it, I saw Ryan and Andy freeze next to me. Big, big mistake.

Before I knew what was happening, Ryan had me pushed to the ground. He'd always been stronger than me, would probably have gone out for wrestling if baseball hadn't been calling his name since the second his dad put him in his first Ranger's jersey. Same as Andy.

Meanwhile, in the four years I'd been playing club lacrosse, Dad had been to maybe a half-dozen games, with Andrea, our nanny, filling in, occasionally accompanied by Paula or Aunt Evie and a completely bored Frannie.

"Did you talk to him about it?" Paula asked, and there was a pause where Freddy looked at me again.

"I don't need to. There's no excuse-"

"Talk to him," Paula interrupted, and there was another pause, followed by brief shuffling.

From closer to the door, his voice sounded, "Fitzwilliam Nicholas Westfall, get your ass up here." I flinched. He'd never lay a hand on me - not that spankings hadn't been out of the question as kids, but more out of principle than anything now. You can't tell your kids emotions make you weak, only to turn on them in physical anger.

"Chris." Paula's voice was admonishing, and I could almost see the look that crossed between them. Paula was one of the few people that can get through to him, make him see any reason when he's clearly seeing red. I pushed up, and Freddy's tiny hand wrapped around my ankle. When I looked down at him, he looked like he was about to cry. I tried to offer him a small smile. He let go, and I did my best not to stomp up the stairs, catching Frannie's eye from the parlor where she was lounging, her nose pressed against her Nintendo. Probably playing that stupid dog game she likes so much.

"Fitzwilliam!" I flinched again.

"Coming." I swallowed, taking the last steps two at a time until I was standing at their doorway. Paula was seated on the tufted lounge at the foot of their bed. She didn't even have a chance to change out of her suit, having come straight from the law firm she works at to pick me up from mall security.

Dad stood in the corner by the door, his arms crossed, and his eyes were the exact same shade of blazing green mine had been when I looked at myself in the mirror earlier. Raging, nose bloody, trying to catch my breath while security pounded on the single-stall bathroom I'd managed to find after running.

"Well?" He raised his brows, his forehead wrinkling to meet his hairline, which was slowly receding, that red hair, almost the same shade as mine, getting thinner each year.

"Well what?"

"Don't give me that shit, Will." His jaw tensed, and I could tell he was trying not to completely let loose on me. "What do you have to say for yourself?"

"I'm sorry?" It came out as a question, and he laughed - it wasn't happy, it never really was anymore.

"You don't even know what you're apologizing for, boy."

"What happened?" Paula's voice was quiet, but its softness set me at ease in the tense room, and I finally looked at her. When I bit my lips, I winced - the top one was split open.

"Does it matter?"

"Yes," they both said, one more spiteful than the other.

"It was a joke." His eyebrows shot up further, and I continued. "Not the, uh," I swallowed, "fight, or whatever. He made a joke."

"About?"

I stalled, trying to decide whether to tell the truth, or spin something. But spinning has always been Frannie's speciality, not mine.

"Mom."

Paula's eyes widened from across the room, and she gave Dad a look that clearly said *go easy on him*. But in true Chris Westfall form, he does the opposite of going easy.

"Will, you don't even remember your mom." Paula sucked in a breath, and I waited a beat before stepping forward.

"That doesn't mean people get to make jokes about her." Wordlessly, my stepmom stood up, striding across the room and coming to stand on Dad's side. She reached a hand out, touching his upper arm as he continued.

"You've got to get this in check, son." His voice was strained again. "If you're going to run this company one day, you can't have a criminal record longer than your arm."

I winced.

If you're going to run this company one day.

There it was.

Fitzwilliam Westfall, family embarrassment, age 12.

"We're worried about you," Paula said, and her eyes shone in a way that twisted my gut.

It'd always been like this. Dad's brash, quick to conclusions attitude and firm belief that emotions were best kept locked deep, deep inside, countered by Paula's attempt to temper him into something kind of resembling a human being.

I don't know how she puts up with it.

"I think it's time we start seriously talking about Geneva." His voice was harsh, but before he could continue, there's the sound of footsteps from behind me, and tiny arms wrapped around me.

"No!" Freddy held onto me for what feels like dear life, and I tensed.

This was really who Geneva would mess up. Being sent to Dad's elitist boarding school halfway across the world would suck, yeah, but without me here to bear the brunt of his crap, this one, right here, would get it.

The expectations. The pedestal. The anger.

"You can't go," Freddy cried, and gripped tighter, his little green eyes welling, and I saw Paula crouch next to dad, holding out her arms to my brother. He shook his head against me. "I don't want Will to go. I need him here. He needs to help me tie my cleats!" A lump formed in my throat.

"Someone else will help you tie your cleats, Fred." Dad was dismissive, but he looked down at Paula, who held her hands out again. Freddy glanced up at me, his tears spilling over, and I squeezed his arm, nodding my head towards Paula. He took it as a sign to run to his mother, and that lump got bigger when she lifted him up into her arms, despite him being almost her size, and carried him towards the door.

Before she exited, she turned to look at both of us, and I watched her. She and Frannie looked so alike sometimes - her hair was a lot darker than any of us, but it still has that red shine to it that shows she's a Westfall. She and Dad had that same light skin, while mine has always made me stand out from the rest of my family.

I hated it. I hated feeling like an outsider in my own house. Because however much I look like the man in front of me, there's pieces of my mom that he can't pretend aren't there.

"We both love your mom, Will," Paula said, her voice shaking. Present tense. Love. Like she was still here.

I supposed Paula could have loved Mom - I wasn't really sure, have never really pried about it. I've seen a picture of the two of them together, just in passing in an old box of photos while trying to find something for a class project.

"Funny way of showing it," I muttered, before really thinking about it, and Dad stepped up until he was nearly in my face. I shrank away as Paula cried "Chris!"

"You watch your mouth, or I'll have you on the next flight to Switzerland without so much as a goodbye to those snotty friends of yours." I fought the comment on the tip of my tongue - that those snotty friends of mine, and their families, have been better to me than he has my entire life. More family dinners, more support at tournaments, more reasonable advice without the ulterior motive of trying to train your replacement from diapers. Like his dad had with him, I guess.

From Paula's arms, Freddy let out a sob, and she glared at Dad before looking back at me.

"We love you, too." She glanced between the two of us, and then down at Freddy. "Your dad wants you to be successful, and I want you to be happy." With a sniffle, she shuffled Freddy to the other hip. "But this fighting has got to stop." She walked out with a final look over her shoulder, and Dad closed the distance between us until I'm practically leaning at an angle to get away from him.

CHAPTER 33

"You can't upset her like that." His voice was even colder, and I heard my own gulp, feeling my muscles tense. "Geneva." He held up a finger in my face. "I'm serious. One more time."

"He's always been like that," I explain, shrugging when Piper asks if that was normal for us.

"Geneva?" She pauses, shaking her head like she's imagining what our lives would have been like if I had been shipped off to Switzerland - that time, or any other time before that when I'd let my feelings get the better of me. Or so Dad had said. "So you just...decided to stop...showing emotion?" She struggles for the words, and I have to admit, I smile to myself a bit. It's not often that she's left without the right thing to say.

"I couldn't risk leaving Frannie and Fred to all of that." I shrug again, rolling onto my back and looking up at the ceiling. "So I decided to suck it up. My fate was sealed, all of the oldest sons have been raised to take over since WHG was founded." Five generations of brash fuckers, each as driven and single-minded as the last. At least my grandfather had the decency to be honest about it. Dad tries to hide his behind family values and PR stunts.

"You really don't remember your mom?" Her voice is quieter, and I glance over at her out of the corner of my eye. She's leaning over to face me, her head propped up on her elbow, a mirror of how I'd been moments before as I shared that memory, so ingrained in my head. I shake my head, folding my hands over my bare chest. Piper reaches out, her nail whispering down my arm.

"But you're a fierce defender of her." I nod wordlessly, savoring the way my hair stands at her touch. "Are you feeling pretty emotionally put out right now?" I turn my head towards her, and she's observing me in a way that tells me it's not a judgment. It's a genuine question, like she's gauging where I'm at. I nod again, and she smiles, her finger stopping, only long enough for her to turn and plop that last pill in her container out, swallowing it down without any water. Damn.

"Let's get some sleep. You can tell me all of your other dirty little secrets tomorrow." The idea is horrifying, but when she pulls my shirt over her head without a second thought, those dark curls bouncing around her bare chest, the worry falls out of my head. When she faces away from me, I wrap my hand around her and pull her close, her warm back against my chest. Roscoe lets out a loud huff, the unencumbered freeloader that he is, when he has to shift to make room for her against me.

"Goodnight," I murmur against her shoulder, pressing a kiss into it just below that line of pearls, and she wiggles against me, completely naked, I realize, because my 2XL Tall t-shirt went down to nearly her knees and she never put pants on.

"Sweet dreams." And before I can even register the sated feeling that drifts through me, I'm out like a fucking light for the first time in a long, long time.

CHAPTER 34

Piper

The first thing I'm aware of the next morning is something cold and wet nudging at my hand.

"Bex," I mumble, pressing my face further into the pillow I'm laying on and taking a deep breath.

Hold on.

I try to twist around, but the arm slung across my back sticks when I turn. I'm a hot sleeper normally, but when that thing nudges me again, I realize I'm not hot, sleeping in my bed, unable to move because Bex is laying on top of me - which does happen occasionally.

A loud, jolting breath on the other side of my head makes my eyes pop open, and I'm face to face with Roscoe.

"Jesus fuck." I start, head rearing back and nearly bashing into what I think is Fitz's nose behind me. Great. Add to the bruises, Delmonico.

With a wince, I close my eyes and let myself feel the complete embarrassment for that one. And when I shift under his weight, finally turning to face him, there is, indeed, a splotch of red across his high cheekbone. I curse to myself, watching his face as he nests further into the blankets half covering his face and trying to pull me closer. Oh no, you don't.

Roscoe's cold nose meets my shoulder and I jump.

"Fuck, Roscoe, I got it." Gingerly, I wiggle out until I've let his arm fall to the sheets, sitting up on the edge of the bed and stretching. In the daylight, this room doesn't look so stark. Even facing the inside wall, the light from the windows over my shoulder washes the room with more warmth. Roscoe comes in front of me, nudging my knee with his nose, and I scratch behind his ear until his foot is thumping lightly on the floor.

Behind me, Fitz stirs, and I look down at his dog. "Let's get your morning started, hm?" I find my discarded t-shirt on the floor next to the bed and pull it on, trying to move across the room as quietly as possible to dig my underwear out of the pile of black lace near the dresser. I smile to myself, watching Fitz turn over again, his shoulders flexing deliciously where they peek out from under the covers. As far as I'm aware, he doesn't still participate in any sports, but clearly he's keeping some sort of routine up with the way he gracefully picked me up and threw me on his bed. I ignore the throb of heat at the thought.

I pick up my phone from the table by the bedroom door as I follow Roscoe down the stark white hallway, until we're back in the kitchen. When I let him outside, I hide behind the door in case any neighbors decide it's a good time for a morning peek over their fence. The curtains are all drawn around the breakfast nook, and in the living room I step into once Roscoe is outside.

I've got notifications like I haven't seen since my graceful visit to the hospital, and I open the message thread with the largest number next to it first.

Group Text (22) *Alex, Carla, Penny, Vic*

Mother of God. I scroll through the messages, mostly inappropriate .GIFs supplied by Carla, finally making my way to the bottom. Fuck me, why am I up so early?

ALEX CALLOWAY
If you don't respond, I'm calling the cops and giving them your location.

PENNY ROBINSON
Chill, A. She's down the street. If Carla needs to go kick down a door, she can.

CARLA MONTGOMERY
Ocupado, mis amigos.

VIC MONTERRO
Since when do you speak Spanish? That was horrible. The feminine is ocupada.
What are you doing besides snuggling with snorterino? You said you couldn't brunch this morning.

CARLA MONTGOMERY
Avoiding her vicious gas.

CHAPTER 34

ALEX CALLOWAY
Back to the topic at hand.
Piper?
Piper?
Piper Giovanna Delmonico Davis, I swear to fucking god.

The last message was sent just a minute ago, and I send a .GIF of someone hiding under a pile of leaves, locking it back up and looking around the room I'm in. It's all so...clean. Clean lines, clean space. Grays and whites and blacks, just like the rest of the house I'd seen. A low, sleek leather sectional stretches across the dark living room floor, centered around a coffee table that looks like it was cut from a solid block of steel. On one wall is a shelf of books, beautifully organized in shades of monochrome with brutalist bookends and small statues, like a Homegoods and a nuclear bunker had a baby. On the other wall, a sleek gray inset bar gleams like it could make me a cocktail itself. If this is the living room, I wonder what the rest of the house looks like.

Hell, he made himself at home while I was asleep. What's the worst I could do?

A lot, actually. I could do *a lot* as a clumsy bitch.

The floor is cold under my bare feet when I make my way back towards the front door, where I know the staircase, dining room, and office are, based on my short observation the night before. The dining room is just as modern as the living space, a black table layered with pre-set dishes and silverware like it's ready for a dinner party at any moment. I snort to myself. Aside from the lack of personal touches, this is my mother's dream. A house ready for entertaining.

When I peer inside the office, past its frosted french doors, it's relatively empty. Based on the way it's laid out, I'd be willing to bet that it was Olivia's space. There are still a few nails in the wall here and there, and in the corner, white plastic tubs are stacked, some of the only clutter I've seen so far. If you can call that disorder. I close the doors softly behind me, and pad back to the kitchen to let Roscoe in, and he happily slops at a self-filling water bowl while I check my messages again.

Group Text (4) *Alex, Carla, Penny, Vic*

VIC MONTERRO
She lives!

CARLA MONTGOMERY
Status report?

PENNY ROBINSON
We need deets!

ALEX CALLOWAY
Do I need to pack up Mickie and head over to beat some wholesale ass?

I snort, and send a quick reply as a message from Carla comes in on another thread.

PIPER DELMONICO
Still in one piece. May have accidentally kneed Fitz in the face last night. All is well. Facetime later?

I curse to myself reading Carla's message.

CARLA MONTGOMERY
Don't forget we have the reunion call at 11!

Fuck my life. That's in...shit. I'll wake Fitz up soon - we should absolutely not look freshly fucked for that call.

Heading back for the front stairs with Roscoe trailing behind, I hold onto the railing, thankful I'm not still in my stockings. There are two bedrooms up here and I wonder to myself why Fitz doesn't have a home office. He seems the type to need a space to set up and work after hours - but like so much else, maybe I'm reading that wrong, too.

I pop into the last room and nearly fall over, looking down at Roscoe like I expect him to be just as amazed as I am.

It's sleek and modern, sure, but it's clearly meant for comfort, because the gray sectional up here is extra padded and huge, stacked with pillows and blankets, in front of a wall where the projector in the ceiling would clearly display whatever's being watched. This is the only room in the house with any sort of personal touches. Signed jerseys line the wall, Longhorn, Rangers, Cowboys, Mavs, even Alamos and F.C. Dallas. In one corner, I spot Fitz's Southwest lacrosse jersey, framed in a dark shadow box like the rest.

CHAPTER 34

Ten Years Ago

"Fuck yeah!" Andy's voice drawled from two tables over in the cafeteria. He inspected the big baseball-shaped patch in his hand, passing it to Ryan, who compared it to his own.

"Yours is bigger," Ryan whined.

"That's what they tell me," Andy responded almost instantly, and I snorted to myself.

Immediate regret filled me when Andy's head turned my direction. Fuck. I should have just kept my mouth shut, my head in the baked potato on my tray, and my eyes on my phone screen. But instead, this testosterone pack walked by, high fiving each other over the new patches they'd picked up from the letterman jacket station outside of the cafeteria.

"Don't agree, Delmonico?" Andy sneered, and those in the tables around us turned too. Vic and our friend Maria looked up from the conversation they'd been having about Vic's newest patch, for his third state championship with the school dance team. I swallowed to myself and made eye contact with Vic, just briefly, before I turned the rest of my body to face the boys. Fitz sat at the table next to Ryan, a book open in front of him next to a can of Monster, surrounded by several other lacrosse and baseball players.

What's the collective term for a bunch of jocks? Gaggle? Convocation? No, too sophisticated. Cluster?

"I wouldn't agree, no." I tried to keep my voice even, but he must have sensed my unease, because his eyes narrowed and he hopped off the waist-high retaining wall he'd been perched on, striding towards me.

"I guess the guys you fucked before me must be rocking chodes then." I bit my tongue. That would be an improvement for him. His eyes landed on the dry cleaning bag hanging on the back of my chair. "You? You lettered?" He snatched it off the back of my chair in a clean grab, and some of the guys from his table sauntered over. Fitz leaned back in his chair, crossing his arms, but didn't move. Brave of him to assume his bestie wasn't about to pull the same shit he'd pulled just a few weeks before, right outside this very room.

Andy inspected the brand new letterman jacket with Delmonico across the back in script, and three patches along one arm.

"MSO? You lettered in MSO?"

"I lettered in MSO, dickwad," Maria sneered from across the table, brushing her long dark curls behind her back. She had fresh extensions installed the week before, and she's feeling particularly invincible. I know the experience well - my own were almost as new, and they feel like a suit of armor sometimes.

"International champion?" he read off one of the patches.

"Two years running," Vic added, and I sagged. The last thing I needed was for Maria or Vic to get hurt again, putting themselves between Andy and I. He wasn't wrong - my visual merchandising display projects had, in fact, won at Internationals both in Memphis and Austin last year. But Andy wouldn't know that, because we weren't friends. Never had been.

I stood, snatching the jacket back and picking up my backpack, followed by my tray. When I was a few steps away, I turned back and looked at Vic and Maria, who were also cleaning up. Then, to Andy.

"Stop overselling yourself, Andy. It's unbecoming to make promises you can't keep about your appendages." And as several of the players behind him snickered, as I fought the smile on my face, I tossed my foam tray in the trash and walked back out into the hall where, not a month before, I'd been face-first on the floor at the hands of that very boy.

Fuck him and his cluster of jocks.

I can't help the small smile to myself staring at that jersey on the wall - that Fitz was so vastly different than the man sleeping downstairs. The man who'd shared intimate details about himself I'd never expected him to tell me, especially not this soon.

The man who'd been inside of me, like, twelve hours ago.

I swallow, shutting the door to whatever mancave I'd just entered and padding back downstairs, landing in the kitchen. Fuck. I've gotta shake these feelings out of my head. All I want to do is go crawl back in bed and convince him to tell me more.

Instead, when my stomach grumbles, I open the fridge and peer inside. Surprisingly full for someone who seems to not be home that often. I'm not usually a breakfast kind of person, but last night's activities have me feeling like protein is necessary, and I'm able to locate a container of eggs and a fresh package of bacon.

I scavenge in the cabinets and drawers, a boppy playlist echoing from my phone, since I'm not brave enough to fuck with the space-edge sound system and risk scaring the shit out of Queen and country. I finally pull out a frying pan and Roscoe eyes the bacon as I pull it out, piece by piece, and start frying it.

While I'm washing my hands again, I look over the counters in front of me - bare, except for where the box of chocolates from the night before sit with the tablet and a pile of papers.

It's an email printout, pink and white, with the words *FOR FNW TO EDIT - NEEDS OOMF* scrawled across the top in a neat, swirly handwriting. Curious, I dry my hands, and with the bacon starting to sizzle behind me, I look the document over.

I'm nosy. Sue me.

It's an email campaign for Cossette, the cute French venue where Maria tied the knot with her college sweetheart, Tony. Compared to the gorgeous space, the email feels plain - lackluster. It's all words and blocks of white with a few pretty pictures.

I picture the sweeping staircase, the lighted outdoor dance space - the gorgeous chandelier hanging above the reception hall.

Pen. I need a pen.

Twenty minutes and two pans of bacon later, I've got notes scribbled all over the three pages that were stapled together, but now sit atop each other, like one, long email - the way it was meant to be seen.

My degree is in marketing, but visual design has always been my niche. Despite not having a lick of spatial awareness in real life, probably for the lack of athletics I participated in as a child (with good reason), on paper, and in a lot of other things, it's my jam.

I can look at someone and tell you their measurements, or close to it. It's a gift and a curse, because it means I'm the token shopping friend, the "does this look balanced" graphic last look from our social team at work, and the forever fixer of hanging art and stacked shelves.

Probably why this space looks so blasé to me. I need things to occupy my brain.

By the time I pour the scrambled eggs into the pan with some of the residual bacon grease, I've stacked the papers back up and put them where I've found them, like it'll erase the scribbles I'd left all over it.

To the beat of a song that came up in my Spotify suggestions last week, I tip the pan from side to side, trying to get an even coat on the bottom before I ruffle them up - a trick my Nona taught Penny and I when we were kids.

I hum to the catchy song, pointing at Roscoe with my spatula and singing a few lines to him while he stares in utter confusion. Clearly this is something Fitz and Olivia never did. Funny, because Bex gets this show *at least* once a week from either Carla or myself.

I'm twisting my hips from side to side, even singing a few lines out loud, before I dial the heat off and turn with the pan in my hand, using the spatula to fluff the last of the eggs. *Take them off the heat before they're done*, Nona said.

"Finally, I found something you're not good at." Fitz's voice makes me jump, so much that I almost drop the hot pan right on the floor. Luckily, it clatters only a foot down to the island in front of me, and with my heart beating out of my chest, I hold the hand that's not gripping the edge of the counter for dear life up to feel the thuds. Fitz stands in front of me, leaning against the entryway to the kitchen in a white tee shirt and the shorts he'd slept in. That bruise is starting to get deeper in color.

His hair is gloriously mussed, though it's clear he's tried to tame it at least a bit, because there are no chunks sticking up at odd angles like mine had been with sweat and pressure.

"I'm perfectly alright at cooking," I finally manage, and then spin to grab the plates and two forks I'd fished out earlier. When I turn back, he's leaning against the island in front of me, putting his body weight on his hands so his shoulders shrug casually as he smirks. Actually smirks.

Fitz Westfall. Smirking at me, in his kitchen, after walking in on me shaking my ass to the latest addition to my favorites playlist. I swallow, trying to act casual as I scoop the eggs onto the plates next to the bacon already on them.

"I meant the singing." I don't even look up as I snort. Fitz moves to feed Roscoe, who skitters over to the bowl so fast his feet slide on the tile.

"Oh, yeah, no, not one of my great skills in life." Penny got the voice of an angel. I sound like glass in a garbage disposal on a good day. Doesn't keep me from a poorly-timed Adelle rendition or the occasional drive down I-35 belting the *Legally Blonde: The Musical* soundtrack. I put the pan in the sink and sit next to him at the island, where he's settled into one of the padded, backless barstools.

"I'm sure you have many redeeming qualities to make up for it, I've already seen a fair few." He gives me a reassuring smile, and then digs into the food I've made, humming in approval.

"There's quite a few I think you'll find much more worthwhile than singing," I say, more to myself, and then add, "for instance, my lack of gag reflex."

The way he nearly chokes on the bite of egg he's just taken has me covering my mouth to keep an unladylike cackle from escaping again. He gapes at me, his gaze flitting between my crinkled eyes and my hand over my lips. In this light, I can see that his pupils are completely blown.

Welp, that had the desired effect, because there's no way I'm leaving this house without fucking him at least one more time.

You know, to at least have some variation to the things I think about when we're no longer at arm's length from each other.

The thought leaves me a little hollow inside - it feels like the last twenty four hours or so have gone by like days, soaking in each moment with him like it's our last. Maybe it's a force of habit after Mickey?

But the way that Fitz is suddenly eating very, very quickly snaps me back to reality, so that by the time I'm finishing up my plate, he's already standing next to me, looking sort of impatient. He takes our dishes and puts them in the sink, and I almost spot a wince as he looks at the pile over his shoulder, crossing the room to let Roscoe outside. When he turns around, back to the door, his gaze is predatory.

And then he stands in front of me, my head just level with his stomach. I give a wistful glance at his crotch before looking up at him. He's smiling at me like I hung the fucking moon.

It makes my stomach clench in a painful, hungry way, but when he moves his finger along the outline of my jaw, my entire body relaxes into his touch. He uses the pressure to pull me to standing, and I wrap my arms around his waist instinctively.

"I don't know about using that mouth on me this morning," he says honestly, his tongue darting out to lick his bottom lip. "Someday soon, maybe. But I don't think I'd be able to let you work your magic and fuck you here on this counter like I've wanted to since I walked in here." And before I can address the throb between my legs, or argue, he hitches his hands underneath my thighs and plops me on the counter like I weigh nothing.

I try not to scramble, but his reassuring kiss, grabbing frantically at the side of my face and one of my thighs, puts any sense of unease to rest as he pulls that ugly orange shirt over my head followed by the one he's wearing. He brings his lips back down to mine, a finger under the back waistband of my panties until I'm lifting my legs up, just enough for him to pull them off, avoiding giving him another bruise. When we separate, just long enough for him to pull a condom out of his shorts pocket and nearly throw the garment across the room, we're both sucking in breaths.

Putting the dishes in the sink, instead of actually cleaning them, may have actually been the closest Fitz Westfall could get to clearing off a surface in a hurry. A moment of calm before whatever side this was came out, and I am not about to complain.

I scoot towards the end of the cold counter as he pulls out the condom and rolls it on, already hard. I run a patient finger down one of his arms, admiring some of the scratch marks I'd left last night, when he positions himself between my legs.

But instead of easing in, Fitz hitches his fingers under each of my knees and tugs, until he's completely inside of me in a second.

"*Fuck,*" I hiss, my legs wrapping around his waist as he leans down to capture my lips in a frenzied kiss that doesn't give me time to think before he's moving in and out of me. I shift in time with him, letting my mouth trail down his jaw and to the crook of his neck with sloppy, toothy nips that have him tensing inside me like it's driving him nuts.

Proving my thought, he puts a hand on my shoulder and pushes me back just enough to grant him access to my own neck, where he starts kissing up. One hand grabs at my ass, trying to pull me closer, and then migrates between my legs.

When he starts rubbing my clit, I tilt my head back, moaning. It gives him more access, and he laughs softly against my skin, a stark contrast to his punishing movements against my center.

"Kingdom come, right?" I manage, fingers threading through his hair as he sucks on a particularly sensitive spot along my pulseline.

"Kingdom come," he echoes, the hand on my shoulder tracing up, up, until he's holding me so tight against him by the back of my neck that the only room between us is enough for his hand to keep working. "*Damn it, Piper.*"

"What?" It comes out as a half-laugh because I'm struggling to breath, struggling to think because this all just feels *so fucking good.*

So good my toes curl and my knees dig into his hips, my free hand clawing at his lower back while he thrusts into me, I realize, in time with the music still playing from my phone in the corner of the room, as he keeps moving over my neck.

"You've already got me so fucking close," he whispers into my ear, and then licks that spot he found yesterday in a way that makes my back arch against him, my nipples driving into the smattering of hair across his chest.

"Then come for me, baby." I don't know if it's the term of endearment, or the order, but when his vigor increases both with his hips and his hand, it's all I can do to hold onto him to keep from falling back against the cool marble as he freezes and spills out into the condom. My hips buck up to meet him, and a second later, I'm shaking against his chest, spasming as he holds me close while I let my orgasm wash over me, slow and lazy, the only part of this morning that feels that way.

It takes a few ragged breaths and separating from Fitz with a satisfying sticky noise to realize that the buzzing sound I'd been hearing wasn't my imagination.

CHAPTER 34

"Is that Kesha?" Fitz asks seriously, like he hadn't just nearly made me black out and my ass wasn't sticking to his counter with exertion and arousal.

It's my phone ringing, I realize. And my watch vibrating, too, on the other side of the room. And then I glance at the analog clock over Fitz's shoulder.

11:05

Fucking hell.

"The reunion call!"

CHAPTER 35

Fitz

"I'll be right back," Piper says quickly, and then turns to the car door. I reach out and place my hand on her forearm - she looks down at it, and then back up at me, and a smile spreads across her face. "One minute, Fitz, and then I'll come fix your face."

I roll my eyes, but still, she leans forward, giving me a quick peck before exiting the car and speed-walking towards the entrance to her apartment building, impressive, since she's back in those heels. I don't even wince when she closes the car door a little too loudly - at least we're in my sedan, and not the MK.

I lean back against my seat, letting out a deep breath and closing my eyes. What the fuck have I gotten myself into?

I knew I was in for it when she bit back at me that day at the Pine - she'd had a spark like that long before whatever her husband and his family did to her. But seeing her defend herself like that, and call me on my bullshit. Hell, if I hadn't been so shocked, I probably would have asked her out then. But instead, it took a traumatic brain injury, weeks of half-conversations and the urging of Seer, of all people, to finally give her - give us - the night we needed together. And I'm terrified to let it be over.

But when Piper slides back into my car, closing the door behind her a little more gracefully, I open my eyes just in time to see her coming at my face with some sort of teardrop shaped sponge dipped in tan makeup.

"Fuck," I mutter, flinching back, and she laughs.

"Hold still." She shakes her head, and then dabs gently at the spot on my cheek where her knee collided with my face last night. I can tell she sees when it crosses my mind, because her lips turn up at the corner. "Stop making that face, or you're never going to make it to dinner with your family."

"I'm fine with that." She rolls her eyes back at me. Was I looking forward to dinner with my family? No. Did I feel eons better knowing that Piper was covering up the bruise I knew would lead to an endless amount of questions and taunts from my family, namely Fred? Yes. Besides, it's Paula's birthday, and canceling would make me an asshole. An even bigger one, rather. Our relationship wasn't tight - but it was a lot better now that I was an adult and could see where she was coming from, trying to preserve both the unity of our family and her relationship with my dad, growing up. Doesn't mean I understand what she sees in him.

"There." She snaps the lid on a little bottle in her hands, and then holds it up. "This shouldn't budge for at least twelve hours. Just don't wipe at it."

"Come here," I breathe, wrapping a hand around her waist and pulling her across the center console. She chuckles against my mouth as I give her a deep kiss, her hand coming to touch my uninjured cheek. "Sure I can't convince you to come with me?" She shakes her head as she sits back, smoothing out her hair. She must have ditched the rest of her stuff in the house, because the only thing she has with her is the makeup. When she sits back, observing the parking lot around us, she looks like she's distracted.

"As much as I'd love to meet the parents less than 24 hours after the first date, I have some stuff I need to get done around here." She looks at the watch on her wrist.

"You've met my parents," I say softly, and she glances at me. "Well, not really. But they've been at several things we've been at together. I'm sure they'd remember you." Her laugh is a little sad when she responds.

"Not sure if I want them to remember red-haired, brace-face Piper." Before I can shoot back that I liked red-haired, brace-faced Piper, her eyes narrow at a car in front of us. I follow her gaze - it's a lime green Mustang. Yikes. "That's Dylan's car," she says slowly, and then glances back at the apartment entrance near us. "*Mi stai prendendo in giro.*" I'm half-tempted to ask what she just said, but it sounded like something angry and I don't know if I want to know the answer. Especially because I've heard her say something similar around me.

"Are you sure?" She fits me with a look that tells me I'm an idiot. Probably right. The car is pretty distinct.

"I'm sure. The sticker on the back window is for his work parking lot." I ignore the twinge of predatory rage in my chest - she had a life before this, after all. But then it hits me, what she's saying. His car is here. And he's not here with her. Which means - oh shit. I guess I was right on that theory. I'm about to ask her what she's thinking, but she plasters a smile on her face - a little too quickly - and then turns back to me, where it becomes more genuine.

"Do you want me to come in with you?" I ask, squeezing her hand on the armrest. She turns and laces our fingers together, giving me a squeeze back, but shaking her head.

"Thank you, though. Have fun with your family." I wince, and her genuine laugh makes whatever thoughts were going through her head float away. "I'll text you later, ok?" I nod, giving her a final kiss before she turns to open the door.

"Piper?" She swivels back around to face me. "I'm glad we got dragged into doing this reunion together." Piper smiles, probably the shyest smile I've ever seen her give, before she nods, exiting the car. I watch her walk back towards her building, but she looks at me over her shoulder one last time, shaking her head and grinning before she disappears. I resume my position leaning against my headrest and try to figure out how I'm going to function for the rest of the day (Week? Month? Life?) with the images of last night and this morning running through my head.

I manage to make it through most of dinner without giving anything away. Frannie tries to corner me the second I step into the kitchen, handing Paula the gift card I picked up from her favorite spa downtown with a kiss on her cheek, but I steadily avoided the questions by picking up Greta from her high chair and twirling her around the kitchen until she's giggling.

"Someone's in a good mood," Dad says from the couch, and I ignore him, letting her little fingers wrap around my thumb. She's got the signature Westfall hair, but those eyes are her dad's - dark and deep. She's gonna be a stunner one day. And then I'll murder anyone who tries to come near her.

This house is smaller than the one we grew up in. They downsized a year or so ago, when Freddy moved into the house they bought near LSSU's campus so he and his friends could have somewhere nearby, but not terrifying, to live. Arden could be beautiful and fun, but that didn't mean that living in college apartments where shit got stolen all the time was appealing to Fred or Paula and Dad. So once he was situated, they put their house on the market while it was hot and found this townhome a few miles from downtown. Close enough to all of their friends to still be involved with the activities they've been doing for the last twenty-something years. Their dining room is smaller than mine, but the six of us still fit around the table easily, with Greta's high chair between me and Frannie, and I help keep her occupied while Fran cuts up bits of pasta in front of her.

"They're talking about a big merger," Dad says to Frannie, who's stirring some applesauce up and giving a spoonful to Greta at a time. "The other firm is in London, but it could lead to a lot of layoffs for some of the roles that can be condensed."

"What a horrible time to lay people off," Paula adds, sipping at the glass of red in her hand. I'd stuck the bottle on the counter when I came in, after Frannie mentioned when she called earlier that we were having veal. I toast to her comment with my own glass. There's never really a great time to lay people off, but I don't say that out loud. "But enough about sad things. It's my birthday." She takes another sip, and when she looks at me over her glass, her eyes are sparkling. "Frannie mentioned you had a date last night."

When my head whips to face my sister, she's vigorously cutting at the veal in front of her, though she's got a smirk on her face. Traitor.

And that's when a big glob of applesauce hits the side of my face, running down my cheek and onto the dress shirt.

"Oopsie," Freddy deadpans, and I kick him under the table.

"Oopsie," Greta echoes, tiny hands shaking and a bubble forming at her lips. I can't be mad at that. Clearing my throat, I wipe at my face with my napkin, and am about to tell Paula the absolute bare minimum, but I see the horrified look on Frannie's face.

Fuck.

"Delmonico knock you around?" Freddy asks, again in a flat voice, and it takes everything in me not to hurl my plate at him for both the implication, and dropping her name at the table. Because as fairly certain as I am that neither Paula nor my father will remember Piper or her family, the idea of having to sit through an inquisition is enough to make my stomach roll.

"No," I say clearly, downing the last of my glass in one gulp, "it was an accident."

"Delmonico?" Paula says from her spot across from Freddy. "You went out with one of the Delmonico girls?"

"Do you know who she is?" Dad asks, putting his whiskey glass down on the table. Paula nods, and I can't quite read the look on her face.

"Her mother is in the Female Litigators Association with me," she explains, and then looks to my Dad. Ah. I forgot that Piper's mom is also a lawyer. "Will you grab me another glass?" Dad nods, setting his glass down and pushing back from the table. She waits until he's out of the room to continue, and I'm a little apprehensive when she turns to me. "It's Piper, right? The younger one?"

"Well Penny is married," Frannie adds quietly.

"So was Piper," Paula says, and that shuts Fran up.

"Are you and her mom...friends?" I ask slowly, and the implications of that run through my head a million miles a minute. Jesus Christ.

"We've gone out for drinks a few times." She nods towards Frannie. "I think the last time we saw the two of them together was right after Frannie's graduation from LSSU."

"You saw them together?" I ask my sister and she shrugs, wiping down Greta's face.

From the kitchen, my dad calls, "This bottle is almost empty! I'm going down to get another."

"We ran into them at the mall." Frannie gives me a small, sad smile. "I think that was right before the funeral. She looked so different from what I remembered, Will. Hollow." I feel a lump in my throat forming, and I try not to picture the girl I'd seen in that obituary picture - sure, she'd looked like Piper, but having looked back at it a few days ago, she wasn't herself. Wasn't bright and buzzing with energy. Like being with Mickey had taken the life right out of her, too.

"That family put her through hell, Will," Paula says, crossing her arms over her chest tightly.

"I know." She looks concerned, but I can't tell whether it's for me, or for Piper.

"I don't want to see either of you get hurt again." Her lips purse, and for the first time in a long, long time, I see her eyes shine.

But then a door closes below us, and she shakes her head, turning to look at her granddaughter, face softening.

"I think after this, Mimi is going to get you some cake, hm?" Greta giggles, stuffing a piece of pasta into her mouth, and I try to sink further in my seat as everyone observes me. For once, I'm thankful for Dad's interruption as he brings in Paula's glass, half full, and a freshly opened, similar bottle.

By the time Frannie, Freddy and I sit down in the living room several drinks and a piece of cake each later, Paula has shooed us out of the kitchen so she can organize the leftovers, and Dad has ventured outside with their labradoodle, Lincoln, for their evening walk.

"Seer and Chloe seem to think things went well last night," Frannie says, curling her legs underneath her and sipping at the wine in her hand. Greta plays with a set of blocks on a mat at her feet.

"I didn't realize the whole Scooby gang would be there." I glance at the kitchen over her shoulder, wondering how much Paula can hear from here.

"You went to *Menagerie*," Freddy points out, lifting his vodka soda as if to say *your fault, dumbass*.

"Yeah, but Seer, Mateo and José in one night? Plus Chloe?" I shake my head, leaning back into the couch. "I'm lucky all their bullshitting didn't scare her off."

"Not everyone is as fun-averse as you." Freddy smirks when he says it, but I eye him. This, coming from the guy who gave up soccer in middle school because he made the mistake of researching sports related injuries for a school paper. Sure, dude could party like no other around people he liked. But put him in a social situation with a bunch of strangers? We were exactly the same, on that front.

Frannie shrugs, scrolling through her phone in her hand. "José likes to be there when a couple of them are working, that's why he told his friends he'd do the sound gig. Mostly for fun-"

"Wait." I lean forward. "A couple of who?" Frannie's eyes narrow.

"Uh, his kids?" She says it like I'm dumb, but I feel dumb, and confused. "Seer and Mateo?"

"Seer isn't José's kid," I reason, sitting my glass on the table in front of me. "Why does everyone keep calling her that?" I'd heard the offhanded comments they'd made on Saturday, but assumed it was a joke, given that José had been clearly working with Seer on her cooking skills.

"His son is married to Seer's brother." Freddy looks at me over his glass, his face pinched together. "They got married at Pearson Place." One of our more modern venues on the west side of Fort Worth, I knew it well, helped open it a few years back. But José's son?

"Mateo isn't-"

"Not Mateo, you loser." Frannie snorts into her glass. "Jesse." *Jesse.* Fuck.

It clicks. Jesse, José's stepson. Jesse, whose mom had married José when we were in college.

Frannie turns her phone towards me, and it's a picture clearly taken at Jesse's wedding. He and the blonde next to him, a very serious juxtaposition to Jesse's dark features, were wearing coordinating gray suits, while the surrounding group was in shades of black and purple. In the crowd, I immediately spot Seer, half a foot shorter than everyone else, and Frannie, just pregnant enough that I could tell. With them was a smiling Chloe, Mateo, José's daughter Andrea, her husband Caesar, and Jesse's twin sister, Jasmine.

"That's how Seer and I met," Frannie says softly, probably because she can see the shock in my face at taking in the whole group. I didn't even realize she and Seer were that good of friends, or that Seer was close to José, until a few weeks ago, so seeing her as such an integral part of that group is surprising. "Remember, Jesse and Mateo lived down the street from us in college?" I nod - Dad had done the same thing for her that he'd done for Freddy years later, bought a house for her and her friends to rent out. "When that last shitbag roommate moved out," she starts, but Paula cuts in from the kitchen.

"Shitbag is an understatement," she calls over the sound of running water, and I wonder how long she's been listening. "I still think she sold your laptop on Craigslist."

"ANYWAYS," Frannie rolls her eyes, "Jesse said I should talk to Seer. José and Athena were dating by then, and Athena is on cast with Seer at Greensleeves. She's basically Seer and Liam's second mom. Seer was even Andrea's nanny for a while." She leans back, locking her phone and taking a deep sip of her drink, her eyes crinkling like she's remembering something bad. But when she says "And then shit hit the fan," I know exactly what she's talking about.

And it all falls into place.

"Is what happened to Seer in college why she's sober now?" I ask slowly, trying to be delicate, because I remember Frannie being affected by it then, now realizing how much more it probably did if she and Seer are still so close.

"You mean being brutally sexually assaulted and then thrown under the bus by LSSU?" Frannie asks, eyebrows raised, swirling her glass in one hand. I rear back at her bluntness, somewhat unlike her, and Fred chokes on the sip he's just taken. She reaches over and gives him a rough pat on the back, which nearly makes his drink spill over the edge of his glass. In my pocket, my phone starts buzzing, and I look down at my watch to see a number I don't have saved across the screen. I swipe it away - spam.

"And you all say I don't know how to be tactful." He wipes the back of his hand over his mouth.

"We love you, sweetie," Paula says as she settles in between him and Fran, "but tact isn't even in your function manual." He gives her an eye roll, but she looks at me. "What Seer went through was horrible." She sips at her glass, looking nearly identical to her daughter next to her. "Honestly, if she got along with Piper, it's probably because they have a lot of similar trauma experiences." Frannie snorts next to her, but it's humorless.

"Yeah, being blamed for the trauma you endured by the people who put you through it," my sister says.

Before I can even dig into that, my watch buzzes on my wrist.

UNKNOWN NUMBER
Answer your fucking phone, Fitz.

I stare down at the screen. Clearly someone wants to get a hold of me. I push up from the couch, and Frannie eyes me.

"Be right back," I mutter, and step out into the hall, far enough that no one can hear when Alex's voice on the other end of the line screams over the sound of a crying baby when I answer.

"What the fuck did you do, Westfall?"

CHAPTER 36

Piper

I wasn't really paying attention the first time I entered my apartment today. I was a woman on a mission - help Fitz cover up the one mark I'd left on him that was visible in the outfit he was wearing.

But I have every intention of figuring out what the fuck is going on when I gingerly open the door for the second time, ready to sneak in and Nancy Drew the shit out of this place.

That is, until I nearly run face-first into Dylan. And when I look up at him, eyes narrowed, he knows he's fucked up.

Truthfully, I've suspected something like this may be going on since that day he showed up at the apartment unannounced. When Fitz had left and I'd walked out to see Dylan and Carla talking on the couch, and she looked defensive as hell, my radars were going off left and right. But he'd said he'd figured out what he needed to, and then left quickly, leaving Vic and Kyle to share a confused glance across the bar.

But, naive little Piper was hoping that the rigorous honesty part of the program was in full force and that if something had happened between the two of them, they'd at least tell me about it.

"Oh hey, P," he says, trying to act casual, and I nearly laugh in his face. "I was just grabbing-"

Before he can say anything else, I point past him at the couch. "Sit."

"Really, I'm good, I just needed-"

"Fucking sit, Anton, before I sic Bex on you." I know it's not much of a threat, but he must see the heat blazing in my eyes because he turns, stepping towards the couch with his head hung like a scolded puppy. "Carla Denise Montgomery." I say it loud enough that I know she's heard me, and I lean against the kitchen counter. A second later, her door creaks open, and Bex comes running down the hall at full force. I pick her up as she squirms against me, trying to lick at my face, sniffing at what I'm sure is Roscoe all over me.

Carla's head peaks out around the corner, and she glances at me and smiles, before seeing Dylan on the couch. Then her smile drops, and heat floods up her face.

"Piper, we were-"

"Sit." I make the same gesture I had at Dylan, and to her credit, she doesn't try to argue, just plops down on the couch next to him. Bex squirms out of my arms and I let her run to Dylan, who scoops her up.

Somehow, that just makes me more mad, and I feel myself loose a string of curses in Italian under my breath before I try to take a deep breath. "How long?"

"Since Christmas," Carla blurts, and then Dylan gives her a look I can't quite read. I sit on one of the barstools and look at them.

"Four months? You've been fucking for *four months* and didn't think it would be a good idea to tell me?"

"We're not *fucking*," Dylan nearly sneers, and I rear back, arms crossing. Then, he puts his hand on top of Carla's on her knee, and gives it a squeeze.

And then they share a look that makes my little romantic heart pitter patter. Shit.

"We've been seeing each other, trying to figure out if this is a good idea." Carla's mouth twists to one side. "We didn't want to hurt you, Piper."

"I'm more hurt that you weren't honest with me, C." I look back down at their joined hands, my own coming up to rub my temples. "Did you really think I wouldn't be able to handle the idea of the two of you together?" The look they share tells me no, they didn't think I could. "Christ, y'all, we're not 14. You can fu-be with whoever you want." I catch myself, but instead of irked, they both look surprised. "Clearly, the problem was me, and not Dylan. I'm the one that lost my shit."

"You're not a problem," Dylan says in a voice that makes a knot form in my throat. He looks at Carla, and it gets tighter. "I told myself we shouldn't be together, at first because it was her first year in the program." Carla smiles up at him, and even though she's more casual than usual for being around someone she's dating, she's basically glowing. "But then we got together and I didn't want to fuck things up with both of you in one epic move." I snort, but he continues. "I've been in love with her for a while, I think." I feel my jaw drop slightly, as he squeezes her hand, and she just gazes up at him. Clearly I'd been misreading the signs about her interest in Kyle - or maybe, the closure from realizing being with her childhood crush wasn't going to happen pushed this into a more tangible category.

"I love you too." And then, like they're not sitting right in front of me, he leans down and pecks her on the lips. I make a retching noise that has Bex jumping off the couch and running back to me, and by the time Carla is laughing at my reaction, Bex is in my arms. "Fuck off. You have a hickey on your neck, by the way." My hand flies up to my neck, the side Fitz had been mauling this morning, and narrow my eyes at her.

"So do you, bitch."

When I sit in my bed a while later, armed with a giant water bottle to rehydrate from the night before, and a fajita bowl in hand, I'm able to sift through the messages I'd either missed or ignored this morning in an attempt to enjoy the last few hours before I needed to go home.

KYLE HOFFMAN
I'm sorry, are you wearing a UT shirt?

And then in the same thread, probably sent just a minute later.

KYLE HOFFMAN
Wait, are you and Fitz in the same room?

Ah, I was wondering if he'd noticed. Of everyone else on the call, he was the only one who knew, besides Carla, that anything had developed between Fitz and me.

PIPER DELMONICO
Yes, we were together, yes I was wearing his shirt.

He responds immediately.

KYLE HOFFMAN
!!!
I got the details from Vic. Naughty, naughty, Delmonico!

I roll my eyes, deciding not to poke that curious bear any further and scrolling through the rest. Mom. Penny and Alex's group chat. I texted our other chat after our reunion call and gave them a brief "We had a great time, getting ready to head home shortly."

Only Penny responded, with a middle finger emoji.

Finally my eyes land on a text I must have missed yesterday, in the frenzy of getting ready for the date.

BETHANI PEREZ
Hey, I went to check in on Facebook and it looks like we're not friends anymore.

And then, when I didn't immediately respond.

BETHANI PEREZ
Honestly, I'm disappointed in you, Piper. I knew we'd drifted apart, but you didn't have to cut us out of your life. Mickey wouldn't have wanted that.

The first text made my heart jump in my throat. The second? My blood is boiling.

PIPER DELMONICO
I don't have social media anymore, because it was becoming too difficult to navigate with the harassment. I'm sorry to disappoint -

I stop myself. Why the fuck did I feel the need to apologize for disappointing Bethani of all people.

PIPER DELMONICO
I don't have social media anymore, because it was becoming too difficult to navigate with the harassment. I also don't speak to anyone who has contact with the Davis' anymore. After seeing very clearly how you both felt about my bringing Chase to your party, I think it was clear whose side you picked.

I click send before I can overthink it, just as Dylan pops his head in my door. "I'm actually heading out this time, I'll see you at fam dinner in a few weeks?" I tilt my head. Dylan, at fam dinner? "Carla invited me. I hope that's ok."

CHAPTER 36

"Oh," I stutter, shaking my head. Fam dinner was a sort of tradition we'd had since Mickey's funeral - a way of getting all of us who'd been through the trenches together in one room, to see each other - to support each other. Carla and Vic occasionally brought people they were dating - but only if it was serious. "Sure, of course. The more the merrier. Just be prepared for the eight zillion questions Mom will have for you once she finds out you and Carla are together."

He shrugs, but his smile is bright, like he doesn't care as long as they're there together. Bleh.

"I'll take what I can get. Talk to you later?" I nod, waving him off as Bex tries to follow him out the door, but he shuts it behind him. My phone buzzes, and I feel my heart lurch when I see the screen.

BETHANI PEREZ
I never had contact with Mickey's family. That was Ken. And yes, we had a type of feeling seeing you move on, but we don't blame you at all. My mom died, and my dad moved on. I get how that feels. But we never judged you for it. And I applaud you for putting yourself first. We all need to do that.
And picking sides? Would you like to elaborate on that?

Whoa. Lots to unpack. First of all, lie. I'd seen the mutual friendship myself, blue and white in shiny pixels on Alex's phone screen. Secondly, "a certain way?" There was a whole lot of pandering going on and not a lot of owning up to the shit they actually did.

PIPER DELMONICO
It felt like I'd spent months trying to keep me and Mickey afloat, and then to see either of you even give them the time of day made me sick. And I was dating Chase. It wasn't like he was some rando.

BETHANI PEREZ
Ken said he wasn't ready to meet Chase yet...is that an issue? I remember this conversation.
You can't blame Ken for talking to Mickey's family. That was his best friend. Sit in your seat sis.

I snort. Actually snort out loud reading that last one. Best friend? *Really*? But the texts keep rolling in.

BETHANI PEREZ
That was Mickey's parents that just lost their son, they deserve the time of day. Become a parent and see how it is.
Think about that for a second. Ken and I have never done anything wrong to you. Relax.
I was just checking on you, but nevermind.

Angry tears start streaming down my face as I stare at my screen.

Become a parent and see how it is? The words hit me like a punch to the gut. Bex, as if sensing my discomfort, snuggles into my side as I use shaky hands to write a long response. Probably too long, but I can't stop my fingers from moving.

PIPER DELMONICO
Ok. It took you this long to realize I'd removed you from my life. You don't get to come in and berate me. I don't have kids because my husband died from cancer. I never said his family didn't go through something. I said I spent months keeping us afloat because I did. They abandoned their precious son and you two saw every day of that, down to that horrible funeral. So don't get on your high horse and try to tell me I'm on the wrong side here. I'm working on trying to put the pieces back together that they broke. I wish you all nothing but the best but I'm not going to get dragged into this again.

I wait until the word "delivered" shows underneath my message, and then I go into the contact and hit block.

I don't realize sobs are wracking my body until I'm throwing my phone across my bed and burying my face in one of my throw pillows, letting out a long, muffled scream.

Fuck her. Fuck her and fuck the Davis' and fuck every single person who stood by and watched it and then claimed that I was the one overreacting.

I gave up my entire life to take care of a man who cheated on me, lied to me, I

CHAPTER 36

married a man I knew had been unfaithful because I fucking loved him so much. And his family knew all of that - and still chose the woman who was, to all of our knowledge at the time, lying about having his child.

They chose a pretty dream over a sad reality and left me to deal with the consequences.

I hear Carla knock on my door, but when she asks if I'm ok, I just call a quick "yeah," and bury my head again, holding Bex close. I let the sobs run through me until I'm only hiccuping, and across the bed, I feel my phone vibrate. I look at my watch - and see that Fitz is calling.

I answer on the third ring with a garbled "Hello?"

"Hey." His voice is soft - too soft - and it makes another sob come out. "Have you been crying? Piper, what's going on?" I sniffle, wiping at my face and trying to pull myself together.

"Yeah, I'm ok. Just, uh -" I pause, and glance at myself in the mirror. Fuck, I'm a mess. "Can I call you back?"

"Alex just called me," he says, and my heart drops. "Wanting to know what I did to make you so upset that you'd locked yourself in your room?"

Carla. That *snitch*.

As quickly as I can without tossing Bex across the room, I stand and plow through my bedroom door until I'm at the entry to Carla's room. She looks up from her perch, cross legged on her farmhouse-chic comforter, and tilts her head at me. Her eyes narrow when she sees my face, but I narrow mine right back.

"Fitz, I'm sorry Alex called you instead of talking to me first," I say with a pointed look at my roommate. "Carla knows better than to tell people things without getting the full story first." Her sheepish look down at her lap tells me she knows exactly what she did.

"You're standing in her room about to yell at her, aren't you?"

"Yep."

"Call me later and fill me in?"

"Yep." Before I've even hung up, I pick up a throw pillow from the chair next to me and throw it at her with as much force as I can muster. I miss, and it knocks over an empty water bottle on the floor. "Well, that's par for the course this week."

CHAPTER 37

Fitz

PIPER DELMONICO
Fuckkkk what kind of detergent do you use?

FITZ WESTFALL
Uh, I'm not sure. I have a laundry service. Why?

PIPER DELMONICO
Of course you do. I'm not sure, I've just been super itchy on my arms. Probably nothing - I'm allergic to dogs and it may just be my body getting used to Roscoe.

FITZ WESTFALL
You're allergic to dogs and you have Bex?

PIPER DELMONICO
I found out I was allergic well after I had Bex. In the grand scheme of things, a little itch is worth it for her. Even if her gas does rival most of the Alamo's team on a bad day.

CHAPTER 37

"What a twatwaffle." I look up from my desk to see Seer and my sister standing in the doorway - three days after our family dinner for Paula's birthday, and I'd managed to all but avoid conversations about Piper with Frannie. I could tell that was where this conversation was headed the second they darkened my door.

"You know this is my office, right, not Fran's?" I ask, setting down the stack of papers in my hands and looking at both women. Couldn't be more opposite, but the way Seer sauntered over to my desk and sat down at the chair in front was eerily similar to the way my siblings did.

"I figured we're besties and all, now. You know, since I charmed your girl." She gives me a grin and picks up an expensive pen - a gift from one of our corporate partners, off the edge of my desk. I reach over and try to yank it back, but she rolls her eyes and puts it back down before I say anything. I adjust it back to where I had it. "But seriously. Piper's friend sounds like a twatwaffle."

I eye Seer, and then Frannie, who stands behind her friend, her purse over her shoulder, and shrugs at me. Clearly she'd shared what I'd told her on Monday, very briefly, about Alex's call and the texts Piper had received after getting home.

"I don't know that they've been friends for a long time," I counter, gesturing between us, "just like we aren't-"

"Ah ah ah." Seer holds up a finger, cutting me off, and I sit back in my chair, crossing my arms. "I came here to further help your relationship with the girl who might as well be a fairy princess to your brooding villain. Or do you not want my assistance anymore?" I glare between Frannie and Seer, unsure of who I'm more irritated with, but give a resigned sigh.

"Lay it on me." She grins, digging in her bag, just as ginormous as Piper's, until she pulls out a pink velvet box the size of a sheet of paper with an elastic bow around it. When I eye them, Frannie tilts her chin up at it, her curtain of red hair shaking.

"We may have done some additional wrapping to help sweeten the deal," she says casually, and I narrow my eyes, taking the box from Seer and sliding off the bow and top of the box.

Nestled inside is a laser-cut gold and white invitation, and when I fold it open, I stare up at the women in front of me.

I don't know that I've ever been more grateful for Seer as I am in this moment, but the urge I have to pull her into a tight hug is serious enough that I restrain myself. Baby steps. Don't want to give Frannie a heart attack.

"Thank you," I manage, slipping the lid and bow back on. I can already imagine Piper standing at her kitchen counter, opening this box once I have it delivered. Preferably with Carla recording her reaction, but that could be negotiated. "You two are lifesavers."

"Just don't let anyone in on the fact that I'm not a completely heartless bitch," Seer replies with a shrug, and I glance between her and Frannie, waiting for my sister to defend her friend's character.

But Frannie isn't listening. She's eying the stack of papers underneath the box.

"Is that my Cosette email?" Frannie reaches out her hand, and I shuffle things around until I'm able to hand it to her. "You finally gave me some usable notes," she says after a minute. "These are really good. I'd never thought about theming the package tiers like the chandelier."

"Uh, actually." My hand finds the back of my neck. "I didn't do those." She looks at me, and then down to her friend, who is observing her. "Piper may have done them while she was over this weekend."

Frannie makes a face like she's going to vomit, just for the briefest of moments, but then she shakes her head, looking back down at the papers in front of her.

"Is she looking for a job?"

Piper

FITZ WESTFALL
Why do you want to know who my childhood crush is?

PIPER DELMONICO
Don't be a party pooper and just answer the question.

FITZ WESTFALL
Excuse me, I hold almost exclusively parties for a living and have never been a "party pooper."
Fine, who was your childhood crush?

CHAPTER 37

PIPER DELMONICO
Easy. Nick Jonas.

FITZ WESTFALL
Not even a second of hesitation there.

PIPER DELMONICO
What can I say, I have a thing for curls. (:
Now tell me!!!

FITZ WESTFALL
See, this was my plan all along. Get your answers out of you and share nothing in return.

PIPER DELMONICO
Jackass

FITZ WESTFALL
Strategic

I stare at the empty chair on my computer screen for a solid two minutes before my therapist, Ava, slides back into view, apologizing profusely. There's something about a therapist with stress-induced IBS that can relate to you on a cellular level to set you at ease.

"Back to what I was saying," she says with a half-laugh, her face coming fully into focus. "It sounds like things are compounding for you, between this new relationship with - Fitz, was it? - right, and the situation with Bethani. I'd also really like to talk about how things are going at work. Last time we spoke, you mentioned that you were concerned about really being able to express yourself."

I nod, looking down at my hands in my lap, where I was holding a Dr. Pepper just below the line of my desk. It was my third of the day, which wasn't unusual - but paired with the venti, triple shot Starbucks I'd started my day with, it's safe to say I'm extra caffeinated and feeling a little uneasy.

"To be honest," I start, using the can as the only excuse not to nervously pick at my fingers, "I've been feeling sort of off for a while." Ava nods, typing away on the keyboard in front of her. "Maybe it's because we're starting to come up on some anniversaries - or just with everything going on personally."

"With Fitz?" Ava asks, and I give her a shrug - still an honest answer, if not one I don't know how to quite articulate. "Is this feeling something that's affecting your work life, or do you think it's the other way around?"

Damn. Right in the feels.

I let her words sink in. Truthfully, there were a lot of things that had me sitting on the edge of my seat lately, one of which was Fitz. But looking back at it - I'd come up with some of my best designs in the last few months. Inspired, beautiful pieces that I'd been told were too much.

I'd made them, because for the first time in a long time, I'm not afraid to be bold and big and gregarious and all of the things that had been attached to so much negativity in my life before. Because the way Fitz had looked at me Saturday night, and again Sunday morning (ok, and then again right before he took me home), that made me feel like bold was the best thing in the world.

When I'm finally off my therapy visit, I step out into the hall to see Carla at the counter munching on a bowl of cereal, Bex waiting patiently at her feet for anything she may drop. Without looking up from her phone, she gestures with her spoon to a box on the counter, pink and velvet with a big satin bow.

"That came for you while you were in therapy." She gives me a glance over her screen. "I managed to snag it from the delivery guy before he could ring the doorbell. I swear, that sign is useless." She goes back to her bowl, but I stare down at the package on the counter.

I slip the small envelope from beneath the bow on the front and slide the notecard out. I recognize it almost immediately - the same kind that had been sent with the champagne and chocolates before.

Consider this my belated birthday present. Looking forward to having you on my arm, if you'll join me.
— FNW

"Any idea what the N stands for?" I nearly jump out of my skin when I realize Carla is standing behind me, so close that her question sends goosebumps up my arms. I smack her a little harder than necessary, and shoo her to the side so I can have my full elbow range to slide the bow off the box.

"You're the one who's been cyberstalking everyone for this reunion," I counter, and when I lift the lid, whatever comment either of us had poised next falls to the wayside.

Nestled on a bed of gray tissue paper is a laser-cut gold lace invitation. I pick it up oh-so-delicately, watching the way the overhead lights bounce off the metallic front. I open the tri-fold flaps, and read the playful script font.

You are cordially invited to...
Fae League of Fort Worth's
Annual Charity Gala
Saturday...

The rest of the card details the location, which I immediately recognize as a WHG venue, along with times, dress code, RSVP information...

I don't even take a second to breathe before I'm fishing my phone out of my pocket. Fitz answers on the first ring.

"I take it you got my present, then?" his low voice asks, and the reaction in my body is nearly visceral. I hadn't heard his voice since we were on the phone together Sunday night, and all it's making me want to do is hop in my car and find myself quickly in his bed, preferably with little-to-no-clothing.

"Mhmmm," is all I can manage as I take the invitation and walk into my room, shutting the door with my foot and falling back onto the bed with a satisfied sigh. "You really know how to woo a girl."

"Well, I had some help." Mentally, I wonder which of my friends - or his friends, I guess - helped him pull this off, but instead I just let him continue. "I figured you'd love an excuse to get dressed up - uh, more than normal."

"It's almost like you've known me for more than half my life," I quip, watching the gold reflect lace cutouts on my dark canopy curtains.

"I have a feeling we're just getting to know each other, Piper." A smile spreads across my mouth. His voice gets a little quieter when he asks "Scale of one to ten, how excited are you?"

"Are you in public?"

"Yeah, I'm at the *Monarch* at a late budget meeting."

"You answered your phone."

"You called." My mouth goes dry and I try to swallow the lump in my throat.

When Mickey and I started dating, there would be days where I wouldn't hear from him, maybe at all. I would call, and he'd always respond with a *What's up?* text instead of actually letting me hear his voice. I later found out that a lot of those days and nights were spent with other women - women I'd forgiven him for, even married him, after.

Fitz had stepped out of a meeting, likely one that included his father and maybe his sister, to speak to me.

"Piper?" I realize I haven't responded, and shake my head to clear my comparison.

"I'll show you how excited I am next time I see you."

"*Damn it*, Piper." It comes out as a hoarse whisper, and I laugh.

"Go back to your meeting, I'll talk to you later." And before he can try to coax anything else out of me, which will likely result in nothing less than a raging hard on, I hang up, setting my phone and the invite next to me on the bed and staring up at the ceiling.

Fuck. Fitz Westfall, the romantic.

CHAPTER 38

Fitz

"Oh, come on!" Piper screams at the TV, and if I didn't know that Mateo was alive and well across town, I would have sworn she was channeling his spirit. Completely pissed, face contorted, fistful of M&Ms halfway to her mouth. This was how he typically looked watching college ball in this room. I was not expecting the same reaction from this woman watching the latest Jennifer Lawrence horror movie.

I try to hide my surprised laugh in a cough, but the side-eye she gives me tells me it absolutely didn't work, so I just reach for the bag in her lap and pull out my own handful of candy.

I'd given myself more flack than I probably needed for asking her to hang out tonight - so soon after our last get together, and not even a full week to digest everything properly. But I don't feel like I need it, need a breather, from her, from this.

I'd half expected her to suggest we go out and do something like couples do on Friday nights. Bowling. Movies. Couples? I'd swallowed a little hard at the thought. We weren't there yet, as much as it already felt like it to me.

But Piper's text after lunch had been "going to a 6:30 meeting and then heading your way. Pls have snacks. Bad, bad day."

So, my first quest was wracking my brain trying to remember what all had been on her nightstand that first time I went over to her house. The second had been to see what horror movies were available for streaming - or purchase, because my gut told me she may have seen all of the streaming options already.

"*Questi fottuti idioti.*" She says it under her breath, just loud enough that I can hear, and I give her hip a squeeze where my hand holds her firmly to my side. Her eyes break away from the wall just enough to give me a wry smile. "Just because you can't speak Italian doesn't mean I can't use it around you."

"I think that's exactly what it means," I counter, "but I know enough Spanish and French to know what *fottuti idioti* means, and I agree. Fucking idiots." She nods her head in agreement, and watches the screen, but every once in a while, I catch her looking in my direction. I don't let on - just run my thumb in smooth circles on the skin where her oversized sweatshirt meets the leggings that were so tight, they looked painted on when she stood in my doorway with Bex in one arm and her purse in the other. She'd changed out bags again - this one is a bright yellow on par with some of the ones Frannie sports. Equally as gigantic, too.

By the time the movie ends in a blood-curdling scream, Piper's halfway leaning in front of me, with my chin resting on the top of her head. Bex has curled herself between us under the blanket and Roscoe is under our feet.

"Do you want to talk about why today was such a bad day?" I ask, not moving as the previews for another movie start to play in front of us. I run my free hand up and down the side of her arm, and she shivers in a way that makes the rest of my body immediately react.

Not the time, man.

Piper's long sigh has me chewing the inside of my cheek. "Just work stuff."

"Same stuff as it has been, or?" She leans back, making eye contact with me, and I see the confusion in her face. "You mentioned the other night that your boss doesn't totally understand your work."

"Oh, right." Piper shifts until she's facing me, leaning her body against the back of the couch and propping her head up on an elbow. "Brianna is just..." She shakes her head, closing her eyes for a moment. Bex burrows out from her spot, clearly not happy with the movement, and Piper absently strokes her head when she opens her eyes again. "It's hard to try to tone myself down when I've spent so long trying to figure out who I am."

"And who is that?" She absently wipes at her nose - free of makeup, but still a fucking knockout with her dark curls wild around her neck, the top half pulled back.

"Piper 5.0," she says with a shrug. I feel my eyebrows knit together.

"Not even a 2? Just jumping straight into 5?" She laughs, the first time I've heard her do so since last weekend, and it makes my stomach jolt a little bit.

"There have been a lot of different iterations of Piper," she says simply, and then reaches out to pull my hand back to her hip. Without questioning, I start the circles on her soft skin again. "1.0 was the Piper you met first. 2.0 is post-junior year and all the shit with Andy." I try to hide my cringe by turning my face towards Bex between us. "3.0 is college and Mickey's Piper."

"What was she like?" I ask, and Piper pauses, her eyes flitting down to where my hand connects with her skin. "We've managed to stay clothed, but the way her big eyes keep looking at me like I'm a steak and she's a woman starved tells

CHAPTER 38

me she's having the same thoughts I am.

"A party girl." Piper shrugs. "I was everyone's friend, but not really anyone's favorite. I was the designated driver and the one who brought all the hot girls with her." She stops herself, like she was going to continue down a path that I suspected may have been self-deprecating, but she catches it. *Good.* "And then I met Mickey."

Ok. *Not so good.*

"We don't have to talk about this if you don't want to," she says softly, and I meet her gaze, which is apologetic. I shake my head.

"No. It's a part of your life. Part I wasn't there for." I give her hip a squeeze. "I want to know." She breathes out like she's been holding it in for a while.

"We met on Tinder, did you know that?" I shake my head - though I'm not surprised. While I've ventured onto the app a few times since my divorce, it was nowhere near the use my friends made of it while rotating between bars in Austin during college. "We didn't really publicize that, it would have given his family more ammunition against us." Her eyes tip towards my ceiling, and I can tell that even mentioning his family has her guard up. "That version of Piper was so..." She shudders. "Basic."

I can't help the surprised laugh that bubbles out of my mouth. Of all the words I thought she may use to describe herself, basic is not one of them.

"A basic Piper?" I touch my free hand to my chest, and she bats it away.

"I was! Seriously. I just...I wanted to fit in so badly, and once Mickey paid an ounce of attention to me and I was part of this little group that Alex, Nolan, Brett, and Penny had, I basically did anything I could to stay a part of that. And I know, *I know* that Alex and Penny would never have abandoned me if we hadn't worked out." She swallows, tilting her head to the side a bit as she glances around the room, still propped up on one elbow. "I did whatever it took to stay with Mickey, even if it meant looking past shit I should have walked away from."

"And what about Piper 4.0?" I ask, trying to get her away from a subject that was clearly touching a nerve. Her expression immediately changed and she let out a dry laugh.

"You mean raging drunk Piper?" She snorts to herself, and Bex starts, staring up at us. Piper just continues to scratch her head. "Piper 4.0 is a time in my life I'd love to forget."

"What was that saying?" I touch the spot on her stomach where I know the words are etched, and a small smile forms on her lips.

"It took a lot of changes to get to this version of Piper, Fitz." And when she says my name, so close to hers, something jumps in my chest. I feel my lips tip up at the corners. "What?" she asks, and I use my free hand to scoop Bex away, pulling Piper into my lap until she's straddling me. She makes a surprised yelp that has Roscoe jumping up, ready to save her, but I wave him away.

From every angle, Piper is gorgeous, but this may be one of my favorites. Because even though I can tell she's a little uncomfortable, which I'll have to dig into later, the way her hands grip onto the back of the couch on either side of my head tells me she enjoys being in a position of power. And I'm more than willing to let her be.

"I know this isn't the same version of you I knew all those years ago," she says softly as my hands travel to her stomach, across the bare skin below her sweatshirt, up, up. My eyes widen when I reach her bare chest, and she lets out a musical little laugh. "Piper 5.0 was tired of wearing a bra for the day." With her sweatshirt nearly around her neck, I cup each breast, taking one into my mouth and sucking on it until she lets out a little satisfied moan. I do the same to the other, until she's rocking in my lap against the erection I'm sporting between us.

With more grace than I'd expected, she lifts the sweatshirt over her head until she's topless on my lap, and I feel the grin on my face before she even reacts to it.

"I approve of this new Piper," I mutter as she arches her back, pulling the clip out of her hair and letting her curls fall around her face.

Goddess. This woman was a fucking Grecian goddess, sitting on my lap, moving against my full hard-on like she owns me.

Maybe she does.

"New Piper just remembered something." Her eyes find mine, and I know I'm in for it with the fire blazing behind them. "And how could I have forgotten? How silly of me." She trails one of her fingernails down my arm, eliciting the shudder she knew would happen, before leaning forward and letting me bury my face in her chest.

"Silly," I echo, though it comes out a little garbled against her nipple. I have no idea what she's forgotten, but it can't be more interesting than this.

"I told you I'd show you just how excited I am for that gala." I rip my attention away from the sight in front of me to look at her face, which is mischievous and a little scary. She throws the blanket back to the other side of the couch and uses the leather back behind me to scoot away, until she's standing between my legs.

Behind her, previews are still playing on my wall, but I don't see any of them as she braces herself on the low coffee table and slips out of those skin tight leggings.

Any restraint I've had immediately goes out the window, with her silhouette outlined by the light behind her. Every curve, every curl. I reach forward, but she bats my hand away.

CHAPTER 38

"Manners, *Fitzwilliam*. Let a lady finish her thought first." Before I can pout, because Christ I just need my hands on her, she settles on her knees in front of me, right between my legs, and any complaint dies on my tongue.

Piper fists her hand in my shirt and uses it to pull me towards her, so aggressively I'm caught off-guard, and when she kisses me it's like we're right back downstairs in my bedroom last weekend. Her hands find either side of my shirt, and she yanks it over my head. I fall back against the couch with a huff, watching her fingers trace up my thighs and feeling every agonizing inch towards my waistband.

"Piper," I rasp out, but she shakes her head, hitching under each side of the elastic. I lift my hips, and she pulls my pants and boxers down in one movement, leaving us both completely naked in the middle of my media room.

I don't know that I've ever done *anything* in this room before. Or in the kitchen, prior to last weekend. Or anywhere outside of my bedroom, for that matter. And the thought has me wanting to christen every surface in this house with the woman in front of me.

As if in agreement, my cock twitches between us, and Piper tries to stifle a giggle.

"Someone's happy to see me." Before I can give her the sarcastic *He's not the only one*, her soft hand reaches forward and gives a delicate stroke that sizzles through my entire body. This time, she does giggle when my hips launch off the cool leather below me, and she takes that opportunity to swallow half of me between those full lips of hers.

I can't help my groan at the wet warmth of her mouth, her soft lips around me, moving with her hand. I watch, mesmerized, when she swallows me whole without a second of hesitation, and without a gag.

"Fuck, baby." I push a curl out of her face, those blue eyes twinkling when her mouth lets me go with a soft *pop*.

"You didn't think I was kidding, did you?"

She's trying to fucking kill me.

Without giving me time to answer, she pulls her hair halfway out of her face with one hand and goes back to what she was doing, and all I can do is lean back and take in every second. Her delicate hands, accented with those rings she loves, moving along my shaft with her mouth. Her tongue on the underside of my head, hitting the spot that makes me jolt nearly every time.

I reach out one hand, helping her hold up her hair, which she seems to appreciate because she makes a garbled noise around me. I feel the vibration everywhere and curse. She can't smile at me, but when she looks up, her eyes twinkle in a look I'm starting to recognize as her *I'm about to do something naughty* face.

And even though I spotted that face, when she releases me from her mouth, brings her free hand up to cup my balls, and licks from base to head, it takes everything in me not to come right then and there. She's already got me teetering on the edge - despite having already helped myself once this morning with the thought of just this.

The reality is so much better.

"Where do you want me to come?" I ask quietly, savoring the feeling of her curls in my hand as she bobs a few more times before answering with a wordless point at her mouth. "You sure? You don't have to-"

Her palm squeezes my thigh, fingernails running down the exposed skin, and I shut up with a small groan. I tighten my fist in her hair and she moans around my cock. Alright. That's something to explore later. When I'm about to finish, I whisper her a warning, and then feel everything drain from me in a slow, hazy orgasm that has my hips swaying up to meet her final strokes.

Piper makes a satisfied little noise when she sits up, shaking my hand out of her hair and swallowing whatever was left of my load in her mouth. One of those delicate fingers reaches up and wipes away a tiny dribble at the corner of her mouth, and the sight almost makes me ready for another round. Almost.

That might be one of the hottest things I've ever seen.

"Thanks," she says with a giggle, and I realize I said it out loud. I don't even care. I'm so sated, it takes me a minute to regain my composure. Piper runs her fingers down my thighs while I come down from the high, and finally, I lean forward, fisting her hair in my hand and pulling her to me in a hard kiss. When she pulls back, laughing, I tighten my grip on her hair, just a bit, and her eyes narrow. "Quite the party trick, huh?" She licks her lips, like she can still taste me on her, and I reach forward, cupping one of her breasts and running my thumb over her nipple. Piper closes her eyes and takes in a sharp breath, letting her back arch. I seize the moment, hoisting her up by her arms and setting her on the long piece of the sectional.

Her doe eyes stare at me from where she lays on the couch, her back against the cool leather, hair wild around her head and her arms splayed to the side. But the grin on her face is nothing short of mischievous when I stare down at her, my eyes drifting from her swollen lips and pink cheeks down to where I'm about to return every one of those slow strokes in turn.

CHAPTER 39

Piper

Bex nearly falls off the couch when Fitz plops me down next to where he'd been seated, but she's the last thing on my mind as I stare up at him, my chest heaving.

This aggressive side of him isn't one I know a lot about - and yet, somehow, it's satisfying to see it. Knowing that I'm what's bringing it out is a mild - ok, major - ego boost.

Fitz kneels on the floor, still completely naked, and the outline of his mess of curls and broad shoulders are clearly visible with the light behind him. In his signature move, he grabs at my ankles, pulling me closer to him, but this time, the friction of my sweaty skin and the couch make a squeaking sound.

We make eye contact for approximately one second before bursting out laughing. Then, as if sensing the opportunity to ruin the moment further, Roscoe saunters over and starts licking at a sweat spot near me. I can't stop laughing, curling into myself and watching Fitz out of the corner of my eye as he laughs too, shoving Roscoe away in mock frustration.

"You're lucky you're cute," he says to his dog, holding both sides of Roscoe's face while he's still at eye level. I look over to Bex, who's been completely ignoring us, licking at a spot of carpet near her foot. Typical. Can't even be mad at them as I put my clothes back on, with an understanding look from Fitz that tells me this is far from over for the evening.

"So what's the dress code for this Fairy Ball thing?" I ask Fitz once we're downstairs, getting ready to crawl into bed. I've returned to just wearing one of his shirts, a look I can't complain about, because I know that in about five minutes, I'll have him like putty in my hands when he presses up against me and I wiggle my ass in the way I've learned he likes. This whole situation feels very, very domestic - but you will not hear an argument from me, sliding into these expensive ass sheets.

Fitz fluffs up a pillow just in time for Bex to jump on the bed, nestling right on top of it. He picks her up, plopping her down on the floor. "I can get Frannie to share some ideas with you. We typically have a table every year." I feel my eyebrows knit together. Bex jumps back up, clearing Fitz's outstretched arms and nuzzling into the same pillow again. He picks her up, holding her in the air like Mufasa showing off a baby Simba, and then puts her down on the floor again.

"You have a table? At the Fairy Ball?"

"It's not just a Fairy Ball, per say," he starts, and then lets out a frustrated groan when Bex jumps up again.

"You'll get nowhere with her," I say with a shrug. "She's a spoiled bitch who's used to having half a queen size bed to herself." He picks her up, holding her in his arms and scratching her head. Roscoe looks at them from the end of the bed like he's about to shit in Fitz's favorite pair of shoes.

"It's a nonprofit group that does these crazy events each year, they call themselves Fairies but they kind of use it as a symbol for agents of change." Automatically, my hand finds my side with the script font across my stomach. "Exactly." He nods down to my hand.

"Frannie goes every year?"

"Frannie usually helps organize it, we host it at a reduced cost at one of the venues each year. Seer is on their board, or something." I snort.

"Or something?" Fitz sits down on the side of the bed, leaning back against the headboard and letting Bex run to settle down at his feet. "You say that like you're not sure." He looks a little sheepish when he answers.

"Truthfully, Piper, I'm not." He scrubs a hand down his face, and I plop down next to him, sitting with my legs crossed beneath me. Partially for comfort, partially because I want to get all the view time I can out of the purple lacy underwear I picked to wear over here. "It's so frustrating, but I've realized the last couple of months just how checked out I've been." My head cocks to one side, and he continues. "I've missed so many things, so many details, since…"

He doesn't finish his sentence, but when he looks down at his hands in his lap, I know he's probably looking for a ring that isn't there anymore. I nervously twist my own ring on my finger.

"Is Seer your sister's best friend?" I ask, genuinely curious.

"I think so?" He doesn't sound sure at all, and he lets his head fall back against the headboard, both hands rubbing down his face this time. "God, Piper, everything just hit the fan all at once for both Fran and I. Hell, I didn't even know she was as tight with Mateo and his friends, much less that Seer was a part of their friend group, until recently."

"It's understandable to have been distracted," I try to soothe, but he lets out a somewhat humorless laugh. "Ok. Distracted isn't the right word."

CHAPTER 39

"Fucking oblivious, more like it." Finally, he looks over at me, and slowly his features melt into a soft smile. Fitz reaches out a hand, and I lace our fingers together. His gaze goes to our joined fingers. "I was oblivious to so many things, for way too long." He gives my hand a tug, and I crawl towards him, letting him pull me back to straddling his thighs. His hands find my ass a lot faster than I was expecting, and I laugh, falling forward and letting my forehead rest on his strong chest.

"Everyone has their own way of numbing their pain," I mumble into his hideous burnt orange tee shirt, much like the one I'd been handed the other night. Thankfully, the one I'm in now is a WHG Fun Field Day shirt from several years before. "Mine just happened to include a lot less work and a lot more alcohol." His chest shakes with a low laugh, and one of his hands runs along my jawline, nesting in the curls at the back of my neck. He pulls my head up until I'm looking at him. His eyes are swimming with something I can't place, those deep greens misty and a little lost. "She really hurt you, didn't she?" He blinks at me, a few times, before recognition hits him. Then, he nods.

"They really hurt you, didn't they?" Immediately, my eyes swim with tears - fuck, I've been like this all damn week - and I mentally kick myself. I'm due to start my period in a few days, and I absolutely can not lose my shit now, here, in front of Fitz. Slowly, I nod, trying to look away, but he turns my face back towards him. Before I can ask what he's doing, he brings his lips to mine.

The kiss starts slow, soft and gentle like he's testing the waters. But as his hand pulls on my hair, the other gripping my hip like he's trying to eliminate any space between us, our tongues start to tangle and it goes from soft and steady to hot and heavy with the flip of a switch. One second, I'm on top of him, using his shoulders for support. The next, I'm laying with my legs half off the bed as Fitz pulls my panties down with a lazy move that leaves a trail of goosebumps down my legs.

"I hope you know," he says, kissing the inside of one knee, then the other, "that I have no intention of hurting you." I swallow the lump in my throat when he slides my underwear off my foot, letting it hit the floor with the shirt I hadn't noticed he'd taken off. He hitches one of my ankles over his shoulder, kissing further up my thigh. "When you're ready, I want to know all the ways, all the places you hurt." He stops a few inches from the place I really want his mouth, starting on my other leg in the same motion. "But for now, I just want you to feel as good as you've made me feel."

And without a warning, without so much as even a pause, Fitz buries his face between my legs with a fury that could truly only be described as a man on a mission. His tongue finds my clit in seconds and I jolt against him, but his arms are locked so tight around my thighs, there's no chance I'll budge.

"Oh, *my God,*" I moan, one hand covering my eyes and the other gripping the duvet as I feel my back arch at every stroke of his tongue cross my already slick core. After a few seconds - minutes? Hours? - he moves one of his hands away from my thigh, which is trembling on his shoulder, and traces a finger along the folds between my legs, until he finally reaches my entrance. "You're such a fucking tease," I breathe out, my chest shaking with each violent wave that goes through me.

His laugh against my clit only makes it worse, and it takes everything in me not to clamp my legs around his head. "Enjoying that?" Fitz asks when he comes up for air, but doesn't give me a chance to answer before he slips a finger inside, adding a second just a few strokes later. He curls his fingers, his tongue returning to that relentless rhythm until I'm practically levitating off the bed, grinding my hips into his face.

And when I come, it hits me so fast and so hard I don't even have a second to warn him as I spasm in his grip, moving so jerkily I'm surprised I don't manage to injure him again. He rides out the last few waves with me, letting each second pass with another stroke, another lick, until I'm a sweaty, melty mess on the duvet, half-covering my eyes from the sheer embarrassment of my own neediness. I about broke his nose. And I was thinking *he* was going to be the putty in *my* hands.

I watch through the small slit left between my fingers as he stands up, crawling up on the bed and giving me that same hard kiss I gave him just seconds after he finished in my mouth. I can taste myself on him, and it does something to my insides when he leans back and I wipe a bit of shine off his upper lip. His dazzling smile returns as he climbs back off the bed, making his way towards the bathroom.

I stare at the ceiling, half-dazed, mind wandering. Fuck.

I see Fitz lean against the doorframe of the bathroom, and in my moment of post-coital, pre-period hormonal clarity, I muse out loud, "Why do your sheets smell different?" There's a soft chuckle, and I look over to where Fitz stands.

"Okay, bloodhound." He moves across the room and settles on the bed next to me. "I asked my laundry service to switch to a hypoallergenic detergent."

I feel my eyebrows knit together, and he meets my gaze with an expectant look. Then it clicks. I'd told him I'd been itchy after last weekend.

"You changed your laundry detergent because of me?" It comes out half an octave higher than intended, and though his gaze flits down to the hair barely covering my chest, he gives me a small smile.

"Couldn't have you scratching up this beautiful skin." He slides a hand down my upper arm, and involuntarily, I shudder.

I'm not sure whether it's because of the sentiment of his switch, or the

CHAPTER 39   261

compliment, or the cold from the overhead fan above me.

All three. It's probably all three.

I wake up several hours later with Fitz pulled close behind me for the second time in a week. I think the combination of our exertion and a long week for each of us left us more than ready to curl up for the night, but it didn't make the ache I was feeling any less real. It took everything in me not to wake him up, pushing my hips against him, but when I tilt my head to look at him, he's just so peaceful. My living room was on the receiving end of one of his less than restful evenings, so instead of rousing him, I pulled the discarded top sheet around myself and went to get another glass of water.

When I pad back in the room, he's turned over, and Bex is curled up against his back, with Roscoe where my feet had been. Hmph.

I set my glass down on the entry table and check my phone - a few emails, some texts from our group chats.

Group Text (3) *Penny, Bianca, Alex, Carla, Vic*

PENNY ROBINSON
Are we still doing fam dinner and races Friday after next? Trying to get carpool sorted.

BIANCA DELMONICO – 911 CONTACT
That's the plan. Any objections?

ALEX CALLOWAY
Nolan's mom will be in that weekend, so we should be good.

I glance at the time. It's almost two in the morning, too late to respond, but I make a mental note to reply later. Out of the corner of my eye, I see a light move across the sky outside the floor-to-ceiling windows in Fritz's room. They face his backyard and have reflective covers to keep prying eyes out, so when I quietly walk over to them to watch the plane I'd spotted fly across the dark sky, I'm not worried anyone will see me.

I've never lived anywhere rural enough to see stars at night. At least, not like they do in the movies, where you can look up and point out constellations like a game of I Spy. Even on my few trips to see family back in Italy, the night sky was dimmed by the bright city lights. But it's never kept me from gazing up at them.

In the days between Mickey's passing and his funeral, Ava told me to write him a letter. Tell him all the things I wish I'd said, or hoped he knew, and leave nothing out, she'd said. A final goodbye after months - years, really - of heartache and grief. I sat under the dim stars and bright city lights near our last home together, where he barely spent a few weeks total between hospital stays and doctor's appointments, and put pen to paper on a notebook I'd had since college.

Pages. I wrote him pages and pages of thoughts, of feelings, of anger and grief and sorrow. Pages of things I wish we'd done together. Pages of the life we could have lived. Selfishly, pages of the things he took away from me when he broke my heart over and over again. And pages of why I'd forgiven him. I put the pages in his casket at the visitation, along with one of Bex's old collars, his baseball mitt, and the coloring pages his niece and nephew had completed while we waited for him to come out of his first grueling, hours-long surgery all those years ago.

But looking up at this night sky, now years later, all of those feelings bubbling up seem so different now. They were raw and real and so very very heightened in that time, every thought and function consumed by them until the feelings were all I had left. And then having spent years tamping them down with avoidance and alcohol...

This feeling in my chest. This ease. This...surety. How could I already be feeling it with the man asleep a few feet away from me, when I'm not even positive I ever felt it with the man I buried states away, years ago?

"Penny for your thoughts?" I nearly jump out of my skin as Fitz's long arms wrap around my waist, securing the sheet wrapped around me. I shake my head, clearing the surprise, and tilt back to meet his gaze. He rests his chin on my shoulder after planting a kiss there.

"Is it heated?" I nod my chin towards the pool at the center of the yard. I feel Fitz shake his head.

"Not right now, we - uh, I - usually keep it off until a few hours before we use it." He looks down at me. "You thinking about going for a swim?" I shrug. "The hot tub is available," he says after a moment, and I crane my neck to peer outside. Sure enough, in one of the corners is a large, covered hot tub, surrounded on two sides by vines and on the third by the wall of the house. When I look back up at him, he's smirking. "I'll be right back."

I stay standing as he disappears, returning seconds later with a towel wrapped tightly around his hips, handing me another. I strip off the sheet and start to wrap the towel around myself when I catch him standing next to the door, fingers on the handle, watching me.

"What?" I ask, feeling my face flush. I use the tie on my wrist to pull up my hair. He shakes his head, like he's clearing a thought, and then holds his free hand out to me, opening the door. Bex and Roscoe follow us outside - it's a rare clear, moderate spring night in Texas, so I'm not shivering as I follow Fitz to the hot tub and watch him fold back the cover, turning on the jets. They bubble to life as he brushes off some leaves from the steps, and then tests the water temperature. He gestures for me to do the same.

I moan. It feels perfect. His lips thin into a line, but he holds his hand out to me again. With a glance around the yard, I see that all the neighbors' lights are off - the only ones around us are the soft lights coming from inside Fitz's bedroom. So, I pull the towel off, setting it on the back of a nearby patio chair and climbing into the warm water.

My entire body melts into the seat on the opposite side from the steps, and I watch appreciatively as Fitz climbs in, leaving his boxers on. Hm. Maybe he's a little more worried about being arrested for indecent exposure than I am? He also lives here - I'm less likely to have to deal with nosy neighbors seeing me naked.

He wades over towards me, and I let him settle on the seat beside me before I turn halfway, letting my back rest against his chest. His arm wraps around my stomach, holding me to him as we rest together. After a minute of comfortable silence, I repeat his words, "Penny for your thoughts?" His chest rumbles behind me.

"Touché." I wade away, turning to face him. "You never told me why today was a bad day." I bristle immediately. What a way to sour the mood.

"Just work stuff," I answer, probably more dismissively than necessary, and he raises an eyebrow. "Seriously."

"Seriously," he echoes, and in the warm water, beneath the bubbles, his hand finds mine. His fingers intertwine with my own, and he lifts them so I can clearly see where they meet. "You want me to open up? This makes that a two way street, Piper." He squeezes my hand for emphasis, and I smile back at him.

"Does that mean you'll tell me more of your secrets?" I give his chest a playful jab with my free hand, but he bats it away, twisting our joined hands until I'm back against his chest. I let out a long sigh, pushing away a drifting leaf on the water's surface. "Do you remember that conversation we had in the office at the Pine?"

"Vividly," he says, almost immediately, and I'm tempted to turn and see his facial expression. He keeps me firmly against him.

"I told you that I stopped making myself small for people a long time ago." He hums against me. "I feel like I'm making myself small again." I feel him still instantly against my back.

"With this?" he asks, and I can tell he means us.

"No!" I try to turn, but his other hand snakes around me, his lips kissing the top of my head like he's relieved by my reaction. "At work. With all this design stuff..." I chew on my lip, unsure of how to phrase how I'm feeling. "I thought for a long time that if I could just get out of marketing, and do something that I truly loved all the time, I'd be happy." I sigh again. "I thought that seeing my stuff in stores, on people, would make me happy."

"And it hasn't?"

"It's not that." I close my eyes momentarily, trying to take in this moment, here, with him. "So much has changed since I started at AllHearts. I've changed." I give his hand a squeeze. "I'm starting to think maybe I need to find something else to do for work, so I can get back to doing what I love under my own terms, not someone else's."

There's a few moments of silence, and I can hear crickets chirping off in the distance when Fitz finally replies "Then let's find you a new job."

With my hand, I squeeze the forearm around my waist, and he loosens his grip, letting me turn until I'm straddling his lap. My wet hands find the nape of his neck, and his eyes flit down to the clear line of cleavage just above the water level.

"Just admiring the view," he says after I roll my eyes. Fitz's fingers trace patterns on the curve of my hip. "Admiring you." I give the sides of his toned neck a little squeeze as a smile plays on his lips.

"I'm admiring you, too." I run my thumb over the sensitive spot behind his ear, and one of his hands trails over the fold of my hip, that gathering of extra skin when I sit. Involuntarily, I swallow, and his brows furrow. "Sorry," I start, and then give an awkward little laugh. "I've always been a little self conscious about that."

Lie. I've always been a *lot* self conscious about that. Even at my "I forgot to eat because I'm too busy taking care of my dying husband" skinniest, the way my stomach folds when I sit has always been a point of contention with myself.

"With this?" Fitz watches my face as he moves his free hand over the soft part of my lower stomach, the way it covers part of the triangle of dark hair - where I'd really like his fingers right about now. A shudder runs down my spine at the thought, and he does it again. "What is there to be self conscious about?"

The laugh I emit is not graceful or ladylike - not that I've ever claimed to be either.

"I've never been..." I search for the words. "I've never been physically fit. Even at my smallest, I've always had folds and creases and-"

Fitz's hand on my hip yanks my body forward, his mouth crushing against mine in a searing kiss that steals the air from my lungs. When he sits back, I'm panting, and now I really want that other hand to go lower. But it doesn't.

Instead, he brings it up to the crook of my elbow, the warm water on his fingers leaving a trail as he traces his hand up my arm.

CHAPTER 39

"You're beautiful, Piper." His hand grips my hip harder. "This is beautiful." He moves his hand across my stomach again. "Every fold." His fingers find the line where my thigh and hip connect. "Every crease." And those fingers keep moving until they're exactly where I want them, pushing through dark hair until he's circling my clit. "Fucking gorgeous."

"You're not so bad yourself," I try to say, but it comes out as a garbled mess as my hips push against his hand. He laughs, and I bury my face in the crook of his neck, hiding my whimpers into the kisses I trail up and down his shoulder.

In just a few moments, with panting breaths from both of us and more than a little sloshed water, he has me right on the edge of a blinding orgasm. His free hand comes loose from my hip and grabs the back of my neck, fingers tangled in my hair.

"I don't want anything but this," Fitz says, emphasizing his words with a tug at my curls. "You. However you look, whatever way you'll let me have you." He presses into my clit harder, and his words send me spiraling, pushing against his fingers and hiding my moans in his chest. I ride it out, rocking on his lap until I come down enough to hear his shallow breathing mixed with the chirp of crickets. When Fitz wraps his arms around me, pulling me into his chest, with the warm water, the post-orgasm bliss, the distant sound of car horns, it's almost enough to make me forget my bad day. Almost.

CHAPTER 40

Fitz

PIPER DELMONICO
You're just saying that because it's me.

FITZ WESTFALL
No, truly. My favorite color is purple.

PIPER DELMONICO sideeye.gif
You don't have to make shit up to win me over.

FITZ WESTFALL
IMG_1098.jpg

PIPER DELMONICO
Are those all socks?

FITZ WESTFALL

CHAPTER 40

Yes

PIPER DELMONICO
You own eight pairs of purple socks?

FITZ WESTFALL
It's the closest you will ever get to seeing this Westfall in anything super colorful.

PIPER DELMONICO
Unsurprising. Your house reflects that.
Wait. *This* Westfall?

FITZ WESTFALL
You haven't met my brother, have you? He is, by far, the color king in the family. He has a bright green Christmas suit he wears to the office Christmas party every year.

PIPER DELMONICO
Does he have an extra one? I bet I could make a pretty convincing offer to get you into it, if so.

FITZ WESTFALL
You sure I can't convince you to come over tonight?

PIPER DELMONICO
I told you, needy, I've got to get this commission done this week or I'm going to have to push this fitting for the second time.

FITZ WESTFALL
I can just sit there and be quiet and watch. I won't distract you. Promise.

PIPER DELMONICO
First of all, creepy. Secondly, that's a filthy fucking lie and we both know it.

When I suggested that Piper invite some of her friends over to enjoy the pool on the first 90 degree summer weekend, I had not expected that group to include my sister.

Was I disappointed by the development? Absolutely not. Because the second she asked, having originally invited Seer, who invited Frannie, I knew it was the perfect opportunity to let Fran try to scoop her up for our marketing department. Selfish on my part? Maybe. But there's a reason her department has one of the highest retention rates in the company, and it isn't our CCO, Brent, and his less-than-sparkling personality, let me tell you that.

So when I'm standing in the hallway, digging through a tub in the closet marked "Summer Stuff," I remind myself that my ulterior motives of wanting Piper at the office with me are secondary when it comes to her happiness.

Until she steps out of the hall bathroom in a bright pink bikini. Then my ulterior motives are all I can think about because...damn.

She blushes at the low whistle I let out, grabbing at her waist where the navy pinup-style bottoms come to an end. The strip of flesh between the top of the shorts and the bottom of the halter top, and the way the top presses her chest together, is enough to illicit an immediate reaction from me, and when I pull her into my chest, her eyes widen, because she can feel it too.

"Stop that," Piper laughs, batting my hand away. This is how it's been the last few weeks - when we're together, I can't keep my hands away. Maybe it's the newness of all of this?

Olivia and I were considered an item long before sex came in the picture. But I've never really felt this need before, this insistent hammering inside my head to be closer, to know her in a way no one else does.

Fuck. I feel like a horny teenager all over again.

"This is a new development," she says somewhat absently, looking down at her chest. I quirk my head to the side, confused. "My body has changed a lot in the last few years." With her arms around my neck, she leans back. "When I got my IUD, I'd been on the pill for, like, ten years. Between the hormone changes, sobriety, and..." she trails off, making an embarrassed face, the same one she does when she's talking about Mickey.

Slowly, she's opened up to me about it - about what she's gone through in the last few years. Sure, she had no problems telling me off when I jumped to conclusions all those weeks ago. But truly sharing with me the things she's been through in the time since I'd last seen her? That was going to take a lot of trust building, something we were slowly working on.

So instead of making her feel uncomfortable for talking about her past, I just give her waist a squeeze, letting my hands fall to her ass, giving one cheek a pat. She rolls her eyes, nearly automatic with how much I've admired that ass recently.

"I've just never had tits before." I choke back a huff of laughter as she presses her shoulders together, her cleavage becoming more prominent.

"Did Piper just say tits?"

Piper snorts. "Did Fitz?"

The doorbell rings behind me, and she looks back with wide eyes. When she pushes away from my chest, she smooths her hands over her waist like she's fixing a dress that isn't there.

"Do I look ok?" she asks. I have to suppress a grin - she's nervous. Nervous to see Seer, to see Frannie - and whoever else she invited.

That question is quickly answered when I open my front door and an unimpressed looking Alex Calloway stands on my porch, a towel over one shoulder and a tote over the other. Seer and Frannie stand behind her, Frannie clearly amused by Alex's immediate attitude.

"These two may be sober Sallys," Alex says, pushing past me and towards Piper, who laces her arm through Alex's as though it's automatic. Alex wags her finger between Piper and Seer. "But mamas," she starts, gesturing between herself and Fran, "need margaritas."

"Pronto," Frannie adds, as if it isn't 10:30 a.m.

Clearly these women have been planning this day, and I've been out of the loop, because from her tote, Alex produces a bottle of tequila and sets it down on my kitchen counter, pushing her oversized sunglasses on top of her head.

I lean towards Piper, whispering, "There was a group text for this that I was left out of, wasn't there?" She gives a knowing smile, patting me on the shoulder and then turning to her best friend.

"I think Seer can help with that one." She hitches a thumb back at my fridge. "I stocked up on a few options for mixers, for them and for us." And just like that, Piper's made herself at home in this house, and all I can think to myself is that it's about damn time someone did.

Piper

Several hours, and several pitchers of margaritas later, we're lounging on the patio while Seer wades in the shallow end of the pool, bringing handfuls of water onto her shoulders. She's reapplied the "waterproof" sunscreen about four times, and I can't blame her - if I was that pale, I'd be careful too.

"So let me get this straight," Frannie says from the lounger next to me, taking a deep draw from her cup. "You didn't know this kid existed for years."

"Correct."

"And when you found out, his parents said the mom was crazy and making shit up?" Seer adds from the pool.

"Also correct," Alex says.

"But then they decided the DNA test was wrong, it's his kid, and you're what's standing in the way of him having a picture perfect little family back in bumfuck, Kansas? Not...you know, cancer?" Frannie sounds less sure of her question the longer it goes on, but I laugh.

"Yes. Yes to all the crazy shit, it happened, I have receipts."

"So do I," Vic chimes in from his seat next to Carla, where they perched at the outdoor dining table a little while ago.

"Fuck me, Piper." Seer shakes her head, dipping down until only her head is above the water line. "I mean, you and I both know there's never an excuse for alcoholism, but damn if that shit wouldn't put me over the edge."

I shrug - I'm so used to talking about all of this, so desensitized to it, that sometimes I forget how crazy it sounds.

"No, ma'am," Carla says, sipping on a glass of the cherry limeade that Seer made for us. "Don't act like you didn't wade through a river of piranhas and come out still breathing on the other side."

"Thanks for that visual." Vic shudders, and Seer splashes water at him playfully. "Hey, now, I'm not disagreeing." He looks between Seer and I, like he's assessing how much I'm willing to share with our new friends - my second shrug tells him what I'm thinking. I have no secrets anymore. My entire life played out on social media like a fucking Lifetime movie. The least I can do is let these women in on that part of me, that part that so impacts my relationship, or whatever I have, with Fitz. "I had to speak at that funeral." Vic drinks down the rest of his margarita in one gulp before continuing, rolling back his tan shoulders like he's trying to push the words out of his chest. "I watched the way they pretended like you didn't exist, like none of us existed." He nods his head towards Alex, the only other person who was there that day with us. "And it fucking sucked."

Frannie lets out a deep exhale, tossing back her margarita too and then picking up her phone from the side table. "I don't know how you did it without going crazy."

"I mean, I didn't do it without going crazy." I laugh half-heartedly, sipping at my own drink. "I pretended I was fine, and eventually I couldn't pretend anymore, and I just drank until I couldn't feel anything." I swallow, the lump in my throat forming as I see Alex looking at me from the corner of my eye. "And then the people who care about me pulled me out of a really dark, deep hole."

"That one," Seer says, pointing at Frannie next to me, "is a huge part of my sobriety." She leans on the white tiled edge, crossing her arms in front of her. "My rock bottom, was..." She makes a face that screams the word "yikes," but points to her ear, and from here I can just see the end of a hearing aid, similar to what my grandad had before he died. Discreet and small, but packs a punch.

"You rang?" I turn in my seat to see Fitz at the door, sliding it closed behind him and looking at his sister. He's been inside most of the day, working on a project I think mostly to let us have some girl time - you know, plus Vic. Over her shoulder, Frannie snaps her fingers, holding up an empty glass. Clearly she summoned him from her phone.

"More libations, dear brother." I snort as he rolls his eyes, looking at Seer in the pool.

"There's another pitcher in the kitchen," she says simply, adjusting her short ponytail. "Just add some ice before you bring it out."

"Any other requests?" His tone is sarcastic, at least, I read it as sarcastic, but I can tell that Vic, Alex and Carla are unsure and immediately look at me for my reaction.

"You could come out here and join us," I suggest, and his gaze immediately softens when it meets mine.

"Let me finish up the email I'm working on, and I'll be back out here." He gives me a small smile before turning back through the door.

"Christ on a cracker," Frannie blurts, and there's a beat of silence before we all burst into laughter. "What? I'm sorry, did my brother just agree to stop working and come have fun?"

"Trust me," I start, "it's almost as startling to me." I pick up a chip from the bowl next to me and plop it in my mouth.

"I'm telling you, it's the promise of unlimited head." Carla knows I'm about to go after her, because she jumps out of her chair, and while she runs away from my aim of one of Roscoe's tennis balls at her backside, it does successfully hit her in the ass.

"There is no unlimited head happening," I snap, swatting at Carla with the spicy vampire romance I'd brought outside with me as she walks by.

"From either of you? Because, truly, he has some groveling to do." Alex gives me a pointed look over her sunglasses, and I hear Frannie make a vomiting noise. "From your blush, though, I'm guessing he's not a Hollister."

I let out a wheeze of laughter, nearly dropping my cup from my hands. A Hollister. Man, it's been a minute since I've thought about that.

"Hollister?" Seer asks as she steps out of the pool, letting water drip from her black bikini - her tattoos swirl up one of her arms and continue down that same leg.

I make a mental note to ask her later who did them. They're gorgeous. I'm a tattoo loyalist, and have been seeing the same artist since my first tattoo in college, but I like having a Rolodex of recommendations.

Carla steps in next to Seer, letting her hair down and leaning back to dip her head in the water.

"You know, *Hollister*," Vic says, as if it's the most obvious thing in the world. "Couldn't find a g-spot with a gas mask and a flashlight." Frannie makes another gagging noise, and I'm half tempted to apologize - picturing Penny and Brett makes me want to vomit, too. But Seer makes her way towards the lounger she was using, picking up her own red drink and holding it up in a toast.

"I think this is the start of a beautiful friendship."

"That's what we need," Fitz says from behind me, and when I turn, he's closing the door behind him, another pitcher of margaritas in hand, and he's wearing a pair of gray swim trunks...with no shirt. "You all teaming up to give me more shit." He gestures between Seer, Frannie, and Alex, narrowing his eyes.

Alex lets out a wolf whistle, and I throw a chip at her. He's probably already dying of embarrassment - he's been so quick to cover up any time we've been naked together, and I doubt being shirtless in front of everyone is at the top of his to-do list. Not shy, not even self conscious. Just too much of himself on

CHAPTER 40

display for his internalized anxiety.

God, even his shoes and swim trunks are pretentious and new looking, though, like he didn't own a pair of well worn...anything.

He sets the pitcher down on the table between Frannie and Alex, and then moves to pick up the pool net by the end of the long handle.

"You can't say you don't deserve it," Alex replies, holding up her now full glass at him. He shakes his head, and I stand, crossing the warm pavement until I'm a few inches from him.

"You know she's teasing, right?" I ask in a low voice. He nods, winking, and I give his shoulder a squeeze before walking towards the pool steps where Carla is. When I look over my shoulder, he's staring at my backside, and I pop my hip out for good measure.

"Get a fucking room with that shit," Alex cries, sharing a look with Frannie as I wade into the pool, trying to keep my neck above the water.

"Like you and Nolan weren't ten levels of disgusting swapping tonsils back in the day." Vic, to the rescue. Fitz and I meet each other's eyes as he walks up to the side of the pool, his flip flops hitting the pavement as he scoops away a few leaves near the edge he's standing at. We were most definitely playing tonsil hockey approximately half an hour before everyone got here this morning.

Seer settles in the chair I vacated, reapplying more sunscreen. "Not to rotate a full 180," she says, rubbing lotion into her tattooed shoulder, "but how's the job hunt going?"

The question is enough to pull my gaze away from Fitz's arms, which are difficult to not look at when they're deftly moving that long stick attached to the pool net.

"Job hunt?" I ask, looking around to see who she's talking to - but then I realize it's me. Fitz makes a throat cutting gesture at her, which he attempts to stop when I turn back to glare.

"Job hunt?" Carla and Vic echo, and his eyebrows knit together.

See, this is why I haven't said anything - because as much as Brianna has made me miserable, Vic seems to be thriving at AllHearts. For a boy who grew up wanting to be in the world of fashion, a clothing department at a company like AllHearts is arguably one of the closest places to get that without moving to a coast with a fashion hub. I lean against the pool wall next to where Fitz is clearing leaves, waiting for Vic's response.

But then, his shoulders sink, and he settles into the chair like he's taking a breath for the first time in ages.

"Thank fuck, because we both need to get the hell out of there."

I feel myself sag in relief - it's not just me, then. Seer sips on the cup she filled with her mocktail mixture, looking at Frannie, and then me.

"This one made it sound like you'd made some pretty good suggestions on that, what was it, Fran? An email campaign?" Frannie nods at Seer's words, leaning forward in the lounger, wrapping her arms around her long legs. Her teal swimsuit is more modest than Seer's, with lace cutouts around the top.

"Really good, Piper. Like, things my team didn't even think of." I feel my face flush and tilt my head back, catching Fitz's eyes while he smirks at me. Then, Frannie continues, "We're hiring in the marketing department, if you want to get the hell out of Dodge and need somewhere to land."

He planned this.

Or, well, expected it. For me to get asked about trying to find a new job, and then poise his sister to try to snag me. And the fact that his smirk is now a full smile down at me confirms as much.

Without much thought, I reach for the net and give it a tug, and with a curse and a splash Fitz falls into his own pool. I just cross my arms as he comes up for air, running a hand up his face and pushing his hair away from his forehead.

"What was that for?"

"Does she need a reason?" Carla asks with a blase tone from her spot on the other side of the pool.

He wades towards me, and braces one hand on either side of my shoulders.

"You couldn't be any more obvious," I say, splashing his chest. "You lined up that job offer like one of Nolan's plays."

"That may be true," he says hoarsely, leaning his head near my ear, "but that doesn't mean you're not in trouble later."

There's a splash as Frannie throws one of the dog toys at us, and Alex proclaims "You two are going to make me puke."

CHAPTER 41

Fitz

"Are you sure you want to stay at my place tonight?" Piper asks for the tenth time as we park in front of her building. "I can just run in, grab Bex, and we can head back."

"We're already here," I reason as Roscoe attempts to stick his head between us, leaning over to the passenger seat to give Piper a lick up the side of her face. She laughs, pushing him back, and then nods. "Good. Besides," I start, leaning towards her, "we haven't done anything at your place."

"That's because I share a wall with a little old lady, and another with a couple and a baby." She points at me, eyes narrowing - her cheeks are pink from being outside a good chunk of the day, having finally sent everyone home from my house just a little while ago. Her curls are still pulled up, but some frame her face in wild tendrils, and all I can think of is how bad I want to sink my hands into her hair with her mouth on me - anywhere on me, at this point.

"I do like a challenge," I manage before she rolls her eyes and opens her car door, one hand holding Roscoe's leash as he bounds over the center console of my Carolla and out behind her. I follow her into the building, stopping to let Roscoe do his business, and we enter her apartment together, the air conditioning sweet relief after the already blistering late spring heat.

"I'd apologize for the mess," she says, and then shrugs, dumping her bag on the kitchen counter and letting Roscoe off his leash to sniff around. He hasn't been to Piper and Carla's apartment, yet, and can probably smell that this is another dog's territory. One that he's comfortable, if not a bit cautious around, at my house.

Bex is in her kennel in the corner, curled up on her little purple bed, her head raised just enough that I can see her eyes shining in the dim light of the living room. When she sees us, she paws at the wire door, and Piper meets my eyes. "You wanna let her out?" I nod, pinching the door open and letting her sniff at my flip flops before jumping out, looking first at me, then Piper across the room, then Roscoe, who doesn't look quite sure what to make of the tiny black furball on her turf.

At one point towards the end of our marriage, Olivia got a tiny little Yorkie thing named Ollie that she carried with her practically everywhere. Looking back, it was probably her way of trying to sate me on the whole kids discussion, but the second Roscoe batted that thing across the room like a soccer ball, I knew they were never going to be best buds.

Bex, on the other hand, sniffs at Roscoe's paws while he stands completely still, towering over her. Then, she starts licking at his toes, and he settles down on the wood floor next to her with a huff, like he's compromising in making this his territory, too. I see Piper's shoulders relax from across the room.

"Be right back," she says, and disappears into her bedroom. I think she's going to change and start to sit down on the end of the couch, but I hear the sound of the shower starting and follow the sound down the hall just in time to catch her slipping behind the striped white curtain.

"And just what do you think you're doing?" I try in my sternest voice, and with one foot in the tub, she turns and looks over her shoulder.

The look of surprise on her face, the way her curls frame her cheeks, the curve of her hips mid-step. I swallow hard, and immediately my body is at attention.

It's these moments that I never expected. The times when I'm caught off guard, when she's caught off guard, and it's like everything in the last ten years is washed away. No - not washed away, exactly. Because as much as neither of us want to admit it, the events of the last ten years have shaped who we are in so many ways that have helped us fit together. Like the things that hurt us molded us into shapes that wouldn't have worked together before, but now, after just a few months of having her in my life, I don't know that I can picture it any other way.

"If you're going to join me," Piper starts, pulling me out of my own headspace, "I suggest you take some of that off." She gestures down to the golf shorts and polo I'd thrown on before leaving my house, and without hesitation, I pull the hem of my shirt over my head. She gives a satisfactory smile, stepping into the water and letting it run over her shoulders before I strip and climb in after her.

Compared to the open space of my glass master shower, this feels small and intimate, the bar for the curtain just barely at my eye level. I duck under the shower head, wetting my hair and switching back with Piper so she's not standing there freezing.

"Am I still in trouble?" she asks, working a soapy loofah over my back.

"Oh, yeah," I answer, though the threat is empty. "I had fun today." I'm not looking at her, but I can practically hear the smile when she answers.

CHAPTER 41

"Me, too. Alex and Seer might be my new favorite combo." I snort, and she swats me with the loofah, suds flying.

"Rude."

"Says the guy who spilled all my secrets." I half-turn to look at her face, but she's still smiling, and can clearly tell that I was worried by her statement. "I'm not upset that you told your sister. I'm just not sure I'd admitted to myself that I needed to leave, really, until recently." I feel her turn the loofah on herself, and pivot to watch, leaning against the shower wall. "It feels like a big change." She moves under the water and I step forward with her, letting the suds wash to the shower floor.

"A good change?" Piper sighs deep, and I wrap my arms around her shoulders, pulling her to me. She's being careful not to get her hair wet, and I'm trying to respect that, but damn if all I wanna do is envelope her with my body and remind her she's safe with me.

"I think so." She tilts her head back so she's looking at me, and her mouth tips up at one side. "I have mixed feelings about working for you, though."

"Working *with* me," I correct, and she grumbles against my chest. "I know, I know. Semantics."

"Semantics, and, you know, self respect." She laughs when she says it, but I still look down and meet her eyes, and can feel the furrow in my brow. "Fitz, this..." Piper pauses like she's looking for the right word. "This relationship is a newborn. And banking my professional reputation on a newborn has never been my style." Her hand travels down my back, and then squeezes one of my asscheeks, and I jump, laughing. "No matter how good the orgasms are."

"Hey, hey, hey." I swat at her other hand, which is moving south at a dangerous speed. "So sue me, I wouldn't mind seeing you every day."

"We live five minutes from each other," she says against my shoulder with a huff.

"Yeah, but I'd much rather have lunch with my girlfriend than over a pile of quarterly reports with my sister." Piper freezes momentarily, and I realize what I've said the second it leaves my mouth.

Girlfriend.

Slowly, Piper tips her head back, and even though I know she's been trying not to get her hair wet, a spray of water hits the back of her head as she meets my eye. I'm relieved to see the look on her face isn't horrified or even apprehensive at my putting the cart before the horse. Her eyes are crinkled in a smile that makes her whole face light up, her cheeks still pink from our time outside.

"How about lunch with your sister *and* your girlfriend?" She gives my waist a squeeze on the last word, and I feel myself relax. "Though, realistically, we could do that now, AllHearts is like four blocks-"

But I cut her off with a kiss before she can overthink, can ramble, like I know she does when she gets nervous, and she melts into it with an ease I don't think I was prepared for. It catches me off-guard, the way we fit together.

Until there's a crash outside the bathroom, and we pull apart, her eyebrows creased in concern as there's another loud noise, and while the moment is gone - I don't think I'll be able to stop smiling.

Piper

I think Fitz is regretting all of his life choices up to this moment. Truly. That's how deep the scowl is on his face as I work my wide-tooth comb through his hair the next morning, twisting lines of curls into ringlets on the top of his head.

"Stop. Moving." I put my hand on his shoulder, trying to steady him where he sits on the edge of my bathroom counter, his head bowed in front of me.

"Easy for you to say," he mutters, "I'm not yanking on your hair."

"Right now," I correct, smirking. "You're not yanking on my hair *right now*." He shakes his head and I squeeze his shoulder. "Stop it."

"Are you almost done?"

"You're an impatient little brat. You think this is bad?" I gesture up to the mess of wet hair tied up above my head with a cotton shirt, which probably looks insane to him - but this man has seen me in a Hannah Montana tee shirt with braces and blue eyeshadow. A little curly girl method isn't going to scare him away. "Try adding another two feet of hair and then tell me how you feel." He huffs, closing his eyes like he's trying to steel himself, and then he reaches out one hand, long fingers resting on my hips.

"Knock, knock." Carla's voice accompanies the sound of her knuckles on my door as it creaks open.

"In here," I call, and Fitz looks up at me in horror, effectively ruining the ringlet I was shaping. "Fucking hell." I squeeze his shoulder again, just in time for Carla to round the corner, where she stops, face contorted like she was about to say something, and then lets out a snort of laughter, covering her mouth with her hand.

"Spa day?" The phone in her other hand comes up to snap a picture, but I bat her away. Fitz may have softened up to me, but I think if Carla posted a picture of this to her Snapchat stories, or wherever else she may share it, even I can't guarantee he'd ever step foot in this apartment again.

"How was Dylan's?" I ask, and Fitz shifts in front of me like he's going to try to get up. I mutter several curses to myself as I finish up the last couple of curls and then dramatically hold my hands up. "See, all done." Shoulders sagging with relief, he slides off the counter and turns to look at himself in the mirror - I stole one of his UT shirts the last time I was over, so he threw that on instead of the polo. When his fingers move towards his hair, I grab his wrist. "Don't you dare."

"Good," Carla finally answers, leaning against the doorway and crossing her arms. "He's excited about fam dinner." She inspects her fresh manicure, which I know is perfect because we went together Friday after work. I also know she's avoiding eye contact because she just dropped a mention of fam night in front of Fitz, knowing full well I haven't talked to him about coming to our regular chaos get together.

As expected, he meets my eyes, one brow raising as he tilts his head from side to side, inspecting the neat ringlets. "Fam dinner?"

"I'll leave you two to noodle on that one," my roommate says, and she meets my eyes, winking before turning to leave. Then she stops, and throws over her shoulder "Any particular reason my Waterford vase is now on top of the cabinets?"

I snort, and Fitz gives me a small smile in the mirror before turning back around, leaning against the edge of the counter and crossing his arms, leaving me to say "Roscoe and Bex might have been a little boisterous in their playing last night." I wince. "I would be careful in the kitchen, glass from that red cheapo vase traveled basically everywhere."

"Yeah, my foot learned that one." Fitz dramatically lifts one of his feet off my tile floor, and I roll my eyes as Carla nods and makes her way out of my room. We did, indeed, spend ten minutes digging a tiny sliver of glass out of the ball of his foot last night, which resulted in a very dramatic spectacle of this giant man squirming away from my tweezers like they were on fire.

"Just gonna need you to get that one down before you leave," she says to Fitz from the hallway. But the second she's gone, he turns to me.

"*Fitzwilliam*," I start, and bat my lashes for added effect as his eyes tip to the ceiling. I put one hand on his chest. "Would you like to come to our regular shitshow of a family dinner on Friday? It's a belated Easter celebration, there will be gifts, even for the heathens who don't go to mass." His eyes travel to the intricately tied shirt holding up the mess of curls above my head, and slowly, his face folds into a smile. "Anyone who's anyone will be there."

"Anyone who's anyone?" he repeats, reaching out and putting a hand on each of my hips. I step between his legs, letting him push the hem of my shirt up enough to rub circles on my skin. I look at my reflection in the mirror behind him and nearly cackle. Me, in my 5K For the Cure shirt, with another ratty, old band tee holding up my hair. Only, the way his shoulders strain against his orange shirt makes me smile, and I slide my palm up his chest, over the curve of his neck until I see my hand, all my gold rings, gripping at him. His body tenses, the touch sensual, despite me looking like a crazy person. "Dylan will be there?"

Ah, so the tensing wasn't just because of me.

"He will." He nods, just slightly, and I put the comb in my other hand on the counter next to him, bringing both my hands to the sides of his jaw and forcing him to meet my eyes. Fitz swallows like he's nervous. "If you'd seen the mooney eyes those two were making the other day," I start, tilting my head towards Carla's room on the other side of the wall, "you wouldn't be giving it a second thought." I stroke his cheek with my thumb. "What do I need to do to convince you that I'm yours?"

That word, *yours*, and *mine*, really, had felt like a declaration that first night in his bedroom, and while filled with lust, with physical need, I didn't think it meant any less than completely. Totally. Because at this point, who are we kidding?

I'd been his after that first kiss in my room, just a few feet away from where we are now. It's terrifying, and a little exhilarating, whatever this is. Fitz Westfall's *girlfriend*.

I watch the furrow between his brows ease, his freckled face less tense as he tilts into one of my hands, pressing a kiss to my palm. "Now that you mention it..." His eyes darken, his fingers on my hips tightening, and I let out a strangled laugh, batting him away and stepping back. "Hey, you asked!" I point towards the doorway.

"Out!" He looks wounded, and I relent. "I need to dry my hair, you loon." I point to the contraption holding up my curls. "Now, out!" I shove at his shoulder, halfway between playing and seriousness, and he stumbles out, looking at me incredulously. "You touch your hair before I exit this bathroom and you die." And then I close the door in his shocked face, leaning against the hollow wood and burying my head in my hands at the sheer craziness my life has become.

After a moment of silence, Fitz's voice comes from the other side of the door. "What should I plan on bringing Friday?"

CHAPTER 42

Fitz

It takes approximately thirty seconds for my brother to notice something is different about my appearance, and another thirty for him to place that it's my hair, but once he does, it's literally all he can talk about.

"She's got you using product," he says like I've grown a third arm, tipping the neck of his beer bottle at me from where he stands in my kitchen.

"Product isn't a bad thing," Todd argues from his place on the other side of the counter, a can of craft local brew between his fingers as he leans forward, weight on his elbows. He gestures up to his own head. "I would look like a fucking idiot without something to keep this tamed."

"I'm not saying product is a bad thing." Freddy takes a long sip from his bottle, eying me, and then gestures to his own mop of hair. "You think this looks *this good* without a little help?" I give my neighbor a deadpan look, but Fred continues, "I'm just observing that this girl has *you* using product."

"She's not a girl." I make a face. No, girl is definitely not the word I'd use to describe Piper. But the doorbell rings, saving me from having to qualify that response to Freddy, who is, arguably, more analytical than I am.

When I open the door, Mateo and Vic are standing on the porch, chatting like old friends - but they both silence when they see me standing there, and immediately look at my head. I feel heat creep up my neck.

Frannie had done the same thing yesterday, when I'd spent a measly ten minutes attempting to refresh the soft ringlets by way of Piper's specific instructions. And while they looked a little less glossy today, it was very much a noticeable difference from my typical "two minutes and out the door" attitude.

Vic holds a six pack of Blue Moon out between us like a peace offering. "She got you with the curly girl method, didn't she?" Mateo snorts next to him, the hand holding a large paper bag moving to cover his mouth like he regretted it instantly. I snatch the bag from his hand, turning and heading back down the hall without another word.

"Oh, someone's touchy." Mateo's voice is audible even as I round into the kitchen, hearing the door closing behind them. "Or should I say, lightly coiffed?" I don't need to see Fred to know the laugh across the room comes from him - my friendship with Todd is still too tentative for him to laugh at a jab like that.

"I've missed you, man," he says to Mateo, crossing the room in a few long strides and bringing Mateo into a tight embrace.

I feel on guard - ever since Freddy and Frannie read me the riot act, I've been hyper aware of the way these people around me interact. People I've known most of my life, who have somehow evolved around me and built friendships I wasn't even aware of while I was wallowing in self pity post-divorce.

And one of those, it seems, is Mateo and Freddy.

"Seriously, though. It looks good." Vic gestures to my hair, shrugging on a black bomber jacket over the tee shirt he's wearing, probably because I have the AC blasting to compensate for the gathering heat outside. He looks put together in a way the rest of the men around me don't - I think, mostly, because they simply don't care.

Todd is a personal trainer, he's always wearing athletic clothes no matter the occasion. I saw the guy on Christmas day last year, and he was in gym shorts. Freddy, for now, is always in a LSSU shirt and chinos or jeans. He's always had a kind of uniform. It's shifted over the years, but he joined the same fraternity I was in at UT when he started college, and between their mandatory event shirts and ones he'd managed to find on his own, it was 90% of his wardrobe. And Mateo, well, Mateo always looked like he was about five seconds away from jumping on the back of his Suzuki and speeding away, all leather jackets and thick, square-toed boots.

It's poker night, and I feel overdressed in my own home, already uneasy from all the attention my hair is getting.

"What did you bring this time?" Fred asks, diverting attention away from me and pointing to the bag still in my hand. I peek inside - it looks like...donuts?

"Bomboloni," Mateo answers, throwing keys and wallet onto the counter and setting down a bottle of wine - he's always been a wine snob, I think way before we were even old enough to drink, probably because his dad has been doing wine pairing menus for longer than we've been alive.

"Are we supposed to know what that means?" Todd asks, coming to stand behind my shoulder and looking into the bag. I pull out one of the dough balls, coated with sugar.

"It's like a donut-type-thing."

"Eloquent," I reply, and then take a bite. Mateo snatches the bag out of my hand as I chew, and the bite of the chocolate - Nutella? - in the middle hits my tongue. Oh, man, these are good."

"Fuck off, no more for you until you learn manners," Mateo says. Fred snorts, reaching in and getting one for himself. "They're Italian. I've been fucking with the dough recipe for, like, six months."

"I'll be a good boy if it means more of these," Fred says, holding up the pastry he's already eaten half of, making a guttural noise. I swallow the laugh at the back of my throat - sometimes he doesn't realize he sounds inappropriate. Wordlessly, Mateo holds the bag out to Vic, who I can tell is trying not to laugh at my brother, who licks his fingers in a way that is immediately overtly sexual.

"Piper's Nona used to make these all the time," Vic adds, taking a bite and giving a satisfied nod. "Close, dude, real close."

"I'll take that as a win, assuming Nona knew how to cook." Vic closes his eyes at Mateo's words, like he's remembering the world's best meal.

"Oh, yeah. You didn't leave the table until you were fat, happy, possibly on the edge of falling asleep." He shakes his head, like he's trying not to reminisce too hard, and then looks at me. "Lady was a spitfire, you're lucky she's gone, or she would have eaten you alive on Friday."

"Let's play some cards," I say, at the same time Freddy asks "Ooh, what's Friday?" and I fight a groan. Fuck, Vic. Left the door wide open on that one.

Hours later, I'm staring at a shit hand of cards across my patio table. Over the citronella candle in the center, I see Todd muttering at his cards, eyes flitting back and forth like he's trying to devise a plan. Next to him, Fred starts to say something, and then stops.

My phone buzzes on the table next to me.

PIPER DELMONICO
How's it going? Is everyone playing nice?

FITZ WESTFALL
I don't know about *nice.* Vic has won three games so far, if he wins a fourth we're calling it a fuckin night and heading to Top Shelf if you two want to meet us for late night snacks and Dr. Pepper.

"Tell your girlfriend we all said hi," Mateo teases, knocking my shoulder with his own, and I don't correct him as I lock my phone, waiting for Piper's response. I see Freddy look at me, waiting for me to grind out a retort, but when it doesn't come, he looks immediately to Vic, who isn't meeting my gaze, but has a smile on his face that I suspect is due to more than just another winning hand of cards. The Long Island Iced Tea at the bar just a block away from Piper's apartment is apparently his favorite - and the stipulation for playing another round was the worst hand buys the best hand's drinks.

"Oh shit," Fred says, setting his hand down. "Yeah, no, I'm out, guys." He turns his attention to me, never one to linger long on his own defeat. "You locked it down?"

"I mean she's not about to change her name to Westfall or anything." I scratch at my ear, setting down my own cards. "Fold."

PIPER DELMONICO
We're in for the night, mud masks on and starting S3 of Vampire Diaries.

FITZ WESTFALL
Which brother is she with now?

"Yet," Mateo teases, and I kick his shin under the table. He jolts, leaning down to rub at it. "Fuck you, Will. I saw how you looked at her." He meets Todd's gaze, which is just as hopeless as Vic's is triumphant. "No dice?" Todd shakes his head, sipping at the seltzer in his hand and setting down his own cards as Mateo mirrors his actions. They both look to Vic, who's still grinning.

PIPER DELMONICO
Aw, you remembered. Color me impressed.

"We don't have to tell Piper about me kicking your ass," Vic says a little *too* sweetly, leaning forward and resting his chin on his knuckles. "Even though she's pretty fucking smitten, and I don't think it has anything to do with your card-playing skills." Something in my chest flutters, but before I can dwell on it, he sets his hand out in front of him. "Full house, boys."

Two Long Island Iced Teas later, and Vic's triumph has him riding a high at the bar. We're clustered around a high-top table, drinks in hand, while Freddy and Todd shoot a game of one-on-one pool.

Vic has his phone in one hand, a ranch water in the other, and the grin on his face doesn't quite feel like it's all due to kicking our asses.

"For someone dishing out shit about Piper being smitten..." I nudge the hand holding his phone, and he looks up, shaking his head like he was clearing a thought away.

"That obvious?" Vic locks his phone, setting it on the table in front of him. I lean forward on my elbows, raising a brow at him.

"You've been checking that thing every couple of minutes since we got to the house," Mateo responds, and even in the crappy lighting of this bar, I can see the color in Vic's cheeks flare.

"I may be..." He searches for a word. "Talking to someone?" It sounds like a question more than a statement.

"You're not sure?" Mateo asks, and Vic pops his shoulders. "Look, I'm not saying I'm an expert on-

"Gay men?" Vic finishes, and I nearly snort my IPA out of my nose. "I don't think even gay men are experts in gay men."

"*Facts*," a passing waiter adds, and I'm glad I'm not mid-sip again. Vic and Mateo chuckle, before I turn back to the man I've known just as long as Piper, but feel that I barely know.

He's such a huge part of her life - Christ, I mean, he *married* her and Mickey - but I don't want to pry if it's not something he's comfortable with.

After a minute, he takes a steeling breath, and then meets my gaze. "It's Kyle."

"Who's Kyle?" Mateo asks. Freddy makes a half-hearted groan as he sinks the cue ball in a pocket.

"Hoffman?" It's a clarifying question on my part, just to make sure that I'm on the same page, but Vic's face reddens again. I turn to Mateo. "We went to school with him, he's helping with the reunion."

Mateo nods in understanding, taking a long pull of the dark bourbon in his glass.

Piper has never mentioned Vic and Kyle dating, or talking, or really doing anything together, for that matter, aside from the few times they've both been at her place helping with the reunion. But before I can ask if he's told his best friends anything, he continues.

"Piper doesn't know yet." I press my lips together, nodding. "Things are too...new. And if it goes bad, I don't want it to sour anything they're working on together."

"Why would it go bad?" Mateo asks, like he's known Vic for ten years and not a couple of hours. The question was on the tip of my tongue, too.

Vic shrugs again. "I've known for most of my life I was gay. It wasn't a huge surprise for my parents when they found out I'd had my first kiss, and it was with a dude."

"But?" I press him on.

"Kyle didn't come out until recently," he says, and I nod. Got it. "It's all still so new for him, he hasn't really dated a lot, and from what I understand, his parents weren't the most...thrilled about it."

"I feel that," Mateo adds with an understanding nod. "That's why my stepmom and her ex separated." Vic and I both look at him, confused. "Jesse, my step brother, came out, and his dad basically threatened to send him to conversion camp."

"Jesus." The word comes out as a surprised huff, and I bring my fist to my chest where it just tightened at that idea. "I didn't know that, man."

Mateo shrugs, taking another sip of bourbon. "People can be bigots. But people can also divorce bigots."

"I don't think they're that level of awful," Vic continues. "He was a full-grown adult, but I think it's a big part of why he moved out and doesn't see them as often. He was afraid to date for so long because he felt like they'd judge him."

I grimace and take a long sip of beer, ruminating on that. Kyle and Vic. Vic and Kyle. In the back of my brain, I can see it. Can see them together. Could maybe see them being happy, maybe because I wish for Piper's best friends to be as happy as we are. At least, as happy as I hope we are.

"I think he'd be lucky to date you, Vic," I say after a long pause, and then clap him on the shoulder. "But you've gotta tell Piper soon, because I don't keep secrets from her, and you and I both know she'll be screaming giddy for this one."

For a Wednesday, we're out pretty late - and by the time we're all heading our separate ways in my front yard, the only two left to leave are Todd and Vic. Mateo's car makes a kickback noise as he pulls away, having favored air conditioning over the "cool factor" he'd always carried riding his bike. Better for me - I love the guy like a brother, but I can only spend so much time with him when he smells like a gas station.

"Nice to meet you, man," Todd says, giving Vic a casual handshake and pulling him in for a half hug. Arguably, Todd's had the most to drink out of all of us, but I drove us the quarter-mile to the bar, and he was walking a whole twenty feet back to his front door.

"You, too." Vic pats his back somewhat awkwardly as Todd steps away, giving me a sort of salute and then jogging back to his house. I watch, mostly to make sure he doesn't find the one rock in his yard to trip over, and then turn to Vic in front of me. He's got his jacket draped over one shoulder, a hand in his pocket and the other on the back of his neck. The universal guy sign for "I'm uncomfortable as fuck."

"Thanks for coming." He gives a curt nod, finally meeting my eye.

CHAPTER 42

"I was sort of surprised when you texted, not gonna lie." I quirk a brow - I thought it would be obvious. He's a part of Piper's life. She's a part of mine. An important part, if we're being honest. Clearly he's important to her. "Outside of our usual crew, I don't usually hang a lot with..." He holds his fingers up in air quotes. "The guys." I fight a laugh, crossing my arms.

"I don't know if this qualifies as 'the guys,' but I'm glad you came." I want to reach out, to give him a pat on the shoulder, but the contact feels foreign to me. So instead, I tell him what I'm thinking. "I'm worried about Friday."

As I kind of expected, he laughs - not a lot, just enough to know I'm probably rightfully terrified. After years of having the Carlson's as my in-laws, the idea of having to completely reorient myself with a new family, with new people who knew I would be seeking their validation, is scary. Especially for someone like me, who isn't exactly a charmer on first meeting. Sure, I know how to convince people to see things my way...but if Mrs. Delmonico is half as stubborn as her daughter, she'll see through that bravado real quick.

"The Delmonicos are chill," he says with a shrug, and then starts his car with the remote on his key fob. Clearly he isn't planning to stick around and offer warm words of encouragement. "It's the rest of the fam you've gotta worry about." He observes me, in my still-mostly-formal outfit from work. "Piper tell you to bring dessert?" I nod, thinking back to her words through the bathroom door last weekend - something sweet, besides *that ass*. I fight the eye roll at the memory. "My advice?" he asks, crossing his arms, and nodding his head towards the street, where Mateo's car had been parked moments earlier. "Tag in your slugger and-"

He pauses, like he realizes what he's said as he's said it, and drags a hand down his face.

"Fuck, don't tell Nolan or Brett I just used a baseball term in real life." He pinches the bridge of his nose. "They'll never let me live it down."

"I'll skip that one if you don't tell them how bad you kicked our asses tonight." Vic laughs, holding out his hand. I take it, shaking my head.

"Deal."

CHAPTER 43

Piper

My nerves are shot and it's not even…I glance at my watch. Noon. It's not even noon, and I've had to stop myself from picking at my cuticles three times.

I'm nervous. Piper Delmonico doesn't do *nervous*. Not truly. Not in a long, long time. Sure, I was a little anxious before my first date with Fitz. But in the back of my mind, I knew it was going to go well. We were both invested, by that point.

But Fitz Westfall and my father at the same table? And *Nolan*?

Shit. I'm reconsidering my belief in a Catholic God just to have someone tangible to pray to right now.

"You're gonna break that if you fuck with it any more," Vic mutters, gesturing to the fidget cube in my hand. I'd resorted to a fidget cube. That's where I'm at right now.

"I'll buy a new one," I seethe back, pushing the joystick with my thumb another three times as I slide open the latest email from one of the production team leaders, with a list of items from each department for the winter launches - many of which are already in manufacturing, or will be soon.

I scan the list, spotting a few of each of our other designer's items, as expected. But when I make it to the end of the apparel list, I stare at my screen, and then scroll back up, reading it again.

None. Not one of my designs made the list.

"You have got to be shitting me." It's out of my mouth before I can stop it, and a few people around us stop typing. Vic rolls out of his cubicle again, eying me. By the thin line of his lips, I know he's just read it, too. "Tell me I'm not seeing what I think I'm seeing."

"Deep breath." The look I shoot him has him gulping audibly, and he rolls towards me. "Piper, it's just one season."

"One season I've designed three times my usual amount for."

CHAPTER 43

Hormones, this has to be hormones, right? This innate rage that has me wanting to fucking launch my fidget cube at my expensive ass double monitor setup? I want to scream. I want to break something. I want to tear through this office like a toddler who didn't win a tiara.

I love designing things that make people feel good about themselves. I love giving people the power of feeling sexy. I love seeing my creations come to life. I love this job.

Well. I loved this job.

I close my eyes, trying to take the deep breath Vic suggested. I meditate all the time. Carla's mom is a master yoga instructor. Deep breathing is my jam.

But right now, all I want to do is breathe fire.

As I open my eyes, I push to standing, setting my fidget cube down on my desk with a little more force than necessary.

"Piper," Vic starts, his tone concerned, and I swallow, fingers wrapping around the edges of my desk.

"I can't do this, Vic." My voice comes out strangled, and I blink back tears. I'm not even sad - I'm angry. Angry that I've spent so much time with my head buried in the sand, dedicated to this job - to these designs - that go nowhere.

Vic's sigh is resigned, and when I turn to look at him, his shoulders are slumped. He runs a hand through his hair, effectively ruining the perfectly styled pouf he had going on.

I don't wait for him to continue before pushing off from my desk, rounding the corner and stepping into the hallway outside Brianna's office. One final deep breath, and I step into her doorway, watching her type at her computer for a second before I knock on the door.

The sound makes her glance my way, just for a second, before she registers who's standing in front of her and her hands freeze hovering above her keyboard.

"Piper, come in," she says quickly, rolling back after a moment and gesturing to the seat in front of her. Staring at the ugly knit fabric, I nearly lose my grit. What am I going to say? Am I going to demand that they change the winter lineup? Shove some of my designs into production fast and dirty?

Before I completely chicken out, I close the door behind me and move to step into the chair, and then pause. No. I need to stay standing for this. It should be a quick conversation - one way or another.

"I saw the production list for winter," I start, trying to keep my tone even. My fingers grip the back of the ugly chair in front of me, and I'm sure they'd be white-knuckled if it weren't for the padding.

"Ah." Brianna sniffs, pulling her glasses off, and the move reminds me of my dad - just a little bit, but enough to catch me off guard. "I was hoping I'd have a chance to chat with you before they sent that out."

"Well, you're chatting with me now." My tone is a little less measured, and comes across as kind of catty, but at this point, I'm lucky I'm not a sobbing mess. Willingly confronting someone when I'm unhappy isn't my style.

Brianna's jaw tenses as she looks up at me, and I can tell she's as uncomfortable as I am - probably more so, with me towering over her. I'm already tall, but in heels I might as well be a giant compared to her small frame.

"Why didn't any of my designs make the cut?"

Whoomp, there it is.

"The brand-"

"Please don't talk to me about the brand," I cut her off, and her eyebrows shoot up to meet where her hair is slicked back in a tight bun. "Bri, I know this brand backwards and forwards."

"It's too much, Piper." I rear back, confused.

"What's too much?"

"Your designs." She sighs, and then rubs at her eyes like this conversation is physically paining her. Good. I need answers. "Piper, they're beautiful. But the brand dictates -"

"The brand dictates exactly what I provided." I cross my arms. "I don't get it, half the designs on the list were on par with mine. They were just..." I trail off, my eyes flashing around her office as I look for the words.

Her degree. Her family pictures. Her perfectly posed wedding shot in a giant frame on her desk. Nice. Neat. Normal.

But not exceptional. Not extraordinary.

Not enough.

And suddenly, the cogs in my brain are whirring.

The designs on that list I'd seen myself - some of them were even more wild than mine. But what those other designers didn't have, what they lacked, was my experience. Where their creativity could shine, mine was also balanced with my time spent building brands, truly marketing, managing, in a way others hadn't.

It wasn't my designs. It wasn't the brand at all.

It was me.

Brianna, harsh, plain, neat Brianna was threatened. She was feeling threatened by me.

For a moment, I push away the thought - threatened by me? Who would be threatened by *me*?

Andy, for a start. He was terrified that I would talk about him, about us, and bring down any sort of image he had with it. So he did it to me first.

The Davis family. They were threatened by me from the moment Mickey decided to stay in Texas instead of going back to Paulsville. So they found someone to replace me.

And fuck, while I can't dwell on it too much, not in this moment - Olivia. Olivia was threatened by me all those years ago. Thinking back to those moments in the hall, at prom, hell, any time after Fitz knew about Andy and I. Somewhere underneath all that cool girl bravado, she knew her statue of a man was starting to melt for me. So she made me feel as small and insignificant as she could.

But Brianna. Brianna is my boss. She's been promoted twice in the last two years. She's valuable to the people above her - enough that they didn't think twice when she didn't put forward a single design from one of her designers.

And truly, really, thinking about it right now...putting my heart and soul into designs knowing they could end up on the cutting room floor at the whims of someone else makes my stomach roil.

"We'll just work on something a little more in-line with the vision for the spring, yeah?" Brianna's smile is tentative, hopeful. I can tell she's trying to placate me, but she can see the wheels turning as much as I feel them grinding against my skin. Words Fitz spoke all those weeks ago in his bedroom come drifting through the back of my head, like a breath against my cheek.

He didn't deserve even a second glance from you.

I deserve better. I deserve more than this.

"They're always going to be too much." My voice is soft, probably softer than it should be. But I'm not wrong. Brianna pauses where she's started moving her hands back to her keyboard, looking at me like I'm not making sense. "My designs are always going to be too much, aren't they?"

"Piper, there's always next season."

"And in the spring?" I ask, gesturing around the room with one hand. My eye catches my wedding ring, light glinting off the stone. I swallow. "I refuse to make myself small."

"Small?" She seems caught off guard, like I've cursed at her. Then I realize she thinks I'm talking about myself physically, as her eyes run up and down my body, settling on the curve of my stomach. I step back.

"I've made myself, *who I am as a person*, small a lot. I'm not about to do it here to make you more comfortable."

"It's not about me being comfortable," she argues, and I guess she's had enough because she stands too, her chair rolling back behind her. "Piper, it's just..." She rubs at one brow again. "You're too much."

"Well." I can't help the half-laugh that soars out of me as I cross my arms again, shaking my head. "I'm not going to apologize for being myself, and if that's how you feel then it's clear I shouldn't be on your team." She blinks at me.

"Piper, I-"

"No, Bri. You've made it quite clear." I don't turn as I step back, opening the door with one hand and staring straight at her. I was nice enough to keep the rest of that conversation quiet, but I refuse to let anyone here pretend that my next action is anything but my own doing. "I quit."

"*What?*" She balks at me, at the open door behind me, and I hear any sound outside immediately stop. No keyboards. No whispers. Utter silence.

"Vic can pack up my stuff. If I'm too much, Bri," I start, backing up until I'm at the doorway, my hands raised at my shoulders in a shrug, which might as well be two middle fingers with the way she's staring at me. "Please, go find less."

And with that, I swing by my desk, trying not to lose my cool when I see Vic sitting in his chair with his mouth half open. I grab my purse, my tablet, my phone and my fucking fidget cube and walk out, separately texting my sponsor, my therapist, my roommate, and my boyfriend before I've reached the parking lot with five simple words.

PIPER DELMONICO
I just quit my job.

CHAPTER 44

Fitz

There is absolute chaos happening behind the red door of the Delmonico home, so loud I'm unsure if I should ring the doorbell to add to it. On my wrist, my watch buzzes.

PIPER DELMONICO
Just come in when you get here.

She doesn't mean that, does she? Just walk into her parents house like it's my own?

I read the text probably three times before I decide she's not kidding, and adjust the bag in my hands before pressing the latch and opening the door in front of me. Immediately, the sounds get ten times louder, and I follow the echoes of voices down an equally red entryway lined with white china plates and family photos of the Delmonicos, which I tell myself to stop and inspect later.

From around a corner, Brett's head pops out, and he smiles. "Hey, man, welcome to the circus." He steps out from behind the wall, and I see that he's got a squirming toddler in his arms. Her hair is wild and curly, just like Piper's, and I can't help the smile on my face. "Aria, Jesus, quit-"

And then her tiny foot hits him in the stomach and he doubles over, letting her down to the ground as gently as a man in pain can. Laughing, she runs off behind him without a second glance in my direction, and I stand there, momentarily stunned as Brett recovers faster than I would have.

"Don't have kids," he warns, and then, still half-way bent, reaches out for the bag in my hands. "Offering for the gods?" I shrug, handing the bag over and letting him inspect the contents. "Ooh, you did good."

I had help, I want to respond. But I don't. I just let him straighten up, motioning for me to follow him back where he came from - one, big open room where the chaos is all coming from. Aria, the little girl with the wicked kick, is chasing around a boy that looks maybe a year older. Both of them share the same curly hair, caramel skin, dark eyes - and I know they're Penny and Brett's instantly. In an armchair, I spot Nolan, who I haven't seen since his wife's water broke on my shoes. He meets my eyes, not stopping the rocking motion he's making with a bundle I can only assume is his daughter - Piper's goddaughter - over his shoulder. He tips his chin up at me, a half smile curling his lips, probably also remembering the last time we'd seen each other.

Next to him, on one end of a tufted, antique looking couch, is Dylan, who raises his beer bottle at me. A possessive, animalistic rage swells in my chest - just for a second, before I feel a hand on my shoulder, and turn to see the mass of curls I'd been looking for. The top of Piper's hair is pulled up into two poofs at the top of her head, the rest hanging around her neck in dark ringlets. She's wearing a tan off-the-shoulder dress with another bodice like the one she'd worn on our first date, only this one has bluish-purple stalks rising from the bottom of the hem like grass. Bluebonnets. They're bluebonnets, stitched into the deep blue fabric. I offer my hand out for hers, holding her at arm's length so I can take it all in, down to the platform sandals that make her just that much closer to being able to kiss me without standing on her tiptoes.

"I take it we changed after we went home," I say quietly, and she gives me a grin that's a lot more relaxed than I expected for someone who quit their job less than eight hours ago.

"Cried, stress-ate my weight in Cheez-Its, re-did my hair and makeup, and then changed, yes." She pops her foot out behind her, and then leans up to give me a peck on the lips.

"Get out of here with that crap." I don't need to look behind Piper to see that Alex is standing in one of the tall archways into the kitchen, but I glance anyway. For a second, her eyes flit behind me - I'm sure, to Nolan - and then she smirks. "Welcome to Fam Dinner, Westfall." I catch Piper's smile.

"*May the odds be ever in your favor.*" Piper's voice is high pitched and prim, I can't help the eye roll as I let her lead me past Alex, who digs at my side lightly with her elbow. From my place in the living room, I could vaguely see a mass of people buzzing around the kitchen, but in full view, I see Penny and Carla standing at a double fridge, drinks in hand, talking animatedly about something. Vic is at the stove with a man I immediately recognize as Piper's dad. I've only seen him a few times over the years, but he shares those same intense blue eyes and dark curly hair.

Vic nods at me as we approach, and it's enough to get her dad's attention - he turns to see us, and those eyes, hidden behind thick glasses, widen. He holds both hands up over his head, his pristine blue button up moving with him as he grins.

"You must be Fitzwilliam." Piper squeezes my hand as Vic snorts, moving to cover his mouth with a hand holding a spatula. Behind me, I hear Alex cackle, but I don't really have time to register it, because before I can say anything, this man I don't know at all is pulling me into a warm embrace, slapping my back.

"Uh," I stutter. Vic gives me a thumbs up, and Penny and Carla both turn to take in the interaction. "Nice to meet you, Mr. Delmonico." I gently pat him on the back, trying to echo as much of the sentiment as my startle brain will allow. He pulls back, holding me by the shoulders as he inspects me. I instantly feel a little better, seeing that we're dressed similarly. But, from what Piper told me, this man dealt in fabric for a living. I'd bet he didn't own a poorly made piece of clothing.

"Luca, please." He gives my shoulders a squeeze, and then looks behind me to Piper. "He's a handsome one." He pats my face with one hand, and I feel myself flush - the familiarity and warmth of this family is in such stark contrast with my own.

"Don't inflate his ego too much, Papa," Alex calls from behind me, and we both look at her. Nolan has moved to stand behind her, and he's slipping a snoozing Mikayla into her arms. He's tall, too, but I wouldn't expect anything less from a professional athlete. I realize, with her words, how close Alex must be to the Delmonicos, to call Piper's father *Papa*.

"Me?" Luca puts a hand to his chest. "Never." His grin is easy, and immediately it reminds me of the wicked one Piper gets - clearly that's from him.

"Here we go!" I hear the voice from another room and we all turn towards it, watching as a woman slips out from a door around the corner, arms full of bags and baskets littered with pastel eggs and plastic grass filling. She stops mid-step when she sees me. "Oh! You're here."

"He's here," Piper replies, and I hear the strain in her voice immediately. The woman, who I know is Piper and Penny's mom, dumps the items in her hands on an empty space on the dark brown quartz counter, extending a ring-covered hand to me.

"Bianca Delmonico."

If Luca Delmonico is all smiles and warmth, Bianca is the other side of his coin, a cool, quiet confidence that radiates stability. And in some ways, that makes me more comfortable than the ease with which Piper's dad immediately accepted me. I was used to wariness, expected it, even, because that's how I am, too.

So, I shake her hand, and the way she grips my fingers like a vice tells me she's sizing me up. From the way her eyes scan, head to toe, I know that she's analyzing me as much as I'm analyzing her. Pin straight dark hair, so in contrast to Piper's. Dark eyes. A narrow nose that I knew Penny had.

"Fitz Westfall." I nod to her, then her husband to her side. "It's wonderful to meet you all." I gesture around me, and as I speak, feel Piper's hand slip back into mine, immediately settling me a fraction. "Thank you for having me."

"Had to get you here for the interrogation," Bianca says dryly, and her tone reminds me of Freddy.

"Here, here!" Nolan jeers behind me, and he's raising a beer in his hands in agreement with Bianca's sentiment. This. *This* is why I was nervous to come tonight. Not just because I'd be seeing Piper's parents again, truly meeting them for the first time - but doing so with all of these other people watching, like a spectator sport. I suppose the baseball game was round one; the hospital, round two; and the day at my pool, round three. Round four introduced several new players.

"Down, girl," Luca coos, putting an arm around his wife's waist and pulling her close, nuzzling a kiss into her cheek as Bianca bats him away, and it's all I can do not to laugh. Of all the things I expected from tonight, learning that Piper's parents were the two of us in reverse wasn't even on the bingo card, but the way she gives my fingers a squeeze tells me she's thinking the same thing.

"He brought an offering." Brett finally makes his way into the kitchen with my bag, presumably having chased his kids through the house. "Well, several." He hands the tote to Luca, who takes it, fishing out the bottle of wine first.

"Good start," Bianca says, taking it from her husband and turning to dig in a drawer. "I presume you drink, then."

"Yeah, Westfall." Nolan steps up next to me, holding out a beer, cap already off. "You drink?" I take it from him, letting him clink the neck against his still-full bottle. Piper mentioned he took it easy during the season, and he's back on the road tomorrow for another three-game series in Miami. Luca sets another bottle of wine, this one a white, on the counter next to the bottle of red.

"Ooh." Luca holds up a large paper bag, grease stains along the sides evident - there's no other way to transport fried food without it getting gummy. He puts the tote down, peeling open the bag and taking a deep inhale of whatever scent was wafting from it.

"What'd you bring?" Piper asks, stepping up to my other side as Nolan leans forward, trying to take a peek into the bag. Piper's parents share a look as Bianca twists a corkscrew into the top of the bottle of red, peering into the bag and then back at me.

"If those are what I think they are," Vic starts, setting his spatula down and speaking for the first time since I arrived, "you're going to want to save room for dessert." Curious as ever, Piper moves between her parents, peering in the bag.

She stills, and then looks back at me, wide eyed.

"Are those bomboloni?" I shrug, hands finding my pockets. Piper watches me, eyes flaring at the gesture.

"Mateo made them, I'm just the delivery man." I give them a small smile. "Vic mentioned they're a family favorite."

"Well." Bianca's hands are frozen mid-uncorking, gazing between the bag and where I stand. "We'll see if they measure up to Nona's." I swear, I see her lips turn up at the corner when she turns to reach into a cabinet, pulling out several wine glasses.

Score one, Westfall.

Piper

"Ok, ok," Fitz relents, holding out his wine glass as my father refills it. Again. Gone are the two bottles he brought, out came Papa's private stash of Italian wine his brother sends for every holiday and occasion (*the good stuff,* he'd muttered to me).

Shit, and people wonder why I had such a hard time coming to terms with the idea of being an alcoholic. Booze flows like water here.

"Thank you," Vic says from the other side of the table, holding up the giant gold-wrapped chocolate bunny she gets him every year. It'll be gone by the end of the weekend, like it is every year. He sets it on the tabletop, which is covered in plastic picnic tablecloths - my mother's pushed two six foot tables together out in the backyard under the shade of my childhood house, an assortment of chairs along either side like a summer garden party. I suppose it is, in some ways.

"Your turn, passerotto mio," my mother says, tilting her own wine glass at me with a smile that makes me anxious. She'd handed me a deep purple box while doling out all of our Easter presents, the kids having long-since ripped their baskets apart and gone inside to feast on chocolate and Nintendo Switch.

"Should I be scared?" I ask, gripping the edges of the box. She settles further into her chair, and I shake my head, pulling up one corner and looking inside.

I snort, tearing the lid off completely and setting it on the table, pulling the box further into my lap.

"You're ridiculous." I scoff at her, easily sliding into Italian as I start pulling items from the hot pink plastic grass. A chocolate flamingo. A flamingo-shaped floating cup holder. A water bottle with a flamingo painted on the side, wearing a pair of oversized sunglasses and a floppy hat. "Seriously, Mama?"

"*Inglese,*" Alex begs from her seat next to me, and Nolan pulls close to her, his gaze burning.

"Baby, you know what that accent does to me," he says, just loud enough that I can hear. I make a retching noise - payback, for all the shit she's given me and Fitz over the last few weeks. She smacks him in the chest, giving me a pointed look.

"That's fantastic." Brett leans over from his seat next to my father, snatching the water bottle to inspect. "Does it come with a matching koozie?" I look up at the sky, willing lightning to strike me down.

"I'm going to murder you all." I run a hand down my face, finally making eye contact with Fitz, whose eyebrows are knit together as he waits for an explanation. "It's an inside joke." I let my eyes flit to my mother, her smirk deepening.

"Peak Bianca, in my opinion," Alex says, tipping her seltzer at my mother with the hand not holding Mickie to her chest. "We were on our way back from vacation one summer..."

"Oh we're just diving right in?" Penny settles down in her chair like it's story time at the library.

"And Piper is listening to one of her Harry Potter podcasts." Penny rolls her eyes, looking at Vic and then back to Alex.

"Listening isn't even the right word. She was giving us a play by play." I flush, feeling embarrassment creep up into my chest.

"Harry Potter podcast?" Fitz repeats flatly, and then takes a long sip from his glass, meeting my eyes over the rim. I feel my nostrils flare at the amusement in his gaze.

"I was a nerd, ok?"

"Was?" Alex snorts.

"Nolan, take the baby."

"Not a chance, bitch." Alex pulls her daughter closer, using her as a shield for what would have been a well-placed boob punch. "Anyways, we're in the car for like, ten hours. And somehow we start talking about what our patronus would be. You know, the weird ghosty animal thing that makes the grim reapers run away." She's talking to the whole table like Fitz isn't the only one who hasn't heard this story ten times before - even Dylan, at the other end of the table, next to Carla, is grinning, because he knows exactly how much of a nerd I am. I bury my face in my hands, both from embarrassment, and the pain of knowing that after years of making her watch Harry Potter, that's how she chose to describe what a patronus is.

"I fucking hate you," I mutter, so only she and Fitz can hear me. She ignores it.

"And this loser says she wants hers to be a flamingo." Alex snorts, loudly, taking a sip of her drink.

CHAPTER 44

"A flamingo," Carla echoes, hiding half her face behind her hands as she cackles. Ok, she's on my shit list, too. Alex continues.

"So Bianca goes 'you want an animal that spends its life on one foot with its head up its ass to defend you?'" She's wheezing by the time she finishes, and I see Fitz's shoulders shaking next to me. "I nearly peed my pants."

"Peak Bianca," Vic echoes, tilting his wine glass towards my mother, who does the same back to him - long before Nolan and Brett were part of this family, Vic was her honorary son.

"I hate all of you." I take a drink of my Dr. Pepper, contemplating which of my family I'm going to get back at first, and how embarrassing I'm going to make it.

CHAPTER 45

Fitz

When I offer to help clear the table, Piper waves me away. "We've got it." She gestures between herself and the other women, who have all stood to pick items up from around the table - plates of nearly demolished roast, mashed potatoes, and the other things Luca and Vic had made. Apparently, they were the cooks of the family, and Penny couldn't be trusted with boiling water.

"It's not as sexist as it looks." Carla laughs as Dylan gives her a look that clearly reads *Are you sure?* "We just like going to have a good gossip."

"They do," Vic agrees with a nod, tilting his chin at the retreating ladies.

"This one is getting picked up momentarily, say your goodbyes." Alex holds Mikayla against her chest, turning so everyone can wave at the sleeping baby - Nolan had mentioned his mother was coming to get their newborn so they could enjoy the night and whatever else was planned.

Piper gives me a smile over her shoulder as she carries a stack of plates through the glass sliding door, and I admire the way her hips sway when she steps up and into the house. That bodice is doing dangerous things to me, and it's only getting worse as I drink more. I'm teetering on tipsy, having turned down the last round of wine that Luca offered after ensuring Piper that the flamingos that apparently littered her relationship with her mother were, in fact, adorable, not embarrassing. I think that made her even more mortified.

"Piper and Bianca's love language is dry humor," Luca says once the door closes behind them, pouring himself the last of a bottle and shaking his head. "They're like oil and water, those two."

"Ain't that the truth," Brett agrees, knocking glasses with his father in law. "All of them are terrifying, sometimes."

"Also true." Nolan holds up his beer in silent cheers, adjusting his baseball cap over his short cropped, blonde hair and then standing to move into the chair next to me. My eyes flicker to Dylan, who has moved into the seat closest to

CHAPTER 45

Brett. I've barely heard Dylan say a word, but while this may be his first time at what they've all called "fam dinner," it's clear they all know him, either from his friendship with Piper, or his brother's role on Nolan's team. His presence, soda in hand, is unnerving for a lot of reasons. "So, Westfall," Nolan continues. Brett snorts, sharing a look with Vic across Luca's shoulder.

"He has a name, Nolan." Vic sounds mildly defensive, and I can't help my surprise - clearly, the effort towards including him has had the added bonus of his loyalty.

"Yeah, like I don't call you Montero on the daily," Nolan says, sitting forward in his seat like this is a casual conversation, and not the Spanish - Italian? - Inquisition I'm prepared for.

"Westfall is fine." I set my now empty wine glass on the table. I'd been keeping it in my hands as a defense mechanism, something to play with so I didn't let my hand rake up Piper's thigh. But she's gone, and so I neatly join my hands across my lap, elbow resting on the arms of my chair in what I hope is the picture of casual conversation. "But before you tell me how badly you'll kick my - uh - butt," I hesitate, and glance at Luca across the table, who smiles, " if I hurt Piper, I feel like I should at least get a chance to say something preemptively." The men around me go on alert - even Dylan, who seems to sit forward in his chair like I'm about to give away the spoiler to the next Marvel movie.

So I look at them. All of them. The men who are so clearly important to Piper - even Dylan, as much as the idea frustrates me. Nolan, next to me, who looks worn out and has spit up on the shoulder of his LSSU tee shirt, loves a woman who gets on my nerves almost as much as my own sister. Brett, arguably the closest to me in circumstances, the partner of the other Delmonico sister, who, based on my brief time with, is very similar to Piper, if not a little less quirky. Vic, Piper's best friend of years and a man who has every reason to hate me as much as she does - but clearly doesn't. And Luca, who, when the light hits right, has the same wide smile as his daughter.

And then, because I can't take the eye contact anymore, I find a stray string on the sleeve of my dress shirt and start to pick at it.

"Well?" Brett flourishes his hand around, and I realize I'd started to make this big admission and then stopped short to contemplate the people with me, lost in thought.

"I'm fully aware my lack of action..." Fuck. It comes out cold, and clinical, and immediately Nolan tenses next to me. I close my eyes, briefly, and swallow. "Shit. Sorry. I'm not good at this."

"Good at what, son?" Luca asks, setting his own glass down and leaning forward to look at me. Before I can answer, Vic catches my eye.

"Feelings," he says for me, and I nod, ever so slightly.

Nolan laughs. "Picked a hell of a woman, then."

"She picked me." It's out of my mouth before I can stop myself, and I see Vic's mouth turn up at the corners. But the rest of them are silent. "It's true, as surprising as it is to you all, it's possibly more surprising to me."

"From what we've heard, you were kind of an ass."

"Nol," Brett says in a chastising tone, but Nolan just shrugs.

"I *was* an ass." I nod, looking back down at my wayward string. "And I didn't do anything to directly hurt people, but what I didn't do was say something when I could have." I pause. "*Should* have." I can't meet Vic's eyes, even though he deserves for me to, but I press on. "I don't deserve her grace, or the grace of anyone my inaction hurt. But…" Finally, I look up, meeting Luca's stare. "I'll do whatever I have to in order to earn it." He smiles, and seems to look at the man next to me as if to ask *That good enough?*

After a moment, there's a deep sigh from Nolan, and I watch him sit back in his chair, scrubbing both hands down his face like he's trying to reckon with something. When he looks up, his gaze has softened, and he meets Brett's eyes, then Vic's. Whatever he'd been planning to say seems to have been washed away by my admission, which I'm grateful for, but now he's unprepared, and clearly uneasy.

"They fucked her up, man." I'm surprised to hear Dylan speak, and when we all turn to him, his hand finds the back of his neck. He's uncomfortable too, but he's seen first hand, from what I've been told, the impact of the last several years on Piper. "Like, a lot."

"They fucked all of us up," Vic agrees, leaning onto the table with his forearms, his shoulders sagging in the crisp short sleeve button up he's wearing. It's effortlessly cool looking, which is something I've come to expect from him. "Mickey getting sick affected all of us in different ways, but the way the Davis' acted, that's…that's the worst part of all of this." His eyes cut to Nolan. "Aside from the fact that Mickey isn't here."

"How much has she told you?" Brett's question is cautious, and I can tell he's truly unsure, like there are parts of the story that aren't his to tell. That's fair. It's Piper's story, too, but they all have a piece in it. They all lived through it.

"Not a lot." I flex my hand in my lap, fingernails digging into my palm. "I don't want to press her for things she's not ready to share. But, I've…seen a few things. Online." I wince as Vic snorts, sipping at his water still on the table in front of him.

"I'm sure that went over well."

"About as well as you can imagine," I answer honestly. "She told me off for jumping to conclusions." I meet his eye. "It was kind of awesome."

"The whole situation is fucked," Brett continues.

"Mickey was my best friend." Nolan looks at me, appraising, his blonde brows creasing, and I try to meet his stare with as much courage as I can muster. I may be tall, but he's built in a way I'm not sure I'd ever be, even under the training habits of a professional athlete. "But he treated Piper like shit, and she deserved - deserves - a lot better than that."

"There were girls," Luca says, and then swallows hard. I can tell this man is probably the most emotional of all of us. "Girls, plural. She found out the day he was diagnosed."

"And she stayed." Vic crosses his arms, leaning back in his chair, like the memory hurts him. "She chose to stay, knowing that he was facing what was likely a death sentence, and his family knew that she was choosing forgiveness. And they still treated her like crap."

"They *knew*?" I ask.

"They knew everything." Nolan's tone is sharper. "Not that he cheated, not before she did. But they knew that she chose to stay, and when he wouldn't move back to Paulsville, she became the bad guy. Undesirable Number One."

I blow out a deep breath, running my hands down my thighs, suddenly heated. "I knew that he cheated, but I didn't-"

"It didn't stop after he was diagnosed," Brett interrupted. "We sat through a ten hour surgery, waiting for him, and two weeks later he was back talking to other girls."

"And she stayed," Vic repeated.

"She stayed over and over, when she should have walked." Nolan takes a deep breath before continuing. "And then Kelsie and Kayla showed back up."

"*Back* up?" I sit forward. "Like, you all knew about her before?" I pause. "Sorry, that sounded really accusatory."

"No," Nolan corrects, "you have every right to be accusatory. I was the only one that knew here in Texas." His shoulders sag, too, like he's hit his limit, same as Vic. "I didn't realize Mickey hadn't told her a damn thing, that his family hadn't said anything, until Alex was about two seconds from murdering him and..." He shudders. "It never came up, and I assumed if they were that serious, he would have told her from the beginning."

"Clearly not," Dylan adds, and Nolan pitches a balled up napkin at him.

"They got married, and she had no idea until Kelsie reached out about some paperwork." Luca sighs. "She'd tried to claim that Mickey was the father a few months after the girl was born, but they got a DNA test that proved otherwise. I'm sure Piper has a copy, somewhere. We found out later, he'd been spending time with them secretly. For years."

"He *what*?" Horror lances through me. It's one thing for someone to say you've got their child. It's another to spend time with them, to build a life with them. Like Olivia had done to me, with Ryan. Nolan reaches behind us, to the cooler just at arm's reach, pulling out two beers and handing me one. It feels like an offering before they drop a bomb.

"Mickey told us it was better for Kayla to grow up having a father figure, than believing that her dad hated her," Nolan continues. "Since Kelsie refused to say who her real father was."

"But man, the second the Davis family got wind that Mickey had invested an ounce of time into any of it, a switch flipped." Brett looks at his best friend next to me, and I can tell this part probably hurt the most. "They spent the last few months of Mickey's life telling Piper how horrible she was for keeping him away from his family, from his *little girl*." He says the last two words with an air of disgust that surprises me. "As a father, if I truly believed I was dying, I would move heaven and earth to be with my children. With my family." He shakes his head. "But by then, Mickey realized that what we'd all suspected from the get go was probably true - Kelsie used him to put down on the birth certificate after the fact, so that when he died, they'd get survivor's benefits. And the Davis' supported Kelsie instead of rallying around their dying son."

I balk at him. I hadn't even considered the financial gain that the legal paperwork might bring.

Nolan speaks before I can even breathe out a shocked response. "That was the paperwork she needed him to sign. And he'd done it incorrectly the first time, so we all thought it was done and dusted, until one day, everyone started posting pictures of the three of them together along with the birth certificate."

"These annoying family pictures," Vic adds. "Kelsie thought Piper knew they were all spending time together, or, that's what she tried to say at the funeral."

I stare at Vic, unsure I heard him correctly. "She showed up to the funeral?"

Luca lets out a humorless laugh, and I twist the top off my beer, taking a deep sip, overwhelmed and mind racing.

"Oh, man," Brett says, pinching the bridge of his nose. "The Davis family walked Kelsie and Kayla into that funeral like they were his family, and we were a pile of trash."

I feel my mouth pop open.

"Yes, exactly that face." Vic laughs, humorless, like Luca. "God, I mean it's not funny, but it is." He looks at the older man next to him. "I've never seen Bianca so mad. I thought she was going to have to be restrained."

"I thought we were going to have to tie Alex and Penny up with her," Nolan adds.

"And Bethani, at the time." Brett trails off, making a disgusted face. "There were so many of us who spent days with them, with him, because we fucking loved him, and didn't want him to be alone at the end."

CHAPTER 45

"She couldn't do it by herself," Vic says with a shrug. "So we made sure she didn't have to."

I feel my heart swell, and every instinct in my body is fighting my growing urge to pull Vic into the tightest bro hug I can muster. Because while I had my head up my ass, he was making sure she was cared for. They all were.

"No one even knew they were married." Luca's eyes close, his head shaking in a reflection of the same horror coursing through my body. "We didn't do anything big, because they wanted it to be private, but once we were able to share, we were screaming it from the rooftops. Celebrating. Sharing with everyone." He scratches at the gray stubble along his jaw. "Piper told us later that most of the people going through the line at the visitation didn't know they'd been married at all. His family was more focused on making up for time lost with their not-so-surprise secret grandchild instead of celebrating the very real relationship right in front of them."

"Why?" I breathe the word out so forcefully, it surprises even me. Vic meets my eyes.

"Why would they treat Piper the way they did? Why would they pretend like Kayla was Mickey's when literally everything said she wasn't?" He looks around the table. "Why would they walk into that funeral and let everyone think they'd been at his bedside every day with his child and her mother, instead of all of us?" He gestures to the men around the table, and then vaguely in the direction of the house, where we can just barely hear voices carrying from the kitchen. Why would someone do that? Why would anyone do that?

"Grief," is Luca's simple answer. Around me, all of them nod, even Dylan. "Grief will drive people to do - to say - crazy things." He takes off his glasses, pressing his thumb and forefinger into his eyes, and then looks at Nolan next to me. "You all did right by her - by both of them." Luca reaches over, patting Vic's hand. "You *all* did."

Before I can agree with his sentiment, which I'm not sure will mean much as an after-the-fact bystander, I hear the door behind me open, and Nolan and I both swivel to see Carla in the doorway. "Incoming!" she says, and a black and white ball of fur comes barrelling out of the house, followed by a plain black one. They whiz under the table, nearly pulling the plastic tablecloths with them, and then go straight through to the other side and into the yard beyond. The patio lights illuminate where we sit, and in the distance I can just make out Bex's tiny little legs, along with another dog I don't recognize.

"Gesù Cristo," Luca huffs, putting his glasses back on and looking over his shoulder. "Sorry about them. Though I suspect you know Bex can be a little crazy. Ernie on the other hand..." He shakes his head, looking at Carla over my shoulder. "Can we come in? As much as I love walking down memory lane, I would love more to sit in a chair with better cushioning."

And then there's a crash from inside the house. I watch Luca's eyes widen, and Vic's face crease with concern as someone yells. "You did *what?*" It's loud enough that I think it's Bianca, though this far away, it could be Penny. Then, the voice continues, screaming in Italian. "*Mi stai prendendo in giro, Piper? Hai lasciato il lavoro?*"

"Oh shit," Vic says, and both he and Luca stand at the same time. I press to my feet, and Vic catches my arm as I try to follow Nolan inside. "I'd stay back and out of the line of fire, Bianca just found out that Piper quit."

CHAPTER 46

Piper

By the time everyone is crowded in the living room and kitchen, Mom has started her typical pacing up and down the space in front of the fridge, cursing to herself.

"I can't believe you would throw all of this hard work you've done away. And for what?" She's going a million miles a minute, a skill I very much inherited, nearly spitting as she throws out question after question in Italian so deep I'm not even sure I understand every word. "It's taken you years to get back to where you're at, and now you walk away? Why? Why would you do this?"

I track her with my eyes, leaning against the counter.

"Love, what's going on?" My father slips past Penny and Alex, who are standing together in the archway, unsure of whether to approach or stay back.

"Your daughter," she hurls, hitching a thumb back at me, "has just casually informed us that she up and quit her job today." She huffs, throwing her hands up in the air. "With no plan. Nothing lined up."

"What's she saying?" I hear Brett mutter to Vic, who snorts.

"Piper's in *trouble.*" He drags out the last word. "She finally kicked our boss to the curb today."

"Thank God," Brett breathes, and I smile to myself. He's been getting an earful for years about my frustrations.

"Don't you dare sit there and *grin.*" Mom whirls on me, finger in my face, and I rear back. Jesus. I feel like I'm back in college, having come home with my first tattoo - the one Fitz likes to trace, just under my bra line, that reads *Just Breathe.* My 19 year old self thought it was oh so creative. "All those years of college, and you decided to go design underwear."

"*Mama,*" Penny says, her tone sharp. Big sister to the rescue.

"Would all of you stop it?" Papa's voice rises above the thrum of conversation happening at a low volume, and everyone snaps to look at him. He's the more emotional one, sure, but my mother is the loud one - only when she's like this.

"I've already got several interviews lined up," switching back to English, mostly for the benefit of the other people around us, so my mother will stop hiding behind a language she knows only we'll understand. She opens her mouth to respond. "And for your information, *all* of them are for marketing jobs." Her mouth snaps shut, and she stares at me. "Yeah, I'm not a total idiot. I've also got savings." I hold my hand up, the other still crossed over my chest tightly. "Mama, you should have seen me in there."

"She was channeling her inner Bee, for sure," Vic says from the living room, and my mother rolls her eyes, seeming somewhat appeased. I look at my friend, and then the man standing next to him, and try not to suck in an audible breath.

God. Even standing in the shitty lighting of my parents darkly decorated home, I want to climb Fitz like a tree.

Hormones. Those are my hormones talking, I remind myself. A long day, lots of stress, a fucked up menstrual cycle. You are at your parents' home.

But damn, those cheekbones.

"You need something else to wear," I finally choke out, and then look back to Vic. "You think you can help him out with that one?" Vic looks at Fitz, sizing him up in about two seconds.

"I think I can do that." He grabs Fitz by the forearm, dragging him towards the front door, but Fitz throws me a look that's part concern, part terror before disappearing down the hall. I look around the room at the other men.

"Did we have a nice chat?"

"Not nearly enough interrogating," Nolan answers, shaking his head.

"Booo." Alex smacks his arm. "You had one job."

"Dude got sentimental," Brett says with a shrug, and I stare at him. Penny snorts, but then realizes her husband isn't joking. Alex and Carla, too, are speechless.

My father says "He clearly cares about you, passerotto mio."

"You told him, like, zero, though." Nolan gives me a look that tells me he told Fitz everything.

"You loose-lipped bastard," Alex groans, her head falling into her hands.

"I mean, we didn't give him all the sordid details." Brett's grin makes me think otherwise. "Just the important ones."

"The ones that make you sound like a badass," Dylan adds, reaching for Carla's waist and pulling her close. "Promise." I toss the hand towel next to me at his smug face while he makes mooney eyes at my roommate.

"Promise, my ass." I whirl on my father. "You said you'd take it easy on him, and instead you let tweedle dee and tweedle dumber tell the story?"

I tip my chin as both Brett and Nolan shout, simultaneously. "Hey!"

"Not to break up this party," my father starts, ignoring my question and taking the baking sheet my mother holds out to him. "But I need to know who is staying here tonight, so I can make up the guest rooms." He wipes a towel at the tray in his hands.

"Just the kids, I think, Papa," Penny answers, and then looks around the group. We all nod. It's a straight shot back home for the rest of us, and she and Brett can get Hunter and Aria in the morning, after they've had lots of coffee, and maybe some adult alone time. I shudder at the thought.

Down the hall, the front door opens and closes, and I hear Vic and Fitz talking, before one set of feet go upstairs, and the other pads down the hardwood hall. Vic comes around the corner to see us all staring, and he hesitates in the entrance.

"I sent him upstairs with a different shirt." Vic meets my eye, and then smirks. "He's headed to your room."

I push off the counter. "Oh, fuck," I stutter, nearly body-checking Nolan, and edging my elbow purposefully at Vic as I race by. I take the stairs two at a time, and when I make it to the first door on the right, I pause momentarily. The door to my childhood bedroom is closed - the words *"Piper's Room: Do Not Enter"* glisten back at me in purple glitter on purple poster board. "Fitz?" I call out. There's a beat before he answers.

"I'm decent." I twist the handle, pushing the door open to see him standing in the middle of the room, arms crossed, the biggest grin I've ever seen him wear plastered across his face as he stares at the walls around him. "You were not kidding about Nick Jonas."

Fitz

"Absolutely not." I hold the shirt Vic handed me out like it's covered in The Plague.

"Take it, or die of heat stroke." Vic shrugs, closing his hatchback pulling the back door open.

"I don't even know where we're going."

It's the truth. And frankly, my head is still spinning - both from all the information I'd gleaned tonight, and from watching Piper and her mother nearly duke it out right there in the kitchen.

"Consider it a group activity," he answers, reaching into the backseat and pulling out a backpack. He slings it over his shoulder, shutting the door and leaning forward to adjust his hair in the reflection. Suddenly, he looks nervous, and I cross my arms, the other shirt still in my hand, watching him. After a second, he looks back. "What?"

"I'm not wearing this." I hold the shirt back up. "It's...what even is this?" I pull it open.

"It's called retro." Vic's nostrils flare. "I got it with a plan to frankenstein it with a few other things, but if you'd rather sweat like a pig in front of your girl and all her friends-"

He tries to snatch the shirt away, but I hold it back.

"Fuck, fine." He smirks, and motions with his head for me to follow him back through the red front door. "Are they always like that?"

"Bee and Piper?" He looks over his shoulder as we cross the threshold. "You get used to it. You should see Bianca in court, it's scary as hell." He shakes his head, pointing at the curved staircase in front of us, framed in a deep burgundy wall littered with more family pictures. Shit. I don't think my family and I even have this many pictures all together, much less ones we display like we actually like them. "First door on the right." He pauses, and then smirks again. "You're welcome." Before I can question him, he turns to walk down the hall back towards the kitchen, and I step up the stairs, stopping in front of the door in question.

Piper's Room: Do Not Enter is written in scrolling, glittery letters.

Vic just may have become my favorite person in this house, aside from the girl whose childhood room I'm about to scope out.

Gripping the shirt tighter in my hand, I turn the knob and move in, shutting the door quietly behind me like I'm in Mission freaking Impossible. When I whirl back around to face the bedroom, a sea of purple and pretty boys stares back at me.

Holy shit. It looks like Tiger Beat and Hot Topic exploded here. What in the actual hell?

The only normal thing in the room is a dark wood double bed, covered in a purple comforter, but even that is littered with beaded throw pillows, one that reads "Team Edward" in a font I distinctly recognize as belonging to Twilight. Posters and drawings litter the wall, and right next to a vanity littered with old magazines and small dumbbells is what may as well be a shrine to the youngest member of the Jonas Brothers.

Behind me, I hear Piper's voice through the door. "Fitz?" A grin spreads over my face.

"I'm decent," I reply, stepping forward as she quietly opens the door, slipping inside and closing it as quietly as I had. "You were not kidding about Nick Jonas." She goes from surprised to horrified in about two seconds flat, and I laugh, turning back around and leaning forward on the foot of the wood bed frame, taking it all in. Piper pinches the bridge of her nose.

"Welcome to Piper 1.0," she says, gesturing around the room.

"Piper 1.0 was very..." I step a few feet towards the wall, running my hand

CHAPTER 46

over the letters someone clearly hand painted around the chair rail. "Unique."

"Fuck off," she says with a laugh, pointing to the words in front of me. "They're all designers." Her finger makes a circle, and I swivel, looking at all corners of the room. Givenchy. Lilly Pulitzer. Michael Kors. Juicy Couture.

"How early-two-thousands of-"

I don't even get the sentence out before she's whirling on her feet, throwing a pillow from a nearby egg chair at me.

"Jesus," I cry, holding my hands up as she pelts me with another pillow. "So violent."

"Oh, you haven't begun to see violence." She makes a move towards the pillows at the headboard, grinning, and I laugh, dropping Vic's shirt on the bed and grabbing at her waist. Piper giggles, half-heartedly batting me away, but she stills, her fingers splaying out on my chest as I settle my hands on her hips. "Well, you've officially seen into my teenage soul." Her eyes flit to the wall behind my shoulder, and she grins. "Hey, look, it's you." I whirl, and my eyes land on a pegboard criss-crossed with purple ribbon. Nestled in one corner is a picture of a group of kids standing in a field, flanked by horses.

"Holy..." I reach my hand up, yanking down the photo and sitting on the bed. Piper settles at my side, leaning over to inspect it with me. Twenty or so of us, all huddled around a campfire, in various degrees of pre-teen awkwardness. "Camp Wildwood, right?" She nods, pointing to a brace-faced little redhead on the front row, kneeling like something out of a Captain Morgan commercial. Come to think of it, that's probably exactly what I was doing on our sixth grade class trip.

"Knock, knock." Alex's voice comes at the exact time she pushes open the door, not waiting for anyone to respond, and she's got her eyes covered like she'd expected to walk in on us completely nude. "Does he have a shirt on?"

"You're all-clear, loser." Alex separates her fingers, turning towards Piper's voice until she spots us on the bed fully-clothed.

"They're not naked," she calls a little too loudly, and Piper hisses next to me. Carla pops her head in the door looking disappointed, and Penny follows. "We had bets going to see how undressed you were." Piper tosses her Team Edward pillow, missing her friend by about a foot.

"Come look at this." Piper takes the picture from my hand, holding it up. Outside, a car engine purrs to life, and I face her.

"Is that my car?" I reach to feel for my keys and find them still in my pocket. She laughs, patting me on the shoulder.

"You're not the only one with a sexy ride." Alex makes a vomiting noise, and as they settle on the bed behind us, Nolan, Brett, and Dylan appear in the doorway.

"Well this is not what I expected," Brett deadpans, and his wife snorts, leaning over her sister. "He's stolen all of our women."

"Aw, look at little baby Fitz," Carla coos, making motions with her fingertips like she's pinching tiny cheeks. "And little baby Piper." My eyes find Piper two rows behind me, her hair blonder than I remember, donned in her signature purple, and Penny laughs again.

"Personally, the blonde was not my favorite." She tugs on one of her sister's curls. "But don't forget the baby Alex." She reaches between us, pointing out an uncomfortable looking blonde next to Piper, who seems to be getting harassed by...

"Andy," Alex says with a scoff, snatching the picture and handing it to the men waiting at the doorway. "Feast your eyes, boys, look at all that middle school glory." Together, they inspect the photo, and Brett smiles, looking up at me.

"You had braces."

"So did you," Penny retorts, scooting off the bed and back over to her husband. Carla follows, taking the picture from Dylan's hand before he can look too close and find her where I'd spotted her, half-distracted by the s'more she was downing.

"I'll take this, thanks very much," she says, at the same time Dylan says "Hey!" "For the reunion." She sticks the picture in her back pocket, glancing around the bedroom. "Any more where that came from?"

"I'll ask Mom to take a look." Piper leans back on her hands, looking at the group in the doorway. "We're right behind you, this one just needs to change." She tilts her head towards me, and Alex eyes the shirt at the end of the bed.

"Vic was not kidding when he said-"

This time, I lob a Tootsie Roll pillow at her, purposefully missing so her husband doesn't pummel me, and she holds her hands up, laughing. Piper points at the door. "Out, all of you. We'll see you there."

They all crowd out the door, Carla the last one out, and as she latches it shut I swear I hear her say "Make good choices!" When I turn, Piper is scrubbing the back of her neck, head bent forward.

"I hate all of them."

"No you don't." I jostle into her shoulder playfully, and she collapses back on the bed with a huff. I lay back with her, joining my hands over my chest, staring at the ceiling fan that desperately needs to be dusted.

"How much did they tell you?" she asks after a minute. I sigh.

"Enough." I tilt my head to look at her. "When I asked if they hurt you, I didn't mean it as the understatement of the century." She huffs a laugh. "I'm serious." I swallow. "It's a miracle you're not in a mental institution somewhere after the shit they put you through. All of you." She squints, meeting my eye.

CHAPTER 46

"Who told you about my grippy sock vacation?" I can tell she's joking, but something about her tone tells me it may not be completely untrue. I stick a pin in that for later. Her hand reaches out, tugging on one of my belt loops. "Not fragile."

And fuck. The movement of my pants rubs against me, and without warning, my cock twitches. It's hard to miss at this angle, and I know she saw it because she sucks in a quick breath. I look anywhere but at her - up at the dirty fan, over to her desk and the neat stack of yearbooks, even to the fucking Nick Jonas shrine.

"You know I don't think you're fragile," I say after a moment, willing myself to ignore how close we are, how weird it is to be in her bedroom and this close to her. She asked me a serious question, and all my body can do is act like a horndog.

"Really?" I look at her, then. Her smile has changed. Gone is the happy go lucky grin. Wicked, teasing Piper is here. "Prove it." My mouth goes dry, and I feel my body react immediately - my skin pebbles, and I'm half hard just from seeing that expression on her face. "Did you hear me?" she asks after a second. "I said-"

I cut her off with a kiss so wild that when I pull away, we're both panting. She looks at me, one hand on my neck, the other propping herself up, chest heaving. Before I can get carried away, I push off the bed, and she starts to protest. I cross the room, clicking the lock on the door as quietly as I can before turning back. Her mouth snaps shut, and she smiles again, that same, wicked smile.

"I want to show you just how *not fragile* I think you are," I start, leaning halfway against the door and watching her lashes flutter as she looks at me. "But I don't want to mess up that makeup and hair you already had to redo today."

Something in her face changes, and she bites at her lower lip. "That might be the sexiest thing you've ever said."

I laugh, crossing back over to her and pulling her up to her knees on the bed, bringing my face down to hers as I work at my belt with one hand. She nips at my lower lip and I gasp, pulling back and looking down at her. Swollen lips, blue eyes staring up at me.

Fuck, I want those lips wrapped around my cock so bad, but I want to feel her come around me even more.

"Hands and knees, we need to be quick." Her eyebrows practically hit her hairline as she gazes up at me like I've gone crazy. "Piper, hands and-"

She's scrambling before I can finish, turning on the comforter while I pull out the condom I'd been wishful enough to stash in my wallet last weekend. She falls forward, catching herself on her hands, and I work open my pants, letting my other hand trace down the curve of her back, down, over the bodice and to where it ends above her hips. She arches into my touch, and I flick back the skirt of her gauzy dress, hitching my finger under the tan bike shorts beneath and inching them down.

"Fuck me." I hiss when I catch the lacy green underwear with my finger too, pulling it all down at once. Piper looks over her shoulder, that wicked smile on her face. This very well may be my favorite position yet, with her leaning down on her forearms, thick thighs pressing back towards me. I tear open the condom, and while I roll it on, already hard and aching, I trail a finger through her wet pussy, bringing it to my mouth to lick it clean, all while she watches. A barely-audible whimper escapes her, and I quirk a brow at her, pressing my thumb into her clit. "Are you going to be able to keep it down?" Her eyes narrow, and I laugh, steadying my dick in one hand and gripping her hip with the other.

"I can be quiet, you know."

I scoff. There's a reason we haven't fucked around at her apartment, aside from lazy morning sex under the sheets with one hand pulling her bare back to my chest and the other covering her mouth.

"Could have fooled me." Before she can bite back with another comment, I sink into her, burying myself in one quick move and then stilling. Fuck, I feel like a teenager, being in this room, with a girl I'd fantasized about more than once, my cock buried in her while her back arches and her mouth opens in a silent moan. She pushes against me, and my hands vice grip around her hips, stilling her. "Don't," I seethe through gritted teeth, and with her breathing erratic, she stares back at me over her shoulder, the dark curls that are still loose cascading over her neck.

Control. I need control, or I'm going to last two seconds.

I slide one arm forward, fingers finding the hair at the base of her neck and pulling her back. She starts to say something, something loud, and I press a finger to her lips. Her hands find my shoulder, my forearm in front of her as she's pressed against me, her position making everything *so fucking tight*.

"It would be one hell of a first impression if your parents walk upstairs to find us like this," I manage, and her chest shakes against my forearms. I tighten my hold on her hair, letting my other hand snake down her collarbone, dipping under the hem of her dress until I can feel one of her taut nipples against my fingers. I pinch it, and she clenches around me. I bite back a moan. "*Piper.*"

"Hmm?" Her head tilts back against my hand, and I can see that glassy look in her eyes - fuck, just the situation must be turning her on as much as it is me. I run my thumb over her nipple, and she bucks back against me.

"Hey," I warn in a hoarse whisper, and she bites her lip. Taunting. She's fucking taunting me. Slowly, I rock back, sliding back into her, and her eyes drift shut, meeting my pace. The hand in her hair slides down, down her shoulder, fingering that painstaking beadwork on her corset, until I can reach around and find her clit with my fingers. She bucks again, and if I didn't know any better I'd say she's drawing blood with the way her lip is snagged between her teeth. "We're gonna go fast and hard, ok?" I feel her head nod against me, and before I can second guess myself, I pull back and thrust into her, building a quick tempo that has the bed shaking.

"Fuck." Her voice is low and breathy, and she writhes into my hands, her fingers locking into my hair. God, at this angle, everything is so tight, so close, my heart is pounding and all I can do is watch as her face contorts in wry pleasure.

She deserves this. Deserves every second of happiness, of pleasure, of forgetting the rest of the world is there so she can just be. And I want to give it to her.

"Tell me you want me," she whimpers, and it almost makes me pause. Almost - because at this rate, I'm not sure there's any stopping either of us. But does she really doubt that? Here? In this moment? "Fitz." I look down, and those blue eyes are staring back up at me.

"Piper, I want you so badly." Her eyes close for a brief moment, and I pull her closer to my chest with my forearm, pressing my fingers harder into her clit as she writhes against my circles. "More than just like this." Without opening her eyes, she smirks, and I know she's picturing all the ways we could be, all the positions we could be in. But I mean so much more than that. "Piper." My hand travels from her breast up to her chin, tilting her so she's looking at me again, and her eyes widen. I slow my tempo, just for a minute, to meet her gaze. "I want you. I want *you*." I tighten my hold. "Not just this." I push into her clit and she presses her lips into a thin line, but her eyes are sparkling. "I don't want you to doubt that, to doubt us."

"Us," she echoes, and then she's pulling me down to meet her mouth, tangling my tongue with hers as she rears against me. I pick up the pace again, as fast as I can possibly go without making the whole damn bed move because fuck, it feels so good.

Her kiss becomes more measured, trembling as we continue, and I can tell she's right on the edge, right where I am, when her fingers in my hair and on my forearm tighten. She tries to pull back, but I don't let her move, letting the crash of her orgasm and the clench of her around my cock springboard me into the one I've been holding back as long as possible.

If I wasn't kissing her, this whole damn block would hear exactly how much I want Piper Delmonico Davis.

CHAPTER 47

Piper

My father may like Fitz more than I do, it seems. Or, at least, that's the impression I get when he stares longingly after us as we pull out of their driveway in Fitz's car. I can see him in the side mirror, one hand around my mother's waist, but his gaze is firmly planted on the beauty we're riding in.

I can't say I blame him.

We turn out of my parents' neighborhood, I look at Fitz in the driver's seat, saying "I thought we were going to have to wipe away his drool." He's looking at me with that same burning intensity he'd had in my bedroom.

Well, my childhood bedroom.

Which was a whole different level of kinky I had not been expecting tonight. Zero percent, did I think that I'd be leaving the evening thoroughly fucked and trying not to make mooney eyes at Fitz Westfall when I followed him down the stairs, but damn, it's what I did.

"Are you going to tell me where we're headed?" Fitz asks, lacing his fingers through mine on the top of my thigh. I can't help but smirk as I look out the window, the streetlights buzzing by as we whip onto the freeway. We have the top up, I don't have the energy in me to do my hair for a third time today, and despite being the one to tell Fitz to drive the MK to my parents', I hadn't thought to bring my hair scarf when riding with Dylan and Carla over here.

"Where would the fun in that be?"

"Rude."

"Karma." I squeeze his hand. "Exit 66, it's just a few miles down." I see his eyebrows pull together, and he releases me just long enough to shift gears. I love old cars, but driving stick is not something anyone wants me to do. I tried it for approximately ten seconds in Mickey's Corvette and nearly ground down the gears with the miserable attempt.

I know the second we're exiting the freeway, he can see where we're headed.

CHAPTER 47

His eyes dart over to me as the bright lights of the speedway come into view. "Drag and Brag."

I grin up at him. "So smart. Have you been?" He shakes his head, his fingers gripping the steering wheel a little tighter. I panic momentarily. "I wasn't expecting you to race."

"It's not that," he breathes out, and then looks at me. I must look like a wounded puppy, because my excited face went sad and now he looks concerned, too. "It's nothing, don't worry about it." He reaches out, squeezing my hand again.

"Is it all the people?" Fitz swallows.

"Yeah, the people." My gut tells me that's not all, but I don't press him. I just watch as he gets in line behind other cars entering the speedway, inching forward until we pull up in front of the tattered wooden booth near the entrance. Fitz rolls down the window, and I can already hear cammed engines and cheering.

"Welcome to Lone Star Speedway," the guy behind the booth starts, and Fitz pulls out his wallet, but I put my hand on his forearm, leaning forward until I can see Josh's face. "Are we just watching, or-"

He freezes, arms mid-air, as he spies me, and then a grin slides across his face.

"I'll be damned, it's little Delmonico." He leans forward, holding his hand out for a fist-bump, and I reach over Fitz, meeting his fingers with my own. "Sweet ride." I smile up at him as my hand settles on Fitz's thigh, using it for balance, but also serving as a reminder that I'm here with him. Any tension he'd shown a moment ago eases away.

"Thanks, Josh." I nod my head towards the man next to me. "This is Fitz, he's not racing tonight but if we can sneak into the center, that'd be great." Josh pulls down his baseball hat, looking between the car and the entrance in front of us. His dark hair has always been long, but now it curls around his neck, already sweaty from the Texas heat, and it's not even nine p.m.

"You and Pen kill me." Josh shakes his head, leaning against the frame of the booth on his forearms. "I just let the rest of your crew in about half an hour ago." His smile turns as he eyes the pair of us. "I take it you were otherwise occupied."

Slimeball. Fitz's knuckles on the steering wheel go white, but I tighten my grip on his thigh.

"Fuck off and let us in, Kimball," I jeer, shaking my head back at him and nodding towards the entrance. A car behind us honks. "We're holding up your line."

"Yeah, yeah." He snorts, and then waves us forward, holding a walkie-talkie up to his lips. "We got a blue MK coming up, they're VIP, let them into the center when there's a break." Fitz doesn't bother with goodbyes as he presses the gas, lurching us forward so fast I grip my seat.

"Jesus."

"Jesus is right," Fitz mutters, and then turns to look at me when we pull up to a man standing with his hand up. He flags the car behind us towards a different entrance.

"Is someone...jealous?" I lace my voice with as much incredulity as I can, but I can read his body language, clear as day.

He gives a dry, humorless laugh, shaking his head and letting his jaw tick. I put my fingers on his forearm, now mostly bare thanks to the shirt that Vic had lent him. It was the right size, but the white, lightly patterned fabric still pulled tight on his arms when he held them like this. It made his skin look tan, his biceps look amazing, and did all sorts of things to my insides. I'd had to stop myself from staring when he put it on after climbing off my bed, off of me, stumbling into the bathroom with about as much grace as I'd felt in my boneless body.

When we pull into the center of the arena a few moments later, my touch on Fitz seems to have eased some of his returned tension. He finds a spot next to a dually with a confederate flag flying in the back, grimacing and then looking at me. "Ok, not exactly the best representation of the people here," I start, immediately on the defense. "But I promise, it'll be fun!" His eyebrows knit together, and I poke at the lines above his nose. "Fun. Remember that word?"

"I'll show you fun." He leans forward, grabbing at my waist, at the corset securely around my midsection, and I smile against his lips.

A wolf whistle breaks us apart, and when I turn to look out his back window, Alex and Nolan are standing a foot from the bumper.

Alex can say she still dislikes Fitz all she wants, but I know she wants to see me happy - the smile on her face says as much, when I close his car door behind me and move to link my arm with hers. Nolan gives Fitz the obligatory *sup, dude?* head nod, and even though I roll my eyes at my best friend, it's clear the vibe here has changed. Whatever they'd said to Fitz, whatever Fitz had said to them, had an impact.

"Where's everyone else?" Fitz asks, clearly trying to ignore the spectators who have stopped to admire his car. Stroking his ego is 90% of the reason I told him to bring it. Stroking mine is the other ten.

"Brett and Penny are off getting drinks, Dylan and Carla went to get seats," Alex says.

Fitz steps into place next to Nolan, behind Alex and I, as we push our way through the crowd at the center of the speedway. I take a deep breath, letting the familiar scents of popcorn and burned rubber pull me in. We'd been doing this for nearly half my life, but the first weekend of Drag and Brag still held magic very little else did in my life. Screeching tires, the buzz of a screaming crowd, it

CHAPTER 47

was like a recharge to my battery that left me grinning for days. Next to me, Alex glances back at Fitz before tightening her arm in mine. "Vic is already lined up," Alex continues.

"Lined up?" Fitz's voice holds the confusion I'd expected, and Alex smirks next to me, not answering as we make our way to the tunnel that leads below the track. Above our heads, two giant trucks with exposed engines barrel by, the crowd screaming as one narrowly beats the other. The tunnel around us shudders as they pass, and I see Fitz give the ceiling a wary look as we near the other end. His hand finds the small of my back, like he's ready to jump on top of me at a moment's notice.

"There they are." Nolan points above our heads to the rest of the group, who are situated halfway up in the stands a few sections away. I stop, mid-step, when I see who's seated on the other side of Carla.

"Look who we found." She grins at me as I slide into the row in front of her, trailing after Fitz with Alex on my tail. She points to Kyle next to her, who is giving all of us a sheepish smile, eyes darting back and forth to his phone. Alex and I share a look before I sit, the metal of the bleachers blessedly not blazing against my thighs as Carla holds a drink between us. "Dr. Pepper for the happy couple?" I take the cup, noting the single straw as I look at Fitz, my eyebrows raised.

This man has had his mouth on my clit, but we have yet to share a drink.

He takes the drink from my hand, taking a long sip before offering it back to me. I lean over, taking a sip, batting my lashes up at him.

Behind us, Carla groans. "I take it back. Give me back the drink."

I snort. "You don't even like Dr. Pepper." Setting the drink on the ground, Fitz turns, looking at my sister and her husband.

"Is this something you all do...often?" He gestures to the crowd around us. Arguably, this is not the scene one would expect to find our friend group in. The semi-pro baseball player and his doting wife; the happy college sweethearts that look like they just walked out of a day at the office (probably because they did); the new couple behind me, snuggled up; and me. And while I'm probably, appearance and attitude wise, the least likely suspect for "who's idea was it to go to the drag race on a Friday night?" It was definitely me.

"I used to come here with my high school boyfriend," Penny explains, tearing off a piece of her cotton candy and feeding it to Brett. "Piper tagged along a few too many times, became friends with the staff, and now they can't get rid of her." I lob a piece of the popcorn I've just stolen from Carla at Penny.

"We came here a lot in college." Nolan's voice is quiet, and I can tell he's probably thinking of the same memories that I am: Friday nights cheering on Mickey and Vic from the stands and then turning around for a late Saturday morning baseball game to cheer on Nolan. "Now we usually just stay till the end of Vic's race." Fitz's eyes widen, and he sits back to meet my gaze.

"Vic's a badass," I say with a shrug, taking a sip of our drink and turning back to watch two older model Chevy trucks face off, lurching forward as the light turns green on the side of the track.

We watch ten more races before they switch classes, and it's only a few more before I see the familiar silver body and red stripes of the Fiat rounding the far corner.

"There he is!" Alex nearly screams, and I scratch at my ear. She shoves at my shoulder, but I'm too busy watching the way Kyle's face has just lit up behind Fitz. I fumble my hand, trying to grab Alex's leg, and when she catches my eye, I nod towards Kyle. Her eyes widen, and her brows shoot up. "Do you think?" I bite my lips, catching Fitz's eye - he's clearly had the same thought, because even my Marble Man is smirking.

"Hah, a German." Penny scoffs behind me as a green Volkswagen pulls up next to him.

"I'll try not to be personally offended by that," Fitz says, rolling his eyes while holding my gaze. "Is that Vic's car?"

"He and Papa fixed it up," Alex says, and then grips my thigh so hard it could bruise. I swat her away. "Sorry, nerves." She shakes her head. "I want to wrap him in bubble wrap."

"Ok, Mama." Penny shoves Alex from behind. "He's got his helmet on, he'll be fine." Fitz takes my hand as the announcer reads out the specs on both cars. We all cheer, even Fitz, with his hands cupped around his mouth, when they call Vic's name.

And then, with a beep, the light turns green and they start down the section of the track, neck and neck. The VW gains on Vic, just for a moment, before, halfway down, Vic shoots in front of him. I stand with Alex, screaming, and suddenly our whole group is screaming, cheering, as Vic crosses the finish line, dusting the VW easily. Even Fitz is laughing, clapping as Penny and Carla whoop, Kyle screaming "yes!" next to us.

Fitz slides his arm over my shoulder, pulling me towards him, and I do a little happy dance in his arms, wiggling. And for a moment, I wonder why he was so worried - he's doing fine, with all of these people. Like being with a group that had no true expectations, aside from childish jabs from Alex, brought out a different side to him. I watch Vic's car pull into the other side of the speedway, where finalists sit before the best in class rounds.

But I feel Fitz's whole body tense over me, and I glance up at him, trying to figure out what's going on. His gaze is far off, staring at a distant part of the crowd. Slowly, his hand retracts from me, and it's like the mask has come back on. His face is emotionless, back to stone, as he leans forward, looking at Nolan.

"Restroom?" Even Nolan can tell that something is wrong, but he cocks his head towards the outer ring of the speedway behind us, up the stairs, and Fitz nods. To his credit, he gives my shoulder a squeeze, not meeting my eye as he brushes past us, walking up the stairs two at a time.

"What the actual fuck?" Carla says, head bobbing between Fitz and where I sat, staring after him, completely confused.

"Oh, shit." When I meet Alex's gaze, her eyes are wide. She nods behind me, and I turn in my seat, tracking where she's looking. My body goes rigid, understanding immediately why Fitz had done the same. Because standing in the front row a section away, staring at us, is an equally shocked looking Ryan Trinh.

CHAPTER 48

Fitz

The person in the mirror looks nothing like me. He's got the same dark red hair. The same green eyes. The same tense jaw that's always stared back at me. But the curls are neater. The shirt isn't something I would ever own. And the intense, burning rage that stares back isn't anything I've ever seen in my face before.

But there's a first time for everything.

I grip the cold porcelain of the sink with both hands, willing the feeling to ground me. To tether me back to reality.

Ryan Trinh.

Ryan *fucking* Trinh.

Of all the people. Of all the places he could have been.

I knew there was a moderate risk. The second I spotted the speedway, I knew. He and his college buddies came here all the time, for regular races and drag. I hadn't seen or spoken to him in years, given the circumstances with Olivia. Had never confronted him for sleeping with my wife, right under my nose.

For being my best friend and tearing my entire life apart with three little words.

I reach out for the sink, turning on the water and splashing it on my face. It's lukewarm, and doesn't hit the way I needed it to, like a cold jolt to the system. I'm wiping at my face with a paper towel when the door opens behind me, and I meet Kyle's gaze in the dingey mirror. Behind him are Brett and Nolan.

I can't blame the girls for sending them in after me - I've been in here for twenty minutes trying to get myself sorted.

"Dude," Brett says, stepping up next to me. "You scared the shit out of your girl."

Your girl. If I wasn't so fucking pissed right now, I'd probably feel a little better about anyone referring to Piper as my girl. I meet Brett's dark stare, my nostrils flaring.

CHAPTER 48

"I know you don't wanna lose your cool in front of her." Kyle crosses his arms in front of him. Based on the way he's dressed, my guess is he came directly from work - black pants, with a black button up, rolled up at the sleeves. "But going AWOL ain't gonna help."

I laugh, scrubbing a hand down my face.

"Losing my cool is the least of my worries." I stare down to the hand still gripping the sink, my own white knuckles, which still have scars from getting battered in lacrosse, from fights as a kid. "If I see him again, I may throttle him."

Nolan crosses his arms too. "Do you care about Piper?"

I rear my head back at his words. Did we not just have an entire discussion about this three hours ago?

"Uh-"

"I didn't ask if you fucking love her, Westfall." I swallow. Love. The thought hadn't even crossed my mind, but now that he's said it... "I asked if you care about her."

"Yes."

He quirks a burly blonde eyebrow at me, his forehead creasing against the band of his backwards baseball cap.

"Are you sure? Cause right now, you seem a little wrapped up in the ex and your shit with her." White hot rage bubbles up in my chest, and I step towards him.

"That was out of line," I breathe. We're even in height, and he just stares at me, arms crossed.

"He fucked your wife." Brett says it with an ease that should really have only been reserved for an old friend. But instead, he crosses his arms too, and the three of them are squaring off at me like they expect me to back down.

But they don't know me. Don't know what happened, how it tore everything apart.

Tore *me* apart.

"He fucked your wife," Kyle echoes, "and-"

"Watch it." It comes out as a near growl, and Kyle laughs.

Actually laughs in my face.

I rear towards him, but Brett grabs at my collar, pulling me back.

Where the fuck did this come from? It's been years since I went after someone physically - since I felt enough to want to hurt someone.

"There's the Westfall we've been waiting for." Nolan's voice sounds amused. "Cracks in the surface finally starting to show."

"He fucked your wife," Kyle continues, "who was a royal bitch, in my opinion."

"That seems to be the consensus." Brett nods.

"And you know what?" Kyle holds his hand up, gesturing around. "It got you here."

"To the bathroom?"

Kyle snorts, rubbing at his forehead, pushing his bangs back. "VP, you're real dumb sometimes." He sighs, leaning against a wall with his arms still crossed. "To all of this. To Piper."

"She said you guys ran into Bethani, yeah?" I look at Nolan, nodding, unsure of where this is about to go. "Bethani may not have fucked her husband, but I think after tonight, you know that anything having to do with that situation is a mess for her." He pauses, hitching a thumb at the door. "Did she go running when you two saw Bethani? Head for the hills and leave you sitting there wondering what you'd done wrong?"

"Piper didn't do *anything* wrong." I sound incredulous, but Nolan just stares at me.

"You shut up, shut down, and walked. And she's out there trying to figure out whether it's because *you* saw *Ryan*," Kyle says, "or because Ryan saw *you* with *her*."

My heart jumps into my throat.

"Oh, fuck."

"Oh fuck is right," Nolan agrees. "I love the dude, but Mickey fucked with her head in a lot of ways." He gestures back towards the door again. "Now fix your shit and get out there before we miss Montero's race." I lean against the sink, gripping it again.

"What do I even say to fix this?"

Brett laughs. "Delmonico women are all the same." I give Piper's brother-in-law a look of disbelief. "Piper may take after Luca, but in reality, they all want one thing." He pauses. "Well, two things. Buy her books and tell her she's pretty." A surprised laugh bubbles out of me. "And of course, reassure her that this had nothing to do with her, and everything to do with your tiny, fragile male ego."

Nolan nods, adjusting his baseball cap.

"In those exact words." He puts a hand on my shoulder, and I have to fight the urge to cringe away. "The night is young, and we might all get lucky if we play our cards right. But you hurt Piper, and I'll have an entire baseball team after your balls." Nolan looks towards Kyle. "You too, dude. I don't know you, but Montero is my brother, and I'll be damned if either of them get hurt."

And it's all I can do to meet Kyle's wide eyes as Brett and Nolan fistbump, leaving us to trail after them in a stunned silence.

# Piper

PIPER DELMONICO
You ok?

I stare at the words on my screen, my text to Fitz unanswered. Fuck. One second, we're fine. The next, I'm getting iced out and walked out on while Ryan Trinh picks his jaw up off the speedway floor. Nolan, Brett, and Kyle went after Fitz ages ago, leaving us with Dylan, who we decided was probably safer out of Fitz's line of sight, as well.

My phone buzzes, and I jump, hoping it's Fitz responding to my text, but it's a group chat.

FAM BAM (1) *Alex, Penny, Brett, Nolan*

BRETT ROBINSON
We're on our way back out. Fitz is coming too.

I suck in a breath, my eyes darting back to where Ryan is still sitting with people I don't recognize. He's aged a little, but for the most part, he hasn't changed since I last saw him at graduation. Same cocky smile, same almond shaped eyes, same-

"Hey," Penny says behind me, and I swivel in my seat to see all four men coming down the steps. We stand, letting Kyle and Brett slide in behind us as Fitz starts down our row. His face has softened, his forehead creased in what looks like concern, maybe determination, as he reaches out a hand for me. Surprised, I meet Alex's eye before moving to sit, but a hand wraps around my waist and I'm spinning around, back towards Fitz.

And suddenly, I'm being bent back in a sweeping, feverish kiss that catches me by surprise, gasping against Fitz's lips. He murmurs a laugh, tangling a hand in my hair and swiping his tongue over my lip until I'm meeting him stroke for stroke, my back arching in a dip straight out of a cinematic ending. I grab at his neck, his shoulder, anywhere I can find purchase.

"Oi, get a room!" someone calls, and for once, it's not Alex, because I hear her tell them promptly where to stick it as Fitz laughs against my lips again. He pulls me back up, meeting my gaze with a warm stare that makes me go a little gooey.

"Uh," I stutter, and he smiles. "Was that to show off in front of Ryan, or?" The lines between his brows return, and his grip in my hair, on my lower back, tightens.

"No." His voice is hoarse as he kisses me again, and Brett whistles behind us. I hear Penny smack his leg. "This is for you. For *us.*" Fitz swipes my hair off my shoulders, leaving my upper chest bare except the pearls I always wear. He touches his finger to them lightly as he speaks. "I don't ever want you to feel like I'm not happy to be with you. Ecstatic, really." His hand traces down my arm, lacing his fingers with mine.

"Ok, now I really am going to puke," Alex jabs as we sit down. Her comment rolls off me like rain on a window, because damn, I feel pretty impenetrable right now. Like Fitz's words are wrapped around me, armor against my self-doubt. And Ryan's shocked face, which I see when I casually glance his direction, is satisfying as hell. Feeling brave, I reach my hand up in a wordless little wave, and he dumbly waves back while one of his friends nudges his shoulder like a preteen boy at a school dance. I laugh into my hand as Carla flips him off behind me.

I can't wipe the smile off my face as Vic's second race starts, against another Fiat with what should be an engine that wipes the floor with him. But when he pulls ahead at the last second and scrapes out a win, I'm on my feet and screaming until my throat feels hoarse. Carla tosses her popcorn in the air like freakin' confetti, and I'm picking it out of my cleavage when we walk back across the bridge, my hand linked with Fitz. Vic's found the parking spot on the other side of Fitz's car from the dually truck, and he lights up when he sees us, holding his little trophy and box car model above his head like it's the Stanley Cup. I don't even get a chance to scream before Nolan rushes past us, sweeping Vic up with a rally cry, and I stand back with Fitz, letting them have their moment of bromance.

"Typical," Alex says, crossing her arms and nudging my shoulder. Nolan lets Vic down, and he fist bumps Dylan and Brett in turn. "Vic pulls all the-"

Her words stop as we watch Kyle swagger up to Vic, grabbing him by the side of his face and pulling him in for a kiss that has my eyes wide as saucers, biting my lip to keep myself from gasping. Beside me, Alex lets out a high pitched squeal as Nolan whoops, and Fitz's arm slides back over my shoulder, smiling like he knew this was coming before I did. I look back at him, then my friends in front of me, utterly confused and internally fangirling.

But as fast as the moment started, it ends when someone tosses an empty beer can in the direction of my friends. They break apart, and we all turn to see three guys leaning against the end of the truck next to Fitz's car, the one with the confederate flag.

CHAPTER 48

"Knock it off with that homo shit," one of them, wearing entirely too much camo, yells, and my whole body tenses. I immediately think of Andy, that day in the hall, beating on Vic and I with his horrible comments. "Ain't nobody wanna see that here."

"No one asked for your opinion, lowlife." Penny's practically growling, and I see Brett and Nolan exchange a look next to us.

"What did you say, you stupid bitch?" The same one speaks, and I see movement out of the corner of my eye. I think it's Brett, then Nolan, but I watch as Fitz crosses the space in three quick strides, his elbow flying back and then clocking the guy so hard, he falls back against the end of the truck. Holding his face, he staggers back, and one of the other men steps forward like he's going to try something, then realizes that Fitz has about a foot on him. Nolan steps up behind Fitz, followed by Brett and Dylan, and they're scrambling to hop into the cab of the truck.

"Yeah, you better run!" Alex screams after them, like she's not five feet tall and 120 pounds soaking wet. But my heart, while still pounding from excitement, from anger, from confusion, and from the absolute joy in seeing the look on Vic's face as he meets Kyle's eye, swells just looking at Fitz. As he turns around, cradling his hand and letting Nolan take a look at it, he meets my gaze and gives me a bashful smile, like he expected me to be angry at him for sticking up for Vic and Kyle.

The feeling in the pit of my stomach is far, far from anger, I realize, letting Carla, Penny, and Alex squeal and pepper Vic and Kyle with questions I truly want to know the answers to as well. Because their kiss came out of left field, blinding me. But so did this feeling in the pit of my stomach.

As surprised as I am by the events of today, the events of tonight, I'm more surprised by one obvious fact now at the forefront of my mind: there is a really good chance I'm in love with Fitz Westfall.

CHAPTER 49

Fitz

"So, I heard you punched a homophobe." I close my eyes, hoping for a second I'm hallucinating. But when I look up, Seer is, in fact, standing in the doorway to my office, grinning.

"Do you ever actually come here for work?"

"Down, tiger." She bats her hand at the air, stepping into my office like I invited her. "I'm meeting with Piper for lunch next door once she's finished with Fran." I let out the deep breath I hadn't realized I'd been holding - I'd told Piper yesterday I wouldn't be able to join her for lunch after her interview with my sister because of an important meeting my father had tagged me in on last minute. I feel immediate relief knowing she has someone to go debrief with.

"Okay." I nod, leaning back in my chair and flexing my fingers. Nearly a week later, and my hand is still aching. The bruising has gone away, thank God, because I wasn't sure how much longer I could hide my hand from my dad. "Did she talk to you about the ball?" Seer nods, her shoulder length blonde hair bobbing.

"We're going shopping tomorrow. Did you talk to her about Saturday?" She looks down at me, though the height difference is minimal and makes what I'm sure was supposed to be a piercing gaze much less intimidating. I hold back the sigh I want to let out - of course, Frannie told her.

"No." I grip my hands behind my head and wince. "I don't know if I want to put her through that shitshow." Seer snorts.

"Your brother's graduation is hardly a shitshow." I give her a flat stare. "Ok, maybe a little bit of a shitshow. But it's the perfect excuse to welcome her to the fam."

"Therein lies the problem."

"You don't want her to be part of the fam?" She crosses her arms, leaning forward against the chair facing my desk.

CHAPTER 49

"It's not that, I-"

I stop myself, caught on that idea. Piper. Part of the family. Part of *my* family. Fuck. You're like, two months in, Westfall. Pump the brakes.

But why does that idea make the tiny, itty bitty - ok, not so itty bitty - caveman part of me gloriously happy?

She's mine. I know she is. But in a way I can't quite put my finger on, the idea of her being a part of my family is both thrilling and terrifying.

"I don't want to scare her off," I finally breathe out, scrubbing a hand down my face. Seer laughs again, and this time, it's got a tone of disbelief etched in it.

"You think your family is going to scare her off, after the shit she went through with her in-laws?"

Ok. She has a point, and I wonder to myself how much of the story Piper's told Seer.

Before I can reply, there's a soft knock from behind her, and we both look to see Piper in the doorway. She's wearing a green blouse with a dark skirt that highlights the dip of her waist. I can just see the faint bruise healing on her shin from where she'd walked into my coffee table last weekend. She needs bubble wrap, I swear.

"Hey." I stand from my desk, crossing the office towards her, and dipping down to give her a quick kiss. She puts a hand on my chest, stopping me. "Whoa, what?"

Her laugh is soft, but her eyes dart behind her, into the bullpen of cubicles outside my office where I know there are people peeking around to get a better look.

"Not here," she breathes, and then flashes a grin that sets me at ease. I'm a little floored, usually the one to deny PDA, not the other way around. "Not if I actually get the job after that disaster of an interview."

I raise an eyebrow at her - disaster of an interview? With my sister? I'm about to ask as much when Frannie steps out of her office, meeting my gaze. Then, right behind her, my father walks out, giving me a tight lipped smile before turning to head to his office down the hall.

"Was he in your interview?" Seer's voice is quiet behind me, and Piper nods, tipping her head in the direction of the elevators.

"You sure you can't come?" Piper's eyes are pleading, and I shake my head, giving her an anxious smile and praying that the light squeeze I give her waist conveys what I need her to know. I have her back. In this, and anything else.

Because if there's one thing I'm not going to let my father do, it's drive a wedge between me and another person in my life.

Piper

I stare down at the cup of tea in front of me, watching spirals of steam ebb off the surface. Across from me, Seer's fingers tap the tabletop, a ball of nervous energy from the second she saw Chris Westfall walk out of that office after his daughter.

Fuck me, what a morning. I already had one grueling interview with a marketing agency across town - doing similar work to what I was doing before I started at AllHearts. But Frannie hadn't even had time to warn me that her father was joining us before their hushed conversation at her assistant's desk, he just plastered on that fake as hell smile and sauntered in ahead of us.

They looked alike, I had to admit that. I saw some of Fitz's best features, the physical ones, anyway, in his dad. The red hair, the strong jaw, green eyes. The smattering of freckles was definitely his, though he was pale in a way that made me sure Fitz got his coloring from his mother. But that was where their similarities ended.

Chris Westfall didn't set people at ease with a quiet confidence the way Fitz did - or, had, before being in the same room with him made my chest seize. He made me incredibly uncomfortable, his posture too tight, his questions clipped as he grilled me about how I felt my time at AllHearts would translate into a position in their marketing department.

He had every right to be protective - over his company, and his son. Olivia had done a number on Fitz, and he didn't know me from Eve, aside from the potential connection between his now wife and my mother, who I learned were both in a female lawyers association together.

Paula Westfall, was, in my mother's words from the brief conversation we'd had on the night of Fam Dinner, rooting for me.

"Finally," Seer breathes, and then scoots over in her chair to allow Frannie to slide in after her. I feel my chest expand with the breath I didn't know I'd been holding as Frannie reaches out to grab one of my hands.

"You are a rockstar." She squeezes my fingers, her eyes creasing behind the teal-framed glasses she had on today, which matched her purse almost perfectly. "Anyone else would probably have cussed Dad out."

"He wasn't that bad." My voice is not convincing, and both of them stare at me. "OK, my watch was telling me the entire time that my heart rate was too high."

"I was wondering why it kept vibrating." Frannie flags over a waiter, who greets her by name, like they had Seer when we sat down. "Unsweet tea and the Cobb salad, thanks, Hector." She gives the waiter a warm smile, turning to us.

"French Onion Chicken for me, and," Seer pauses, catching my eye. I nod,

CHAPTER 49

handing my menu over to Hector. "French Dip with the parm fries, extra garlic aioli. You'll have to key the specialties in, but the kitchen should know what to do." Hector looks like a deer in headlights as he takes the stack of menus, going to put in our order. Seer turns on her friend. "How did he even know she was interviewing today?"

"He must have seen my calendar blocked off this morning." Frannie gives a deep sigh. "I'm so sorry, Piper, if I'd known he would do that, I would have moved it to make sure he wasn't in."

"It's fine." Seer gives me a look, sipping on her Diet Coke. "I mean, it's not. I thought my heart was going to fall out of my butt."

"Glad that didn't happen," Frannie deadpans, stealing her friends' water to gulp while waiting for her drink. "I got an earful when you two left."

"Yeah, he's texted me already." I hold up my phone half heartedly. The second we were on the elevator it dinged, and he hadn't stopped. I appreciated the check in, but I think part of him is freaking out more than I am. I look at Frannie, gauging her before I continue. "They don't get along at all, do they?"

Frannie freezes momentarily, eyes sliding to Seer for just a second before she looks back at me. "Will and Dad are...more alike than they want to admit." She wrinkles her nose. "Oil and water sometimes, but other times, it's like they're on the same wavelength."

I snort. "That's what my dad says about my mom and I." I take a long draw from my tea, glancing around the restaurant on the bottom floor of The Monarch. It's hidden enough in the back of the lobby that I'm not worried about anyone seeing us, hearing our conversation - and if it'll get back to Chris Westfall. I am, however, worried about something else. "Is your friend going to get mad that you're here with me?" The two women across from me share a look, clearly confused. "The one that showed up here the other night, when we were at Menagerie." Recognition sinks across Seer's face.

"She means Savvy," Seer explains to her friend, and Frannie nods in understanding.

"I know someone told her I was here with Fitz, at least, that's what he figured." I pause, looking for the right words. "I would hate for the two of you spending time with me to put a dent in that relationship." Frannie toys with the roll of silverware in front of her.

"Savannah is..."

"Savannah," Seer finished for her, and then sips from her drink again. "I make it a point not to talk about people behind their backs, but if there's one thing you should know about Savannah, it's that nothing - no one, really - holds her attention for too long." She shrugs to herself, then looks at Frannie. "She's had a crush on Fitz for years, but I think she's finally figured out that she's not going to be able to sway his attention."

"My brother can be a tool." I nearly spit out my drink at Frannie's brutal honesty, but she just gives me a half-smile. "Both of them can be, really. But after Liv..." She leans forward on her forearms. "Piper, she hurt him. A lot. And he won't admit it to any of us, but I think he buried himself in work, and pointless shit outside work, just to get through the day." Then, her half smile goes full Westfall grin. "But then he started seeing you."

"Ok, Shakespeare." Seer waves a hand at her friend. "Chill it with the life-changing circumstances shit." Hector comes back with Frannie's drink, but when I turn to see why he's still standing there, I realize that the aproned man isn't Hector at all, but Mateo, the man I'd met briefly the night of my first date with Fitz. "Ah, perfect timing. Look at that." Mateo grins at us, pulling a chair up and sitting in it backwards, his chest pressed against the upholstered fabric. "We were just talking about how Piper doesn't need to worry that Savvy will be jealous of us spending time with her." Mateo nods, but I see something else in his eyes - hesitation, maybe - as he replies.

"Jealousy, no. She's not the jealous type." He shrugs, his fingers thumping on the top of the chair back. "Really, she just needs a new job."

"Welcome to the club," I reply, drinking my tea.

"She's really talented, but she puts a lot of her energy into relationships with pointless people instead of the ones worth her time, friends, and otherwise." Seer shrugs. "I think she was hoping that she'd be able to use her experience here to springboard into something more her forte, but so far, no dice."

"What does she want to do?" I ask, both curious about this girl that captured Fitz's attention, and someone that was clearly close to the people around me who, from what I could tell, came with Fitz like a packaged deal. I'm not complaining - Seer's neverending barrage of dry humor and memes throughout the day kept me going on some rough afternoons.

"Weddings." Frannie takes a long sip of her drink. "But not the venue side - I think, long haul, she wants to do actual coordination and planning, but for now..."

"For now she's working for Hitler." I nearly blow hot tea out my nose at Mateos words, and turn to look at him. "Seriously. Her boss has the little pedo stash, right here." He points to the area in between his upper lip and nose. "And that's it. No other facial hair."

"He does not," I snort, and Mateo just continues to nod.

"She went to work at Emily's after she left the concierge job here," Seer explains, and I make a face. "Yes, exactly that."

Emily's was a quantity over quality venue chain, a far cry from the personalized catering and white glove service at the WHG properties I'd been to. I'd also

CHAPTER 49

heard they paid shit.

"Does she have any interest in florals?" I sound thoughtful, and I don't meet their eyes as my fingers tap on the side of my china cup.

"She's been doing her own arrangements since we were in middle school." Mateo's voice is laced with annoyance, but I can tell he means it teasingly. "Why?"

"My sponsor is a florist." I shrug, meeting Seer's gaze. "I can send you her info, she's always looking for more help. Especially during the crazy seasons."

"Her and everyone else in this industry," Frannie whispers, and my phone and watch vibrate.

FITZ WESTFALL
Do you have any interest in attending my brother's college graduation Saturday morning? And then lunch after with my family?

For the second time in two minutes, I almost choke on my drink, setting it back down on the saucer with clumsy fingers as I read over the text again. Frannie raises her eyebrows at me, and for a second, she looks so much like her brother. I tilt my phone towards her, and her eyes glide over the screen before she brings two fingers to her temple, eyes closing as she shakes her head.

"That boy has less communication skills than anyone I know." She stifles what looks to be a yawn, looking back at me before continuing. "Sorry, Greta has been a nightmare to get down lately. Would you really want to help Savannah, knowing that she was with my brother?" I try my best to keep my head from rearing back in surprise.

"I'd help just about anyone."

There it was. The truth. Plain as day. The people-pleaser in me on display for the world to see, my heart on my sleeve and my fingers in my ears to keep out the people talking sense.

Instead of pressing me further on that, she says "We're going to my place after graduation, sort of a party thing. You're welcome to join us after lunch with Mom and Dad."

"I thought you lived in..."

"Middle of nowhere?" Mateo finishes for me, and I nod. "Yeah, they both do. It's like driving through the freakin' Hills Have Eyes out there."

"Fuck off," Seer chides, tossing her straw wrapper at the man next to me. "What he means to say is, yes, we live in a quaint small town about a quarter of a mile apart, and it makes for the perfect space for a good party." Mateo rolls his eyes.

"Does Fitz usually go to your parties?" My question is laced with disbelief that's only further confirmed by Frannie's unapologetic shrug.

"No, but I think you could ask him to spend Saturday night picking up dog poop and he'd do it, if you were there with him." Heat creeps up my face, and I bite my lips to keep the smile from spreading the way it wants to.

"Oh my god," Seer breathes, crossing her arms. "Look at that, she knows you're right." She leans forward, looking around with a conspiratory glance. "Was Carla right? Is it the promise of unlimited head that keeps him in check?"

"Aaaaand that's my cue to head back to the kitchen," Mateo says, standing up at the same time Frannie mimes vomiting into her tea.

CHAPTER 50

Piper

Five Years Ago

The rain pounded on the window outside, but the room was quiet, still. Nearly everyone was asleep, sprawled out on couches, the floor, pallets made haphazardly with blankets so that they could all be together.

I was at one end of a couch, curled up under an old blanket too small for my frame - the only one I could find after everyone else claimed theirs. Mickey's feet were pressed into my side, and his head lay in Melissa's lap. She was running her fingers over his scalp, his hair still short from chemo, and muttering to Liz, his sister, who sat on the other side of a small coffee table.

They thought I was asleep. They didn't know that in the hours that passed since we finished watching the final Cars movie with his nephews, and they'd been quietly planning their attempt to keep him in Kansas - to force him to move back, to give up his treatment and come live with them - I'd been listening.

"I just can't believe she's doing this to us," Melissa said.

"It feels like it's out of spite," Liz responded, and I heard her husband, Tyler, snore loudly. "She just keeps him from us because she doesn't want us to make memories with him before he's gone."

"Meanwhile, she's getting to make all the memories she wants." I bit the inside of my lips, willing myself to keep my eyes closed. "While she acts like we don't matter. Like his daughter doesn't matter."

My breath caught in my chest.

His daughter. Kayla. The daughter I didn't know about until days before. The daughter they hadn't mentioned in the years we were together, until confronted with Mickey's lies and his sickly appearance when we'd arrived for this visit.

The daughter that DNA said wasn't his.

Not that I cared about that. I was the last person to believe that blood meant anything, with the chosen family that had stood by us during years of chemo, of hospital visits, while the people in this very room stayed states away, musing their feelings on social media. No, the DNA was just a pin in the thing I'd said since the second I found out about Kayla. To me, it was interesting that this child and her mother seemingly weren't involved in his life until after he was diagnosed with a terminal illness.

And the cold, visceral feeling that had run down my spine when she'd messaged me the day we left to head to Kansas for this trip - asking me to speak with Mickey about signing paperwork for their daughter, like I'd known that they had been seeing each other for years under my nose - shot into me again.

"Kelsie won't tell her who her father is, I just wanted her to have someone she can look up to," Mickey had said when I confronted him. After I'd called his father, who, just as shocked as I was - or so it seemed - told me that they had put this issue to rest years before. Kelsie had accused Mickey of fathering Kayla, and he'd taken a DNA test that proved otherwise. I had personally gone to get a copy of it myself the day we arrived in this shithole town. And when those results came back, his family moved on with their lives.

Until Kelsie had messaged me, and Alex, my mother, and I slowly unraveled years worth of lies, of secret meetings that he'd hidden from me since reconnecting with the child who thought he was her father, despite every piece of evidence I had saying otherwise.

So when Kelsie had shown up at the Davis family house, while I sat on the couch next to Mickey, trimming his nails because he was too weak to do it himself, every inch of my soul wanted to confront her. Calling her out for taking advantage of a sick - dying - man, and his family. For lying to the child she claimed to love.

But then, Melissa and Oscar had physically blocked me from even coming outside. Literally held the door closed so I couldn't be a part of the conversation they were having about my husband. About the man that I'd been taking care of since his diagnosis, sacrificing my career, my livelihood, my health, all so they could sit in the comfort of this living room and garner sympathy from their small town. About the man I loved.

So hours later, hearing them talk like that was painful - but not surprising. They'd been trying to convince him to move back to the town he escaped from practically since his diagnosis, and his insistence had never wavered. I didn't think it ever would.

CHAPTER 50

"What about this one?" Alex holds up what's got to be the eighth turquoise dress of the day, swaying on the hanger as she attempts to get it high enough for me to see.

"No," I call, not even bothering to really give it a look.

Turquoise looks good on Alex, who's blonde and fair skinned and currently huffing at my reaction to her suggestions. It washes me out, makes my hair look too dark, and truthfully, is often unflattering on my curves.

"I feel like we're less close to finding something than we were when the day started," Seer muses from the rack next to me. I can't help but agree.

We'd come to the mall with four main objectives: 1. An outfit for our reunion; 2. An outfit for the fairy ball; 3. A new pair of running shoes for our upcoming 5K for the Cure, which was the day after the ball, and 4. A gift for Freddy for his graduation. After what feels like ten different stores, we're currently stuck on 1.

"Ok." I huff, digging in my purse for my phone. I scan the mall directory. "Let's find the tennis shoes, then we can circle back on the reunion and ball."

"Thank God," Alex says, and I follow her and Seer towards the entrance back into the bustling hall in the mall. For a Friday mid-day, it's surprisingly busy, but we fall into the flow as Alex checks her texts. "Mickie is all good, Vic said he's meeting us up here after lunch with Carla."

"How'd his interview go?" I ask, and she clicks away at the screen. Vic took a PTO day for an interview this morning, and while he wouldn't tell me who it was with, he seemed excited. I think the prospect of having to sit next to whoever AllHearts hires to replace me is pushing him out faster than he'd originally intended.

I've had a total of four interviews this week, with more lined up for next week, but honestly - the one I was interested in the most was on Frannie's team at WHG.

Carla insisted I take some time to think on it - like any good Alcoholic friend would. But even without the promise of seeing Fitz every day in the office, or working on a team lead by Francesca Westfall, who I'm learning is a force to be reckoned with, the position is alluring. Brand Manager? Make things pretty for a living and still have the creative energy to design on the side? 401k match, 100% of health, vision and dental covered, five weeks of vacation plus sick time and parental leave? A millennial's wet dream, that's what the job is.

"He didn't say, but considering there is no mention of tequila shots, I'd guess well." I feel myself ease a bit, and look over to Seer.

"Is it hard, bartending when you're sober?" She doesn't even pause at my words as she slips through crowds of people walking the wrong direction, going straight ahead like they're going to plow into us.

"Not really." She hitches her bag higher on her shoulder, a well-worn designer tote with a silver charm hanging off the handle. I'd realized earlier in the day it was a constellation - Scorpio, to be exact. "I was never really much of a bar drinker. Like, sure, I'd have one here or there." Seer shrugs. "But I did my worst blackout drinking by myself."

"Same." I nod, understanding completely. These were the things that varied from drunk to drunk - were you a social drinker, or a loner? Liquor, or beer? Do you need three meetings a week to cling onto your sobriety, or did you stop and never look back?

Seer didn't strike me as the three meetings a week kinda girl, but I could be wrong.

"Honestly, I keep alcohol in the house now." I feel myself freeze when she says this, just for a moment. "The idea of picking it up to actually drink it again makes me physically ill."

"In the house?" I echo, and someone bumps into me from behind. I shake myself out of it, catching up to her and Alex, who's half paying attention while scrolling through what I assume are pictures of Mickie from her mother in law.

"After this," Seer starts, and then points to her ear, where I can just make out one of the tiny hearing aids, "it's not AA keeping me sober. It's the idea that one drink, and I could kill someone, because I know that after one drink, I'm gone." I nod again.

"Fitz hasn't told me any of your story." She glances at me, and I swear I see a smile at the corner of her mouth.

"I'd be surprised if he knows any of it, to be honest." She makes a quick turn, and we cut through one of the stores at the center of the mall which I know will lead to the sports outlet on the other side. "He was too busy with his head up his ass to notice anything."

"Ain't that the truth," Alex chimes in, and I realize she's paying attention again. "I don't think I could bartend knowing I'll never have another drink again."

"It's not the alcohol, really." Seer sniffs, clearing her throat after we make it through a cloud of salesmen spraying cologne mid–air. I try not to cough. "After a while, in the program or not, you realize that the alcohol isn't the problem. The problem is you, and it's how you own up to that idea that determines your success."

She's not wrong - it's an idea that's taken years of expensive therapy to unravel.

"Ok, Gandhi." Alex laughs, throwing an arm around Seer's shoulder, which is

CHAPTER 50

low, even for my best friend. "Let's get these tennis shoes and then some lunch, Mama's starving."

"Is Mama going to continue referring to herself in the third person?" I ask.

"Mama will bitch-slap you if you keep testing her."

Lunched and set with a new pair of running shoes, we meet with Vic and Carla in one of the anchoring department stores, where I find a wide-brimmed tan hat and put it on, striking a pose.

"What do we think?" I ask, tipping the brim down. "Does this read country glam, or wanna-be influencer?"

"Watch it," Seer warns with a smile, "I have that one in white."

"Actually." Vic reaches for the hat, plucking it off my head and leaving my hair a mess. I glare at him as he continues. "With the right accessories, this could be a super fun piece." I want to say I'm totally kidding, but Carla cuts in.

"You know there are stores that do that, right?" She sniffs a candle on a nearby home decor shelf, making a face and then setting it back down. "Like, at the Stockyards, even in Deep Ellum."

Vic snorts. "Yeah, for like, $200 a pop." He holds the hat out at arm's distance. "I'd be willing to bet Piper already has everything she needs to make this one fabulous." I eye the hat. He's not completely wrong - some leather cording, maybe a line or two of chain. The white feather I'd been saving for some sort of hat for Greensleeves. This seemed more pressing.

"For the low price of," Seer takes the hat, examining the price tag, "$35, sold!"

"This was not on the list," I remind her, and she just stashes the hat with the armful of items she's planning to try on. This girl may rival my mother and her shopping problem - I mean, habit.

"No." Vic has turned on his heel, and he doesn't move as he keeps talking. "But that was." I follow his gaze to the mannequin halfway across the clothing section, eyes squinting.

"That? What was on the list?" I cross my arms. "For the reunion? Or for Freddy?" Vic snorts.

"Neither." He holds his hands up, making a frame with his fingers. "You still have those lace appliques, yeah? The ones with the rhinestones?" I think on it - I'm pretty sure I have them stashed in a drawer somewhere, leftovers from a piece I'd finished last year. "A little tulle here, some more rhinestones there. Ooh!" He steps towards the mannequin and we follow, like a pack of dogs waiting to be fed. "We could make you one of those badass chain shoulder things."

"I can never wear those," Seer sighs, looking down at her chest through the Marina and the Diamonds shirt she's wearing. "The girls are just too big and they're made for people with giraffe necks."

"Lucky for you, Vic and Piper know their way around needle nose pliers."

Carla would know, she's stepped on them enough around the apartment. Seer perks up, crossing her arms and looking at the dress in front of us, then me.

"It could work." She taps at her chin. "Fitzwilliam would need to wear something more than his usual boring suit."

"I'll handle Fitz," Vic says with a wave, and I narrow my eyes at him.

"Did one shirt make you his personal stylist?"

"The man could have gone to jail for defending me." He shrugs, but his face is sincere. "The least I can do is make sure he looks good with my girl."

"I think you mean *his* girl," Alex cuts in, and I roll my eyes.

"I think you're all idiots."

"Maybe," Carla answers, reaching out to slide one of the layers of the dress in front of us between her fingers. "But you're an idiot who's gonna make his jaw hit the floor when he sees you in this, once you've worked your magic."

CHAPTER 51

Fitz

Quiet Piper is scary. I didn't think I could be more scared of her than I was that day in the office at The Pine. That cold fury radiated off of her in waves at the insinuation she'd been the one in the wrong with the Davis family. But here, sitting in my passenger seat, not saying a word for the forty five minutes it takes us to get parked at the Lone Star State University colosseum, is terrifying.

"Are you sure you're ok?" I ask for what feels like the tenth time.

"Mhm." She nods, flipping down the mirror, again, smoothing chapstick over her lips, again, and swipes under her eyes, again.

"You look great." I reach over to squeeze her knee, but when I try to pull my hand back, she grips my fingers in a way she hasn't the entire car ride. I feel my shoulders relax a little. There she is. She closes the mirror, fidgeting again with the small gift bag in her lap - I told her she didn't need to bring anything, but she promptly told me where I could stick that idea, so I left it alone.

"I don't know why I'm so nervous." She pauses, watching a family cross the parking garage, toddler screaming at the top of their lungs. "That's a lie. I do."

"They're going to love you." I watch her whole body freeze the second the word love is out of my mouth, and I want to wrangle it back in. Stuff it back in the jar it came from. But instead, I squeeze her knee again, and barrel through like it didn't happen. "We're going to be late if we don't go in." She glances at her watch.

"It doesn't start for another half hour."

"It'll take us at least twenty minutes to get through security," I argue. Her brows knit.

"You're the kind of guy who likes to be early to everything, aren't you?"

"Yes." She sighs, reaching up to pat my cheek while she puts the gift in the backseat.

"I apologize in advance for any undue stress I may cause you, then." I'm a little scared to ask what she means, but before I can, she plops out of the car, pulling her curls to one side as she adjusts her purse on one shoulder. As I pull myself out of my seat, I see her nervously smoothing over her waist, glancing around, and then adjusting her chest. I bite my lips to keep from smiling. "Oh, shut it." Even with that tone, she holds her hand out to me, and in what's become my new normal, I take it, letting her lead me out of the garage and into the warm late May air. I forget, sometimes, that this was her alma mater, too. Not just Fred and Frannie's. She probably knows these streets better than I do.

And she proves it, when, while crossing the road to get to the colosseum from the parking garage, she J-walks diagonally through the intersection.

"Jesus," I call after her as she nearly jogs. "That's not how those work." Piper snorts, walking backwards as she nears the sidewalk at the other corner.

"How would you know, Westfall? Maybe here in Clifton, we all walk across intersections-"

But she doesn't finish, because the back of her heel catches the curb and she nearly tumbles backwards. I watch her face flash with panic and reach out my arm, catching her around the waist before she can truly fall.

"That's what you get for calling me Westfall, *Delmonico*." Her face scrunches up at me, but her hand's still gripping my upper arm through my suit jacket - one I'm regretting putting on, now that it's a sauna out here.

"I don't like it when you call me that."

"Now you see how I feel." I pull her up to standing, and she adjusts again, like she's fallen into a pile of dog hair or burrs. I pick at an imaginary Bex hair and she almost thanks me, before realizing that I'm teasing and smacks my arm.

"Hey, that's my job!" We both turn to see Frannie half-running across the intersection, the same way Piper had, and the only saving grace is that Greta is not with her.

"You two are going to kill me," I state plainly, looking between them.

"What'd I do?" Frannie asks, breathing jagged as she catches up to us.

"I was just telling Fitz that it's an unofficial tradition to completely disregard crosswalks on campus." My sister nods.

"It's true."

"True like the white raccoon?" I ask, and they stare at me. I'd been teasing, only bringing up the albino raccoon as a joke, the sort of unofficial mascot of LSSU that I knew had several fan pages and a variety of inside jokes that I never quite understood.

"We never joke about Lucky," Piper says, one hand to her chest.

Oh god, she's being serious.

"Lucky?" I feel my brows knit together. "It has a name?"

"It has a family." Frannie's voice is loud enough to garner attention from the people walking in front of us on the sidewalk, who turn briefly. "Of course it's got a name, Will."

These women are going to be the death of me, and that's all I can think as we make it through security. It does, in fact, take 20 minutes, which I point out to Piper before we trek to the other side of the arena where my parents are already seated in the VIP section, right above where the big WHG logo is plastered around the sideboard.

"Easy to spot," Piper mutters to me, and I smile, squeezing her hand when we spy Paula waving like a mad woman. When we finally make it over, Frannie slides into the row behind them, giving Paula a hug over the seat while I shake Dad's hand. He's his usual self, a little terse, phone in one hand, but he gives Piper that same tight-lipped smile he'd had for her the other day at the office.

It took everything in me not to lay into him on Thursday, mostly for how uncomfortable I know Piper must have been meeting him for the first time while also interviewing for a job. There'd been no warning, just hurricane CW heading out for destruction. In its path? My relationship. The only reason I didn't let him have it was Frannie, who assured me that despite his thorough grilling, Piper held her own against my father on questions that would have made other people crumble.

He didn't really know, or had forgotten, what this woman had gone through. A few questions about working in the business of pretty undergarments wasn't about to phase her.

"Piper!" Paula holds out her arms, and tentatively, Piper steps into them, letting my stepmother embrace her like she had Frannie. "It's so good to see you, sweetie." She pulls back, taking one of Piper's loose curls in her fingers. "You look so good." Paula grins. "So happy."

I can't help but notice the glance Piper shoots me before answering, "I am."

Shit. My heart gives a little jump at that.

"It's good to see you again," Dad says, adjusting the leg of his pants as he sits back down in the stadium chair, turning to look at us.

"Surprised you didn't scare her away." Paula's voice is light, but there's an edge to it that after years of listening in on their conversations, I pick up on immediately. As we sit down, Frannie looks at me over Piper's shoulders. She must have said something to her mom.

"I would hope it'll take more than one conversation to scare someone away." Dad raises one graying eyebrow at his wife, then back at me.

It's on the tip of my tongue, what I want to say about that very conversation, but from behind us I hear "Shit, shit, sorry we're late!" right as the commencement music starts, and I pivot in my seat to see José, Mateo, and Andrea jogging down the stairs.

It's been a minute since I've seen Andrea, Mateo's older sister and our former nanny, but three kids and fifteen years later, I wonder if she's ever seen a wrinkle in the same way her father's retained his eternal youth.

"Hey, sis," Frannie calls as Andrea slides into the seat behind her, reaching forward to kiss Frannie on the head. Dad and I shake Mateo and José's hand as they find their seats behind Piper and me, and José leans forward between us.

"I see you haven't run away yet."

"Why is everyone so convinced I'm going to run off screaming?" Piper asks with a laugh, hands half-raised. "Are there bodies in a closet I should know about?" I share a look with Mateo that's more suggestive than anything, before he bursts out laughing and I smirk at Piper. Andrea reaches over and introduces herself, and I realize it's probably the first time we've all been in a room together in a decade, save Freddy, who I'm trying to spot in the crowd filing into the stadium floor.

"There he is!" Paula nearly screams, pointing towards a figure half a foot taller than the girls on either side of him, and sure enough, it's Fred, the navy cap pressing down on that mop of red hair in that way that's not particularly flattering on anyone. "I can't believe it!" She leans on Dad's shoulder, and he gives her arm a pat. "Our baby is graduating college." She gives a big sniff, and I can tell by the way she's wiping at her nose she's forgotten tissues.

I'm about to offer her my pocket square, because honestly, I'd rather have her snot on that than hear Dad complain about his jacket later, but Piper's fishing something out of her purse and holding it out next to Paula's head before I even get the chance.

Paula and my dad both look at the pack of tissues between them, and then back at Piper. Paula gives her a watery smile, taking a tissue and then offering it to Dad, who declines them. He glances at us over his shoulder one more time before returning to the ceremony in front of us.

I think he's unsure of what to make of Piper Delmonico, and at this point, neither am I. But there's one thing I do know about this girl - this woman - next to me, who finally seems a little more relaxed as she settles into her chair.

With every beat of my heart, every time she presses her lips to mine, I wish she hadn't gone through the things that hurt her. But I can't help but be thankful that the changes she went through, to make her into who she is now, led her to me.

CHAPTER 52

Piper

"How does it feel to be officially an adult?" Frannie asks her brother, yanking on one of the seemingly endless cords around his neck. He's got one for pretty much every accolade a psych major can get, which is, apparently, a lot.

"Fred's an adult when I'm rolling over in my grave," Andrea shoots out, and then jumps in the picture with Frannie and her brother. Even though we've long since left the coliseum in the middle of campus, Paula forced Freddy to stay in his gown and accessories long enough to get pictures. Thirty minutes later, and we're still sliding person after person into a variety of poses so that they can get every shot possible in the back room of one of the only nicer restaurants in Clifton, The Rise.

"Can we please be done now?" the center of attention asks, to which both his mother and sister respond "No!" Freddy gives a noticeable grumble that sounds an awful lot like the man standing behind me. I lean back against his chest, tilting my head to look at him.

"You ok?" His face is tighter than usual, almost pinched looking.

"Yeah," he breathes, and I let my hand move back, searching for his. When I find it and give one of his fingers a squeeze, he seems to relax a bit. "Sorry. I just hate pictures."

"You haven't even been in any yet," I reply, quirking a brow. He looks down at me with a look that could wither a pansy in perfect health.

"Yet."

As if hearing our words, Paula's voice calls "Alright, Andrea, you and Fitz trade places." Andrea, who I might have become best friends with in about two heartbeats after seeing the Kindle stuffed in her crossbody, slides out from under Freddy's arm.

Fitz's brother isn't quite as tall as him, and is a little bit more lean. His skin is pale in a way that reminds me of his sister, his mom, but he shares the same freckles as all of them. His long, red hair falls in soft waves around his face, and I wonder to myself how the psych major younger brother figured out how to style his hair before the appearances-and-aesthetics-matter Westfall.

The stark contrast between the three of them becomes apparent the second Fitz slides in where Andrea, José's daughter, had been. His tan skin is shades darker than theirs, and while their eyes are green, they border on hazel. He's bulkier and taller, and I can't help but think what his mother must have looked like for him to get all of these beautiful traits, clearly the best of both his parents.

"Piper, you get in there for one!" Paula calls, breaking me out of my reverie. I laugh, shaking my head at the incredulous ask. "Come on, you're part of the family now!"

Fitz's body language tells me immediately he's caught off guard by the phrase, but he holds an arm out for me as Frannie and Mateo chant together "One of us, one of us!" Chuckling, I sidle up next to Fitz, finding space under his arm and letting him drape across my shoulder. Paula takes about eight thousand pictures, and when we're done, I look up at him from my cozy spot. He's already looking down at me, and while the creases between his brows are there, there's no other tension in his face like there had been when the pictures first started.

By the time we're seated and have ordered drinks, I can tell that his social battery is all but zapped. He's got one hand on my thigh and seems to be listening to a story his brother is telling, but I recognize that idle tapping with his thumb at this point. The only people that stayed for lunch were José's family and Paula's sister.

"So," Chris says, all but cutting his youngest son off as he looks at Fitz and me. "How's that reunion planning coming? Only a few weeks now, right?" His tone is casual, but my hackles raise the second he speaks.

"It's going well," Fitz responds for both of us. "We should have a good group there. Piper's roommate has been working on getting in contact with everyone."

"And your roommate is..." He trails off, looking at me.

"Carla Montgomery." He quirks a brow at Frannie, who's seated on the other side of Fitz.

"Don't we have a Montgomery on staff too?"

"Chloe," Frannie deadpans. "She's one of my best friends, Dad."

"Right." Chris holds up his whiskey glass like he's just unearthed a precious memory. "So your roommate is connected with us, you're helping with the reunion...and now interviewing for a job at WHG?" I can practically hear the swallow I make, nodding. "Forgive me." He looks at Fitz, but nothing about his gaze is apologetic. "I just don't remember Piper here being among your friends in school."

Fitz's hand on my thigh tightens, and I settle mine over it.

CHAPTER 52

"We weren't close in high school, no." Understatement, but sure. "The reunion reconnected us."

"Which is *adorable*," Andrea pipes in from the other side of Frannie. I think both of them are thoroughly enjoying some kid-free time, they've been attached at the hip and swapping complaints since we got here.

"Adorable," Chris echoes, and then sips his whiskey. He gives us a faint smile, but I can see Paula's appraising look on her husband from next to him. "I know Francesca has several top candidates for the position on her team. I just want to make sure that whoever she hires is..." He eyes me, and for a moment, I feel like he has x-ray vision and I'm immediately uncomfortable. "Dedicated to WHG, not just one person there."

"Chris." Paula's voice is low, and the grip on her wine glass is so firm I'm a little worried it's going to shatter. But I'm hardly noticing - because there's a ringing in my ears, the flame of embarrassment creeping up my cheeks.

"Piper is more than dedicated," Frannie says, leaning forward, "and more than qualified."

Chris quirks a brow.

"Did you even look at her resume?" Fitz asks quietly, and all heads swivel in his direction. I'm trying not to dart out of the room, my conflict aversion at DEFCON 1, and truthfully, this whole conversation isn't fair to Freddy, who's looking almost as uncomfortable as I feel. This is his day, not an opportunity for his dad to grill Fitz's new girlfriend. Again. Fitz's words, his stories about his father, all come rearing to the surface, fueling the rage bubbling under my skin. "Or did you just see AllHearts, hear we were dating, and make up your mind then and there?" Chris lets out a little surprised noise.

"Of course I looked at her resume, I was in her interview. I just don't see what years of designing-"

"I have a degree in marketing." It's out of my mouth before I can stop it, and everyone swivels to look at me. Fuck. Delmonico, what are you doing? "I have a degree in marketing from this school, right here, the same one your daughter went to." I gesture towards Frannie, finding my voice. "I was a three time MSO international champion, which I also know means something to you, considering you helped fund several of those trips while Frannie was involved." He looks a little taken aback, so I keep rolling, even as Fitz's hand might as well be a vice grip on my thigh. "And prior to AllHearts, I worked for what's arguably one of the largest marketing and public relations agencies in the country, on accounts with annual marketing budgets three times WHG's total budget." I pull my napkin out of my lap, setting it on the empty space where my plate would normally go.

"So I'm sorry, Mr. Westfall, if you don't think years of designing for a multi-million dollar company is relevant to the work I would do at WHG. And maybe it's not." I push my chair back, standing. "But I do know what I want, and what I need, and what I needed after my husband died was a change." Mateo does a near spit take next to me, choking on his water. "My time at AllHearts has run its course, and I'm trying to find somewhere to land where I don't feel stagnated or made to feel less than I am. But if this is the way business is conducted, maybe I should rethink my application."

Pretty much everyone's mouths are hanging open, and Freddy's head bobs between looking at me, and his father across the table, who's just as shocked. But I don't care. I turn on my heel, heading for the bathroom, locking the single door behind me with a click as my heart practically beats out of my chest. My head falls forward, forehead on the cold wood, and I try to even out my breathing, my heart rate, which my watch is telling me is too high. No, shit.

From the other side of the door, there's a soft knock.

"Someone's in here." There's a moment of silence before the response.

"It's me." Fitz's voice is low, but I know it well enough, and click open the door to see him on the other side, his chest heaving as much as mine, eyes blazing like he wants to burn down the world. Good. Maybe I'll let him. He pushes past me into the single room, and I shut the door behind him, locking it. I lean back against the linoleum counter of the sink, crossing my arms. He doesn't say anything, he just looks at me, into me, and I feel uncomfortable again.

"I'm sorry," I say finally, and his brows knit together. "This is Freddy's day, and I just ruined it by-"

Before I can finish my sentence, he's crossed the room, grabbing both sides of my face. I make a surprised yelp, but Fitz crashes his lips into mine in a ferocious kiss that I'm so stunned by, it takes me a second to realize what's happening. Once I figure it out, I melt against him, one hand finding his hair and the other on his hip, pulling him into me. His kiss is so heated, so needy, that when we pull apart, we're both gasping, and I look up at him, blinking through my lashes.

"I, uh," is all I can manage, and a smile slides across his face. I realize I can feel him, hard and standing to attention against my thigh, and I glance down with a surprised laugh.

"That was," he says, still meeting my eye as one of his hands reaches down, pulling the hem of my dress up until he's sliding his hand across my thigh, up the shorts I have on underneath, "quite possibly one of the sexiest things I've ever seen."

I can't help it. I let out an unladylike, surprised snort. He just beams down at me, his hand cupping one of my asscheeks.

"And if we weren't in a public place, these would be off and I'd be showing you just how much I enjoyed watching you tell my dad off." He gives my butt a pat, and then lets my skirt fall back down. I pout, and his throaty laugh sends a shiver up my spine. "But the last thing we need is to get arrested for indecent exposure on Fred's graduation day."

"It wouldn't be indecent exposure," I argue, surprising even myself, but he just laughs and runs his thumb over my lip. I want to take it into my mouth, remind him exactly what I can do to him, but at this point, I don't think that's fair to either of us.

"Do you want to get out of here?" His gaze changes, the lust clouding it moments before gone as he observes me quietly. "We can just kill time until we head to Lawrence?"

"No," I sigh, closing my eyes and giving a resigned groan. I turn in his arms, facing the mirror and attempting to adjust myself. In the harsh lighting of the bulbs above the mirror, both our eyes shine brightly. The deep blue dress I'm wearing is pretty well coordinated with Fitz's navy suit, and we look...good together. "Hm," I muse, one hand reaching up to feel the lapel of his jacket. I meet his eye in the mirror. "You sure I can't convince you into a quickie?" He laughs, snaking his arms around my waist and leaning down to set his chin on my shoulder.

"You probably could, but I'd much rather take my time with you." He tilts his head, his nose finding my hair, inhaling deeply. "Thank you for coming today." I meet his eye again.

"Of course." He breathes in one last time, and then separates from me, the cold air hitting my back and making me frown. As he adjusts himself, he leans forward, giving me a quick peck before I turn and open the bathroom door.

What I was not expecting was Paula Westfall, sitting on the leather bench outside the bathroom, looking up at us with a huge grin on her face.

CHAPTER 53

Fitz

I meet Paula's eyes, and then watch them flit down to my hand connected with Piper's.

"We weren't, uh -" she stammers, but Paula just shakes her head, waving a hand and then gesturing for Piper to come sit next to her on the bench. She meets my gaze for a second, before moving to sit next to Paula, smoothing her skirt under her thighs.

I watch her move - her legs crossing at the ankles, hands folding in her lap. It's ladylike and poised, which isn't always Piper's forte, but I've noticed the way she changes around authority figures, especially people she wants to like her. It's probably the little remaining piece of what she points out is making herself small for others. Taming her into something less than what she is.

The observation makes my chest a little tight. The fact that she felt she had to make herself small around my family hurt. The fact that it's taken me this long to notice those things about her hurts more.

"I wanted to make sure both of you were alright," Paula starts, leaning forward and putting a hand affectionately over Piper's. She looks up at me. "Chris is wound so tight right now, and..." She trails off, an apologetic smile on her face.

"I don't think that's an excuse for what he just did." I lean against the wall next to the bathroom door, looking down at her.

"No. It's not." Paula's sigh is deep as she recrosses her legs, her body language telling me all I need to know. She's uncomfortable, probably not as uncomfortable as Piper, but enough that I can read it all over her. "It's not an excuse, but your father is an investor in that company we were talking about at my birthday. VistaTech?" Piper's eyebrows shoot up, and she glances between us. "Their merger with that London company is this week, and it's apparently not going well from a PR point of view."

CHAPTER 53

"That's what happens when you lay off thousands of people." My tone is flat, but I can see the way Piper's reacting, and quirk an eyebrow at her.

"Penny and Brett work at VistaTech," she says quietly, and then when Paula looks confused, she adds, "My sister and her husband." Paula nods, patting Piper's hand.

"It doesn't sound like it's affecting anyone here, just at the London company they bought." I see Piper's shoulders sag, just slightly. "But I think Chris is holding his breath until it's over." I open my mouth to argue, but she holds up her other hand. "It's not an excuse, I know, I've already said that." She swallows audibly, bringing both hands to smooth down the sides of her hair. "I think he's also feeling a little bit of Deja Vu right now."

"Deja Vu?" Piper says what we're both thinking, and Paula nods, sighing.

"You two...God, it's like stepping in a time machine." Piper and I share a confused look, but Paula holds her hand out to me. "Will, give me your wallet." I raise a brow at her. "I'm not going to steal your credit cards, just let me see your wallet for a second." I'm thoroughly confused, but dig my wallet out of my jacket pocket, handing it over to her. She flips open the worn brown leather, sifting in the pockets until she finds what I'd half expected her to.

With a look of triumph, she sets my wallet in her lap, lifting up a tattered photo. I haven't looked at it in years, but it's always been there, since I was old enough to carry a wallet. And when she hands it over to Piper, I know that she's thinking the same thing I am.

Because unconsciously, I'd found a woman that looks strikingly like my mother, in the best ways. I know that Paula is pointing out Mom's tan skin, the dark, curly hair, the way her nose wrinkles when she's laughing, which you can just barely see under the strain of the sun in the picture of her in front of the Eiffel Tower.

"This is Fitz's mother, Tessa." Piper looks up at me, and then back down to the picture Paula is pointing at. "She was also my best friend." Both of our attention snap to Paula, who laughs. "I don't know how many times I've told you we love your mom, Will. I wasn't making that up."

"I know that." I feel a lump in my throat. "But best friends?" Sure, I'd known they were all close - that Paula had been there when my dad was falling apart, and that's how their relationship began. But I'd never pressed for details, never wanted them, never needed them.

"When Tessa died," Paula starts, and her eyes begin to shine with tears pooling at the corners. "Your father was doing everything he could to keep her alive. Every treatment, every procedure possible. But in the end, she was hurting so much." A tear slips, and she swipes at it. The lump in my throat gets bigger. "We'd all been friends since high school, and if he wasn't there with her, I was.

But, Will..." She purses her lips, dabbing at her eyes. "Losing your mother nearly killed him. Nearly killed both of us. We weren't the people we'd been before she got sick. Didn't know how to be those people again." Paula lets out a watery laugh, looking between us. "And truthfully, I don't know that we could have. Because your father was a broken man, missing half his heart, and I was hurting in a very different way. But we both loved - love - your mother fiercely."

"And that's what brought you together?" Piper asks quietly, handing Paula the picture. She takes it, settling it in her lap, not letting it go. Her fingers absently trace the edges, which are worn and creased.

"In some ways, yes." She nods. "Will, I'm not blind. I know I'm never going to replace your mother, but-"

"I don't want you to." It's out of my mouth before I can stop it, and she rears back a bit. Piper gives me a wide eyed stare, and I try to course correct. "I mean, what I mean, is, uh - I wouldn't want you to replace her."

"Especially not if she meant that much to you," Piper finishes for me, and I try to give her a grateful smile. "To both of you." she reaches out, taking Paula's hand. "And of course, it makes sense that Chris would be protective of Fitz. Not just after Olivia, but after knowing what it's like to lose someone, like I have, like you both have." She glances up at me. "Like you all have."

"It's not an excuse," I repeat, and Paula nods, her other hand settling over Piper's, the picture still between her fingers.

"It's not, and trust me when I say we'll be discussing that when we get home." The look of determination on her face is the one I saw too many times as a kid, usually reserved for court prep or cleaning a stubborn grass stain out of Fred's soccer uniform. "But please, Piper." She squeezes Piper's fingers. "Don't think that this has anything to do with you, personally. I've been hearing your mother rave about you for as long as I can remember." Paula looks at me, then. "And I think you're good for each other."

And while I keep the thought to myself, letting Piper and Paula hug it out in the hallway before following them back to the table, where no one speaks of Dad's outburst and we continue through a family style lunch, she's right. I think we are good for each other. And I'm starting to think Piper Delmonico might be the best damn thing that's ever happened to me.

Piper

"Ok, so let me make sure I'm following," I start, pointing the neck of my bottle of root beer at the group spread across Frannie's living room. I gesture to the man sitting next to Seer, whose hair is blonde like hers, curling around his ears in

CHAPTER 53

a messy mop. "You're her brother." I point back to Seer, and Liam nods. "And you're married to her brother." I point the bottle at Jesse next to Liam, who also nods, leaning back on the couch and tracking his husband's moves with icy gray-blue eyes, a stark contrast to his deep, smooth skin. I swear I've seen this man before, or at least someone that looks like him, but I can't put my finger on it.

I move to point at Mateo and Andrea, who are in a corner with Andrea's husband, Caesar. Their kids are running around upstairs, presumably working off some of the cake Mateo brought with him to celebrate Freddy's graduation. "Your dad is married to his mom." I point back to Jesse, and everyone nods.

Liam is Seer's brother. Jesse is Jose's stepson, and is married to Liam. Andrea and Mateo are Jose's kids.

This feels like a middle school standardized testing word problem.

"Alright, I think I've got it." My voice does not sound confident at all.

"Can't forget Chloe, Jas or Savvy," Mateo says, sipping at his beer. I know Chloe is working, because I asked Carla this morning if I'd be seeing her. I have no idea who Jas is, but I can guess on the last one.

"Right." I turn to Seer next to me, wholly overwhelmed with the amount of people I've met tonight. "Is Savannah coming tonight?"

"She'll be here later," Seer says with a note of surprise in her voice.

"Good." I point to my purse, tucked into a corner on the bartop of Frannie's modern farmhouse kitchen. "I brought one of Lisa's cards with me." From his spot next to Freddy on another couch, Fitz gives me a confused look, and I mouth "later."

I take a look at my phone - there's a conversation going in our group chat about what we're wearing to the reunion, and I'm feeling pretty triumphant, having already squirreled away most of my outfit. I see a text from my mother about Hunter's upcoming birthday dinner after the 5K next weekend, and an email from one of the companies I interviewed with this week - a thanks, but no thanks.

I try not to let defeat cloud the moment too badly, and lock my phone, staring at the wallpaper. *Life isn't about finding yourself, it's about creating yourself,* the scroll text reads, gold on a purple background. My motto for the year - to create a life I want to live, not to hope I find one by happenstance. And if the recent months are any indication, I'd say this is a pretty good start to creating that life.

But something catches my eye.

The date.

I stare.

It can't already be this late in May. Not being at work every day, seeing time and date stamps on emails and submissions, not crossing days off my calendar, I didn't even notice.

For the first time in years, the middle days of May passed by without a second thought. The anniversary of Mickey's death, of the shitshow of a funeral, of the days leading up to and the days following May 16. Those days haunted me like the worst kind of poltergeist, the grief creeping up unseen and unheard. But just like that, the days had passed, and I hadn't even noticed. Because I'm happy. God, jobless, unstable financially, but gloriously happy and creating a life I love.

FITZ WESTFALL
You ok?

I look up, meeting his eye across the room, and he raises a brow. I give a silent nod, tucking my phone under my thigh, letting the conversation still happening around me wash in like a tide, taking away any thoughts of Mickey and those days with them. I deserve to be happy. To forget those times, just for a while, and live in the now, not the past.

Behind me, the door opens and the alarm system beeps. From upstairs, I hear one of Andrea's kids scream "Auntie Jas!" and there's the sound of feet thundering down the steps and a quiet "oof."

"Hey there," a familiar voice says, and I turn to catch Fitz's attention again. After a minute, the feet make their way back upstairs, and around the corner walks Jasmine Norton. We both spot each other at the same time, and the squeal she emits is near comical as I barrel off the couch, throwing my arms around her in the biggest bear hug I can manage.

It's been years since we've seen each other, and with my lack of social media presence, I couldn't even tell you what she's been up to. But as I hold her at arm's length, looking over her, she looks like she's glowing. Her deep skin is always flawless and dewy, and her tightly coiled hair has blonde highlights in it that give her a summery, vacation-ready look.

"Will someone please explain what's going on?" Freddy says dryly, and we turn to face the rest of the room, who are looking at us with confused gazes.

"Sorry," I say, a little out of breath from my excitement. "Jasmine and I went to color guard camp together, what was that, fifteen years ago?" I catch her eye, and she nods. "She also photographed my wedding."

"Hold on," Fitz says, raising the hand that's not clutching a beer. "You were in color guard." It's not a question, more of a statement of shock, and I glare.

"Yes, yes I was." Next to me, Jasmine laughs, shoving playfully at my arm.

"For, like, a whole six months."

CHAPTER 53

"What an interesting development." Seer gives Fitz a look. "She can't handle a sword, but she can do rifle tosses?"

"I didn't even make it that far," I say honestly, "I fell and hurt my ankle the week before school started and spent the whole freshman football season in a boot on the sidelines."

"And how did we hurt our ankle?" Jasmine asks playfully, and this time I shove her.

"Felldownmyfrontporchsteps," I grumble. Seer holds a hand up to her ear, hearing aid clearly visible.

"Sorry, can't hear you, what was that?" Her face tells me she heard exactly what I said. I wheeze out a laugh, pinching the bridge of my nose.

"I fell down my front porch steps, okay?" I sigh, running a hand down my face. "On lunch break from drills, went home for an hour, went to get in the car and fell down three steps."

"I always wondered what that boot was for," Fitz muses out loud, and I cut him a look. He'd noticed my boot?

"Why they let me have a flag, I'll never know, I nearly knocked myself out with that thing more times than I can count." I wave my hand as they all laugh at my expense. "Yes, yes, Piper is a clumsy bitch, we're all aware." I move to sit back down next to Seer, and Jasmine sets her purse down. It's only when she's about to sit down next to Jesse, and I see the two of them next to each other, that it clicks. "Hold on." I point at the two of them. "He's your twin, isn't he?" Seer snorts next to me, leaning her head against the back of the couch.

"Well spotted," Liam teases, and I roll my eyes.

"I'm off social, ok? I don't even know what's happening in the news most days, much less who everyone is related to."

"I wish," Frannie says, running a hand through her long auburn hair. "You do realize when you're on my team you're going to have to do something about that, right?" I nearly choke on the sip of root beer I've just taken.

"*When* I'm on your team?" I question, and she gives me a shrug, like it's obvious.

"I mean, the job's yours, if you want it." I bob my head between Frannie and her brothers, to Seer, who's smiling like she knew this was coming. But I just stare. "Hello, earth to Piper?"

"Sorry, sorry." I shake my head, trying to get my shit together.

"I can put a more formal offer together on Monday, and you two will have to sign a form for HR." She points between Fitz and me, and he just shrugs, leaning forward to rest his elbows on his knees, which are still in those navy dress pants that work wonders for his thighs. "But yeah, I mean, you can start next Monday if you want." I squeal, climbing over Seer on the sectional until

I'm hugging Frannie in a way that is definitely not professional, nor ladylike, but I don't care.

"Cuddle puddle!" Frannie calls, and suddenly I'm being engulfed by Seer, by Jasmine, even by Jesse and Liam, whom I've just met but already know I like. And as much as I know this is probably the first time Fitz is spending time with this group at large, as uncomfortable as I can tell he is, when I feel a squeeze on my shoulder through the cuddle puddle and look up to see him standing over the back of the couch, the smile on his face is genuine. Because I think he needs this, needs days like today, as much as I do. He just wasn't willing to admit it.

CHAPTER 54

Fitz

"Motherfucker, God damn -

"Whoa there." I laugh, bending over to try and meet Piper's eye as we sit on her bed after Fred's graduation party. We left Frannie's after a couple of hours - the drive back to civilization was long, and I knew Piper wanted to work on something for the Fairy Ball next weekend. What I hadn't been expecting was for her to pull out a full tub of beads and a needle and thread, and start sewing tiny pearls onto a piece of lace just bigger than her hand. "You good?"

"No," she moans, sitting back against the bed and letting her head fall on my shoulder. "I think I've sewed my finger more than the fabric, at this point." She holds her hand up, like she's looking for an invisible tremor. I spot the little prick of blood on her finger, and reach over to the side table, handing her a tissue. "Thanks." She sets her work down on her side table, holding the tissue to her finger as, in front of us, some sappy scene plays out between the main characters of the Hallmark-esque movie she'd picked. Normally, we debate back and forth on what to watch, but after watching her take down Chris Westfall with a couple of sentences, I think I'd let her do just about anything with no argument from me in sight. At least, for today.

"She plays the dragon lady, right?" I ask, pointing up at the screen where I'm pretty sure the woman from Game of Thrones is visible. Piper quirks a brow at me.

"Dragon lady?"

"You know," I continue, shrugging. "Derius whats-her-face and-

I stop, because the look she's giving me is both incredulous and insulted, and I try to stifle a laugh. I fail miserably. It's the wrong move, because she's leaning forward, setting the tissue down and turning to look at me fully.

"Are you talking about Daenerys Stormborn of House Targaryen?" She says it with such ferocity that I sit back, staring down at her.

"Uh, sure."

"First of Her Name?" Piper continues, throwing the fluffy blanket she'd had on her lap onto the floor.

"Hey!" I protest, picking it up and throwing it over Bex, who burrows out to watch as Piper stands, climbing on the bed where she'd been sitting and towering over me.

"Queen of the Andals and the First Men, Protector of the Seven Kingdoms?" And now she's jumping, bouncing on the bed while her curls fly, getting so close to me I'm genuinely worried she's going to land a foot in my lap and injure me. "Mother of Dragons, the Khaleesi of the Great Grass Sea, the Unburnt, the Breaker of Chains?"

"Jesus Christ," I breathe, trying to get her to come down, but she just keeps going.

"You dare disrespect her by calling her dragon lady?" She's laughing now, and I stare up.

"You're such a nerd." I grip at her thighs, but she bats my hands away. "Sure, whatever you say, Daenerys Stormborn, and - uh." I look up at her sheepishly. "All the things you just said." She gives a satisfied *hmph*, falling back onto the bed with her legs curled under her as I scrub a hand down my face. "You're going to kill yourself to make a point one day."

"I know." She shrugs, but her eyes are blazing with triumph, with amusement. "Being a nerd is one of my best qualities."

"Among many," I reply, and while my tone is teasing, she smiles, and it makes my heart jump. "You have lots of qualities that I like." I reach forward, pushing one side of her hair behind her shoulder, my fingers brushing her collarbone, her string of pearls that I swear she does everything but sleep and shower in. "Lots that I love, too." She stills at my words, and I feel like we're both holding our breath. My heart is already pounding, but it just gets louder in my ears.

"Love?" she echoes, and I nod, my hand sliding down her arm to her hand, which I take in mine. I bring it to my mouth, kissing her knuckles, letting her set her palm against my cheek and then turning into it.

"I think I've known for a while." My inner dialogue is screaming at me to shut the fuck up. Am I really about to do this? "Probably a lot longer than I'm willing to admit, because it was all so easy."

"What was easy?" Her voice is raspy, and she clears her throat. The other side of my dialogue, like the angel on my shoulder that just wants me to be happy, is screaming something else entirely.

Do it.
Say it.
Tell her.

CHAPTER 54

"Falling in love with you."

There's a heartbeat, maybe two, of silence, and I panic. What did I just do? Did I really just say that to her?

But before I can spiral out too far, her face splits into a megawatt smile and she launches herself at me, climbing into my lap and peppering my face with tiny kisses until her thighs are straddling me.

A surprised laugh falls out of me, and I grip onto her hips, letting her shake her hair out of her face. Piper stares down at me, swallowing before she replies "It was easy for me too." She takes a breath, and then says "I mean, not at first, because you were kind of an asshat, but-"

I cut her off by pressing my lips to hers, holding the back of her head to me until we're breaking apart, panting, and I let out a strangled sound.

"I tell you I love you, and you call me an asshat."

She gasps. "That's not what I was saying, or what I was trying to say, I-"

I kiss her again.

"Fitz, you've got to let me finish-"

When I press my lips to hers again, she nips at my bottom lip so hard I draw back, shocked.

"I love you, too."

Oh, shit. The words do something to my insides - they go molten as I stare into Piper's baby blue eyes, which are shiny and filled with something I can't place. No, I can place it, I realize. Because it's the same look she gave me after I punched out the guy at the races. It's the same look she had today in the bathroom, meeting my gaze through the mirror.

It's love. True, unbridled, passionate love from a woman just as unbridled as that feeling. It bores into me in a way I feel to the tips of my toes, like a shock to the nervous system.

When I kiss her again, it's long and languid and that shock just keeps rippling through me, hitting me in waves like the crest of an orgasm but in a way that's making my heart flutter, not beat wildly. And she kisses me back, just as passionately, wrapping her arms around my neck, my shoulders and pulling me to her. Slowly, that kiss turns into tangling tongues, and I pull away, tilting her head back and kissing down her neck, trailing the same spots with my tongue and feeling the way she shudders against me. It takes just a second for my body to react, and when it does, she's grinding against me, the fabric of our shorts bunching together while she makes soft little moans that go straight to my dick.

Gingerly, I thread my hands into her sweatshirt, feeling her skin underneath and finding that she's naked again - my favorite kind of surprise from this woman in my arms. She gives me a wicked smile, her head still leaned back, eyes half closed as my hands rake up her sides and back down to the hem. I tug up, pulling it over her head and letting her curls fall over her shoulders, now bare except for that string of pearls. Without hesitation, I lean forward, letting her grab my shirt and tug it over my head, until our chests are pressed together and I'm kissing a line across her collarbone, across her shoulders, the tops of her breasts.

"I love you," I breathe into her skin, and her hand in my hair tightens. "Of the handful of people I've ever said that to, I mean this the most." She lets out a watery laugh, and when I meet her eyes, she's crying.

"Fuck, what-"

"It's fine," she garbles out, waving a hand between us. "I'm sorry, I'm just an emotional mess all the time." She sniffs, wiping at her eyes. "I'm also on my period, which isn't helping."

Ah.

I swipe her curls behind her ear, letting her forehead press to mine.

"I love you, and it terrifies me," she says after a heartbeat. I try to sit back, but she holds my head to hers, both hands on the back of my neck, her eyes fluttering closed. "I'm terrified to love someone again, to *let myself* love again. But damn it." She sits back, startling me as her eyes meet mine. I notice the way her breasts bounce when she moves, and it's like a straight shot to my groin. Focus, man. "We both deserve love."

"We do," I agree with a nod. Piper presses her lips to mine again, this kiss long and sweet, and when she leans back, I shift her off my lap, standing.

"What?" She looks confused, a little hurt, but I hold out my hand and she stares at it. "What are you doing?"

"Getting the woman I love in the shower," I answer, shrugging. "And if I'm lucky, she'll let me hear how much she loves me when I make her come on my fingers." Her eyebrows shoot to her hairline, but that wicked smile slides across her face as she pushes up, following me into the bathroom and letting the door click behind us.

Piper

We were not, in fact, quiet enough in the shower on Saturday, as Carla has reminded me about sixty times this week, practically every chance she gets.

"I don't ever want to hear those noises again," she says dryly, pushing around the cereal in her bowl, an afternoon snack we're both partaking in like a normal Saturday afternoon. Except, Carla is fully clothed, ready for an afternoon of final prep for the reunion, while I'm standing in our kitchen with my hair in curlers, in a robe and just my underwear.

"Like you have room to talk." I tilt my head back, looking at the ceiling, willing my voice to go a little higher. "Oh Scottie, baby, oh, right there."

"Jesus fucking -" Carla launches across the bar, nearly clamping a hand over my mouth as I shove her arm off. She and her ex were practically loud enough for the whole complex to hear.

"Watch it," I warn, gesturing to my face. "I literally just finished my makeup. You fuck it up, you can have that conversation with Jesus when you see him, cause I'm sure he'd be angry about wrecking this masterpiece too." I point my finger over her in the sassiest move I can muster, and she just rolls her eyes, going back to her Reese's Puffs.

"Everything good to go for tomorrow?" she asks through a mouth of cereal. I nod, sipping at some of my milk.

"I think so, I got everyone their shirts this week, so it should just be a quick morning and then we can head to my parent's for Hunter's party."

"Penny has a death wish, trying to do both the 5K and the party in one day." I shrug.

"She and Brett wanted Nolan there. He's only out this weekend and then he's back on the road for another two weeks. He's flying in for, like, eight hours for the reunion, and then flying back to Utah."

Alex and her mother-in-law aren't exactly BFFs, but I have a feeling that by the end of this season, my best friend will sob when Vicki leaves.

"Does Fitz know what he signed up for?" Her voice is a little softer, and I meet her eyes over the rim of my cereal bowl.

"I mean, he knows we do it every year for Mickey. I didn't exactly give him a play by play." She quirks a brow. "Don't give me that look, it's not like the first year where they pulled my sobbing ass on stage to thank everyone."

"Hits 'em right in the checkbooks," Carla says, a hand to her heart. I point my spoon at her.

"There will be no sobbing. There will be walking, and laughing, and then some Mexican food. And then a toddler party with enough superheroes to wage war against Thanos." She snorts.

"If you say so."

"I made it through May without a total breakdown," I remind her. "I think I can handle this without any problems." Carla sits back, raising her hands. "I'm good, Fitz is good. Promise."

I don't even believe my own words, and I know she doesn't. But Fitz had vehemently insisted on supporting us - all of us - at the 5K, with a generous donation to our team and a promise to walk right alongside me.

I had mixed feelings at first, the idea of having him there felt like melding two worlds that I'd worked so hard to keep from bleeding into each other back when Mickey was alive. I don't think Mickey ever heard a word about Fitz, because until recently, he just wasn't on my mind. But now, the idea that Fitz is doing something to honor him, makes my stomach clench in a way I can't quite decipher.

And it's that feeling that's still low in my stomach when my phone buzzes on my vanity a few hours later. I'm unwinding the curlers from my hair while I check it.

FITZ WESTFALL
At your front door. Finally read the sign. You're right, shit does get awkward when Bex goes full psycho.

I laugh to myself, and at the picture he snaps of my front door, where the vinyl sign I printed is on full display.

Please do not knock or ring the bell. The dog will bark, I will scream, things will get awkward.

"Carla, can you grab the door? I'll be out in a minute."

"Yes, master!" she calls as she walks past my bedroom door, and then stops, turning back around. "Hot damn."

"Shut up." I toss a roller at her, which hits the door frame next to her face. She just raises an eyebrow at me.

"You're staying at Fitz's tonight, right?"

"Uh, yeah."

"Thank God, I can't listen to you two when he gets you out of that." She gestures to me. "Are we wearing the secret special underwear?" I flush, meeting her eye in the mirror.

"Maybe."

"Yeah, definitely don't come back here, then. I've got Bex." She doesn't even give me a chance to reply before she turns on her heels, and I hear the door open and close. "Don't you dare come back here tonight, Piper," she calls from the living room, and then reappears in the doorway. "You two are going to eat each other alive." I make a gagging noise, all the chins on display as I shake my head at her.

"Piper?" Fitz's voice calls, and my eyes go wide.

"I'll be out in a second, stay there!" I stand, slipping off the robe and setting it on the bench I'd just been occupying. I smooth a hand down the front of my dress, adjusting the hemline at my bodice. "How do I look?" It comes out a little more reserved than I'd meant it to, and Carla steps into my room, taking my hands away from where they'd been fidgeting with one of the lace pieces on the sleeve.

"You look gorgeous, P. Seriously." She adjusts a curl across my chest, big and bouncy in a way I haven't had my hair in years. Then, she turns, gesturing towards the doorway. "Now go get your man." I take a steadying breath, heading towards the doorway, when her hand collides with my ass through the layers of my skirt.

"Hey!" I cry, moving to protect myself. "Rude." She just laughs, pushing through the door before me. I follow her out, peeking around the corner to see Fitz standing in my entryway, clasping a bouquet of white flowers like it's a lifeline. I step around the wall to get a better look, and he meets my eyes, grinning before his gaze slides down my body. His mouth goes a little slack, and I feel a tentative smile on my face as I give him the same appraising look.

Fitzwilliam Westfall looks like something out of a romance novel fanart. His dark red curls are just long enough to sweep across his forehead, and I see the flush creeping up his neck, which is bobbing as he swallows, his eyes not leaving me. Vic was not kidding - he had handled Fitz, and in the best way, because damn. He's wearing a black dress shirt with a collar that comes up around his neck on the sides and backs, curving and accented with gold stitching that meets in the front and goes down the seam of the gold buttons. The same pattern dances around the cuffs of his shirt, and I know it's Vic's handiwork - I'd recognize it anywhere. With black pants and a pair of black dress shoes, he's giving the morally gray, dark haired villain vibes even before the look in his eyes goes molten.

Because I know I've set a complete trap for this man in front of me - I've spent all week talking about how excited I am about this dress, this piece that isn't totally mine, but is enough to make me feel like I created something beautiful. I feel beautiful, and based on the way Fitz is looking at me, he thinks so too.

I give a girlish giggle, twirling in my kitchen to let him get the full effect. The tight bodice with built-in cups, the way it hugs my waist and highlights my tiniest point while still making my chest look fantastic. The gold tulle that hugs the fabric over the satin bust, coming up on the sides to make long, bell-shaped sleeves just transparent enough that you can see my arms through them. The tulle gathers at my waist, cascading long and full over my legs, but there's a generous slit up one side that Fitz's eyes zero in on immediately. The whole thing is accented with cream lace, seed pearls, and rhinestones that match the ones on my cream colored heels. It feels ethereal, and whimsical, and I feel fantastic as Carla wordlessly takes the bouquet of what I now see are tulips from Fitz's hand. He barely notices her as he reaches for me, pulling me closer but still far enough out that he can appreciate the way I look.

"Piper," he breathes, and the word sends a shiver down my spine, the same way his mouth on my neck had last weekend. I can tell he's thinking the same thing, the way his green eyes sharpen, watching my deep gulp. Fitz reaches out, pulling at one of my dark curls, which are tamed and smoothed into soft, gigantic waves and ringlets that read more 50's glamor than wild electrocuted toddler, which is my normal go-to.

"You like?" I ask, tilting my head to one side, then the other, popping out a hip.

"I love," he says, and then dips down to kiss me. I smooth a hand up his chest, and my fingers are toying with the neck of his shirt when he pulls back.

"I do too." He holds an elbow out to me, and I reach towards the counter, picking up my overnight bag and pearl clutch, which I never get to use.

"Ok, Cinderella," Carla starts, ushering us towards the door. "You two have fun, just don't stay out too late. We have to be at the park at 8." I groan, looking back at my roommate. "You signed us up for this, Piper!"

"I didn't know when I signed up I'd be going to a literal ball the night before." My voice is whiny, and I gesture to Fitz. "Blame him."

"Excuse me?" Fitz sounds incredulous, rounding on me, and I laugh. "We can just go back inside right now and I can strip you out-"

"La la la la," Carla screams, one hand covering an ear as she shoves us out the now open door. "No one's stripping, go do fairy shit, be safe." And then she shuts the door so fast, it smacks my butt behind me.

CHAPTER 55

Fitz

Ten Years Ago

The room around us was dark, modern radio music blasting out of the DJ's speakers as we bumbled away from the dance floor.

"My feet hurt," Olivia moaned. I wasn't surprised. The strappy, silver shoes peeking out from under her lime green dress looked incredibly uncomfortable, and I'd told her that before she bought them.

"Take your shoes off," I answered simply, and she gave me a look, leaning more heavily into my arm as she held it. Her incredible distaste for feet, even her own, had existed as long as I'd known her, and we were edging on thirteen years of that.

"I'm just ready to get the real party started," Andy mused from behind us, and I could see him snake an arm around Becca, his date, from over my shoulder. The real party being the not-so-small get-together he'd planned at a property not far from his house, which would be littered with cans and bottles by the morning.

We were finishing the year on a high note - going out with a bang and one final hurrah before we all go our separate ways over the summer. But Andy started pre-gaming before he even put his tux on in the hotel room above us at The Monarch, where our prom was taking place.

"I think it's started," Becca muttered, giving Andy a slightly disgusted look as he swayed with her. We weaved between tables, making our way to our own, when behind me, Andy stopped.

"Barton!" Andy barked. Shit. Where Alex went, so did...

I turned on my heels, and Oliva stumbled slightly, catching herself on my other arm as she gave me a glare.

"Don't you look...good." I could tell by his tone that it isn't what he was originally going to say, but Alex's date, a guy I vaguely recognized from the graduating class before us, is a big dude, and was practically seething as Andy's eyes scanned over her glitter-speckled chest.

"Fuck off, Andy, go find a cow to tip or something." Next to her, I saw Vic stifle a laugh with his deep purple jacket sleeve. Seated beside him was Piper, who I didn't immediately recognize as herself. She looked different. Her normally bright red hair looked darker - maybe she had dyed it for graduation, so it didn't clash with our hideously orange caps and gowns. It was pulled back on the sides, tendrils hanging by her face. Her tight-topped, deep purple dress matched Vic's suit, the long sleeves covered in a deep lace, dotted with pearls and rhinestones.

"That wasn't very nice," Olivia cackled. She may have pre-gamed a little too hard with Becca as well.

"Yeah," Andy agreed, and then spotted Piper in front of him. "Piper and I are friends, right, Delmonico?" Her eyes widened.

"Not the time, Andy," I urged, putting my hand on his forearm, but he shook it off.

"Friends," Piper repeated stoically. She put her napkin on the table and stood, her back to Andy. Alex and Vic stared at her as she turned slowly to face him. "We weren't friends when we were fucking, Andy, and we aren't friends now." I blinked at her. That was the first time I'd heard her speak about whatever it was they had together, and her plainness surprised me. "So please, get your ill-fitting suit and your..." she leaned forward, sniffing, "whiskey breath out of here before your coach informs your mother you've been speaking to me." She nodded over his shoulder, where, sure enough, Coach Vaughn was sipping at a cup of punch.

Andy didn't know what to say. Hell, I wouldn't know what to say either. It was like the months since the incidents in the fall had steeled something in Piper.

I took the opportunity to lead a slow-thinking Andy back to our table, where he mumbled under his breath for the remainder of our time in the room.

"I will literally pay you any amount of orgasms if we can turn around and walk back out this door," I breathe in Piper's ear as we stand in the lobby of Starlight Grove, one of the WHG properties on the west side of Fort Worth. She laughs, the sound making me smile, even though she smacks my chest.

CHAPTER 55

"You couldn't pay me any amount of orgasms to leave." The line in front of us moves, and I follow behind her, watching the way she teeters on her feet like a kid in a candy store.

I can't blame her. The atmosphere for this event has always been exactly what Piper loves so much about her fantasy novels, or so she's told me. Extravagant outfits, beautiful makeup and jewelry, whimsical decor and worldbuilding. It's a night that drips otherworldly, and it's right up her alley. It's absolutely not even near mine.

"There you two are," I hear from behind me, and we turn to see Frannie striding towards us.

She stops about five feet from us, taking in what we're wearing, eyebrows shot to high heaven. She crosses her arms. "Damn, y'all. I look like a kid in a costume compared to you two." She gestures down to the frilly blue dress she's wearing, her hair pulled back by an elaborate tiara.

"You do not," Piper muses, reaching out to take Frannie's hand. "You look great."

"*You* look great."

"Yes, we all look great," a man behind us in line cuts in. "Can we please move, now?" I look behind me to see that the line has, in fact, moved, and we're holding it up.

"So sorry," Piper cries, stepping out so they can move forward, as Frannie mutters "Rude."

"Everyone else is already at the table, well, except Liam and Jesse," my sister says, still holding Piper's hand. She pulls us towards the open double doors behind the registration table. As we pass, she leans over to one man wearing prosthetic pointy ears and a green suit covered in fake ivy. "These two are with me, WHG table." He nods up at Frannie like he's been taking orders from her all day, which he likely has, if she's been here helping organize like she normally does.

The inside is just as eccentric as the exterior, with fake tree limbs climbing up the corners, lanterns hanging from the branches. It gives an air of mystical forest, which is why this event is held here every year - and why it's quickly becoming one of our most popular venues.

A string quartet is already playing in the corner by the door, situated close to a short stage that has more trees, lit by candles and strings of tiny lights weaved through the branches. The room is dark enough that the lights on each table sparkle, giving the silky linens and mossy centerpieces a mystical glow. I look to Piper, who's gazing around the room like she just walked into heaven - for her, this probably is akin to that.

"What do you think?" I ask, leaning over to whisper in her ear. She doesn't respond, just keeps swiveling her head around so fast, I'm worried she may crack her neck.

When we make it to the table, Freddy, Mateo and Chloe are already seated with a couple of people I don't recognize - a girl, who introduces herself as Amy, Mateo's date, and Chloe's date, Tyler. All of the other men are in plain suits, and I instantly feel a surge of heat as they look over my choice in outfit.

In my defense, I had argued with Vic for about twenty minutes when he finally showed me what he'd done with the shirt I'd ordered and had sent to his house. It was frilly and not my style, but seeing Piper's reaction made it worth it.

Fuck me, Piper's reaction - seeing Piper in that dress. All I've wanted to do since she walked out of her room is rip her out of that dress, but that seemed like a poor decision, so I've settled for ogling like a schoolboy.

"We would have been here sooner, but someone decided halfway here they needed caffeine." I throw Piper a pointed look, and she scoffs.

"You try getting in and out of the MK in this thing." She lifts her skirts slightly, and Chloe just reaches out, her fingers sliding over the fabric.

"It's gorgeous." She looks up at Piper's face. "Did you make it?"

"Sort of," is Piper's response.

Before Fred can ask the question I know he's about to, someone says from behind me, "Drinks, losers?"

Fuck me, she's everywhere.

"Two more Modelos," Mateo calls as I turn around, finding Seer standing close with a tray of empty glasses and beer bottles.

"Usual for me, Blue Moon for Fitz, and..." She trails off, looking at Piper, who shrugs, taking in Seer's appearance. She's dressed in a deep green velvet jumpsuit with prosthetic ears, a pair of iridescent wings jutting a foot out from behind her. Used incorrectly - or, correctly, I guess, if you're Seer - they could double as deadly weapons. She seems taller...but then I look down, and see she's got at least three inches of platform on.

"Surprise me," Piper answers with a shrug, and she reaches out, touching Seer's shoulder, which is dusted with a sparkly powder. "You look *so* cute."

"Right back atcha, hot stuff," Seer says with a shoulder shrug, and then waves me off like I'm an annoying gnat. Piper finds a seat next to Chloe, and I sit next to her, watching people mill around while we wait for our drinks. From across the room, I see Liam and Jesse slide through the door, and immediately feel better about my outfit, no longer the man at the table in the most elaborate outfit. They're both dressed in matching deep green blazers, the same velvet as Seer's jumpsuit, with the same kind of pointy ears. The top of Liam's hair is braided back into a sort of half man bun, and Jesse is wearing smudged eyeliner. Piper

CHAPTER 55

stands from her chair, greeting them with the rest of the table. "Ah, I see my dates have arrived," Seer observes as she comes back with a tray of drinks.

"Are you actually working tonight?" Piper asks, taking the cloudy drink Seer hands her. Seer shrugs, waving around.

"People are still getting here, once things settle, the board and I will..."

But she trails off. I stopped listening about five words ago, because I can feel something tickling at my ear. It feels like a feather - looks like a feather out of the corner of my eye, and I can see everyone around me staring over my head where there is clearly someone standing.

Piper moves her hand to her mouth to stifle a laugh, and I turn in my seat to see a couple in full fairy gear, vine-covered clothing and glittery everything. The girl is holding the feather up, covering her mouth in an "uh oh" gesture.

"Can I help you?" is the only thing I can think to say, and Piper lets out a snort before the whole table starts laughing at me. I shoot Mateo and my brother a look.

"They can't talk, they're fae," Seer says, as if it's the most obvious thing in the world, and I look back at the couple behind me. "They're here to cause mischief."

Mischief, my ass. It's bad enough I'm being dragged to this thing in the first place, but to be taunted and teased by two grown adults holding feathers all night? No thanks. Public mockery is one kink I'd like to stay far, far away from.

"I wouldn't do that if I were you." Fred's voice is deadpan as the man behind me reaches one hand up, clasping a black feather between his fingers.

"You could always pay them to stop," Frannie says from next to me. "Pay to play, or, I guess, not to play, in this case."

"How much?" My voice is dry. Seer raises an eyebrow, one hand on her hip, the other holding up the empty tray.

"Minimum donation is fifty." Wordlessly, I pull out my pocket, handing over a crisp $100 bill to the woman behind me.

"I'll give you an extra $50 to get that one." I hitch my thumb back at Mateo, who's laughing his ass off, and he sobers up real quick when both fairies look fit to burst. He's grumbling as he pulls out cash from his wallet, and his date and Piper snicker together.

The festivities start shortly after our run in with the extortionist fae, and Seer is talking into the microphone on the small stage while I chew the chicken on my plate. It's a little dry, and I make a note to talk to the chef after the evening is over.

"This event would not be possible without our gracious hosts, WHG. I would like to invite one of our most adamant supporters, Frannie Westfall to the stage to say a few words." I glance at my sister, who takes a deep breath before pushing out of her chair, applause surrounding us as she crosses the small dance floor. She holds her skirts up as she steps onto the stage, giving Seer a side hug before taking the microphone.

"Thank you, Saoirse. And thank you all for being here today." She holds a notecard in her hand, and I see her look down at it, just for the briefest of seconds. Frannie has always been the better public speaker, between the two of us. Sure, I had a few moments over the years, but my power has always come from being the calm in the storm. Frannie is the storm, she's the excitement and the joy behind every project, every campaign. Everything she's ever put her mind to, she's given 110%, even her shitty husband. "As you all know, the Fae League selects a nonprofit each year to receive the proceeds from this event. This year..."

I catch Piper out of the corner of my eye, watching Frannie. "She's incredible," she breathes.

"Sounds like someone else I know." Piper's eyes narrow, and she taps my back with her finger, nodding towards the stage.

"Pay attention to your sister, dummy."

Once the plates have been cleared and dancing starts, Chloe immediately pulls Frannie and Piper to the dance floor, where several people stop Piper to comment on her dress. I have to agree with them - it's breathtaking, and falls in a way that makes her look like something off a Grecian urn.

"Fitz?" I turn at the sound of my name, and standing behind me is arguably one of the last people I'd expected to see tonight - Savannah.

"Oh, hi," is all I can manage, noticing that Mateo and Jesse's conversation falls quiet as Savannah sits in the chair Frannie had been occupying.

"I'm not here to cause a scene," she starts, and I deflate a little. Her summery, highlighted hair is pulled back into a slick ponytail, and she's wearing arguably one of the tamest outfits here, a black gown with a high neckline and giant black earrings.

We haven't talked really, not since that day in my office, and if we're being honest, she has every reason to cause a scene. I left her on read, stopped responding to her messages, and then turned up with a girlfriend after months of telling her and anyone else I saw that I was not interested in commitment.

Turns out, I was just waiting for the right person to commit to.

"I just wanted to say that I'm really happy for you." Her voice sounds genuine, and she wraps the end of her hair around her hand, tilting her head to look at the dance floor over my shoulder. "She looks really good, you two look really good. Together, I mean." She smiles, and it's a little sad, but before I can respond, she's standing. I feel a hand on my shoulder, and look up to see Piper standing over me, smiling and catching her breath as the song ends, and a slower one starts.

"Hi, Piper," Savannah says, and then sticks out her hand, commencing one of

CHAPTER 55

the most awkward handshakes I've ever seen in my life. To Piper's credit, she hides her surprise well, until I hear Savannah say "Thanks again for connecting me with Lisa."

I whip my head back to Savannah. What did she just say?

"Not a problem," Piper says, squeezing my shoulder, "I hope you're able to lend her a hand. She's swamped right now, and between commissions and the new job..."

"I heard you're starting on Fran's team Monday," Savannah continues, and I feel like I've stepped into the Twilight zone. In what dimension are Savannah and Piper on speaking terms? In what dimension have they ever actually talked to each other? "I'm glad she's got someone besides Jas to keep her rolling full steam ahead." Piper quirks her head to the side.

"Jasmine is on her team, too?" Savannah nods.

"She does most of the photo and video for WHG."

"Does everyone work here?" Piper says with a laugh, looking down at me. I shrug.

"We like to hire good people. Clearly we surround ourselves with good people."

"Agreed," Savannah says, and then reaches out, touching Piper's shoulder. "You look beautiful. Thanks again." And then she turns and walks off, leaving me looking up at Piper, utterly confused.

"What in the hell was that about?" I ask, but she just smiles down at me, her hand lifting from my shoulder to hold out for my own.

"Dance with me?"

I'm about to tell her there's no chance in hell I'm dancing on that tiny dance floor when she gives me a pleading look. To add insult to injury, Fred breezes past, a blonde girl at least a foot shorter than him on his arm, heading straight towards the throng of dancers.

"You're lucky I love you," I breathe, taking her hand.

"I know." Piper squeezes my fingers, and I let her lead me to the edge of the floor, where she turns to face me, her arms wrapping around my neck. I take her waist as we sway.

"I'm gonna need an explanation at some point." I keep my voice low, and she smiles up at me, a glint of mischief in her eyes.

"I may have helped Savannah find a new job." I freeze momentarily, staring down at her. "What? Lisa, my sponsor, needs some help on weekends. Savannah wants to go into weddings." The woman in my arms shrugs, as if she hadn't helped her boyfriend's former fuck buddy secure employment.

"You are..." I struggle to find a word appropriate for the situation.

"Incredible?" she asks. "Stupendous? Amazing? Fan-flipping-tastic?"

"All of the above." She laughs as I pull her towards me, bringing her chest flush to mine as I give her a peck on the lips.

"Mind if I cut in?"

My whole body tenses, and Piper can tell when we pull apart that something is wrong, because I know exactly who's standing behind me without having to turn. But I do, tightening my grip around Piper, as we both look at my dad.

CHAPTER 56

Piper

There are very few things that could surprise me more than Chris Westfall asking for me to dance. Alex backing down from a fight, an un-stylish Vic, Fitz on a unicycle come to mind. And those are the thoughts I keep in my head as I try my best to smile at the man behind Fitz, whose arms feel like vices around my already tight waist. He keeps this up, I'm going to puke.

"Sure," I breathe, and Fitz swivels to look at me, narrowing his eyes. I place a hand on his chest. "I'm sure Mr. Westfall will be more than courteous." I look over his shoulder, directly at Chris. "Right?"

"Absolutely," he replies, and Fitz lets out a humorless laugh. "Son, you don't-"

"Don't *son* me." Fitz's voice is a little louder than I think even he realizes, and several heads turn our direction, including Freddy, who has a cute blonde in his arms. *Go Freddy.* Fitz lets go of my waist, one hand on my lower back as he steps towards his dad, bringing me with him. "I'm not about to try to tell this woman what to do," he starts, glancing towards me, and my heart stutters a bit. "But I'm not stupid, and I'll be standing right there in case you try anything." He points to a vague area just off the dance floor, and Chris nods, offering me a hand.

I take it, barely touching him as he guides me back to the dance floor. Fitz steps off, his shoulders squared as I watch Mateo slide up next to him. He's shed his suit jacket and is now just wearing a white button up, the sleeves rolled to his elbow.

"Piper." Chris Westfall's voice drags me back to my body, to where I'm standing with the father of the man that I love - the father who hurt the man that I love. Who made him feel like he couldn't express an ounce of emotion, for fear of looking weak.

So I answer "Chris," letting him settle one hand on my waist while I find his shoulder, our other two hands up in a formal stance that gives plenty of space between us.

"Piper, I would like to apologize for my words last weekend." I swallow, staring at his face, watching the lines crinkle around his eyes like Fitz when he's anxious.

"Just last weekend?" I say, before I can stop myself, and one of his graying eyebrows raises at my words. Well, shit. I've already started on the crazy train. Might as well see it through to the next station. "You've hurt more than just my feelings, Chris."

"I'm not sure what you-"

"Please don't patronize me." I don't think this man is used to getting interrupted, because he's floundering, mouth half open. "Your insinuation that I'm using your son for a step in my career, and that I'm not qualified to work for your daughter, are moot points, seeing as I'll be starting with WHG tomorrow."

He gives a curt nod. "Yes, Francesca told me she extended a formal offer to you."

"And I took it. But not because I love your son." I pause. "Ok, that's a lie. It's partially because I love your son." I swear, the corner of his mouth turns up just a bit. "But also because I want to work for someone who recognizes talent, and who looks to build that talent while working towards a common goal." I nod my chin towards Frannie, who's standing at the opposite edge of the dance floor from Fitz, Seer next to her, and their eyes are firmly planted on me and her father as we sway.

"That sounds like Francesca."

"It does," I agree, nodding. "But more than your insinuation, you've hurt your son, and I'm not sure that this," I gesture between us, "and your apology to me will be enough to start us down a different path." He seems unsure of what to say, so I continue. "I know that you lost the woman you love."

Like his son earlier, Chris freezes, just for a moment, before his eyes lock with mine. "I did."

"I lost the man I love. And I think you know more than anyone else in this room what that does to a person." Slowly, he nods. "But there are lots of different paths, trying to find your way through that darkness, and your path left some casualties behind." He swallows, his gaze darting towards Fitz and Mateo. Fitz, I notice, has unbuttoned his sleeves, and he rolls them up his arms while I watch every second, Shit, it's like watching him get naked.

"I'm fully aware I'm not father of the year material." I snort, shaking my head.

"That's not a conversation I'm willing to have here." I nod my head down, towards the dance floor. "And I don't think that's a conversation you need to have with me. You need to have it with him." I tilt my chin towards Fitz and Mateo, trying to ignore the way his arms are flexing as they cross over his

CHAPTER 56

chest. "You made that man think he isn't allowed to have feelings, and that's not something I take lightly. You let your feelings, your grief, drown everyone else around you until they bend to your will." As the song comes to a close, I pull my hands loose from him, giving a small bow.

And then I leave Chris Westfall standing on the dance floor by himself, at a loss for words.

We barely make it in the house before Fitz has me literally pinned to the wall in his entry way, his mouth moving over my jaw, my neck, the swell of my chest, his fingers dipping below the hem of my shirt.

"You rip this and I will hurt you," I breathe, my voice husky, but he doesn't even seem to notice, just pushes his thigh harder between my legs, to the point where I'm writhing against him, trying to get any sort of friction through the layers of fabric. From down the hall, we hear a whine, and he comes up for air, cursing. Roscoe.

"He needs to go outside." Fitz's voice sounds bored, uninterested in his dog, but I laugh, shoving his shoulder.

"Go let him out before he pees somewhere." I turn, making my way towards the bedroom, glancing back over my shoulder. "I'll be waiting." He's already moving lightning fast, kicking off his shoes and hopping down the hall on one foot as he peels off one sock, then the other. My laugh echoes around the hall, and I find myself planted at the foot of the bed, a halo of silk and tulle spread around me like a picnic blanket. By the time Fitz makes it into the room, I've checked the twenty texts that came in while we were at the ball, the last of which were from Frannie and Seer asking what had happened on the dance floor with Chris.

PIPER DELMONICO
Starting out strong at WHG by telling the head W in charge that he hurt the man I love.

Instead of responding with the chastisement I'd been expecting from Frannie, my new boss, I get *Love???* followed by a heart eyes emoji.

"What's so funny?" Fitz asks, closing the bedroom door and digging his keys, wallet and phone out of his pockets. He throws them on the entry table, and I toss my phone on the nightstand, turning so he knows he has my full attention.

"Your sister is very cross with me," I joke, but Fitz looks genuinely concerned, so I add "Kidding. She just wanted to make sure I was okay." He nods, smoothing a hand down the side of his hair. His eyes trail from my head, down to my chest, and then to the pool of fabric around me.

"You really do look incredible." His voice is quiet, just audible enough that I know it's not my mind playing tricks.

"So do you," I reply, smiling. I reach both hands out, primping my skirt like a princess. "Now come get me out of this thing like I know you've wanted to all night."

Fitz's face spreads into a sly grin, and he crosses the room, standing in front of me. My fingers find his belt, then the buckle, and I move to undo it, but he pulls my fingers away. "I have a better idea." I meet his gaze, watching as he drops to his knees in front of me.

He pulls one of my feet into his lap, unbuckling the little snap on one side of my shoe, sliding it off my foot with a measured, graceful movement. He does the same thing with the other, taking his time, before setting them together at the foot of the bed. His hands move up my calves, to the inside of my knees.

Suddenly, there's a mess of flying fabric as he disappears under my skirt, and I hear him breathing, feel him against my thighs, warm and wet. I know the second he's reached my underwear, because he stills against my legs, and then slowly slides out from under my dress. His hair is a mess, but it's rivaled in color now by the flame in his cheeks, the heat in his gaze intense.

"Have you been wearing those all night?" he asks, and I nod, smiling.

"Thought it would be a nice surprise for-"

But I don't get to finish, because at the same time his hands hitch behind my knees, he's submerging himself back under my skirts, pulling my legs until I feel his hot breath where my blue velvet crotchless panties part to give easy access.

To his credit, Fitz takes full advantage of the easy access, and when I feel his tongue slide across my clit, I let out a breathy moan, falling back against the duvet. His fingers grip my thighs so hard it feels like they might bruise, and all my sounds do is cheer him on, pulling me firmly against his face as he works me over.

When he emerges again, I'm half-dazed, edging on an orgasm, and his face is red, lips swollen and glistening. The rustle of the fabric of my skirt is the only sound as he prowls on top of me, eyes burning, planting a hand on either side of my head as he kisses me, hard, fierce and rough. I taste myself on his mouth, and the satisfaction of knowing Fitz Westfall burns for me, loves me, only makes me kiss him harder, letting his tongue tangle with mine until we're both sloppy, grinding against each other.

Again, I reach for his belt, but he doesn't stop me this time - just keeps my gaze as I unbuckle, unbutton, unzip him, hitching a finger under one side of his underwear and pulling it all down at once. He's already hard, springing free and leaving a warm trail on my thigh.

I put a hand on his shoulder, pushing him to lay back on his bed, following him to leave kisses across his chin, his neck, unbuttoning his shirt with my free hand and then letting my fingers trail down. When I take him in my hands, he lets out a little gasp, his head falling back on the bed.

"Fuck." It comes out as a little moan, and it's all the assurance I need before I sit up, hoisting my skirts until I'm able to straddle his lap, the fabric pooling around both of us. He looks up at me with a surprised grin, grinding his hips up so he's rubbing against my clit, and I rock against him, leaning forward to give him a deep kiss.

Still holding me to his chest, Fitz sits up until his back is against the headboard, still grinding into me with a delicious friction that's edging me closer and closer to the orgasm I almost had moments ago. He leans over, I'm sure to grab a condom from his night stand.

And something in my buzzing little horny brain tells me to stop him. So, I do.

I reach my hand out, grabbing his wrist as he moves to open the drawer. He looks back at me, his eyes narrowed in confusion, still burning just as bright. I put one hand on the side of his face, shaking my head.

"I want you now." I push forward, so he knows exactly how wet I am, how ready I am for him. "Just like this."

"Piper," he says, almost at a whimper, closing his eyes for a moment before meeting my gaze again through hooded eyes. "Are you sure?"

Instead of answering, I slide my hand to the back of his neck, crashing his lips into mine in a kiss I hope tells him exactly how sure I am.

It does the trick, apparently, because he's shifting under me, positioning himself right at my entrance and breaking apart only to meet my eye again. I nod, pressing my forehead to his as he pushes in, nothing between us except the gathering of fabric around my waist, and his head falls back against the headboard, eyes shut until he's nestled inside me completely.

I reach out, stroking the side of his face, and he takes a ragged breath before looking at me.

"Feel good?" I ask, and he nods. "Good." I lean forward until my mouth is right next to his ear, savoring the way the angle changes and my muscles tighten around him. "Now give me something to think about when I see you at work on Monday."

I sit back, watching a lazy grin slide across his face. His hands reach under my skirts, gripping at the curve of my hips, tangling in the sides of the underwear that's just barely covering anything, pulling until I'm sliding up his length, and then letting me go so I fall back down, inch by inch. I meet his gaze, watch his throat bob as I mimic the same actions again, pressing up onto my knees and then letting myself fall again.

On the third time, he meets my hips with a thrust once I settle back down, and the moan that falls from both of us is all he needs to pick up the pace. He meets me thrust for thrust, while I wrap my arms around his neck and grind into each movement, desperate for pressure on my aching clit. One of his hands slides up, finding just enough space to press his fingers against me, moving in tight circles that zing through my body with him inside me.

He buries his head in my neck, breathing me in while he wrings me out, a jumble of curses and moans falling from his lips and into my ear until we're both shaking and panting and the rhythm of his hand on me and his hips against mine are all I can think about.

"I love you so fucking much," he stutters out, just barely loud enough that I can hear it, and my heart clenches, my fingers gripping the back of his head as I move to rest our foreheads against each other, so close to the edge again.

"I love you." My voice is a hoarse whisper, as I continue, "To kingdom come, right?" I see the smile that crinkles his eyes, and then lean my head back as a spiral of pleasure comes from him hitting just the right angle inside me.

"To kingdom come, Piper." He presses a kiss to the center of my chest, where I know I'm probably covered in glitter and sweat and who knows what else from our night. But he doesn't care, just lets me fall forward into his embrace.

And I keep falling, down, down, until I'm crying out, my fingers digging into his shoulders as I ride him, ride his hand, the circles on my clit never stopping as he tenses under me. I feel him jolt inside me, and when I finally lean back to meet his eyes, he's trembling slightly.

I wipe at a glisten of sweat on his cheek - and then realize it's not sweat.

Holy shit, it's a tear.

"Sorry," he breathes, closing his eyes as another one falls, and I wipe it away for him, letting him press his forehead to mine.

"Don't ever apologize for your feelings." I swallow the lump forming in my throat. "Especially not to me."

I nuzzle my nose against his, which feels incredibly silly with him still inside me, making what I'm sure is a fine mess of my underwear and the sheets below us.

"You're exactly what I need." His voice is still raspy, but he continues, "Exactly who I need. So please don't let my father or anyone else tell you differently."

CHAPTER 56

I laugh, sitting back to look at him.

"If you think *your father* is going to scare me away, have I got news for you." He smiles, and then sniffles, and my heart melts. "Seriously, babe. I'm here." I run my thumb across his cheek, still slightly damp. "I'm here to stay."

CHAPTER 57

Fitz

I look at my phone for what feels like the tenth time tonight, and the numbers 3:45 stare back at me.

Fuck. This is not good. My mind is racing, my heart is clenched like someone's got a fist around it. I turn, seeing the back of Piper's head where she's folded in on herself, a little mass of curls and curves in a fetal position next to me, the blanket wrapped tightly around her.

If the sight didn't make my heart clench more, I'd probably wake her up just to slide my arms around her, feel one of her heavy breasts in my hand, feel her nipple pucker under my thumb and-

Fuck my life. Seriously. What is this feeling in my chest? I feel it deep, like a rock in the pit of my stomach.

I try to move as quietly as possible when I slide out of bed. Roscoe raises his head from where he's laying at my feet, but I give him a pat on the head, pulling my boxers on and padding out into the living room. I find the decanter of whiskey on the bar, pouring myself a couple of fingers and collapsing into one of the chairs in the living room, phone in hand. Mindlessly, I flip through all the pictures I've been tagged in from the night, approving and denying them depending on whether they're halfway flattering or not.

There's one of our table, all of us gathered around one side while we smile up at Jasmine, who took the picture on Fran's cell phone before gathering a few with the professional camera she was using for the evening. Another shows the look of abject horror on my face while Piper holds a plastic crown over my head, teasing like always.

The one of the two of us, pulled together on the dance floor, chests flush together, makes that pang hit again. Fuck. What is this?

It's not regret. Not a lack of surety, or affection. It's not pain or sadness. It's not something I've ever really felt, and I search for the words.

CHAPTER 57

Love. The word dings in the back of my head, lighting up like a neon display, captioned by the words "that's what it is, you idiot."

And I sit back in my chair, draining the last few remnants of my drink in a single gulp, ruminating on this feeling. Love. Is this what actually, truly being in love with someone feels like? A weight you carry around with you?

No, not a weight, I realize. A blanket. A cocoon of warmth. A secure, tight feeling that's wrapped so hard around me I feel like I may explode. A clear, unwavering knowledge that the woman asleep in my bed loves me, truly, and has no problems showing me, showing the world.

I glance back down at my phone in my lap, looking at the way my arms grip Piper's waist. It looks small and fragile in my long fingers, but I know she's not fragile. I smile to myself - definitely not fragile. You can't really see my face, but you can see hers, and the clear way she's looking up at me as we dance.

That look. That's a look I've never seen before. Not even on Olivia, I ponder.

That's the way she looked at me when she said I love you for the first time, when I felt this feeling wracking my body that I hadn't been able to place at the time. The vice grip those words placed around my heart. And the thought that I'm not sure I ever want to let this feeling go.

I manage a few hours of sleep, pulling Piper to my chest and breathing in her usual warm, sugary scent, until the alarm on her phone goes off and she blindly reaches for it between the sheets.

"It's on the nightstand," I groan, rolling away from her and rubbing at my eyes. She reached over further, finally turning off the electric pop music she'd set as an alarm tone. She yawns, scrolling on her Home Screen before looking at me.

"Morning." She props herself up on her elbows, and I lean down to meet her halfway for a kiss. "Coffee?" Piper moves to pull the blanket from off of her body, but I wrap my arm around her, pulling her close again. "Fitz," she says with a laugh, but then snuggles into my arms. "We need to get up."

"We need to do a lot of things," I agree, giving her a squeeze. She lets out a strangled sound, but I know it's a joke because the squeeze was gentle, and she's being dramatic to get a rise out of me. I lean my head forward, my lips next to her ear. "I can think of a few things we can do before we get out of this bed." She laughs again, swatting at my arms as she untangles herself. "I'm hurt." I press a hand to my chest. "Absolutely offended that you wouldn't-"

A pillow comes flying at my face, and I barely have time to deflect it before she's reaching into her overnight bag, making a beeline for the bathroom so fast I don't have time to pull her back into bed with me, which is really where she belongs.

I'm on my third cup of coffee by the time we make it to the car, and Piper's grumpy morning attitude has turned chipper as she drinks out of her travel mug, flipping through the pictures on my phone from the night before.

The phone buzzes in her hand, and she looks at it for a second before turning to me. "It's your dad."

"Hmm," is all I say, and I put my free hand on her leg, my thumb smoothing over the stretchy fabric of her leggings. "What does he want?"

"To get lunch tomorrow." She pauses. "With both of us." I raise my eyebrows.

"What exactly did you say to him last night?" I turn into the parking lot at Windsor Park, following a line of cars filing into spaces down the long rows. "You never told me." She watches as I back into a spot, waiting until we're in park before she responds.

"I may have told him he fucked up, and took his grief out on you." Piper shrugs nonchalantly, sipping at her coffee, and I just stare at her.

I would probably have continued staring, if the sound of something hitting my hood didn't jolt me out of my stupor. We both jump, and look out the front window to see a group gathered in front of my car.

"You scared the shit out of me," Piper says as she all but slams my door closed, feigning a punch at Alex's arm. Like the rest of us, she's clad in the same neon green shirt, only hers is half covered by the baby she's wearing across her chest.

"No cursing around the baby." Alex covers Mikayla's ears like the infant can understand us, and Piper snorts.

"Like you didn't say ten times worse changing her diaper last week."

"It was a nasty one, ok?" Alex's voice is defensive. "Also, these shirts are atrocious." She gestures to the group around us - Nolan, Penny with Brett, their kids, Piper's parents, Carla, Dylan, Vic, even Kyle, and a woman who introduces herself as Nolan's mom, Vicki.

"It's not like I designed them." Piper pulls her baseball cap further down on her head and crosses her arms.

"Well whoever did should be drawn and quartered. This color isn't flattering on anyone, and we look horrible." Vic is not a morning person, I'm gathering.

"Yeah," Kyle says with a yawn, throwing an arm around Vic and Carla. "But we look horrible together."

"Aww." Carla sticks a finger in his ear and he rears back, and that's the attitude we go into the morning with, making our way across the parking lot and through to registration for the 5K. Piper hands us each our numbers, which are really just for show because not one of us is actually planning to run this thing. A group stroll through a beautiful park is how Piper sold it, and after several minutes of announcements and information, the shotgun start sounds, earning a wail from the once-sleeping baby in Alex's arms.

"Fuck," she says in a low voice, bouncing on her knees, "It's ok, sweetheart."

CHAPTER 57

It's just one loud sound." We follow as she treds forward, the movement seeming to sooth the baby. "Now we just get to hear the sounds of sweat dripping down Mommy's back, hm?"

Vic makes a gagging noise from my side, and Piper's vision for the morning is pretty dead on - we spend the hour or so at a glacial pace, letting walkers and runners alike pass us, talking about anything and everything. Nolan tells us about one of his teammates getting locked outside of his hotel room butt ass naked. Vic shares that he's got a second interview this coming week with a company that shall remain nameless, though Piper tells me behind her hand she thinks it's Tera Bella, a bridal design company headquartered near where he lives. We talk about the fairy ball, and Alex scrolls down my profile, liking every picture from the night before and leaving me with two dozen notifications by the time she's done.

They talk about Mickey, and I listen with Dylan and Carla as they throw around stories, bouncing off each other to add details about the time he nearly got run over when a car slipped into neutral while he was working on it. They talk about his diagnosis, how hard he fought, continued to fight, despite everything.

I don't know that Mickey and I would have been friends - hell, sometimes, the way Piper talks about how he hurt her, I wish he was still around to punch the daylights out of. But I think I would have appreciated, at least, the way he clung onto life, onto this group of people he considered family, who stuck by him when his own family didn't.

As we cross the finish line, volunteers are there with noisemakers and blow horns, and Alex covers Mikayla's ears while Brett and Penny's kids run through a shower of bubbles. "Mommy, can we get bubbles on our way home?" Hunter asks, his eyes wide as he stares up at Penny with a look I immediately know could sink a thousand well-thought out plans.

"Maybe," is Penny's determined answer, but behind her, Brett nods at his son, earning him a thumbs up from the kiddo, and a stern look from his wife. Piper laughs, squeezing my hand in hers and then letting go as Aria drags her towards a chain link fence, decorated with posters for each team - Piper must have turned ours in earlier this week, because it's already up, a picture of Mickey in his baseball gear front and center with other photos all around.

Piper hauls Aria up until the toddler is sitting comfortably on Piper's hip, little arms wrapping around her neck as she looks back at the photos. "Is that Uncle Mickey?" Aria says, pointing at the pictures, and Brett nods, stepping up behind Piper.

"Sometimes it feels like yesterday." Nolan's voice is gruff, and I look over my shoulder to see him tucking Alex underneath him, pressing a kiss to Mikayla's forehead.

"Hey, strangers," a warm voice calls from behind us, and Piper pivots to where a blonde woman, dressed in the same ugly shirt as us, smiles at the group.

"Dr. Sanford!" Penny says brightly, and the woman pulls her in for a hug. Penny takes Aria from Piper's arms, and the two embrace. I hear the woman saying something to Piper, who stiffens at her words, and when they pull apart, she's giving Piper a tight smile. "What is it?" Penny asks, but then immediately adds "Oh, shit."

I follow her gaze, follow Piper's gaze, to a group of people making their way towards us behind Dr. Sanford. I don't need to have seen their faces to know exactly who they are, based on the buzz of reactions from the group around me. Alex reaches into the wrap around her shoulders and then hands her daughter to her mother in law, like she's a bull who's seen red and is rearing for a fight. Maybe she is. Because the absolute look of shock and disgust crossing her husband's face tells me that the people coming towards us are the Davis family.

CHAPTER 58

Piper

I've played out this scene in my head a thousand times. It's like that last big scene from Breaking Dawn - the future playing out in my brain, imagining every possible worst case scenario playing out until I've seen them all. Sometimes I'm calm, cool, and collected, breezing by the Davis family like they're a bug on my windshield. Sometimes I bitchslap Melissa across the face.

In no scenario was Fitz Westfall settling his hand on my lower back while I stare, dumbfounded, as a little girl runs across the field, throwing herself at Dr. Sanford, who looks almost as surprised as I feel.

Immediately, I know it's Kayla. Years later, and she still has that same wild dark hair, the hair they said was further proof she's Mickey's child.

I swallow the lump in my throat, glancing at Nolan and Alex, the latter of whom looks ready for a throw down. Nolan moves his hand to her arm, and she lets out a jagged breath.

"Aria, Hunter," Vickie starts from behind me, "Let's go find some of those bubbles." She grabs my niece and nephew by the hand after slipping Mickie into the baby carrier she's wearing, having switched off and on with Alex throughout the walk. If I wasn't in the middle of an oncoming shit storm, I could kiss the woman.

"And who do we have here?" Dr. Sanford asks, squatting down in front of Kayla. She knows exactly who Kayla is - she heard me talk about this enough, about the turmoil we were going through, as she oversaw his palliative care towards the end of his life. His parents met her a handful of times, but never has she set eyes on Kayla or her mother. Which tells me that his family likely sent Kayla over to greet us, like a pawn in a chess match they're willing to sacrifice for their greater good.

"I'm Kayla," she says brightly, and my chest clenches, wind leaving my lungs so fast I ball my hand into a fist. Kayla points at the poster behind me. "That's my daddy."

"Is that so?" Dr. Sanford answers, ever the queen of tact in a way I wish I could be. Her calm, soothing voice had smoothed out the wrinkles in several conversations - well, disagreements - between myself and the Davis family, about Mickey's care, about his wishes. Kayla smiles at our group, and I realize she probably doesn't remember any of us - we all look different, have aged in the time since we've seen her, and I wouldn't be surprised if trauma clouded her memories as much as it clouded mine.

"You're all Daddy's friends, right?" She stares up at Nolan. "I've seen you on the TV, Pawpaw says you play baseball, like Daddy." I try to regulate my breathing as I watch Nolan - watch his throat bob, watch his eyes slide to Melissa and Oscar and Kelsie, to Liz, Mickey's sister, and her husband Tyler next to them, their kids at their heels. To Zander, who looks as morbidly uncomfortable as every other time I've seen him, though he appears to have grown about a foot. My eyes track the group, and stop when they land on the cherry red hair hiding in the back.

You have got to be fucking kidding me.

"That's right," Nolan says, and I know he's trying to keep his tone even, his demeanor cool around the kids still with us, even though every fiber of his being is telling him to lash out. I know, because I'm feeling the same way.

"And you had a baby?" Melissa asks, peering around our group. "Did you not bring her with you?"

"Mikayla is with her grandmother," Alex seethes through gritted teeth.

"Shame, I was so hoping to meet her." A strangled scoff comes out of - no, wait, that's not that Alex, that's me.

I take a steadying breath, trying my best to not make eye contact with Bethani or Kenny, who seem a part of the group, but not quite, hovering in the back like they're getting ready to watch a pay per view cagematch. To play devil's advocate, it had almost happened at the funeral, so to expect it here is less than surprising.

"What are you doing here?" Comes Penny's measured voice, saying what all of us are thinking.

"We figured we'd just come to support our son," Oscar gruffs out, crossing his arms. "Bring his daughter to visit some of his favorite places."

The laugh that bubbles up from me isn't intentional. It's near psychotic sounding, like Harley Quinn on a particularly crazy day. But it draws everyone's attention, and I have to fight not to cover my mouth in shock.

"I'm sorry." I shake my head, stepping forward. "You chose *now* to support your son?" Fitz's hand on my back presses a bit, and Oscar opens his mouth to say something, never one to back down, but it's Melissa that cuts in.

CHAPTER 58 387

"We were supporting him long before you came around."

"And we were there long after you abandoned him," Alex hisses. God, this is why this woman is my best friend.

"Abandoned him?" Liz's voice is sharp, and she wraps an arm around her son's shoulder, which nearly hits her waist now. Fuck, that shouldn't hurt, but it does. All the years I've missed with these kids, who should have been, could have been, hearing the best stories from his best friends, instead of the pick and choose truth from these people in front of us. "That's rich, coming from the woman who couldn't be bothered to show up at his gravesite."

In front of me, Kayla steps back until she's flush against her mom's legs. She may be young, but she's old enough to know what's going on here.

"But I see," Melissa starts, eying the hand Fitz has on my back, "that it hasn't taken you long to move on."

"No, it didn't," comes Bethani's voice, and in a flash, I see Alex lunge next to me, Nolan wrapping an arm around her waist to hold her from ripping out one of Bethani's bad hair extensions, an Alex Calloway signature move.

And everyone is screaming, curses are flying, Tyler and Brett are in each other's faces in a heartbeat, Nolan is physically restraining his wife from lunging at Bethani, at Kelsie, at anyone daring to say anything, and I look back at Fitz, who's just taking it all in with raised eyebrows.

"I can't believe Nolan married trailer trash like you," Melissa snaps at Alex, who cackles.

"Sounds like the pot calling the kettle black, or should I say, *racist?*" I nearly cringe, but she's not wrong - small towns aren't exactly known for their diversity, and Paulsville, Kansas is no different.

"You left him," Penny's saying to Liz, squared up, though Penny is at least half a foot taller. "You all left him because you couldn't get through your thick heads that-"

"Enough." Alex looks my way, even Nolan, but the screaming is still happening. I take another breath, and then dial it up to Delmonico level. "*Enough.*"

Everything goes still, and beyond our group, several conversations cease as people look at us. I swallow, taking another step forward, away from Fitz's hand, his embrace. From the corner of my eye, I see him move back, next to Carla.

"We are not doing this here." My chest is rising and falling much faster than I want it to, giving away my stress level. My watch buzzes on my chest, I'm sure to tell me my heart rate is high again. "We are not doing this in front of them." I glance pointedly at Kayla, at Michael and Mickey, my nephews, god, my nephews that I baked cookies with every Christmas, that I spent years letting into my heart. My nephews who I didn't get to see grow up, because these people were too damn selfish to see past their own delusion.

Kayla looks up at me, and hell, I see it. I see the way her gaze is the same as Mickey's, the way her smile tips up at one side like his does. Did. Like his *did*. I've seen it for years, known it for years, that there was always a possibility that she was actually Mickey's. That this family had railroaded Kelsie back in the day, the same way they later railroaded me, throwing the truth out with the bath water.

Silently, I squat down in front of her. She looks up at her mother, and then back at me, eyes wide. "Kayla, right?" She nods, her fingers gathering in the skirt she's wearing under the same ugly neon shirt as the rest of us, about three sizes too big for her. "I'm Piper."

"Piper?" she repeats. I nod back. "You were..." Her eyes find Melissa's. "You kept Daddy away from us."

Again, the wind is knocked out of me, like a punch straight to the chest. I'm pretty sure I hear a sob from behind me, unsure whether it's from Alex, from Penny, from my mother, hell, from Nolan, at this point, because the only time I've ever seen that man cry was at his best friend's bedside the day he died, and at his funeral watching shit hit the fan. Everything was - is - out of his control.

I give Kayla the best smile I can muster. "I'm sorry you feel that way. Your daddy and I..." I swallow. "I love your Daddy very much, and I want you to know that." I tilt my head towards Nolan. "I bet if you ask your grandma, she can show you some pictures of Nolan and your daddy when they were your age." I try to smile conspiratorially. "He and my friend Alex just had a baby, do you want to know her name?" Kayla nods. "Her name is Mikayla, but we call her Mickie."

Her eyes widen as she looks up at her mother, and I can't tell whether Kelsie is furious, or sad, or uncomfortable. Or all of the above. Because as much as my gut told me then that this woman was trying to make a quick buck off a dying man, there's always been a lingering feeling that she may have been telling the truth from day one, and things got so messed up that I couldn't wade through the muck fast enough to tell heads from tails.

Leaning forward, I pull the hat off my head, smoothing out my ponytail as best I can. I hold it out to Kayla. "This is one of your daddy's favorite hats," I start, pointing to the Jayhawks on the worn blue fabric. "I held onto it, but I think it'll look better on you. What do you think?" Kayla and I both look up at Kelsie, asking the same permission, and she nods down at her daughter. I see the tight swallow she makes as I look back down at the child in front of me where she's sliding the hat over her head. It's one of the last items of Mickey's I kept, and now, just like that, it's hers.

She could be his. She could be his, could be the child of my husband, and I never even got a chance to know her. Will probably never get the chance to know her. And none of that was my choice, my doing. Those choices were taken from me by the lies Mickey and his family spun at every turn until the only truth I knew was that I loved him, and I clung to that, clung to it like the last shred of my dignity, and they'd taken that too.

"It looks great on you." I tap the bill, and she giggles, and God, the way my heart hurts for this little girl, who doesn't know what's going on, just knows that I'm the mean lady that kept her from her Daddy.

I pop up from my squat, nearly losing my balance, and before I can fall Fitz is back at my side, taking my hand and steadying me. I see Liz staring at the places we're making contact, see Melissa's look of disgust - genuine disgust, not the playful, loving kind that Alex and Frannie hurl at us - and the last thread inside me snaps.

And I'm about to let her have it, let them all have it, when Fitz squeezes my hand, and looks back down at Kayla, who I realize is watching us with a huge smile on her face. She doesn't know. She has no clue that I was married to her father - or, father figure - because his family never acknowledged it, much less celebrated it. She's just seeing a man being chivalrous, being loving, and she's happy about it. Hell, I'm happy about it too, despite the underlying pain radiating through my body at the way I'm restraining myself, holding back all the things I really want to say.

I take another calming breath, and let my face slide into the cool, collected smile I haven't used in weeks, not since I was at AllHearts, pretending everything was fine. It's the same smile I wore at Mickey's funeral, at his burial. It feels like a mask, like a frosted window sliding shut over me so you can see the outline of who I am, but no clear details.

They don't deserve the details. Don't deserve to know any more about me, about my life. They ruined enough of it already.

I step away from Fitz again, and let the emptiness, lacking his touch, fuel my words.

"I am going to say this once, and I'm going to say it as kindly as possible because I have more respect for these children than I do for you all." I raise my brows, gesturing to the group of adult-sized toddlers all glaring at me. "You were my family. All of you." I give Kenny and Bethani a pointed look, and see Ken shrink back. "But the second Mickey decided to do something you didn't like, I became the problem. Not your son, not the way he -" I catch myself, trying to watch my language. "Not the way he messed up. I was the problem."

Melissa opens her mouth to speak, and at the same time I hold my hand up, Nolan says "Let her say her peace," and Alex seethes "Shut. Up."

"You made me the villain in your story. In her story." I nod down to Kayla. "But these people behind me? They showed up while you all sat in Kansas on your high horse, letting everyone think you were busting your butts taking care of your sick son."

I give a pointed look at Oscar. "You posted on social media about the big fight against Cancer."

I look at Liz. "You told me we were waiting on the unexplained miracle, and I needed to let him come home to his family."

To Melissa, I say "You told us how upset you were that we didn't include you in our wedding, while at the same time, proving exactly why we didn't involve you. And instead of asking your son what he wanted as his final wishes, instead of letting me do what he asked, you jumped the gun." I look between this woman and her husband, who raised a man that I'll love for the rest of my life, knowing full well I loved him through the end of his. "If you'd taken ten seconds to ask me instead of lawyering up, you would have known that we agreed to have money set aside from his insurance to pay for college for Zander and all of your children." I point to Liz, whose mouth gapes slightly. "I sincerely hope that money went towards what he asked, at least in part."

Finally, my eyes slide to Kelsie. "And you? I don't know what they did to you, or what you're doing to them, if we're being honest." I glance down at Kayla, who just looks confused at this point. "But for the sake of that little girl, I hope that the truth doesn't break any of you the way this all broke me."

"She is his daughter," Melissa huffs.

"And I was his *wife*." It comes out as a strangled sob, a scream, and if people weren't looking at us before, they are now. I feel Alex's hand on my arm and pinch the bridge of my nose. "She was his daughter, and I was his wife," I repeat, just loud enough for those around me to hear. "For better or for worse, I committed myself to your son. Knowing everything he did to me, knowing that we probably wouldn't see another new year. I was his wife.

"I was his wife, as much as none of you want to admit it. And I watched - we watched - while you acted like none of us existed. Like this part of his life didn't exist." I laugh, humorless and dry. "And now you come here to show his daughter some of his favorite places." My chest heaves, and the words on the tip of my tongue are some of the hardest yet, the hardest to speak out loud. I meet Liz's icy stare. "I haven't been to his gravesite because I'm not stupid enough to think that you all haven't convinced that entire town that I'm the devil incarnate. I know that the second someone spots my car, I'm in for the same barrage of harassment we all got the day after the funeral, when you all made quite the show as the spurned family who lost a child.

"You carved her initials into his gravestone," I choke out, and I bury my head in my hands. I'm trying my hardest not to lose my absolute mind, but Alex's hand on me just makes me sob harder, and through my tears I say "You

CHAPTER 58

carved her initials on the gravestone that I paid for, after you abandoned him, abandoned us, and had the gall to use his name, his love for you, to make a quick buck."

Melissa just gives me a blank look. "He would be so disappointed to see you talking this way to us." I suck in a breath at her words, but she doesn't stop. "And he'd be disappointed to see the way you've..." Her eyes trail up and down my body. "Grown."

Red flashes across my eyes, hot and furious, but I'm holding Alex back with one hand and moving the other in front of Fitz, who steps forward so fast I barely see it. And before either of them, before any of them can say or do anything, I'm an inch away from the face of the woman who made my life hell from the moment I heard the word "cancer."

"Don't you dare think for one second," I spit, "that I would not let them pummel you to the ground. All of you." I tip my chin at the people behind her. "But not one of you is worth a felony record, so I'm going to say this one more time to get it through your head." And like an angry school teacher, my finger is in Melissa's face, and she's flinching, and a flicker of power seeps through me knowing that I can get a rise out of her that fast. "You were my family, all of you. And you treated me, treated us, like we were nothing."

"I pray that none of you ever have to do what Piper did," my mother says from behind me, speaking for the first time. "To take care of the person you love the most in the world while watching them die in front of your eyes."

"To feed him, and change him," Alex adds. "To do things most people assume you need a medical degree for."

"Mostly by herself." Nolan looks over at me, and I want to hug him. "Knowing that Mickey was too proud to have any of us there to help him at the end."

"We would have helped," Liz says.

"But you didn't." I give them all a sad smile, stepping back. "You can sit there and say you would have helped, should have been able to help, but you didn't. I wasn't barring you from visiting, didn't physically keep you from being involved in his life the way you did to me." I give Melissa a pointed stare. "You had every opportunity to come down, to be here for all of it, and you didn't. And then you made those of us that were here feel like shit." I don't even try to stop the last word from coming out, just spit it like it's a bad taste on my tongue. "You made me the villain, and you can scream that from the high heavens, telling everyone how horrible I am." I hold up my hands for emphasis, because at this point, why not. "But don't forget to tell people the part where you made me that way."

"I highly suggest you make yourselves scarce," Penny says, and she crosses her arms over her chest. "Because as much power as you think you wield in Bumfuck, Kansas, I think you'd be surprised to know just what this group of

Mickey's insignificant Texas friends - family - can pull off." Next to her, I see Dr. Sanford step up, not even realizing she'd left in the middle of the shitstorm, toting a uniformed police officer with her.

Oscar mumbles something, and Alex holds a hand up to her ear. "What was that? Can't hear you hiding behind your wife."

"I think we should be going." He looks like a dog with its tail between its legs as he takes his wife's arm, yanking her away. Melissa and Liz give us seering glares, and I realize that neither Zander nor Kenny said anything the entire time - either too chicken, or too shocked to do so. But as I watch them retreat, Kayla looks over her shoulder, pressing that hat to her head.

I feel my shoulders sag, and as fast as my heart is beating, as ragged as my breaths are, when I look at Alex, and she mutters "What the fuck just happened?" All I can do is shake my head, blinking.

Because for the first time in years, I feel like I can breathe. Truly, really breathe, all the weight of those words off my chest, the man that I love beside me, and my friends, though stunned, smiling sheepishly at each other like we just won a drag race while climbing down the track on the world's most stressful vehicle.

CHAPTER 59

Fitz

When I hear an unexpected knock on my door, I'm half expecting to see Seer standing in the frame, waiting with some quippy remark. But when I look up, I'm staring at an apprehensive Chris Westfall, hands in his pockets.

We steadily avoided each other the last couple of weeks, following the complete crapshoot at Freddy's graduation lunch, but now he looks sheepish in a way that tells me Paula definitely read him the riot act. Internally, I score one for my stepmom.

"You have a second?" he asks, not waiting for my response before stepping in, closing the door behind him. Burying a scoff, I look down at my watch.

"I thought we were meeting downstairs at noon."

"I wanted to chat for a minute before we meet the girls for lunch." The girls. He says it like they're silly, and twelve, and possibly wearing pigtails with skinned knees.

Ok, the skinned knee part might be on par for Piper, but not my sister.

"They're not girls," I correct, all pretense out the window. Maybe it's Piper's words from the day before that have been echoing around my brain all morning. The way my heart pounded watching her tell the Davis family exactly how she felt, no qualms about it. And then I soften my tone, repeating, "They're not girls."

Dad looks stunned, halfway between standing and sitting in one of the plush armchairs in front of my desk. After a second, he seems to recover, sitting down.

"You're right, they're not." He unbuttons his suit jacket, and for the first time in a long time, I look at my father. Really look at him.

We look alike. I know that. Fred and I both have a lot of the same physical characteristics as my dad. But while Fred is lean and toned like Paula, I'm bulkier, particularly around the middle, if I'm not careful - which is one of the reasons I drag myself out of bed at the asscrack of dawn to run with Roscoe every morning.

And it's also why I had to tell Mateo to stop bringing his failed - or successful - desserts up to the office.

But my father is getting old. Not in a "can't walk, needs caregiving," way. But in a groans-when-he-sits, salt and pepper facial hair kind of way that has me silent for a beat too long.

"What's wrong?" he asks, and it shakes me out of my stupor.

"Nothing, sorry." I set the stack of PTO reports in my hand down on the desktop. "Yesterday was just a long day."

"Francesca told me a little bit," he starts. "So did Paula." I raise a brow at him. "It seems Piper's mother and she are closer than we realized."

"Figures," I sigh, sitting back in my chair and lacing my fingers over my chest. "Bianca Delmonico is terrifying. I'd be scared shitless to go up against her in court."

"Paula said as much." He rakes his hand through his hair, thinning at the front, giving a gravely laugh. "They're all scary, to be honest."

"Who?"

"Women," he says. I bark out a laugh, scrubbing a hand down my face. "But that's not what I'm here to talk to you about."

I stay silent, and after a moment of awkwardness, I wave my hand out in a gesture that clearly says *go on*.

"I wanted to apologize. To you and to Piper." I'm about to tell him he needs to apologize to Piper's face when he holds up a hand. "Give me a minute. I promise, I'll let you get a word in." I shut my mouth. "Thank you. I'm sure Piper told you what we discussed on Saturday." She kind of had, but left it vague. "But she gave me a lot to think about. A lot to talk about, really."

"Paula let you have it, didn't she?" Dad's laugh is actually a real one for once, and he tugs on his ear, a nervous habit he shares with Freddy.

"She did. I told her what Piper said to me on Saturday, and it was like a floodgate opened." He sighs, mirroring me by leaning back in his chair. "I think she's kept a lot of stuff pent up for a long time, and it all came bubbling up yesterday." I run my fingers over the side of my mouth, shaking my head.

"Welcome to the club. Sunday from hell."

"I don't know about that," he continues with a shrug. "But it was probably one of the most open conversations I've had with your - with Paula - in a while." He takes a deep breath, like he's about to break into song, or scream. "And between her, and Piper, they made some good points." He looks at me then, his eyes appraising, and I try not to wither under his stare. "I wasn't a very loving father."

Like Piper the day before, I feel a laugh coming up from my throat that I can't control, and steeple my fingers in front of my mouth. Once I know it's passed,

CHAPTER 59

I tip my hands towards him in a motion to continue.

"To any of you, really. I wasn't loving." He sighs again, nodding his head back towards the door, like Frannie is standing on the other side. "I wasn't affectionate-"

Hold on. Frannie *is* standing outside my door. I can see her peering in through one set of blinds, with Piper in the other, and it takes everything in me not to narrow my gaze at them because they're both staring, wide eyed.

"I wasn't particularly supportive." I nod, like I've heard everything my father is saying, like there isn't a two person comedy act outside my office door. "You can disagree at any time, Fitzwilliam."

And then I snort. And damn it, I need to stop hanging around Piper's friends so much, because I never snort, and my dad's shocked face all but confirms that it's out of character. I want to reel it back in, to bottle it up and pretend like it didn't happen, but he just raises a brow at me.

"And I don't know that I've ever heard you make that noise in all of your life."

"It's a recent development," I deadpan, and he smiles. My father actually smiles across the desk. "So is that." I point to his face.

"It's a recent development." He rubs at his forehead. "I also skipped my botox this month, so I can actually move my face a little better."

I stare at him, unsure of whether he's joking or not, but when he rattles on, I realize he's being completely serious, and I pocket that tidbit of knowledge to press my sister about later.

Botox? How long has Dad been getting *botox*? Does Paula get botox? Does Frannie? Does *Freddy*?

"You're spiraling," he says after a second, and I shake my head. "I can practically see the wheels turning."

"Sorry, I just..." I press my still-steepled fingers into my mouth. "This all just feels very surreal." He looks confused, so I continue. "This whole conversation. This week." I tip my head forward, staring down at my desk. "This whole year, to be honest."

"I can't imagine I've made that any easier."

"Did Paula physically threaten you?" I ask, because this side of my dad isn't something I'm used to seeing at all, much less so freely.

"Not in as many words." He joins his fingers over his belly. "But she told me to get my head out of my ass, or else."

"Or else?"

"Or else I'm going to completely push my children, push you, away."

There's a knock on the door behind us, and we both call "One minute." He smiles at me, because he knows as much as I do that the response is automatic, timed almost exactly the same.

"If you think Paula is scary, you should be terrified to see her and Bianca Delmonico together," I say finally, because I'm not sure what else to add to the conversation. I am spiraling, but I think it's going to take longer than the few minutes before we're late for our lunch reservation for me to figure it all out.

"I heard Piper is also quite the spitfire when she wants to be." He taps the side of his nose, and I sigh, shaking my head.

"She's... something else, that's for sure." He looks at me again, that same appraising stare.

"You love her a lot, don't you?" I nod, swallowing.

"I think more than I ever loved Liv." I blink back at him. "Is that horrible to say?"

"No." He pushes himself up, out of his chair, buttoning his suit jacket. "It can be a different kind of love, too, Will. It's not all the same." His throat bobs as he stares down at me. "Take it from someone who has been lucky enough to have two great loves in their life. And from someone who went through something very similar to what I hear Piper experienced." He scratches at the corner of his eye, and part of me wonders if he's trying to hold back a tear or two. I haven't seen him cry since the day his father died, and that was really just the aftermath of him locking himself in the bathroom for four hours before coming out bleary eyed and red faced.

I stand, meeting him around the corner of the desk, and when he reaches forward to open the door, I see Piper and Frannie standing strangely close to the doorway, almost like they'd had their ears pressed to the door. From behind my father, I raise a brow, and my sister laughs nervously, smoothing over her pencil skirt at the same time Piper runs a hand over her hair. It's still tamed and straighter than normal, big bouncy curls that don't look like the Piper I've grown so used to, but I'm not about to say that to her. Still, there's a part of me that can't wait for wash day.

My God. *I can't wait for wash day?*

"Uh," Piper says, "Hi, Mr. Westfall."

"Chris, please," Dad corrects, putting a hand on Frannie's shoulder. "Are you two lad-" He seems to catch himself, looking at me before continuing. "Are you two ready for lunch?"

"Starving," Frannie whines, grabbing her purse from Georgia's desk. My assistant is staring at the lot of us like we'll put her in an early grave, which isn't totally off base with the way we've been trying to pull reports for the last several months. She may throw her computer out the window if I ask her to cross-check one more spreadsheet.

"How's your first day going?" I ask, falling in line behind my father and sister,

CHAPTER 59

reaching my hand down to squeeze Piper's.

"Good." She tucks a strand of hair behind her ear, and it feels shy, feels reserved.

It feels so not Piper.

"We'll meet you down there in a minute," I call to Frannie and Dad, and they both look at us as they step into the elevator. "Go ahead and get our drinks."

"Dr. Pepper and water?" Fran calls, and Piper nods, just in time to see my sister roll her eyes as the doors slide closed. I take Piper's hand, pulling her into a quiet corner of one of our conference rooms.

"Fitz, what are you...?" I put a hand on either of her shoulders.

"What's your name?" She looks at me like I've grown another arm, but I stare down at her. "What's your name?"

"Uh, Piper." Her eyebrows crease in the middle.

"And who are you?" I ask. The crease gets deeper. "You're a badass, Piper. A badass who told a whole cluster of people to go fuck themselves yesterday." She laughs, one hand coming to cover her mouth. I bat it away. "Stop it. You are a badass, with a beautiful laugh, and you're going to have to admit one of those two things to me before I let you leave this room."

"Or else?" Her eyes sparkle, even in the dim light, and I do my best not to notice the way her skirt hugs at her waist, the length highlighting her toned legs.

"Don't distract me." I set my jaw. "Who are you?"

"A badass," she mumbles.

"What was that?"

"A badass," she says a little louder. I squeeze her shoulder.

"That's better. Now, for the love of all things holy, don't spend your first day trying to fit into whatever tiny little box you've made for WHG Piper." She looks up at me, and suddenly there's water pooling in her eyes, and oh no - "Jesus, don't cry." I squeeze her shoulders again, because all I want to do is hug her, but the last thing I need is for anyone here to think we can't work together without being professional. "Piper."

"Sorry." She gives a watery laugh, snagging a tissue from a nearby table and holding it to the corner of each eye. "I needed that. I've been so nervous all day."

"There's nothing to be nervous about. They're going to love you just as much as I do." Her smile dials up about ten notches, and I make a mental note to add more sugary sweet, doting phrases, because she clearly thrives off them. We make our way to the elevator, and when the door closes, she reaches out, grabbing my hand.

"Thank you." I nod, giving her fingers a squeeze.

"You think that was good, you should hang out with my sister more often." She looks at me, brows furrowed. "She and Seer and Jasmine have this weird thing I saw them do a few weeks back, apparently it's something they started in college." I tip my eyes towards the ceiling of the elevator, shaking my head at the memory. "They set a timer, and for, like, a minute, all of them give one person as much praise as they can handle." Piper looks impressed.

"It's like a snap cup," she says confidently, and I'm immediately lost. She rolls her eyes, squeezing my hand and snapping with the other one. "You know, *We'll find harmony and love in the old snap cup!*" Her singing is so off-key, I wince, and she's smacking my arm just as the elevator doors open, revealing Frannie and Dad.

"I knew I liked this one." Frannie laces her arm through Piper's. "What did he do this time?"

"He didn't get my Legally Blonde reference," Piper says, as if I've set off nuclear bombs on the whole of Europe. Dad and I share a look behind them. "I need to know more about your super special praise time." Frannie pauses, looking confused.

"The thing you were doing with Jas and Seer the other day in your office," I add, and then realization crosses her features.

"Oh, the snaps," she says, her tone understanding, and Piper just throws me a look over her shoulder like I'm a complete idiot. "Also known as high praises, because Mateo refuses to call it snaps."

"Understandably." My voice is low, but Frannie cuts me a look.

"I see why you hit him." I shake my head.

"I've made a grave mistake." We step outside into the blazing Texas heat, and I'm thankful that in about a minute, I'll be back in the air conditioning, but as we're crossing the street, I add "Seer's not working today, right?"

Frannie laughs. "Of course she is, I let her know we're on our way in. She's in the kitchen today." I bite my lips together, but Dad speaks for me.

"Is the grave mistake putting together a group full of women who know all the places to hit you where it hurts?" I nod. Hit the nail right on the head. He holds the door open for Fran and Piper, and I grab it above his head, letting him sneak in front of me. "Welcome to being a Westfall man. We like stubborn women, and have daughters even more stubborn."

"Hey," both women call over their shoulders, and I shake my head, trying to clear the thought of a tiny, blue eyed, curly red haired child kicking the shit out of me the way Aria did to Brett.

CHAPTER 60

Piper

"Sorry, sorry, sorry," I cry, pushing into the bridal suite at the Pine with my garment bag over my shoulder, an arm full of tote bags held out in front of me. "Bex decided to sneak into a bag of tortilla chips this morning, I had to drop her off at my parents before I came this way." Across the room, Carla meets my gaze.

"Those were my tortilla chips."

"I'll buy you new ones tomorrow." I huff out a deep breath as I dump the bags on the table in the center of the room, and immediately, Carla reaches her greedy little hands into the one she knows all my presents are sitting in. "Ah, ah, ah." I swat at her hand.

"Boo." Fallon meets my gaze in the mirror she's sitting in front of, curling her hair, and I feel like I'm backstage on opening night of the school musical again.

Except, then, I'd spent every day seeing the same old faces, over and over again, miserable. I haven't seen these people in ten years - haven't shared updates outside of the women in this room - well, women, plus Vic, who's helping Jackie with her makeup. But the flutters are the same. The weight on my shoulders feels palpable as I stick the garment bag on a rolling rack, pulling the dress out to let it hang free.

"We may need to steam a few things." Jessica is talking more to herself as she pushes into the room, holding a cream table runner. "These are still all wrinkly." She stops when she sees me, and grins. "Girl, oh, my God." She drops the runner on a small table near the door, coming up to clutch both of my arms, like we're two best friends about to have a gossip. "You and Fitz?"

Ok, I guess we are about to have a gossip. I stare over Jessica's shoulder at my roommate, who shrugs, taking a bite of the sandwich she was munching on when I left several hours ago to get the bags she'd left sitting on our kitchen counter.

"I didn't even have to tell her." Carla's voice is blase as she scrolls through her phone, probably texting Dylan. "His tagged pictures did all the talking for him." I close my eyes. Well, shit. I hadn't even thought about that, thought about the implication of those pictures and not completely blasting to the world that Piper and Fitz were not only together, but had stared lovingly into each other's eyes in a public space. One shocker at a time, ya know?

"Those pictures," Jessica squeals, gripping my arms tighter. "You should have heard the way I screamed to - oh, perfect timing." She watches as a woman backs in through the door, balancing a tray of what looks like bagged favors on a clearly pregnant belly.

"Hey, babe, I'm not sure-"

She freezes, mid step, staring between Jessica and I, before setting the tray down on top of the table runner and putting her hands on her hips in what I'm sure is exactly what this woman will look like when that child misbehaves. "Well, let me guess, you must be Piper." Her voice is all sugary sweet southern charm, and I shake loose one of Jessica's hands, pointing between the two of them.

"I'm guessing this is your wife?" Jessica nods, and she blushes. Actually blushes, visibly. How had Penny described Jessica's wife? Oh, yeah, a gorgeous specimen. Well, I mean, this woman has big blonde hair, a tiny frame, and is holding a basketball between her hips, but I could agree with that sentiment. "Lizzy Baker, pleased to meet you." I hold out a hand, but she pulls me into a hug that leaves me trying to maneuver around her stomach.

I like this Lizzy. I'd trade Mickey's sister Liz for this Lizzy any day.

"Back to the most pressing questions," Jackie says from across the room, and Vic grabs her arm, steadying her underneath the brush he has precariously close to her eye. "What? When? How?"

"I thought you two were going to kill each other when we first got together." Fallon's voice is matter of fact. Carla snorts.

"They were. It wasn't all sunshine and rainbows."

"I may have yelled at him when I came here the first time." I glance around the suite, not adding *after I showed him my vibrator, and then nearly puked upon seeing Andy for the first time in a decade.*

"About *what?*" Lizzy sounds scandalized, and holds her hand to her chest like a woman in a Baptist church clutching her pearls.

"He was being an ass and putting the cart before the horse," Vic answers dryly, but I see the smile on his face. I think his budding bromance with Fitz may be happening just as fast as my relationship did.

"Sounds about right." Jessica sighs, looking at her wife over her shoulder. "Ten bucks says Liv makes a scene."

"Liv is coming?" I ask, and feel the color draining from my face. When I'd last asked Carla a week ago, neither Liv nor Ryan had RSVPed yes to the multiple invitations. We figured that they wouldn't want the drama of being in the same room as Fitz or deal with the commentary it was likely to bring, but her tight lipped look across the room gives me the answer I need. "Fuck my life," I breathe, moving to drag a hand down my face, but Vic screams "No!"

"Don't make me start all over." He points the brush in his hand at me "Or I will come over there and kick your pretty little ass."

"Say it again," I moan, covering my eyes.

"Pretty? Or little ass?"

"Yes." The room laughs, and I feel an arm snake around my shoulders, looking up to find Jessica next to me.

"If anyone deserves to be happy, it's you. And I think I speak for everyone in this room when I say that Liv did not make Fitz happy."

"Facts," Jackie agrees as Vic adds a bit of a wing to her eyeliner. The door opens behind me again, and Frannie slides into the room, holding a plate of cookies, with Seer on her tail, a bottle of champagne and several glasses on the tray in her hands.

"Ooh, treats!" Lizzy's voice is high pitched and excited, and I meet Jessica's mooney gaze, giving her a thumbs up.

"She's great," I mouth.

"I know," she silently screams back, hands on her heart.

"This," Seer says triumphantly, holding up the bottle of champagne, "is non-alcoholic, and courtesy of WHG as a thank you for hosting your event with us." She gives me a wry smile as she pops the champagne, making Jackie jump and Lizzy squeal again. I wonder how many times Seer has had to say that as a WHG employee, or how many times she's specially requested to work, even at properties she's not assigned to.

Frannie slides into place next to me, watching Seer pour the bubbling drinks and handing them out to everyone.

"Carla told me about Liv," she says, and when my head snaps to her, she grips my upper arm. "She didn't want to freak you out."

"Mission *not* accomplished." I take the glass Seer holds out to me. "Does he know?" Frannie nods, taking the other glass from her friend.

"She told both of us together, I think so I could talk him off the ledge."

"Did he *need* talking off the ledge?"

I can't imagine Fitz on a ledge. What does that look like?

But Frannie shakes her head, sipping at the drink in her hand and then giving it an appreciative look.

"This isn't half bad for no booze. And no, he was weirdly calm about it." She pauses. "I mean *weirdly* calm."

"Well, that's terrifying." My new boss gives me a pointed look that says *I know, dummy*. Because of course she does. She's been monitoring his emotions her entire life. And in the week I've been working with Frannie Westfall, there are a few things I've come to learn. One of those is that, like me, one of her top five strengths is individualization. And while for me, that comes out with my nurturing side, finding what people need and then giving it to them, even to the detriment of myself, it comes out in the middle Westfall child in an entirely different way.

Frannie Westfall is more observant than people give her credit for, possibly having taken all of the observation skills left to the Wesfall name and leaving her poor younger brother without any ability to read the room. But she spots those needs, those desires, and she uses them. Her brother may make big, lofty speeches, and write eloquently worded emails that make you think that yes, yes you are fully committed to meeting quarterly sales goals as part of the WHG team. But Frannie, oh, Frannie Westfall is subtle. She can walk through a room and meet ten new people, convincing them all she's the hottest shit since our last 100+ degree day. Frannie figures out how to get her foot in the door, and then she keeps it open, sneaking the occasional suggestion in through the crack.

As opposed to Seer, I've learned, who blasts the door open, reads you like an open book, and then tells you the deepest, darkest secrets about yourself that you don't even know. I'm overwhelmingly thankful that, though I've come to really like Seer, she's not my boss, because on a scale of sugar coated to dark chocolate, I take criticism at a solid cavity-inducing sweet level, and Seer hands hers out mixed with 99% cacao.

There's a knock on the door behind Frannie, and then I hear Kyle's voice call out "Is everyone decent?" There's a chorus of "Yes!" and he pushes open the door, Fitz hot on his heel, and his eyebrows are knit together with a tension that tells me they've been like that all day. He meets my gaze, and the lines immediately melt away. Seer holds out glasses to the men, ushering them in the room as Frannie closes the door behind him.

"Thanks for the drinks, big man." Fitz looks confused at Jackie's words, and then glances down at his sister, and the cup in my hand.

"Yes, thanks, dear brother, for this refreshing bottle of non-alcoholic champagne, so everyone can join in on the festivities." Frannie holds up her glass, tilting her head pointedly at Lizzy, Carla and I, and he rolls his eyes.

"It's coming out of your budget."

"Bet," Frannie and I say at the same time, and then look at each other, wide eyed. She laughs, finally taking in what I'm wearing.

"Please tell me-"

"Jesus." I feel self-conscious, tugging at the pair of bike shorts I'm wearing

CHAPTER 60

under a giant tee shirt. "Of course this isn't what I'm wearing." I point behind her, to the dress hanging on the rack, and she gives an appreciative nod.

"To the best planning committee a girl could ask for," Jackie's voice suddenly calls, and I realize she, Fallon, and Vic have joined us on the other side of the room. She holds up her glass, and we toast, even Seer and Frannie. I take a sip, letting the bubbles settle over my tongue. My lips purse, and they all stare at me.

"Even when I was drinking, I hated champagne." I hand my glass to Kyle, who shrugs, tipping back the glass.

"More for me."

I look at Fitz, nodding my head back towards the corner of the room, near a window looking at the garden on the backside of the venue. I snag the bag Carla was digging in, pulling out a purple box and handing it over. He takes it, and looks like he instantly regrets it when glitter clings to his hands, to his shirt.

"Oops," I manage, hiding my smirk behind my hand. He sets the box on the arm of the couch, sliding the lid back and pulling out the long tan belt coiled inside.

"What's this?" He holds it in his hands, pulling it until the gigantic belt buckle is between his fingers, where he eyes the giant F square in the middle of it.

"I made it." My voice is quiet, but I press on. "I thought you might like something to match the rest of us, I made one for Kyle too, but it doesn't match mine, and-"

"I love it." His voice is equally as quiet, and his hand moves to my face, pulling me into a hug and pressing a kiss to my head.

"This is too sweet," Lizzy calls.

"I think I'm going to puke," says Frannie at a deadpan.

Carla's voice is close as she asks "Does this mean we can open presents now?"

"Ooh, presents?" I roll my eyes at the excited tone to Seer's question.

"They're in the bag, have at it." Carla digs in like a kid on Christmas morning.

"I've been watching her work on these for weeks, I have no idea what we're all getting, though." I'm not really paying attention as she hands out each bag, because I'm watching as Fitz undoes his belt buckle.

"Take it off!" Fallon cackles.

"I'm going to murder someone by the end of the night," he says under his breath, tugging the belt through the loops of his jeans - arguably, the first time in ten years. They're worn and tight in all the right places, and my, oh my, does Mr. Westfall look fantastic with a belt buckle the size of his gigantic hand front and center.

"Please don't." I pat the side of his face. "You're too pretty for jail."

Fitz

I'm in jeans. I'm in jeans, and a checkered shirt, with a big ass belt buckle above my crotch, at a WHG venue, and every instinct in my body is telling me to go hide out in the office until tonight is over.

But I may get killed if I do that, by an undetermined number of suspects who shall remain nameless, but are all wearing matching accessories with tooled, dark flowers etched into the leather by the lead suspect herself. At least, that's what I remind myself as I scan over the crowd of people pressing into the Pine, where I hug the wall, occasionally giving a "Hey, man," waving.

I'm easy to spot, I know. I've never really blended into the crowd, and it was one of my favorite traits back when I was around these people every day. It got me what I wanted, got me where I wanted on the lacrosse field. But even my old teammates aren't quite sure how to approach me, probably because I look like I just swallowed a bitter pill.

"Would it kill you to smile?" Frannie stands next to me.

"Yes." She sighs, leaning against the wall, crossing one of her legs over the other. I haven't seen her in jeans in a while either, but she's gone full country with boots, and even a hat that's almost as big as the one Piper is wearing, which is also visible across the room. "What are you even doing here? Tif was scheduled."

"I told her to take the night off," Frannie says with a casual shrug, crossing her arms so we're standing in the same pose. "Her boyfriend is in town from the rig." Ah. "Plus." She nods her chin towards Piper, who's been in the same conversation with Vic and her friend Maria, who greeted her like no time has passed, since this thing kicked off an hour ago. Based on what Piper told me, it's been several years since she and Alex have seen Maria, having gone to her lavish New York wedding together after college. She lived a very different life than either of them, and they seemed ok with that.

"The party has arrived," a voice I immediately recognize calls, and through the door walks Alex Calloway, taking her gigantic sunglasses off and holding out her arms like a star on the red carpet. "Please, don't all crowd me at once."

"You're obnoxious." Nolan wraps an arm around her from behind, so I know he means his jab affectionately. He seems like the kind of guy I would have been friends with, looking back a decade ago. From what I've heard through their friends, he and Alex took several years to finally date, and in that time he was mixed signal city, because he was so hard to read, and so focused on getting recruited out of college.

I wonder to myself if I'll ever be that at ease with Piper, that free to be affectionate, loving, with other people's eyes on us. I'd had a taste of it a few times over the last several months, and it was still something my brain was trying to process. But maybe he is too? Maybe the affection is just something he does because he knows, like Piper, that Alex feels more secure when he does it.

That idea makes me feel a little better inside as I watch them make their way to the bar. Seer's already making their drinks when they walk up, and she turns to me, waving a hand.

"Hey, boss man!" I stride over to the corner of the bar, and Nolan claps me on the back over Alex's head. She looks up at his arm like she's about to bite it. Seer holds a near-empty bottle of Moscato up. "Can you grab me two more of these from the fridge?"

"I'm not working tonight," I say dryly. She gives me a withering look - because my name is on the side of the building, or her barback is the new guy she's still training, or she'd rather ask me than my sister, who actually *is* working tonight, I'm not sure. "Fine." I take one last look at the label before heading for the kitchen, where I spy Mateo dishing out orders on the fly.

"All good out there?" he asks, and I nod, clapping his shoulder as I walk by.

"All good, Chef, the bartender is shit and didn't stock up like she's supposed to."

"I'm telling her you said that." I can't see his face, but I know he's smiling into the bowl of pico he's mixing.

"Go right ahead." I open up the fridge door, shifting tubs of guac and cheese until I find the stash of chilled wine in the back. When I turn, bottles in hand, Mateo is standing in front of me, and his demeanor has gone from teasing to deadly serious in a matter of seconds.

"I'll take those." He snatches the bottles out of my hand, setting them on the workstation beside us, and I stare at him. "I need you to, uh, take a deep breath for me, man." Mateo mimics what could only be compared to breathing they do in a birthing class, taking quick, short inhales, and then one deep exhale, his hands moving with the gesture.

"What the fuck you doing?" I move to pick the bottles back up, and he steps between me and the work station. "Seriously, Mat, what is your-"

"Liv is outside the kitchen door."

CHAPTER 61

Fitz

I freeze, my entire body tensing, and I close my eyes for just a second, willing his words to be a hallucination. A daydream. A stroke. Anything is preferable to my-ex wife actually showing up to this thing.

Silently, I turn on my heel, and sure enough, I see the top half of Olivia's face through the diamond-shaped window in the kitchen door. Her eyes narrow when she sees, taking in my appearance.

I reach back out for the bottles again, but Mateo moves faster than me. "You don't need to take any projectiles out there."

"Projectiles?" I'm about to ask if he thinks I'll throw something at her, when I see Ryan's face in the window beside her.

I see red.

Faster than it had at the races, faster than the moments reading those texts over and over until my eyes crossed, I see *red*, and Mateo grabs at the collar of my shirt as I hurtle towards the door. But before I can fight him off, before I can formulate a coherent sentence, we hear a voice from outside the doors.

"You've got some fucking balls showing your face here." I blink, the red seeping away as Mateo and I look at each other, because that voice is one we both know too well. Liv and Ryan's faces disappear from the door, and Mateo doesn't try to stop me, but follows me out. And I have to blink several more times to make sure I'm seeing things correctly.

Ryan and Liv, a very pregnant Liv, cornered near a seating area while my sister waves her arms around like a cartoon character, hair flying, practically spitting as she speaks.

"If you thought for one second you can set foot on WHG property without a problem, you're dumber than I realized." She points a finger in Liv's face, and she rears back, against Ryan, who wraps his arm around her. Around his wife, I surmise from the rings on their hands.

CHAPTER 61

"You don't get to speak to her that way," Ryan has the gall to say, and Frannie laughs, a loud, outrageous cackle that turns the attention of several people waiting in line for the bar.

"What's going - *oh shit*." Alex halts next to us, mid step, her drink halfway to her lips when she spots the catfight about to ensue. As if his husband senses are tingling, Nolan rounds the corner behind her, quickly takes in her shocked state, and then tries to turn her away, but all she does is hold her drink up to him. He takes a deep breath that I recognize all too well, having already done the same several times today.

I tell myself I'm probably spot on the money - in another life, Nolan and I would have already been friends - as he takes his wife's drink.

He looks at Mateo. "Ex-wife?" Mateo nods, crossing his arms, and Nolan shakes his head, glancing over at me. "Want me to go get security?" He nods towards the opposite corner of the room, where, behind the buffet full of people piling up their plates, a cop sits, yawning to himself.

"I think they've got it," Mateo answers for me, gesturing to Frannie and Alex, who steps up behind my sister, taking off her gigantic earrings and stuffing them in her pocket. "Shit, she means business."

"She's still mad about last weekend," Nolan says dryly, leaning against the wall next to the door like Alex isn't laying into Liv and Ryan. "She's wanted to knock Melissa Davis out since the first time they met."

"She's so...angry." Mateo sounds less judgemental, more appreciative. "Like a Seer-sized ball of cursing and trash talk."

"I heard that," Seer calls from the other side of the bar, and pushes the swinging door next to Nolan open. "You gonna call off the wolves?" She nods her head at Alex and Frannie, who, at this point, seem to be feeding off each other.

"I will." Piper's voice comes from behind me, and I turn at the hip, meeting her gaze where she stands just behind Nolan.

She changed into a purple, gauzy dress with a belt to match mine just before everyone got here - a smart move, since in the span of an hour, she spilled on herself no less than four times. The hat she's wearing, she told me, is something she and Vic designed together, with a strip of the same floral leather wrapping the top. The same hand-made, painstakingly stitched work she'd given to all of us - belts, bracelets, a mug strap for Seer, she explained, so she can use it at Greensleeves to attach her cup to her dress. I didn't even know that was a thing until she held it up, latching and then unlatching it.

Her hair is back to those wild, messy curls that make me want to sink my hands into them, and seeing her in full form makes my frozen body thaw a little, not even realizing it'd gone cold with Olivia here. With Ryan here.

Piper's eyes slide to mine. "If that's ok." She nods her head towards Frannie and Alex, and when I give her the go ahead, she says "Alex." Alex doesn't respond, still babbling. "*Alex.*" No response. Finally, she slides her thumb and forefinger into her mouth, letting out a loud whistle that makes the entire room go silent, including Frannie and Alex, who turn to us. Both of them are breathing hard, like they've run a marathon, and Nolan turns back to the room.

"Nothing to see here, people," he calls, holding up the drinks in his hands. "Carry on."

They do not, in fact, carry on, even as Jackie tries to get everyone's attention with the slideshow on the projector screen. Through the crowd, Carla and Dylan emerge, Vic and Kyle on their heels, the whistle a Bat Signal for Piper's friends.

"Jesus, dude," Ryan breathes, meeting my eye for the first time since I'd come out of the kitchen. Red blurs at the edges of my vision, and I try to blink it away. I feel Mateo's hand on my arm.

"Like my sister said," I start, my tone more even and measured than I'd been expecting. "You've got balls showing up here." I eye Liv. "Both of you."

Liv scoffs, pushing off from Ryan like he's a springboard and she's a gymnast about to land a perfect trick, a smile sliding across her face as she smooths over her hair, which is flat against her head.

I look at her, then. Really look at her.

Polished, proper Liv, the woman I was married to, isn't who's standing in front of me. Not just her appearance, the dark circles under her eyes, the dull sheen to her skin and hair. She was meticulous, always putting up the perfect front, the perfect image. Much like my family growing up, I realize.

"I had to see for myself if the rumors were true." Liv's voice is incredulous, her eyes scanning the group around us. Though I can't see it, I can feel more eyes on my back, staring into our little corner near the front of the venue.

"Rumors?" Frannie bites back, crossing her arms.

"Well, not rumors." Liv smiles at me, and it's sickly sweet. "I guess it's not a rumor if it's plastered, plain as day, all over your tagged pictures." Her gaze falls to Piper, and her eyes narrow, a viper, ready to strike. But before she can make a move, Alex takes a step towards her.

"Watch it," she warns, gesturing down to Liv's stomach. "I dropped a ten pound baby out of my hoo-hah two months ago, but I'll still beat a bitch." I hear a snort from behind Nolan, and Seer is covering her mouth.

"Can't fight your own battles, Fitz?" Ryan asks, settling a hand on Liv's back, and I note the gesture, raising a brow at him. "So you send women in to do your dirty work for you?" Alex takes another step towards them, and they shrink back.

"Keep testing her, man." Nolan chuckles, sipping on the beer in his hand.

"She's wound pretty tight and I can't make any promises she'll fight fair." Ryan looks at Nolan, and something - recognition, maybe - crosses his eyes, before they land back on me.

"So you found a new girl, and a whole new friend group?" He laughs, looking down at Liv in front of him.

"Yeah, I did." Several heads whip towards me, but I press forward until I'm a few inches behind Alex. "And you know what?" Liv gives me a droll look, like whatever's coming next is the least interesting thing she's ever heard. "They're better friends to me than you ever were." I look back up at Ryan. "Either of you."

"You and Delmonico?" Ryan says, his tone critical and disbelieving. "I'm sorry, in what world-"

"In a world where you fucked my wife." It's out of my mouth before I can stop it, and I hear Piper's sharp intake of breath next to me as I repeat the words Nolan, Kyle, and Brett had all said to me just a few weeks ago, mid-panic after seeing Ryan for the first time in years. "In a world where you fucked my wife," I point to Liv, "and you fucked my best friend, and I was left to pick up the pieces." I turn back to Piper, and her hand reaches for mine. Silently, I lace my fingers through hers, and she gives them a squeeze. Liv lets out a dry laugh, crossing her arms over her stomach.

"And you expect me to believe that this is *real*?"

"I don't expect you to believe anything, because I don't give a shit what you think." Her head rears back. "And honestly, Liv, this," I hold up our joined hands, "is ten times more real after a few months than it ever was with you." Piper blinks up at me, shock clear across her face, but the second the words are out of my mouth, I know they're the truth. They've been at the back of my brain since I watched my dad and her from the side of the dance floor, praying he didn't fuck up another thing in my life, knowing full well that Chris Westfall wasn't going to scare Piper away.

"Well isn't that just sweet." Ryan's voice drips sarcasm, and I open my mouth to tell him where he can shove it, but someone steps up between Piper and Nolan, effectively cutting off anyone else trying to inch their way into the corner.

"Is there a problem here?" I have to blink several times to make sure I'm seeing things correctly, because it looks like Andy is the one standing there, crossing his arms over his wide chest.

"Uh," is all that comes out of Ryan's mouth. And I realize it's probably been just as long since Andy and Ryan have seen each other, that long, stressful day, far away at another WHG venue, when I tied myself to a different woman than the one holding my hand. I doubt Andy remembers most of that day, but I'll take what I can get as he squares up, taking in everyone around him. If there's one thing Andy Martin is, it's a big presence, always rivaling my height but now doubling my weight, and Ryan shrinks under his gaze.

"You've got to be kidding me," Piper mutters under her breath, and I feel the side of my mouth tip up at the corner. We can laugh about the irony later.

"I think it's pretty clear that no one wants you here." He raises a brow at the couple in front of us. "Either of you." Ten minutes ago, I would have said the same thing to him, had I realized he was in the room. Now, it's all I can do not to give him a fist bump across Piper's shoulder. Too much? I think that would be too much.

"I wouldn't test these ones." Mateo points his finger at Piper, her friends, and I. Our friends, I realize, because as much as they're her friends, with the way Alex just laid into Liv and Ryan, that can't all just be for Piper, right? "Westfall already took down a homophobe this month, we can add a shitbag ex best friend to the roster if we need to." There's a snicker from behind me that I know is from Vic, who I see move his arm to give Piper's shoulder a squeeze. Several people look at me, including Andy, but finally, Ryan takes the hint, grabbing Liv's hand. She hesitates, looking back at us.

"You can't be serious." Her voice is incredulous, her eyes scanning over all of us. At my hand with Pipers, at Andy, jumping into the middle of whatever this was. Of Alex, with her baseball-star husband, and Vic with his newly minted relationship. Even Jessica and her wife have sidled up on the other side of the bar, with Lizzy leaning against the bar top, cradling a bottle of water.

"Don't let the door hit you on the way out." Frannie's dry comment wrings out several laughs, and Ryan all but drags Liv out the large wooden doors. I crane my neck, watching them climb into his car without another word, and I let out a breath, feeling my shoulders sag with the tension I didn't even realize they held.

"If she hadn't been like eight months pregnant," Alex says under her breath, taking her drink from Nolan's hand and downing it in two gulps.

"Four," Andy says, and we turn to look at him. "She's four months pregnant."

"What?" Alex blinks up at him.

"With twins." There's a smile on Andy's lips, like he's thinking exactly what I am. Ryan may be one of the most mess-averse people I know, with his spotless car and tidy workspaces that I know drive him nuts with a pen out of place. He is *fucked*.

"Three under three." Jessica's voice is flat as she looks at her wife. "Yikes."

"Yikes," Alex echoes, and then takes Nolan's beer, ignoring his protest as she downs that, too.

"Oh, go get another one, it's not like we're not friends with the bartender."

CHAPTER 61

"I'm not," Nolan corrects, and Seer pops back out from the door next to him.

"Yes, you are." She looks between us, her finger pointing around. "The husband of my best friend's brother's girlfriend's best friend is my friend." I don't even have time to riddle out what that means before Mateo disappears to the kitchen, and Piper moves in front of me, her hand finding my chest.

"Are you ok?" I take another deep breath, shaking my head and meeting her eyes. They look about as shocked as I feel.

"Yeah, I think so." One of my hands moves to cover hers against my rapid heartbeat, the other finding the back of my neck. Someone clears their throat, and we both turn to see Andy still standing there, arms still crossed, like even he's not sure what just happened.

"Piper," he starts, and we both tense. "Can we, uh, talk for a minute?" His eyes slide to mine. "In private."

CHAPTER 62

Piper

"Not a chance." I don't think Fitz means for it to come out like a protective asshole, but that's what it sounds like, and we both look at him, my chest shaking with a stifled laugh.

"Anything you need to say to me, you can say to both of us." I drop my hand from his chest, lacing my fingers with his again between us.

"That's fine." Andy nods, looking around, and - I realize with a start - he's embarrassed. Whatever he has to say to me is making him feel ashamed, and if there's anything more surprising than Alex Calloway squaring off against Liv in Fitz's defense (ok, sort of his defense), it's a shame-filled Andy Martin. "I'd still like to talk...not here." He looks pointedly to one side, and I see Alex's eyes widen from where she's peeking around the bar.

"Sorry!" she squeaks, and then there's giggles from several people as she retreats, head ducking away.

"There's an office," I say quietly, appraising Andy as I point towards the staff office, and he nods, gesturing for us to lead the way.

He follows us into the office, and when Fitz clicks the door shut behind us, he meets my eye for a split second, and I give a minute. He can probably tell that I've noodled out whatever Andy is about to say, but I'd like to let the man work for it. You know, for old time's sake.

He moves to stand next to me in front of the desk, leaning against it and settling his hand on my back. My reaction is immediate; I inch closer to him, and his thumb traces up and down on the fabric right above my panty line. Andy tracks the movement, his eyebrows creasing.

"Were you two together the last time I saw you here?"

"No," we say at the same time, and I fight a laugh again. "Not that it's any of your business," Fitz adds.

"I deserve that." I stare at Andy, and he puts his hand on the back of one of

CHAPTER 62

the uncomfortable chairs in front of us, his knuckles turning white as he grips it. "I deserve a lot worse." He pulls his cowboy hat off, running a hand over his close-cropped, receding hair. He's nervous. Actually nervous to say whatever he's pulled us in here for. "I've been trying to figure out how to apologize to you, Piper, to make amends-"

I hold up a hand.

"Are you about to Ninth Step me?" Fitz's head snaps towards mine, and Andy's mouth is moving, but no sounds are coming out as he looks between the two of us. "Ninth Step," I repeat, staring at Fitz in frustration, and then scrubbing my hand down my face. My voice flattens as I look up at the ceiling. "How the fuck did I get here?"

"You're telling me." Andy laughs, but he stops the second we both look at him. "Sorry, I know exactly how I got here." He scratches the back of his neck. "I deflect with humor, a lot. It's my biggest character defect. Mostly poorly timed." He swallows. "And poorly aimed."

"If you're here to try to get her to forgive you," Fitz starts, but I hold up my hand again.

"Andy, I forgave you a long time ago." Those were not the words either of them expected, clearly, and they both stare. "Fourth step," I add with a shrug, "a searching and fearless moral inventory. Nothing like having to make a list of all the people who've fucked you, or fucked you over, to make you really take a harsh look at your life." When I finish the sentence, I mull on it for a moment, and realize what I've said, my hand coming to my mouth. It slides up, over my eyes and I look down, my thumb and forefinger pressing into my brows.

"Sorry, Andy. I think I had a small stroke, and forgot you were in here." But Andy's chest is shaking as he looks up at the ceiling, same as I had.

"In what world is Piper Delmonico an alcoholic?" he asks, leaning against the back of the chair with his forearms.

"In the same world where I'm a widow." My voice is matter of fact, and it doesn't strike Fitz in quite the same way it clearly does Andy, his eyes widening.

"And where Liv cheated on me with Ryan," Fitz adds, and both Andy and I wrinkle our noses, the thought thoroughly disgusting.

"Look," Andy says after a minute, and he shakes his head, swiping at his nose like it's a nervous twitch. "I hurt you." Fitz raises a brow as he stares at me, catching the way my throat bobs out of the corner of his eye. I'm clearly uncomfortable, holding back. "More than hurt you." Andy Martin sighs, long and deep, and then he's looking back up like he'll be able to read what he needs to say off the wainscot ceilings. "I humiliated you, shared things that should have been kept private." His hat dangles from his fingers, and it looks like Fitz is concentrating really hard on the hat, and not on whatever thoughts are spinning beneath those auburn curls. "I...fucked you over." I think he omitted several words, because his pause is punctuated by a clear look at Fitz. Probably for the best, not saying he fucked me in a confided space with both of us.

"You did." I nod, just slightly, and cross my arms over my chest, a clear defensive move. Fitz's hand keeps moving on my back. "You ruined my reputation, you hurt me physically, emotionally. You hurt my friends."

"I ninth stepped Montero about thirty minutes ago," Andy interrupts, and I shoot him a withering look. "Right, sorry."

"You were a shitty friend to me, and an even shittier person when we were more than friends. You made me feel like less than I am, less than I'm worth, and a piece of that has always been with me, through everything." And then I look at the man next to me, just briefly, before I sigh. "But this one hasn't told me a whole lot, and I think you and your family may have taken up for him growing up. Being there for him." Andy's gaze meets Fitz's, and he nods. That, he's willing to concede to. "I forgave you a long time ago, Andy."

"I don't deserve it."

"You don't," Fitz agrees. "Neither of us deserve her forgiveness, because I sat by and watched the shit you threw her way, and did nothing." I press my hand into the side of his leg.

"There was nothing you could have done." Andy runs his hand over his head again. "I was drowning, even back then, sneaking drinks wherever I could find it. Your wedding is the only reason I'm standing here."

"I'm sorry, what?" He laughs, nodding back towards the door.

"Your sister threw me in an Uber, paid the driver to make sure I got home ok, and then called Alice and told her to help me sort my shit out." He winces. "I puked in the backseat of the Uber, and had to help Fran get her account reinstated."

For a moment, Fitz stands in stunned silence, staring at the man he once called his best friend, who has clearly just told him some news about his sister.

"Be that as it may," I cut in, effectively shaking Fitz out of his spiral. "You've said your piece, I think it's time you head back out to the party."

"Nah," he says, tipping his hat back on. And for a second, that cool, cocky face slides back on, and we're back in the halls at Southwest. "I've said what I came here to say. I've got a beautiful lady and a Ranger's game waiting for me when I get home." When I stare, he adds, "the lady is a dog, by the way. A husky."

"Out," I order, pointing to the door, but I can't help the smile that threatens to slide across my face at the idea of Andy Martin, home alone on a Saturday night, cuddling with a husky. Andy holds his hands up, backing away.

"Got it, got it." He pauses, mid step. "By the way, was that Nolan Calloway out there with Barton?"

CHAPTER 62

"Out," Fitz repeats, nodding with his chin.

"Ok, sheesh." He's got the door halfway open before he turns back again.

"What now?" I whine.

"He's always had a soft spot for you, you know." Andy adjusts his hat, nodding towards Fitz, and he looks like he wants to curl inward on himself as my head bobs between the two of them. "Even back in the day, we could all tell that-"

Fitz picks up what's closest to his hand, a staple remover, and chucks it at him, and unlike me, his aim doesn't completely suck. Andy has to deflect it with his hand where it nearly makes contact with his face. When the door clicks closed behind him, Fitz scrubs both hands down his face, his fingers separating to look at me.

"What the hell just happened?"

"I think Andy Martin just ninth-stepped me."

Fitz makes a face.

"Please don't ever say that again." I laugh, letting him wrap his hands around my waist, and I press my face into his chest, breathing him in. Breathing this in. After a moment, he pulls back, looking at the office around us. "I distinctly remember," he starts, and his eyes twinkle, "that the last time we were in here, you were showing off some samples-"

"I wasn't *showing off* anything," I cry, pinching lightly at his arm, my voice high in mock surprise. "I was trying to find...well I don't remember what I was trying to find, but I'm sure I wasn't showing you my brand new vibrator."

"Sure, that's what they all say." I tilt my head back, meeting his eyes.

"They all?" My lips come up on one side, and his hand tightens on my waist.

"Only you, Delmonico." I roll my eyes.

"Sure, Fitzwilliam." He huffs a laugh, and I wrap my arms around his neck, pulling him close. "Kingdom come?" Fitz's eyes narrow at me.

"Well I was thinking entirely wholesome thoughts, but now that you say that-"

I cut him off with a kiss, knowing that it says everything my racing brain wants to scream. Every thought of him, every moment over the last few months, getting us here, back here.

When he breaks away, pressing his forehead to mine, his breathing is ragged. It's a sight I would have told you was impossible, all those weeks ago, standing in these same spots - Fitz Westfall, breathless from kissing Piper Delmonico.

Widowed. Recovering alcoholic. Stuck designing for a manager who wouldn't know silk from satin.

Still widowed, but very much in love with a redheaded man that sometimes makes me want to beat my head into my steering wheel. Still a recovering alcoholic, but no longer stuck designing for a manager who wouldn't know silk from satin. Instead, settling into a new position, a new life, blending with my old one like two seams folding together and meeting in all the right places.

Fitz's hand moves across my jaw, fingers lacing into my hair. "Kingdom come," he says finally, and then he's stepping back, holding a hand out to me. "Now, let's actually go enjoy this reunion before we miss tacos and what I'm guessing is a tipsy Alex."

There are a lot of things I would do for my friends without protest. Looking at the man in front of me, I know there are a lot of things he'd do for them, too. Giving up a precious Saturday, several precious Saturdays, to help plan the reunion I wasn't even going to attend, wasn't so bad. Especially if that means getting to spend the rest of them with the people who made sure I got through all the bad days to get here.

EPILOGUE

Fitz

"Piper, you ok in there?" I stand outside the door of the master bathroom, my ear pressed against the cold white wood, trying to figure out what's taking her so long.

"I'll be out in a minute," she calls, and then lets out a garbled sentence.

"Are you sure you're ok to go tonight?" I try to wiggle the door knob, but it's locked. "Come on, baby, is it your stomach?"

"We may live together, but there are some things a girl needs to do in private." That sentence is crystal clear, and I pull my head away. Point taken. I turn on my heel, glancing around the bedroom of the house I've called home for the last several years. Well, we called it a home, but it didn't really feel that way, not until, after her lease expired in September, Piper invaded with her colorful bookshelves and throw blankets on every surface possible. It feels like a home now - a messy, chaotic home that gives me anxiety.

And I know that's what Piper is working through now, the stress of everything going on - the impending move, from this house to our first home together, a real home, that we picked out one cold December morning after seeing the *For Sale* sign on our way back from Frannie's.

Am I looking forward to living so close to my sister I can see the rooster on her weathervane from my front porch? No. Am I looking forward to also being less than ten minutes from Seer? Absolutely fucking not. But moving further east means being closer for the Friday nights we already spend in that direction, with her friends, my friends, *our* friends.

There's a flush, and then running water from the bathroom behind me, and the door opens. Piper flips the light off, drying her hands on a towel as she leans against my arm. I reach down and kiss the top of her head.

"You good?"

"Not even remotely," she answers with a sigh, and then shrugs. "But I can't miss birthday night." She steps aside, throwing the towel back onto the counter blindly. It takes everything in me not to go hang it up on the hoop, which is literally a foot from where she threw it.

Focus, Westfall.

"Especially not for your birthday," I add, sweeping my arms around her from behind and settling my chin where I'd kissed seconds before.

"Especially not for my birthday," she echoes, and then wiggles her butt against me. I squeeze my arms around her.

"Don't start something you can't finish." She tilts her head back, meeting my gaze.

"Bet." I smile down at her, giving her a peck on the lips and she sighs again, this time a little less sad sounding. *"Four years sober."*

"How does it feel?" Piper sways in my arms, moving to music I'm sure is playing as background noise under all those curls, the perpetual soundtrack she likes to hum, off key, when she thinks I'm not listening.

"Good." Her phone buzzes in the pocket of her pants, and she pulls it out, inspecting the screen.

CARLA MONTGOMERY
We're getting ready to head that direction, you still good for movie night after?

SEER BRADLEY
Happy birthday night! Liam wants to know if you'd like anything from the U.K., his friend will provide snacks upon request when visiting this summer.
Liam's words, not mine. I do not make promises of snacks for men I do not know.

Her chest shakes as she reads the messages, moving to reply to Carla first. "You still good for movie night?" I ask, and she nods, her fingers clicking at the screen.

"The media room isn't packed. If it was, I'd say no." She looks up at me, catching her lip between her teeth. "Don't tell them I said this, but the last time we went to their place, that couch Dylan refuses to trash gave me back cramps for days."

"I thought it was just me," I breathe out, shaking my head. "Ok, movie night here." She nods, sliding open Seer's text. "Tell her I want a couple of boxes of

EPILOGUE

Flakes." Piper freezes, and then looks back at me, brows furrowed. "What? I like British stuff too. I'm cultured. I'm *hip*." She snorts, typing my request with the "From Fitz" caveat at the beginning, and then following up with a request for several different candies, because when it comes to chocolate, this girl has a *problem*.

She locks her phone, sliding it back in her pocket as my own phone buzzes, and I look down at the watch on my wrist. A text from Alex pops up, asking if we're still on for lunch tomorrow afternoon. Piper stares down at it, and then back up at me. "You two planning something I should be aware of?"

"We're colluding on your birthday present," I answer honestly, and her eyes narrow. "Will Bex get the pair of tiny Uggs, to match yours, or will you get a new watch to replace this?" I lift her wrist, the screen on her watch nearly unreadable beneath the plastic cover, the victim of a particularly nasty fall while trying to set up her sewing station at the new house. Floor meet, Piper. Piper, meet floor.

As if in response, Bex gives a yip from her place on our bed, and then returns to the bone that Roscoe is eying.

I'm glad I have Piper held like this, looking around at the half-packed bedroom we've shared since basically after the reunion. Because when she's looking away, she can't see the way I'm totally unable to hide the smile on my face.

It's a weird feeling, being so happy you're not able to mask your emotions. It's something I've been working through with my therapist, a pretty cool guy named Cody, who's helping me get over some of the things I know Piper doesn't need to take the brunt of, in the same way I know she works through her issues with Ava, her therapist.

I was being honest, and I'll always be honest with Piper, but she doesn't know that in addition to the watch, and the tiny Ugg boots, I'll be stashing away a ring fit for the woman in my arms.

I'll save it for the perfect moment - or, at least, as close as we can get it to perfect, between the move, her commission work, and the two new venues we're launching this summer - and it all seems to hit at once, like it always does.

Piper hums against me, and I feel it in my chest, letting her sway us to the music in her head, forever at the beat of her own drum, and I can't help but think that I wouldn't have it any other way.

WHAT'S NEXT?

Thanks so much for reading Go Find Less. The next story in the Recovering Good Girls series features...Seer Bradley and one very handsome, tatted Scottish man.

Intrigued? Join my newsletter for sneak peeks, updates and more: www.theaclaireauthor.com

Scan the QR code below to join my Hype Squad Reader Facebook Group!

Leave a Review

Loved Go Find Less? Help other people find Piper and Fitz by reviewing on your favorite book platforms! Find links to all my listings at www.theaclaireauthor.com

ACKNOWLEDGEMENTS

Long before there was a Thea Claire, there was a little girl in a Texas suburb, watching her parents kick ass and take names as real partners in life. Without the drive and passion of my mother, who taught me I can live as many lives as I want to, without the constant, calming force of my bibliophile father, who showed me what it looks like to be with someone who really supports you, I wouldn't be who I am today. Words can't express how thankful I am for their sacrifices to get me here. Also, about the content of this book - #SorryNotSorry

Thank you also to:

My beautiful Aunt L, who helped me get through the hardest moments in my life without a second thought, and to my sister HG, who I think has a totally new appreciation for her snotty goody-two-shoes older sibling.

JT, the man who put my heart back together and gave me the space and time to create the person I am, and who fills my life with more laughter and love than I could have imagined.

HH, my best friend, who stood with JT and held me up when the world around me crumbled at my own doing: I'm proud to watch each day of your family's journey, and to count you all as part of mine. (Love you too, CH.)

Lindsey, my other hype half and the woman who helped reignite my passion for writing: your unwavering support and immediate renewal of our friendship after so long apart has daily been one of my favorite things about this journey.

Tiff, J, and my B Girls - you hold such a big piece of my heart, and the constant support and warmth you give to not just me, but everyone around you, is incredible. I'm proud to be your little sister and HP.

The T Family - BD&F, K, T&G, T&T - and all the cousins, extended family, and sort-of-relatives that I hope aren't reading this, cause, ya know - who welcomed me with open arms in a way I've never experienced before: you are the biggest blessing to JT and I, and I'm eternally grateful for you.

My friends who stuck it out through the muck and the mud - NW, SK, VO, SP - you will never know how much I needed you, or appreciated you standing by T & I when times were tough.

My fabulous Sparkly Unicorns, Alphas, Betas, and ARC Readers – those who helped me shape this book and Fitz and Piper's story: you are some of my favorite people in this entire world, and without you, this wouldn't have been possible. Katy, Ashley, Tasha, Danielle, Keegan, and Kieran – thank you.

Lyssa at ForeverBooked for the beautiful covers that present this story to the world.

My Kickstarter backers, who helped kick off this story in the best way by funding in 24 hours, and who believed in this book before it even hit shelves. Special thanks to Monica and my sister in widowhood, Melinda.

My author mentors and friends, Kim, Rebecca, Evie, Amanda, Ruby, Gala & DL, Ashley & Tiffany, who reminded me each day that this is possible. The bookish community, Rina, Becky, Shannan, IBP&I Discord, Self Pub Authors Discord, and every person who silently cheered me on from the sidelines.

Morgan and Lee, for giving me stability while I was adrift.

To TBH, who changed my life in more ways than he knew.

And last but certainly not least - *you, gentle reader.* You getting this far means you're more dedicated than most (I mean, who reads this far into the acknowledgements?!) and that deserves recognition. But, seriously. From the bottom of my heart, thanks for taking the crazy train to the end of this trip. I hope you've enjoyed (or at least cried at) every minute of it.

About the Author

Thea Claire is a storyteller at heart. A North Texas native, she loves to write about strong characters creating beautiful lives for themselves and those around them. Thea has been an avid reader and sometimes-writer for more than 15 years, and has worked in a variety of fields as a communications and events professional. She is a proud mental health advocate, neurodiverse writer, and member of the LGBTQ+ community.

Learn more about Thea at www.theaclaireauthor.com

SCAN TO FIND THEA ONLINE:

Milton Keynes UK
Ingram Content Group UK Ltd.
UKHW011808010124
435297UK00005B/481